Praise for Oliver North and

## *HEROES PROVED*

**The suspense-charged *New York Times* bestselling novel that only someone who has actually "been there, done that" could write!**

"A heart-thumping 'must read' for every American who cares about the threats we face and where we're headed. Oliver North says *Heroes Proved* is a novel. I say it's a wake-up call—a warning shot across the bow of complacency."

—Sean Hannity, host of *The Sean Hannity Show* on radio and *Hannity* on Fox News Channel

"This is my friend Oliver North at his best. *Heroes Proved* hits the mark on the beauty of South Carolina's 'Low Country,' the courage of our people, and their patriotism. He's crafted a gripping tale of good versus evil, political intrigue, and the consequence of being faithful in an uncertain world. I'm glad he's on our side."

—Jim DeMint, former South Carolina senator

"Oliver North is one of our nation's heroes. *Heroes Proved* reflects his experience and understanding of what it takes to protect our way of life and preserve our Constitution. It's inspiring truth in the form of a novel. Don't plan to sleep until you finish—because you can't put it down. Bless you, Ollie, for writing this."

—Lt. Gen. Williams G. "Jerry" Boykin, U.S. Army (Ret.), founding member of Delta Force

# OLIVER NORTH

# HEROES PROVED

POCKET BOOKS

New York   London   Toronto   Sydney   New Delhi

Pocket Books
A Division of Simon & Schuster, Inc.
1230 Avenue of the Americas
New York, NY 10020

This book is a work of fiction. Names, characters, places, and incidents are products of the author's imagination or are used fictitiously. Any resemblance to actual events or locales or persons, living or dead, is entirely coincidental.

First Pocket Books paperback edition October 2013

POCKET and colophon are registered trademarks of Simon & Schuster, Inc.

For information about special discounts for bulk purchases, please contact Simon & Schuster Special Sales at 1-866-506-1949 or business@simonandschuster.com.

The Simon & Schuster Speakers Bureau can bring authors to your live event. For more information or to book an event, contact the Simon & Schuster Speakers Bureau at 1-866-248-3049 or visit our website at www.simonspeakers.com.

Manufactured in the United States of America

10  9  8  7  6  5  4  3  2  1

ISBN 978-1-4767-1455-4
ISBN 978-1-4767-0632-0 (ebook)

For Betsy,

*"Draw me after you and let us run together"*

SONG OF SOLOMON 1:4

# HEROES
# PROVED

# HOUSTON, WE HAVE A PROBLEM

**NASA HILTON HOTEL**

3000 NASA ROAD ONE

HOUSTON, TX

SATURDAY, 11 SEPTEMBER 2032

0100 HOURS, LOCAL

Only six of the sixteen expected to live. The other ten, all volunteers, did not intend to survive the experience. That's just one of the things that make them different from us.

Two of them, aboard the Venezuelan tanker moored at the Exxon Mobil facility in Baytown, died precisely at one in the morning when their suicide bombs detonated and ignited the ship's cargo of benzene. Nine unwitting crewmen aboard the vessel and twenty-three refinery workers ashore were killed in the conflagration.

Thirty seconds later, two others perished in a ball of fire when their sixty-ton truckload of ammonium nitrate fertilizer mixed with diesel fuel exploded as planned on the East Loop bridge over the Buffalo Bayou–Houston Ship

Channel. Seventeen motorists in eleven cars also died in the explosion or when their vehicles plunged into the water, more than 130 feet below.

The four who disembarked from two cabs in front of the Hilton NASA hotel at three minutes after one all anticipated dying within the hour. Though it actually took longer, they did succeed in taking seventy-nine innocent guests, eleven hotel workers, thirteen Houston police officers, and eleven fire and rescue personnel with them. Among those killed were twenty-one women and fifteen children; six of them, babies in their mothers' arms.

\* \* \* \*

When gunfire and grenades erupted in the lobby, the three men, who had checked into the hotel as guests on Monday, immediately set the "e-cell" microcircuit timers on the explosive charges they previously planted in their rooms on the second, fifth, and seventh floors, then headed for the stairwells and raced to the penthouse level. Dressed in gray slacks and blue blazers with matching lapel pins, they arrived at the twelfth-floor Presidential Suite just seconds after the hotel emergency alarm began.

As he saw them coming, the identically attired security guard, an off-duty Houston patrol officer posted at the front door of the suite, reached for the phone on the desk instead of reaching for his weapon. It was his last fatal error.

The first of three silenced .25-cal bullets hit him in the chest, instantly reminding him of another deadly mistake: before going on duty at midnight, he decided the heat and humidity were too high for wearing his police-issue ballistic protective vest.

The shooter bent over the inert body, pulled the dead security guard's police credentials out of his wallet, glanced at the name, picked up the desk phone, and dialed 71201. When the phone was answered he said, "Sir, this is Officer Vargas at the security desk. There is an emergency in the hotel and we need to get you out of here, quickly. Please put on some clothes. We'll be waiting at your door."

As his two colleagues prepared to drag the security officer's body down the hall to dump it into a housekeeping closet, the shooter removed the dead man's badge, weapon, and holster and fastened them to his belt. Finally, he grabbed the policeman's Personal Interface Device—a clear plastic membrane, less than a millimeter thick, about twice the size of an old-fashioned credit card. Using the dead man's thumb and forefinger, he pinched the thin ceramic strip along the edge of the card and a piezo-actuator instantly illuminated the screen to the downloadable media the officer was watching an instant before the first bullet struck.

From the card came the voice of an announcer, covering the highlights of the afternoon's college football games. "Vargas" grunted, deactivated the fingerprint security option, pinched the ceramic switch to mute the device, and shoved it into his trousers pocket. All three men were arrayed like statues, facing outward when the door behind them opened and the occupant of the Presidential Suite shouted over the din of the emergency alarm, "I'm ready. Where are we going?"

The shooter turned and said, "We cannot use the elevators. We must use the emergency exit fire escape. There is apparently some kind of altercation going on downstairs. We need to get you out of here."

The tall, thin man in the doorway, clad in a lightweight exercise suit and running shoes, didn't look his age—seventy-seven. He held a flat leather case in one hand and a small gym bag in the other. Neither his eyes nor his short, gray hair offered any sign of whether he had been asleep or awake when the alarm started less than four minutes earlier. Over the incessant Klaxon he said, "Perhaps we had better call in to the duty officer at the NASA conference center before we leave."

"No time!" shouted the shooter. "There is a fire and gunshots from the front of the hotel. We're going down the south side, toward the marina. We have to get out of here to safety." With that he gestured to follow him, turned, and headed down the hallway toward the illuminated exit sign.

The four men raced down eleven flights of stairs, the older man following "Officer Vargas" and one of the "security guards." As they neared the ground floor, the stairwell filled with thick, acrid smoke and other frightened guests, all fleeing some unspeakable horror. Several women were weeping and children were wailing as they stumbled down the stairs.

When the crowd of refugees burst out of the building onto the deck above the marina, "Vargas," now brandishing a badge in one hand and an automatic pistol in the other, yelled, "Follow me!" and headed east toward the finger piers and boat slips, past knots of frightened guests huddled with nowhere to go. Outside, with the interior alarms muted by the walls of the structure, the sound of gunfire and explosions seemed dangerously close.

As the four men hastened past the hotel restaurant toward the stairs to the dock, there were screams and a sudden burst of gunfire from inside. An instant later, an armed man wearing a black jumpsuit burst out a door in front of them and nearly bumped into "Officer Vargas."

The gunman looked stunned, lowered his weapon, and said what sounded to the older man like "Ahmad . . ."

Without hesitating a second, "Vargas" pointed his pistol at the man's head and pulled the trigger. The old man recoiled in horror and said, "What the . . ."

"Vargas" spun, grabbed the old man's warm-up jacket, and snarled, "Come, now, to that boat," and pointed with his weapon to the end of the main dock. There a long, low, dark-hulled craft with a blue flashing strobe on its foredeck was idling.

When their "protectee" seemed to hesitate, the other two "security guards" in blue blazers came up on either side of the old man and took his arms as if to assist him. Traumatized guests, some prone on the deck, others peering from behind tables outside the restaurant, watched as they hustled the man in the warm-up suit out to the pier and then into the cockpit of the dark-hulled boat.

Once aboard, things suddenly changed. The man who called himself "Vargas" shouted to the two visible crewmen waiting in the cockpit, "Take him below! Go! Now! Hurry!"

The man at the helm immediately shut off the flashing blue light and pushed the throttles forward to their blocks. The two water-cooled, turbocharged racing engines spun up with a roar and the boat leapt forward. In seconds the black, Kevlar-reinforced, fiberglass hull was racing east without lights across Clear Lake at better than 25 knots.

Below, in the tapered, low-ceiling cabin, the two "security guards" and a third man he hadn't seen before ripped the leather case and the gym bag from the old man's hands, pinned his arms behind his back, snapped handcuffs on his wrists and ankles, and pushed him onto a narrow bunk.

Just before they covered his mouth with duct tape, he

asked, "Who are you? Where are you taking me?" He received no answer. Instead his "protectors"-turned-captors proceeded to wrap his entire body in heavy aluminum foil and then duct-taped him to a long board they shoved beneath him. Completely immobilized, he stopped struggling and was only somewhat relieved when one of them poked two holes in the foil beneath his nostrils. Less than fifteen minutes had elapsed since he picked up the phone and heard "Officer Vargas" tell him there was "an emergency" in the hotel.

## WHITE HOUSE SITUATION ROOM

1600 PENNSYLVANIA AVENUE
WASHINGTON, DC
SATURDAY, 11 SEPTEMBER 2032
0227 HOURS, LOCAL

If twenty-one years—five of them as senior watch officer—in the White House Situation Room had taught Ben Carver anything, it was that the "red phone" never chirped with good news at this hour of the morning. He adjusted his headset, made sure the lip mike was in front of his mouth, and glanced at the "DNI" icon flashing red on the flat plastic panel on his console serving as his computer screen.

He touched the plastic pane and said into the mouthpiece, "Sit Room, Carver."

"Ben, Bill Vincent, DNI SWO."

"Go ahead, Bill," Carver replied.

"We have multiple ongoing events in Houston. Looks like a vessel moored at the Exxon Mobile Baytown facility blew up, damaging the Fred Hartman Bridge. There was also a very large explosion on the East Loop I-610 bridge, which may have brought down a span. There is also an ongoing Houston PD and Texas DPS police action with an apparent hostage/barricade situation near the Johnson NASA Space Center. We don't know if these events are related—"

"Any imagery up?" interrupted Carver.

"Yeah," Vincent replied. "A Global Hawk border surveillance UAV out of Dyess Air Force Base picked up the infrared flares from the explosions. We're up with DHS and have reprogrammed the bird for Houston. It should be overhead in ten minutes or so. I'm sending you the Houston TranStar traffic camera grabs of both detonations and a live feed of the ongoing effects. The Coast Guard is transmitting IR from one of their Galveston Bay aerostats and they are getting ready to launch a helo with a FLIR pod. We also have a download from the security cams at the Space Center, but they don't show much, just a lot of police activity—the usual flashing lights on the highway. We're picking up lots of chatter on social media about casualties."

Carver reached to touch the plastic screen, bringing up the imagery, and asked, "Are there any threat-warns or foreign indicators? Anybody claiming credit?"

"Nothing new," Vincent responded. "Last year, leading up to the thirtieth anniversary of the 9-11-01 attack, we had lots of 'threat-warn' and of course, nothing happened. This year all we're seeing and hearing is the usual anti-American garbage from south of the border and typical 'Anark' right-wing trash talk up on 'Radio-Free Montana,'" Vincent responded. "We aren't picking up anybody overseas mentioning a specific attack, nobody here calling home, as it were—but as you know, the jihadis have been very quiet lately."

"What is Houston Emergency Management Center telling DHS? Do they think it is domestic, international, or just three coincidental events?" Carver asked.

"Hard to tell," Vincent responded. "The folks at HEMC have their hands full right now. We're monitoring all of their encrypted comms and they don't seem to know who or what is responsible. There are apparently lots of casualties from the two explosions and whatever is going on across the street from the Johnson Space Center. Just between you and me, we are tapped into the hotel's internal security cameras and there are a lot of bodies."

Carver simply grunted at the DNI watch officer's admission that they were monitoring and recording a private security/surveillance system without a warrant. Turning to another screen, he glanced down a checklist and asked, "Any indications of radiological, biohazard, or hazmat release?"

"Air sensors say no to the first two," responded Vincent. "There is a large petrochemical smoke plume drifting southeast on the offshore breeze from the Baytown fire. Houston EMC has alerted all first responders and will post a public warning once they get a better handle on things."

Carver pondered this for a moment and asked, "If this is a 9-11 anniversary attack, why Houston? Is there any connection?"

"Not that we're tracking," Vincent answered. "According to the Houston PD they have a bunch of their off-duty cops doing security work for some kind of energy conference coming up at the Space Center, that's about it."

"Energy conference," said Carver aloud, as he touched the electronic pad on his desk and brought up a calendar

on a screen titled "2032 SIG EVENTS." He scrolled to
September and found:

11 SEP:  31st Anniversary Ceremony of 9-11-01 attacks.

         0945–1045 POTUS Wreath-laying Ceremony,
         Pentagon 9-11-01 Memorial. POC: WH COS
         MUNEER MURAD

12–14 SEP:  International Alternative Energy Conference,
            Johnson Space Center, Houston, TX.

12 SEP:  1130 EDT POTUS DEP S/LAWN ENR AAFB: MARINE 1
         1200 EDT POTUS DEP AAFB: A/F 1
         1510 CDT POTUS ARR EFD
         1530 CDT POTUS DEP EFD ENR SPACE
         CTR: MARINE 1
         1600–1800 POTUS Welcomes Conferees &
            Attends VIP Reception POC: WH COS MUNEER
            MURAD. PRESS CLEAR: USSS CRED.

         VIPs Attending:

         U.S. Energy SEC Donald Colbert
         UK Energy Min., Sir Reginald Smythe
         OPEC Oil Min., Sheik Adnan bin Faisal
         CAN Energy Sec., Donald Gregory
         MEX Energy Min., Rafael Hernandez
         RUS Energy Min., Viktor Lebed
         PRC Energy Min., Xiong Guangkai
         UN Energy Coordinator: Amb. Sun Lee [PRC]
         Dr. Franklin Pfister: Cal Poly [US]
         Dr. Martin Cohen: MIT [US]
         Dr. Melvin Larsen: Copenhagen Royal Acad. [DEN]
         Dr. Davis Long: Univ. of Calgary [CAN]

Dr. Steven Templeton: S. Alberta Inst. [CAN]

Dr. Bern Vaclev: Petersburg Scientific Inst. [RUS]

Dr. Lu Weiying, Qinghua Univ. [PRC]

Dr. Shimizu Yoshiaki, Tokyo Inst. of Tech. [JPN]

Carver's mouth was suddenly dry and he sat upright in his chair. With a flick of a finger on the desktop pad, he copied the file and sent it to the DNI watch officer. As he did so, Carver said, "Bill, I'm sending you our SIG Events file. Take a look at who is due in Houston tomorrow."

The file, labeled "WHSR-SENSITIVE," was transmitted instantly over the secure fiber-optic network connecting all of Washington's government agencies—and every major U.S. military command. When the DNI senior watch officer looked at it, he sucked in his breath, as Carver continued: "All of these people must have PERTs. Check their ident codes and find them. Don't bother with Energy Secretary Colbert, he's here in town, I'm showing him on my succession locator and he is scheduled to accompany the president on Air Force One to Houston. See if any of the people listed are already in Houston. And if they are, stop the presses on the PDB. Let me know if I have to wake up POTUS."

### JENNINGS ISLAND CHANNEL

CLEAR LAKE, TX

SATURDAY, 11 SEPTEMBER 2032

0145 HOURS, LOCAL

It took the black-hulled speedboat less than thirty minutes to reach the narrow, winding Jennings Island channel at the east end of Clear Lake. At the helm in the cockpit, the pilot slowed the craft to a crawl and negotiated the passage by getting in line behind two other powerboats headed out on the tide. While the kidnappers wallowed in the wake of the craft in front of them, "Vargas" reached into his pocket, pulled out the PID he had removed from the police officer he killed in the hotel, pinched it to switch it on, and placed the plastic rectangle on the cockpit dashboard.

The man at the helm looked at the device and asked, "Why did you do that?"

The killer smiled and replied, "The authorities may be checking who we are. This will tell them we have one of their local police officers aboard."

As the vessel made the final turn to pass beneath the power lines and the RFID panels beneath the Bayport Boulevard bridge, two very loud, nearly simultaneous explosions ashore lit up the horizon to the left and right of the bow.

The first, at the intersection of Bayport and East NASA, forty gallons of gasoline mixed with kerosene and accelerated by a canister of nitrous oxide, was detonated in the back of a rented SUV by a hand grenade. It spread flaming debris across all four lanes of traffic.

Seconds later, south of the bridge, six propane tanks, vented into a rented panel truck at the intersection of Bayport and Marina Bay Drive, were exploded by a cigarette lighter. In both cases, the perpetrators died instantly. So did nine innocent Americans who just happened to be in the wrong place at the wrong time.

As the black-hulled speedboat cleared the channel into Galveston Bay, it once again picked up speed. Fifteen minutes later it was off San Leon Point doing 45 knots through a light chop and an outgoing tide. By two thirty they were abreast of the breakwater north of Pelican Island.

To avoid being challenged by the Coast Guard's Vessel Traffic Center, they kept their speed down transiting the sea-lane south of Port Bolivar, but once they were abreast of the sea buoy, "Vargas" told the pilot, "Faster." As the man at the helm pushed the throttles all the way forward and headed due south into the Gulf of Mexico, the killer flipped the dead police officer's PID over the side. In the tiny cabin belowdecks, all but the man wrapped in foil began to retch as the boat pounded through the swells.

An hour before sunrise, the speedboat pulled alongside a rusty coastal tanker, the *Ileana Rosario*, seventy-five miles south of U.S. territorial waters. A cargo net lowered from the deck of the larger vessel sufficed to transfer their aluminum-foil-wrapped cargo while five of the six men scrambled up a rope ladder lowered over the side—glad to be on anything larger than the black boat.

After the others departed, "Officer Vargas," flashlight in hand, went through the boat, looking for anything they might have left behind. Satisfied the craft was "clean," he reached into the bilge, twisted a large valve, then hurried back on deck and up the rope ladder as seawater flooded the small vessel.

As the rust bucket churned away to the southeast, the black hull sank in a thousand feet of water. By dawn, the only evidence remaining of the rendezvous at sea was a thin layer of high-octane gasoline seeping from the speedboat's fuel tanks as they were crushed by water pressure. The rising sun quickly evaporated the colorful film.

## WHITE HOUSE SITUATION ROOM

1600 PENNSYLVANIA AVENUE
WASHINGTON, DC
SATURDAY, 11 SEPTEMBER 2032
0610 HOURS, LOCAL

Houston Emergency Management Center is reporting that the hotel is now secure," said Bill Vincent over the encrypted, secure video link. In the Sit Room, Ben

Carver simply nodded. Seated beside him was General John Smith, the National Security Advisor. Smith arrived at the WHSR at 0233 from his apartment at the Army and Navy Club on Seventeenth Street—just two blocks from the Northwest Gate at the White House.

At 0300—after Carver's rapid-fire briefing—Smith called the president over the White House internal secure voice circuit. Then, at 0307, he ordered "Gateway"—the National Security Videoconference Network—activated and called for updates at the top of every hour. This was their third update.

The Gateway network is officially described in U.S. government budget documents as "a contractor-provided and serviced, encrypted fiber-optic system to provide continuous, uninterrupted secure communications in the event of a national emergency." It was originally constructed in the aftermath of the 9-11-01 terror attacks when conventional telecommunications services were overwhelmed by the sheer volume of calls—and tens of thousands of sensitive voice and data messages were intercepted by foreign intelligence services and hackers.

Gateway links the White House Situation Room to operations centers at the Directorate of National Intelligence, the National Counterterrorism Center, Central Intelligence Agency, the departments of State, Justice, Treasury, Defense, Energy, and Homeland Security, the FBI Operations Center, the National Military Command Center, the Federal Aviation Administration, and Northern Command headquarters at Peterson Air Force Base in Colorado.

The Gateway network can also link the WHSR directly via secure audio, video, and data to any U.S. military or diplomatic mission overseas with compatible encryption software and the appropriate satellite communications antenna. In this case, the Houston EMC was patched into the network through the DHS Ops Center. In accord with protocol, only senior watch officers speak on the Gateway SVT network when a "principal"—in this case, General Smith, the National Security Advisor—is "on the line."

"Do we have any word on casualties?" Smith asked.

"No final tally yet, sir," said the DHS SWO. "There appear to be more than one hundred dead and perhaps twice that number wounded. Most seem to be at the NASA Hilton. From what Houston EMC is saying, there were a lot of first responders killed and injured by three explosions about an hour after it all started. It will probably be an hour or more before we have a firm number."

Smith continued with his questions: "Does anyone at DHS, DNI, NCTC, or NORTHCOM have any indications of radiological or biohazard release?"

A chorus of "No, sir."

"Any claims of responsibility?" the National Security Advisor inquired.

"Not that we have received at DNI," Vincent responded. "We have NSA up on the step, as is the NGA [National Geospatial-Intelligence Agency] at Fort Belvoir. No phone chatter and nothing we have picked up on the MESH. Now that the press services have picked up on it, there are a lot of MESH bloggers, social-network types, and hackers speculating and making accusations, but nobody taking credit."

"FBI?"

"We have no traces of anything but people speculating on the phone and on the MESH about who may have done this. We have no fixes on any group, domestic or international, claiming responsibility or any organization that might be in the neighborhood and able to pull this off."

Smith then asked, "Any confirmation that any of the

VIPs from this upcoming energy conference were targeted? Have we located all of them?"

Silence. Then Vincent at DNI spoke up: "General, there are a lot of people on this network right now. This is a very sensitive issue, and I think you and I—or perhaps you and my boss—need to talk 'off-line' about this one."

"Hang it!" Smith exploded. "This isn't time for playing games, Mr. Vincent. Everyone on this SVT has a 'need to know.' What have you got?"

Vincent clearly looked uncomfortable, but he shrugged and said, "Yes, sir. Shortly after we sent out the initial alert on this event, the White House Sit Room asked us to track down the principals attending the upcoming Alternative Energy Conference at the Space Center. As you are aware, sir, international treaties, a UN convention, and our own domestic law all prohibit us from using PERT data for surveillance on law-abiding citizens. Government agencies are restricted from using PERT info for anything except border clearance, immigration enforcement, and fugitive apprehension—"

Smith interrupted. "Look, Vincent, we all know how the system works—and that it can track specific individuals. We don't need a seminar on international law or electronics at this hour of the morning. Get on with it."

"Yes, sir," the DNI watch officer continued. "We have determined that only two of the people listed on the conference agenda were already in Houston. Both of them arrived yesterday and both were apparently at the NASA Hilton when it was attacked. One of them, Dr. Franklin Pfister from California, an expert on solar power, appears to be dead in the hotel—along with his wife and ten-year-old daughter . . ."

The general was agitated and it showed. "What is this 'apparently' and 'appears to be' crap? Why are you hedging?"

"Because we don't have DNA or even a visual confirmation yet from the DPS, Houston PD, or the FBI," replied Vincent, bristling in return. "As you can see from the Houston PD vid-feeds and the press cameras outside the hotel, they are bringing a lot of dead bodies out of there. A temporary morgue has been set up across the street at the Space Center to confirm identities. But we know Dr. Pfister's PERT is immobile in a corridor of the hotel's fourth floor—as are his wife's and daughter's."

Calmer, General Smith asked, "And who is the second VIP?"

"Sir, it is Dr. Martin Cohen, a physicist at MIT. He—"

"*The* Martin Cohen," Smith interrupted. "The retired U.S. Navy admiral, Dr. Martin Cohen, who has been working on a high-power fuel cell?"

"Yes, sir. He checked into the hotel yesterday afternoon," said Vincent. "His PERT data confirms he was in the hotel when the attack occurred, and according to the Houston EMC he had a PSD of off-duty officers from the Houston PD and the Texas DPS."

"DPS?"

"Texas Department of Public Safety."

"Well, is Dr. Cohen alive? Is he okay?" Smith asked.

"We don't know."

"What do you mean you don't know?" demanded Smith. "What do his PERT life signs show?"

"Sir, his PERT signal stopped transmitting—or at least we stopped receiving his PERT geolocation and biometric data—at 0114 CST this morning," Vincent replied. "His PERT transponder may have been damaged or destroyed in the attack. He may have been wounded during the attack and transported to a hospital, or he could be one of the deceased inside the hotel not yet identified. It is also possible that he, ah, er . . . escaped."

"What do you mean—escaped?"

"Well, again, sir, we're on the edge of propriety here, but—"

"Vincent!" thundered Smith.

"Yes, sir." The DNI SWO plunged on. "As soon as we were aware of the attack, we tapped into the hotel security camera system and scooped up all previously recorded and real-time video imagery. We're having our experts examine the imagery now, but it appears that shortly after the attack began, Dr. Cohen's PSD may have escorted him out of the hotel via a fire escape—"

"Good. So where are they—and more specifically, where is Dr. Cohen—now?" Smith interjected.

Vincent swallowed and said, "We don't know, sir."

Smith shook his head. Rising from the chair beside Carver's, he said, "Send me all the imagery you have of Dr. Cohen at the hotel. Contact the Houston PD and the Texas DPS to find out where their off-duty officers are and tell them to let us know ASAP what they learn about Cohen's whereabouts and condition. Have your boss call me in my office."

## CENTURION SOLUTIONS GROUP OPERATIONS CENTER

22570 RANDOLPH ROAD
DULLES, VA
SATURDAY, 11 SEPTEMBER 2032
0630 HOURS, LOCAL

Located 1.2 miles from the end of Washington Dulles International Airport's Runway 1-Left, the Centurion Solutions Group (CSG) Operations Center is a sixty-thousand-foot, windowless, two-story, gray concrete-slab building, surrounded by a sixteen-foot-high chain-link fence. The entire structure is "TEMPEST hardened" with copper foil lining to prevent the "leaking" of all but intentional electronic emissions from the building. There is no corporate "signage," only the street number—22570—mounted high on the wall facing Randolph Road.

From the street, no doors, windows, or vehicles are visible—only an apparently unmanned security-guard station and a heavy rollback vehicle gate. A dozen high-resolution cameras mounted on the roof and atop tall "mushroom cap" poles cover every inch of the building exterior and the surrounding perimeter. Parking and building access are in the rear, out of sight to passersby unless they are willing to "break brush" east from Lockridge Road to approach the facility. There is no mailbox. Visitors are rare.

On the recessed roof of the building are seven satellite dishes pointed skyward at various angles and directions, four 200-kilowatt diesel generators, eight water-cooled air-conditioning units, and an array of radio and microwave antennas. None of this is visible from street level.

The interior of the building is divided into four functional areas. The communications center—lined with racks of electronic equipment, computer servers, fiber-optic switches, telephone circuits, radio receivers, and relays—occupies nearly the entire top floor. The ground level has twelve offices and a theater-style conference room with 150 seats. Forty feet below ground level is the CSG Operations Center, where twenty-four 5'x8' wall-mounted sheets of plastic, less than two millimeters thick, serve as flat-panel holographic screens for the eleven watch officers standing duty in the temperature- and humidity-controlled environment. There are no wires or electric sockets inside the facility. All lighting and electronic devices within the structure are powered by electromagnetic resonance coils that distribute electrical energy wirelessly throughout the building.

Icons on fourteen of the screens display geographic
identifiers for every major U.S. government installation
and military unit around the globe. Five screens provide
details on the locations and assignments of CSG's 5,327
employees, 41 offices and "training sites," 65 "Centurion
Aviation" aircraft, 7 ships, and 2,541 "independent security contractors" deployed around the world. One screen,
in the center of the west wall, is a Mercator projection
of the earth showing day/night, time zones around the
globe, the tracks of debris from the original International
Space Station, and all 779 operational and disabled satellites in geosynchronous and rotating earth orbit. Like all
the other active screens in the room, it is labeled TOP
SECRET/NOFORN. Only the four screens bearing the
CSG logo are labeled UNCLASSIFIED.

In accord with a classified contract with the White
House Communications Agency (WHCA), CSG main-
tains and monitors "Gateway," the encrypted, secure
video-teleconference (SVT) link connecting the principal
departments and agencies of the executive branch of the
U.S. government. Another of CSG's many government
contracts requires the company to "operate and retain
in a state of constant readiness, no less than five robust,
remote operating sites capable of maintaining world-wide
executive branch communications in the event of a 'de-
capitation strike' on the Seat of Government."

\*   \*   \*   \*

When the National Security Advisor in the White House
Situation Room ordered the Gateway SVT link opened at
0307 EDT, the communications watch officer in the CSG
Ops Center manually activated the network by entering
a password on his computer keyboard and pressing his
right thumb against the "screen" for biometric validation.

In less than a second, red lights flashed in a dozen U.S. government operations centers. Cameras and receivers were automatically activated in all of them as a computer-generated voice announced: "The White House Situation Room has initiated a secure video teleconference. Senior watch officers and principals only on this SVT. Please acknowledge."

At the same instant, on the top floor of 22570 Randolph Road, an automated digital data file began recording and time-coding every image and word spoken. Two stories below in the CSG Ops Center, the four screens previously displaying nothing but the company logo now showed the faces of the National Security Advisor and the others on the teleconference in a split-screen array.

Whenever words were spoken in the link, voice recognition software in the computers on the top floor of 22570 Randolph Road digested every name and place mentioned, searching for "relevance" with other information stored in their data banks. When a correlation was found—as in the case of Dr. Franklin Pfister—the computer generated a message to the CSG senior watch officer:

Dr. Franklin Pfister: Cal Poly [US]: CSG PSD 31074 dur visit to Brazil, 17–26 Jan 2031. State Dept Contract ESS DV5852G76. No Sig events. No subsequent contact. Retrieve File? Y/N

Don Gabbard, Master Gunnery Sergeant, USMC (Ret.), the CSG senior watch officer, glanced at the entry and mentally noted that "CSG PSD 31074"—a CSG personal security detail, #74—had protected Dr. Pfister when he visited Brazil in January the previous year—all in accord with a State Department contract. Seeing no other information pop up other than open-source media reports about the alternative energy research he was conducting, Gabbard pointed a finger at the *N* on his computer screen and the entry disappeared.

But a few seconds later, immediately after Bill Vincent, the DNI SWO, mentioned Dr. Martin Cohen of MIT, a new computer-generated entry appeared on Gabbard's screen:

*** ALERT ***
SWO ACTION REQUIRED

Dr. Martin Cohen: Prof. MIT [US]
Admiral, USN (Ret.)
Spouse: Julia
Daughters: Janice, Juliette
PROTECTED FILE
PERSONAL/PROFESSIONAL FRIEND OF CSG CHAIRMAN
NOTIFY CSG CHAIRMAN ASAP OF ANY SIG EVENT

Gabbard quickly scanned two hundred more lines of public-domain information about Dr. Cohen spewing from the computers two floors above. He noted that Dr. Cohen was a U.S. Naval Academy graduate, Class of 1978, a nuclear submarine officer, and an expert on propulsion systems, now teaching at the Massachusetts Institute of Technology. There were several press and MESH blog squibs about Cohen's experiments with fuel cell technology. Gabbard then scrolled back to the top and took a deep breath.

In his eleven years working in the CSG Ops Center—eight of them as a senior watch officer—Don Gabbard had seen the "notify CSG chairman" instruction pop up on his screen only once before. In 2025, when a preliminary DoD field report declared the CSG chairman's son "MIA—Presumed Captured or Dead," Gabbard delayed passing the information until after the Marine Corps made their official next-of-kin (NOK) notification. Though he and the chairman of CSG served together as Marines, the decision to postpone passing the information had nearly cost him his job. He wasn't going to make the same mistake twice.

Gabbard slipped his headset on and as he reached to punch the red button on the console beside the plastic panel that served as his computer screen, he glanced at the digital clock on the pane: 06:33:17 EDT. He listened as the phone rang twice and heard the electronic "ping" as the automated voice encryption engaged. Then a voice he knew well said, "This is Peter Newman. Go ahead, Don."

# CHAPTER ONE

# DUTY CALLS

**NARNIA FARM**
1776 RIVER ROAD
BLUEMONT, VA
SATURDAY, 11 SEPTEMBER 2032
0634 HOURS, LOCAL

When the call came in from the CSG Ops Center, Major General Peter Newman, USMC (Ret.), was nearing the end of his morning ritual—twenty minutes on a NordicTrack elliptical exercise machine, twenty minutes of calisthenics and weights, and twenty more minutes on the elliptical. For a few seconds he listened to Don Gabbard's verbal report over his PID's wireless earpiece—then coasted the machine to a halt, dismounted, and walked across the room to a wall-mounted plastic panel displaying a digital photo of the Newman family assembled in front of a Christmas tree. The general touched the picture with his right index finger. Instantly the family photo disappeared, replaced by the live image of his former ops chief.

In the CSG Ops Center, Gabbard could now see and hear his former commander, the high-def sound and image transmitted by tiny visual and acoustic sensors invisibly embedded in the flat plastic panel. Perspiration was running down the general's face.

"Thank you for the heads-up, Don," said the general in his sweat-soaked T-shirt when Gabbard finished. "I can access Dr. Cohen's file here. Keep me posted on what's happening in Houston."

"Aye, aye, sir," Gabbard replied. He then asked, "Is there anyone else you want me to notify?"

"Not now," Newman answered. "Keep an ear on the Gateway link and send me the feed right away if they find Dr. Cohen, ID the perpetrators, or if anything else happens somewhere else in the world on this awful anniversary. I will talk to James about this and one of us will get back to you once we see where this is going. Thank you, Don." With that he pointed his PID at the screen and it instantly reverted to the family Christmas scene.

Newman walked to the door of the little gym, waved a hand at a wall-mounted sensor to shut off the lights, and tapped the miniature screen on his PID to lock the door as he strode toward the main house. The sun had already crested the Blue Ridge and the late summer day was becoming warm and humid. He stopped at the gate as the two Dobermans came trotting up to meet him. When they caught his scent—or recognized him by sight, he could never tell which—both dogs just turned and ambled back to the house.

As he reached the porch steps, he again used the PID to unlock the back door, then said to the device, "Call James." In the invisible earpiece the general heard the ringtone twice and then a younger version of his own voice: "Good morning, Dad. Why aren't you working out?"

"Good morning to you, James," the general responded. "If it makes you feel any better, I just finished. What are you doing for breakfast?"

"Mmm, breakfast . . ." came the muffled response. In the background there were several thumps and then squeals. "If it makes any difference"—*thump*—"I just got back from a run"—*thump*—"and I am in the midst of a pillow fight with two boys who don't want to get up and face the day"—*thump*. "They are saying something about it being Saturday and they need to sleep in." *Thump*.

Despite the gravity of the news he had just received from Don Gabbard, the old general couldn't help but smile as he listened to the mayhem occurring a mile up the mountain to the east. After a moment he said, "I don't want to spoil the fun, but after you finish pummeling your pups and take a shower, come on down to the house and have a bowl of cereal with me. Something has come up."

"I may have to bring some lounge hounds with me," came the answer—and another thump. "Is seven fifteen soon enough?"

"Sure. Bring 'em along. We'll put 'em on a punishment detail, cutting hay with dull scissors and mucking out every stall on the farm with dinner forks."

* * * *

Peter Newman and his wife, Rachel, simply called it "the farm." But their children, James and Elizabeth, began calling it "Narnia" when they were still young—after they read C. S. Lewis's *Chronicles of Narnia*. Every bedroom had a wardrobe. There was a lamppost—plenty of furry animals—even a stone lion. The Narnia name stuck.

Tucked into a fold of the Blue Ridge Mountains and bounded by the Shenandoah River to the west, the

Appalachian Trail to the east, and hardwood forests north and south, the farm had been in Rachel's family for generations. The original house, a log cabin, was built in the early 1790s by a veteran of the Revolutionary War.

When her mother died in the spring of 2002 and then her father later that same year, Rachel inherited all her parents' property: Narnia, another farm near Charlottesville, and two "vacation" houses—one on Boot Key in Florida and another at Pawleys Island, South Carolina.

In 2008, after Peter was promoted to major general and assigned to the Marine Corps Combat Training Command at Quantico, Virginia, Rachel sold the places in Florida and Charlottesville. Her timing was impeccable. Just months after the sales closed, the real estate bubble burst and the American economy began a precipitous decline.

By the time the Great Recession hit hard, Rachel had renovated the old house at Narnia, turning it into a comfortable home for her family. She built a stable, where she kept four horses and boarded four more, started raising organic beef for sale in local markets, and planted a twelve-acre organic vegetable garden. Until the U.S. Food and Drug Administration banned the sale of "nonregistered food products," she was well on her way to keeping her vow of "making this place pay for itself."

At Pawleys, Rachel invested much of her remaining inheritance to convert the beachfront cottage where she spent so many childhood summers into a year-round home on the north end of the barrier island. The children named it "Cair Paravel," another of C. S. Lewis's mythical places. Rachel said at the time she hoped Peter would retire from the Marines and they could live out their years in quiet contentment between Narnia in the Blue Ridge Mountains and Cair Paravel on the Atlantic Ocean. She got half her wish.

In May 2011, the Marines tried to make Peter Newman the Deputy Chief of Staff for Operations and Plans—and give him his third star. He was duly nominated for lieutenant general but the Senate Armed Services Committee refused to confirm the appointment. The Secretary of the Navy called him to give him the news. On 7 June 2011, at the age of fifty-five—exactly thirty-three years after he accepted his commission as a second lieutenant of Marines at the U.S. Naval Academy in Annapolis—Major General Peter Newman, USMC, "entered the retired lists."

For nearly two years he puttered about between Pawleys Island and the farm, pretending to write his memoirs, painting shutters, fishing in "the creek" behind Cair Paravel, bird hunting in the Carolina low country—and occasionally heading out into the Gulf Stream for some "deepwater" game fish. At Narnia he planted and harvested crops, pruned the fruit trees, took cows to livestock sales, cut miles of oak fence boards and locust posts on their sawmill, and built run-in sheds for the horses using poplar boards from trees harvested and milled on the farm. He hunted the west slopes of the Blue Ridge, fished the Shenandoah, drove James and Elizabeth to sporting events—and drove Rachel crazy inspecting for "dust bunnies" under the furniture.

Friends urged him to run for political office. He turned them down, saying, "No thanks. I remember what happened to Oliver North when he tried that."

Then, on the morning of 2 April 2013, an unusually damp, cold Tuesday, just minutes after Rachel told him, "Peter, you are going to drive me crazy if you don't get on with something other than hanging around here!" he received a call from Henry Hodson, a federal judge in Richmond, Virginia.

In the 1990s, the Newmans and the Hodsons were

neighbors in Falls Church, Virginia. Then, Henry was an up-and-coming assistant U.S. attorney and Peter was a major in the Marines. In the years since, Hodson went on to head the U.S. Marshals Service, then to an appointment on the federal bench while Newman conducted "special operations" in the Corps. They had a lot in common, stayed in touch, and occasionally hunted together. Both men were members of the National Rifle Association, until the organization was banned as an "illegal extremist entity" for advocating that American citizens violate the United Nations Treaties on Small Arms and Arms Trade by refusing to register privately owned firearms.

"Peter," the judge said when Newman answered the phone, "I have a deal for you."

"Oh, what's that, your honor? Is this a belated April Fool's joke? Can I cop a plea for a lighter sentence?"

"This is no joke," Hodson answered. "As you probably know," the judge continued, "in order to comply with the UN Convention on Small Arms Control and the International Arms Trade Treaty, Congress, in its infinite wisdom, has made it illegal for U.S. corporations to do any business outside the U.S. that involves the use of firearms."

"How is that a 'deal' for me?"

"I'm getting to that," Hodson said affably. "And General, just in case no one has ever told you before, patience is not your strong suit. That's why you're such a lousy turkey hunter."

Peter smiled and replied, "Okay, your honor, I'm listening."

Hodson continued, "I've just been handed the Chapter Eleven bankruptcy cases for three of the private security companies put out of business by the new law—"

"I thought bankruptcies were handled by some administrative court. How come you have this kind of case?

Did 'Hang 'em High Henry' get booted off the bench for
cruelty to convicted felons?"

"Very funny, General," said Hodson. "You are correct.
Bankruptcies are normally handled by the U.S. Bankruptcy Court—right here in this same building. But there
have been so many of them the last few years that all the
judges in this circuit are taking them now. And besides,
these three are special cases and I need to appoint someone as U.S. trustee who knows what he or she is doing."

"And you want me to . . ."

Hodson finished the sentence: "Get off your big general's butt, come down to Richmond, and get sworn in as
the U.S. trustee for three of the biggest private armies on
the planet. And do it before their heavily armed employees march on Washington."

"I see," replied Newman. "How long do I have to think
about this?"

Suddenly completely serious, Hodson answered,
"Peter, I'm imposing on our friendship—but I need your
help with this one. Can you come to Richmond this afternoon?"

\* \* \* \*

Three hours after hanging up the phone, Major General
Peter Newman, USMC (Ret.), was in the chambers of
Senior Judge Henry Hodson on East Main Street in Richmond, Virginia. Two days later, the retired Marine was
appointed as U.S. trustee for the three security companies.

On Wednesday, 1 May, after twenty-seven days and
nights of furious work, and countless meetings with the
security companies' owners, creditors, clients, lawyers,
employees, and accountants, Newman filed a consolidated
disclosure of assets and liabilities and presented his reorganization plan. It called for merging the three companies

into a single entity, incorporated as Centurion Solutions Group.

Judge Hodson approved the plan with one caveat: the owners, clients, and creditors had to agree to have the retired Marine oversee compliance with the reorganization for the next twelve months. Newman and the other parties all agreed, but the arrangement didn't last that long.

At a regularly scheduled meeting of the court-appointed Creditors' Committee on Monday, 2 December 2013, the owners and creditors of the former companies unanimously nominated Newman to take over full-time management of the new, consolidated corporation. He talked it over, first with Rachel and then with Judge Hodson. Both urged Peter to take the job. Two weeks later Peter Newman became the chairman and chief executive officer of Centurion Solutions Group, Inc.

By 2018, the year James Newman graduated from the Naval Academy, CSG had contracts to provide a menu of telecommunications, logistics, security, intelligence, and "quick response" support for seven U.S. government departments and agencies and fifteen American corporations operating in the United States and overseas. The company also operated Centurion Aviation, a highly profitable, worldwide "air taxi" service that quietly advertised "terror-free flights to where you want to go." CSG even had its own medical staff, disaster relief operations, and a "counterpiracy service" for international shipping.

Though the global economy was still sputtering in the midst of the Great Recession, CSG was quietly flourishing. Despite new laws forbidding American citizens or the foreign employees/contractors of U.S.-owned companies from carrying or using firearms overseas, CSG's "security and protective services" continued to grow and prosper.

How Peter Newman managed to pull this off was a

constant source of frustration to the media. Press reports and left-leaning MESH bloggers repeatedly referred to him as a "mercenary" and called CSG employees and contractors "hired guns." Centurion Aviation was routinely castigated for "profiling" their passengers instead of subjecting them to U.S.-government-approved, FAA-certified "biometric validation," full-body scans, and pat-down searches.

During a rare interview in 2022, the general was asked, "How can your CSG company manage to defy the laws of economic gravity without breaking other laws?"

Newman attributed the company's success to "being blessed with the ability to discern what needs to be done, then finding the right people to do it faster, better, and at lower cost than anyone else."

What Newman didn't say was that he personally ensured that all CSG employees—including those running Centurion Aviation—were former military, CIA, FBI, Secret Service, or DEA personnel with top secret clearances. By the time James left the Marines in 2026 and joined CSG as chief operations officer, the company had grown to nearly 2,500 full-time employees, along with nearly 6,000 contract personnel, and was billing more than $2.9 billion a year.

\* \* \* \*

James and two of his four boys arrived for breakfast at the stroke of seven fifteen. They raced down the hill from their house on mountain bikes and came charging up the back porch, past the two bewildered Dobermans.

"Halt! Who goes there?" shouted Peter Newman as they burst into the kitchen, out of breath.

The twelve-year-old replied first: "Lance Corporal Seth Newman, reporting as ordered, sir!"

Then, from the boy two and a half years younger and a foot shorter, "Private First Class Joshua Newman, reporting as ordered, sir!"

"Very well. Advance and be recognized," replied the old general with a smile and a wink at James, standing behind them at the doorway. Then, after hugging them all, he said, "Who's ready for chow?"

As they scrambled for their seats, Rachel came down the stairs and said, "Not so fast! Aren't the troops going to wash their hands first?"

While the boys went to the kitchen sink to do their duty, Rachel poured fresh-squeezed orange juice into glasses and set five places at the old oak table she bought years before at a foreclosure auction. When they took their seats, they joined hands around the table and bowed their heads while Peter said a quick thanksgiving for the food, a habit from his days at "Canoe U"—when midshipmen were still allowed to pray on government property.

From a glass jar on the table, Rachel spooned into their bowls healthy portions of her homemade granola—produced from oats, wheat, corn, and honey from the farm—and covered the cereal with fresh Narnia strawberries. As the boys added cold milk from a stoneware pitcher, Peter poured cups of steaming hot coffee for the three adults.

During their meal, they chatted about the pains of "never-ending homeschool homework" and the pleasures of a lazy Saturday. When they finished, Peter said, "You know, I saw some really big bass in the pond below the barn. Why don't you guys grab your fishing poles and see what you can do about catching us some dinner."

Both boys were ready to go in an instant—but only after asking "Nan," their name for their grandmother, "May we please be excused?"

Rachel looked at the clock on the wall, shook her

head, and said, "Fifteen minutes, elapsed time; pretty quick breakfast." But then she smiled and said, "Certainly, gentlemen." And in a flash they were gone.

As the boys bounded off the porch, James turned to his father and said, "When you called, you said something had come up."

Peter asked, "Have you seen the news this morning?"

"Only what has come over this, from our Ops Center," James responded, holding up his PID. "It's a lot more accurate than the media reports." He continued, "I've already checked. All CSG sites and personnel have been alerted. We don't have any active PSDs in Houston. Why did the Ops Center contact you about Dr. Cohen? He's not one of our protectees."

The old general sighed and said, looking at his son, "Marty Cohen was my roommate at the Academy. If it weren't for him—"

"Yeah, I know, Dad," interrupted James. "I grew up on the stories about how you and Mack Caperton, your other roommate, wouldn't have passed physics or thermodynamics . . . might not have gotten through the Boat School . . . and how Marty Cohen was number one in your class and how he dragged you guys on his back all the way to graduation . . ."

"Well, he did," Peter responded quietly.

The son grimaced at the father. "Dad, are you forgetting I went there, too? I know all about how Marty Cohen went on to four stars as a nuclear submariner. But you were in the top third of your class. So was Mack Caperton. You became a major general in the Marines. Caperton went on to become a SEAL and a U.S. senator. Cut yourself some slack . . ."

"James!" said Rachel, who had stopped picking up the breakfast detritus. "Your father and Marty Cohen are friends. Julia Cohen and I are friends. Marty is missing! I was on the phone with Julia just before coming down to breakfast. He was in Houston during the attack. He's now missing. She is beside herself . . ."

Her eyes welled up with tears and she sat down beside her husband. Peter put his arm around her, turned to his son, and said, "James, I know we all had other plans for the rest of the weekend and next week, but I need your help with this."

The son was silent for a long moment, looking at his parents. Then he leaned forward and said quietly, "Okay, Dad. I think I know a little bit about what a person will do for a friend. I'll get on this right away. When Seth and Josh come back from fishing, tell them I've gone up to the office."

James rose, patted his father on the shoulder, went outside, got on his bike, and pedaled the half mile up the hill to the CSG office. Eight hours later, he was on his way to Dulles Airport for a scheduled commercial flight to Chicago and on to Calgary. He couldn't take a company plane. Centurion Aviation was barred from using Canadian airports because it profiled passengers in violation of Canadian human rights laws.

### TREATY ROOM, WHITE HOUSE RESIDENCE

1600 PENNSYLVANIA AVENUE

WASHINGTON, DC

SATURDAY, 11 SEPTEMBER 2032

0800 HOURS, LOCAL

Ulysses S. Grant used this room on the east side of the White House second-story residence for cabinet meetings. President William McKinley employed the space for a ceremonial signing of the peace treaty ending the Spanish-American War. Since then it has been called simply the Treaty Room.

From the room's full-length windows, the view across the Truman Balcony takes in the Ellipse and the Washington Monument. Most modern presidents have used the room as a study and for small, private, off-the-record meetings.

During the tenure of Presidents Lyndon Johnson and Richard Nixon, the Treaty Room was one of the few places inside the eighteen-acre White House complex where conversations were not monitored and recorded. The present occupant of the White House insisted on the same requirement. As the chief executive exploded in anger, General John Smith, the National Security Advisor, reflected on the wisdom of that decision.

"This is outrageous! A terror attack, fifty-one days before my reelection!" the president shouted, interrupting the briefing Smith and White House Chief of Staff Muneer Murad had come to deliver. "We had a deal! How the hell can he do this . . ."

"Madam President," Murad interrupted. He was one of the few in her inner circle who dared do so. Before she could cut him off, the chief of staff pressed on: "As General Smith just said, we don't know who did this. But what we do know is that it is too dangerous for you to go to Houston tomorrow and we need to cancel your attendance at the Pentagon 9-11 Memorial ceremony an hour and forty-five minutes from now. We also need time to take a careful look at your upcoming campaign appearances—"

"No!" she said emphatically. "I will *not*, I repeat *not*, be taken off the campaign trail by this. Now, you listen to me, both of you. I didn't get to be the first woman president just to be driven out of office when I'm on the verge of being reelected. Use the Secret Service, the military, whatever you need, and make sure I can keep my campaign schedule."

"But . . ." Murad tried to interrupt again.

"Shut up," she snarled at her chief of staff. He complied.

Then, turning to her National Security Advisor, she continued, "John, you and M&M work out a statement I can insert into my remarks at the Pentagon. Since you just told me you don't know who did this—blame it on 'Anarks.' This will give us a good reason to crack down on these crazies who breed like rabbits and won't play by the new rules. Have the FBI go out and arrest a bunch of them. If the Attorney General squawks, tell him his job is on the line." Both men nodded, sensing their jobs were as well.

"Now," she continued, "is there anyone out there who is going to contradict us if we say the attack in Houston is the work of Anarks?"

"Well," Smith began. "Even though no group has claimed credit yet, it is possible, I would say likely, that someone will. Though one or two of the perpetrators appear to be Hispanic, we won't have any DNA tracking data from recovered remains for at least a few more hours. But you have to understand, the attacks in Houston have all the telltale fingerprints of an Islamic Jihad attack or one of its affiliates. There were at least three suicide bombers we know of, perhaps more—"

"Stop," the president ordered. "First, for years I have been telling everyone my dear departed husband's 'Framework for Peace' and my Mideast Peace Treaty solved the problem of radical Islamic terrorism. We've staked my reelection on the success of all the measures we have taken to make it a fact. I've told the voters that PERT technology has stopped illegal aliens and terrorists from getting into this country. They believe me. We're not going to confuse people now with some new revelation. If some group makes such a claim, deny it."

Smith nodded, but said nothing.

"Second," she continued, "our 'Revitalize America' and 'Better Deal for All' economic plans are just about to pay off in getting unemployment below ten percent with good-paying government jobs. If people think we're vulnerable again to Islamic terror attacks, or if the price of oil goes sky-high again, it will all go down the drain. Who would be able to contradict the idea that this is the work of a domestic, right-wing extremist, Anark fringe group?"

The general was silent for a beat and then said, "I would guess that most foreign governments and their intelligence services will follow our lead. Certainly, your cabinet officers will. Of course, we can't control pirate broadcasts out of reach of the Communications Fairness Division of the FCC. And I suppose there is always the possibility of a leak from one of our contractors who do most of our domestic and foreign intelligence collection."

"Okay," the president said, "let's stop talking about this. I have to get ready to leave for the Pentagon." She paused for a moment and then addressed both men: "Put out the word that the attack in Houston appears to be an Anark operation, with ties to Mexican drug cartels and Jewish fanatics upset about our Mideast Peace Treaty. Anyone—contractor, broadcaster, MESH blogger, and whether it's an individual or a group—who disputes that is subject to arrest under the Spreading Fear Statute and our anti-extremism hate-speech laws. This Supreme Court has upheld them both. That's how we shut down the NRA. Now go."

As the two men headed for the door, Murad's stomach was churning. He despised the "M&M" nickname she inflicted upon him. And though he tried very hard to never let it show, his Arab heritage seethed at taking orders from a woman. As they exited, they both had PIDs in their hands, summoning deputies to meet them in their respective West Wing offices.

Just as they reached the top of the stairs to head down to the ground floor, the president stepped out of the Treaty Room into the Center Hall and said, "M&M, there's one more thing."

They both stopped and Murad replied, "Yes?"

"When I return from the Pentagon," she said, looking directly at her chief of staff, "I want you to get your friend the Caliph on the secure line. If he has broken the pledge he made to me about no terror attacks until after the election, there is going to be hell to pay."

Murad simply nodded and turned to go down the stairs.

That's when Smith noticed the Secret Service agent posted beside the entry to the Treaty Room. She was wearing a dark blue two-piece pantsuit and standing immobile with her hands clasped "fig leaf" style. Their eyes met for an instant. There was no hint in her expression that she had even heard what the president just said.

That was, after all, her duty. That is why it's called the "Secret Service." But as Smith walked toward his office, the retired general made a note in his PID to find out her name.

# CHAPTER TWO

# WANTED

## MAPLE LEAF ROUTE 1, TRANS CANADA HIGHWAY

CALGARY, ALBERTA, CANADA
MONDAY, 13 SEPTEMBER 2032
1045 HOURS, LOCAL

James Newman knew he was a wanted man. He just didn't know why.

The unmarked, dark blue sedan in the old Harley's rearview mirrors had been behind him since he pulled out of the University of Calgary. It followed him on Twenty-Fourth Avenue as he headed east toward the southbound ramp of Crowchild Trail.

Newman punched the car's license number and a "?" into the PID mounted on the motorcycle's handlebars, hit SEND and less than five seconds later he had a four-letter answer: "RCMP"—the Royal Canadian Mounted Police. As he accelerated past the stadium at Foothills Athletic Park, he noticed a second, identical car joining the chase, fifty yards behind the first.

For an instant he considered making a break for it. Except for motorcycles and the big, twenty-four-wheel, Inter-American freight haulers and petro-tankers, the highway was almost devoid of traffic. The Harley Nightster's 73.4-cubic-inch engine might be twenty years old, but Newman knew it could easily outrun any government hybrid.

Instead he throttled back, downshifted, thumbed his right-turn signal, and exited the four-lane highway on the Sixteenth Avenue ramp, following signs to the eastbound lanes of the Trans Canada Highway. With the two blue hybrid sedans trailing, he settled down to an easy speed-limit pace until he saw the sign SOUTHERN ALBERTA INSTITUTE OF TECHNOLOGY, 1 KM.

As Newman slowed to make the exit into the North Hill Shopping Center, adjacent to the engineering campus, the lead blue sedan suddenly flashed its lights, sped up, and pulled even with the black motorcycle. A loudspeaker beneath the hood blared, "Pull over, police."

Newman obeyed, slowly coming to a stop in the nearly empty shopping center parking lot. With the Harley's distinctive exhaust cut to a murmur, he touched a button on the handlebars and spoke into the microphone inside the motorcycle helmet: "Pulled over by RCMP. Plot my GPS location. Stay tuned for more. Out."

As Newman unzipped the black leather flight jacket and removed his bright blue helmet, the lead car pulled in front of the bike, stopped abruptly, and all doors but the driver's flew open. Three well-built men emerged, all identically attired: dark blue suits, light blue shirts buttoned to the collar, no tie. In the Harley's rearview mirror he could see the second car, ten yards behind him—a camera lens visible inside the windshield.

"Good morning, James Stuart Newman," said the

oldest of the three as he approached the bike and rider, holding out his badge and credentials. "Senior Inspector Christopher Jackson, Royal Canadian Mounted Police. What's your business in Canada?"

"Good morning yourself, Inspector," replied Newman with a smile. "Aren't you supposed to warn me of my rights first? Am I suspected of breaking any laws?"

"Ah, you're a clever one, aren't you, eh?" said the police officer, not smiling at all. "Just like in the Lower Forty-Eight, we're required to record every stop and detention. So I have to tell you, for the benefit of the cameras, that you are not being apprehended or detained."

"Then why did you pull me over?" asked Newman, still sitting astride the motorcycle, eyeing not only the inspector but his two colleagues, who stood with their coats unbuttoned, hands at their sides, about ten feet behind their superior. They were spread far enough apart so if they had to, they both could get a clear shot at the man on the Harley without hitting the inspector in front of him or the sedan behind him.

"Well, to be quite honest about it, Mr. Newman, I don't quite know why you are of interest to my superiors in Ottawa—but I do know my provincial field office was directed to see to it that your business here is concluded and you depart Canada expeditiously. Apparently your PERT data is transmitting intermittently. According to our data you have an implanted PERT. Where is it?"

Newman held up his right foot and said, "Between my third and fourth toes."

The RCMP officer pulled a scanner about the size of a TV remote from a holster on his belt, waved it over Newman's raised foot, looked at the digital readout, shrugged, and said, "Looks like your PERT is working to me. You know it's contrary to the North American Union Treaty and forbidden by laws in your country and mine to tamper with your PERT signal, right, Mr. Newman?"

"Of course," the motorcycle rider replied. "So may I go now?"

"Well now, it depends on where you are going," said the inspector. Then he added through a tight smile, "I'm trying to be pleasant about this, Mr. Newman. Please remember, we're Canadians. We're the *nice* North Americans. So where *are* you going, Mr. Newman?"

Newman looked at the policeman, shrugged, and said, "I'm headed back east to watch the trees change color."

The officer was no longer smiling. He reached into his pocket, pulled out a PID, and said, "Let's stop playing games, Mr. Newman." The inspector touched the screen to activate the device and continued: "Your PERT informed us when you arrived Saturday night on Air Canada flight 5081 from Chicago—less than twelve hours after serious criminal activity took place in Houston, Texas. We know you stayed Saturday night and all day yesterday at the home of Professor Steven Templeton. We know at five thirty this morning, an unusually early time of day, you accompanied him to the university's Applied Sciences Laboratory. Do you want more?" asked the policeman.

"Sure," James replied with a shrug.

"Very well," the Mountie continued, looking at the screen. "We know at eight fifty-five this morning you placed a call to Dr. Davis Long at the Southern Alberta Institute of Technology from Professor Templeton's laboratory phone and talked for exactly six minutes and thirty-one seconds. We know the Harley Davidson Nightster motorcycle you are riding is registered to Stanley Templeton—the son of your professor friend. And now we want to know where you are heading. You know you can't hide. How about it, eh? We're going to track you anyway."

"Who is 'we,' and why are 'we' so interested in where I am going, Inspector?" asked Newman.

"As far as you are concerned, I am 'we,' Mr. Newman, and 'we' are responsible for preserving law and order, enforcing international agreements, and protecting security in this province of Canada," Jackson replied, his voice hardening.

When the man on the motorcycle said nothing in response, the inspector placed his hand over the wireless microphone embedded in the RCMP pin on the lapel of his suit coat and bent down so Newman's head masked the camera mounted in the police car behind the motorcycle.

The inspector continued, barely above a whisper, "I was in Canadian Special Forces during the Shindand campaign in 2025—back when this country still had a military. I know what you did then. I don't know why you're in Canada now, but I do know you are in danger. From whom—or what—I don't know. But you need to get out of here—quickly."

Newman still said nothing and he tried hard to keep the surprise he felt from registering on his face. Finally, in frustration, the Mountie reached into his trousers pocket, withdrew an object, held it in front of the motorcyclist's face, and said, "Now do you believe me?" Clutched between the policeman's thumb and forefinger was a tiny metal fish.

"I have one of those, but that's not in my PERT file," said Newman, still wary.

"I know," said Jackson. "Those of us who carry these are in a different database—at least for now." As he put the little ichthys back in his pocket, he said, "You need to get out of here, do you understand me?"

"Okay. I'll leave. But first I need to go next door to meet someone," Newman said, gesturing toward the Southern Alberta Institute of Technology campus, across the Fourteenth Street expressway.

"Who?"

"Dr. Davis Long, in the engineering department," Newman responded.

"Don't bother. Professor Long is dead."

"Dead?" Newman was visibly stunned. "How? When? I just talked to her less than two hours ago."

The Canadian lawman, still covering the microphone on his lapel, said, "We know. Apparently she committed suicide by jumping off the roof a few minutes after you and Professor Templeton hung up the phone. Her body was found on the pavement of Fowler Drive. The death is being investigated by the campus and municipal police. They haven't located anyone who saw her fall. Any idea why she might want to kill herself?"

"No. But I know she wouldn't commit suicide."

"How do you know?"

"Because she also carried one of those little metal fish," Newman said emphatically. "I need to get to her office right away. Can I go there?"

The big Canadian cop thought for a moment, then stood erect, took his hand off the lapel mike, and said, "Follow me."

The motorcade started up again, this time with the deep-throated Harley between the two sedans. They exited the south side of the nearly abandoned shopping center, turned left on Fourteenth Avenue, crossed over Fourteenth Street on the overpass, and turned left on Fowler into the campus. They stopped at the yellow police tape.

Jackson ordered the rest of his crew to stay with the cars and motioned for Newman to follow him. James shut off the ignition, removed his helmet, dropped the kick-stand, dismounted, and followed the broad-shouldered Mountie into the building.

Immediately inside the door they were stopped by a uniformed campus police officer who said, "I'm sorry, gentlemen, you can't enter right now. There is an ongoing police investigation."

Jackson merely nodded at the policeman and said curtly, "Check my ID on your PID, Officer Thomas," and headed for the elevators.

The uniformed officer glanced down at his personal interface device, mounted on a police wristband, looked up, and said, "Excuse me, Chief Inspector Jackson. You'll want the third floor, room three twenty-one."

When the elevator doors closed, Newman was surprised to see Jackson reach under his coat and switch off the lapel mike's tiny wireless transmitter fastened to his belt. With that done, the inspector turned to Newman and said, "Look, you are going to have to trust me. What are you here for? Does this have to do with the work Dr. Long was doing with Dr. Martin Cohen and Professor Templeton before Cohen disappeared?"

Newman shook his head, trying to grasp all that had happened since leaving Templeton's laboratory. Still uncertain about how much to tell the Canadian lawman, he said, "You probably know this anyway, Inspector. Professor Templeton, Dr. Cohen, and my father are all classmates from our Naval Academy. Class of 1978. They are lifelong friends. My father and Professor Templeton care about Dr. Cohen and his family—"

"And Dr. Cohen, Professor Templeton, and Dr. Long were all working on some kind of advanced fuel cell technology that didn't sit well with the Caliph. I suppose you know that in this part of Canada, the Caliph and the

Chinese are competing to buy all our oil and natural gas business," added Jackson, helpfully.

Newman nodded without speaking as the elevator doors opened to the third floor. Everything the Mountie had just said about the three scientists was true—and public knowledge. There was a media frenzy six months earlier when it was announced that Cohen, Templeton, and Long had achieved a scientific breakthrough for making high-powered hydrogen fuel cells commercially viable. That this news was not well received in oil- and natural gas–rich Russia, Mexico, Brazil, Venezuela, and the Caliphate was also well-known. So too was the fact that cash-rich Chinese companies were buying every energy resource they could.

"Does this have to do with the Cohen-Templeton-Long discovery?" persisted the Canadian law officer as they walked down the hall toward a group of uniformed police officers. "What are you looking for here in Canada?"

Seeing the crowd gathered outside room 321, Newman suddenly realized he needed the chief inspector's help. "I'm here to pick up a digital memory card," he said softly. "It's in the bottom drawer of Dr. Long's safe."

The inspector simply nodded, walked up to the four uniformed officers standing outside the door, flashed his credentials as a courtesy, and said, "Chief Inspector Jackson, RCMP."

One of the officers in a Calgary Police Service uniform checked his wrist-mounted PID, then stepped forward and said, "Christopher, this is our investigation. Is the RCMP taking it over?"

Jackson smiled and said, "We'll have to see about that, Jonathan. You know how it goes—the Mounties always get their man—even if it means taking credit for your work." Then, more seriously, he said, "You have

Cummings in there. I need to talk to him. Won't take a minute. Excuse us."

With that, Jackson stepped between the men in blue uniforms and opened the door. Newman followed him into the spacious office. Two crime-scene investigators attired in paper coveralls were painstakingly document-ing the chaos with tiny digital cameras equipped with UV strobes. One of the investigators looked up and said, "Sorry about the disorder, Chief Inspector. Seems as though someone 'tossed' the place looking for something before we arrived."

"I should hope it was before you arrived, Cummings," Jackson said, surveying the mess. "Any prints?"

"Sure, lots of 'em," the investigator replied. "But so far they all match student or faculty prints in the national registry. No 'bad-boy' matchups yet. Whoever did this was probably wearing gloves."

"Well, whoever did this may have been here before-hand—without gloves," Jackson said. "Any surveillance images or PERT records?"

"First thing I asked for when we got here," replied the forensic investigator, while snapping images of an upturned lamp. "According to all available PERT data we have, Dr. Long was alone in here this morning. There are audio and video sensors at the main entrance, on the elevators, and in the hallways, but none in the stairways or inside this office. It's primitive time lapse; fifteen-second interval; useless. The perps probably knew that and timed their entry and exit so they wouldn't get imaged."

"Perps? How do you know more than one person did this?"

"Because Dr. Long was on the phone from this office less than fifteen minutes before she fell, jumped, or was pushed off the roof," answered Cummings. "Unless her office was like this while she was here, this was all done between the end of her last call and her sudden stop on Fowler Drive. The campus police were in this office within ten minutes of her death. One person couldn't make this mess in that length of time."

Jackson nodded, looked at Newman, then at Cummings, and asked, "Do you know who she was talking to on that last call?"

Cummings now paused in his work, pulled a PID from the pocket of his coveralls, thumbed the screen until he found what he was looking for, and said, "She arrived in the office at eight-oh-five. Apparently came directly from her home after stopping at Tim Hortons for a doughnut and coffee. Over the course of the next forty minutes, she placed three phone calls: two to members of the faculty and one to a student. At eight fifty-five she took a call from the office of Dr. Steven Templeton at the University of Calgary. Seven minutes later she placed her last call. It lasted less than five minutes. At nine twenty-five her body was found on Fowler Drive."

"You didn't answer my question," said the chief inspector at the end of the recitation.

"You're correct," replied Cummings. "Because her last call was to the switchboard of the U.S. Senate in Washington, D.C. And as you know, Inspector, the North American Union Treaty does not permit us to monitor those calls."

Jackson nodded, paused a beat, and asked, "Is there an alarm system in here?"

"Of course not," said Cummings, grimacing. "Come now, Inspector, if people did all these things, they would put me out of work."

"Where's the safe?"

"Over there, if you can get to it," Cummings replied, gesturing toward an anteroom full of file cabinets—and a four-drawer safe. "But before you touch anything, please put these on," he added, handing Jackson and Newman each a pair of latex gloves.

The inside of the file room was even worse than the office. File drawers were opened and documents were strewn everywhere. As they made their way through the mess, Jackson said, "Apparently Dr. Long missed the memo about going paperless." The safe was the only unopened cabinet.

Jackson stared at the heavy steel box and said, "Now there's an antique. Old S&G government model from the last century. Manual dial combination and all. Unless we have the combination, we'll need a torch to get into that thing."

"We don't need a torch" was all Newman said. He reached into his jacket pocket, withdrew a PID, pulled off his right glove, touched his forefinger to the screen, and it immediately lit up. He scrolled down on the screen and four numbers appeared. As he put the latex glove back on he looked Jackson in the eyes and said, "Professor Templeton knew the combination. He gave it to me this morning."

With the inspector watching, Newman spun the dial, left, right, left, and right again, finally stopping at zero. He then rotated the little toggle in the center of the combination dial, spun the wheel a quarter turn until it stopped, and pulled down on the lever mounted on the drawer. There was a resounding *thunk* as the lock pinions disengaged.

The top three drawers were tightly packed with neatly labeled files. But as Newman pulled the bottom drawer open, both men could see it was empty except for a single silver digital memory card, less than an inch long. As Newman reached for it, Jackson said, "Stop!" Newman looked at the big policeman, who then added, "Before we touch anything, I want Cummings in here with his handy little camera." He turned and went into the outer office to summon the forensic investigator.

In the thirty seconds it took for Jackson to return with Cummings, Newman reached into the drawer, pulled out the tiny card, held it against his PID, and touched DOWNLOAD on the screen. By the time Jackson returned with the white-clad Cummings and his camera, Newman had the PID back in his pocket and the memory card back in the drawer.

It took Cummings, camera in hand, nearly five minutes to "image" the contents of the safe. Just as he was completing his work, there was a commotion at the hall doorway, and two men—both attired in pinstripe suits and shirts buttoned to the collar without ties—practically burst into the outer office.

The lead intruder turned toward the file room, his eyes widening above a closely trimmed beard. "Jackson, what's going on in here!" he shouted. "This isn't your purview."

The chief inspector let out a groan and said under his breath to Newman, "Ahh, the Calgary chief prosecutor. This will be interesting. Close up the safe and follow me."

Cummings watched Newman close the drawers of the safe and spin the combination dial. Then both men followed the big Mountie out of the file room and back into the office.

"I'll have your badge for this, Jackson!" yelled the prosecutor, waving his arms about furiously. "This isn't your investigation. If you and your leather-jacketed goon aren't out of here immediately, I'm calling Ottawa and having you sacked! Do you understand me?"

"Okay, Mr. Al-Nouri," said the Mountie with a shrug. "I was just trying to help. We're on our way. Come on, James."

As they exited the office, both men peeled off their latex gloves. Newman stuffed his into the rear pocket of his jeans—and never noticed when one fell on the floor as they stepped into the corridor. The gaggle of officers outside the door when Newman and Jackson arrived was now at the opposite end of the hallway. As the elevator door closed, Jackson asked quietly, "Did you get what you came for?"

Newman, mindful of what Cummings had said about surveillance cameras in the elevators, simply said, "It's still in the bottom drawer of the safe." Jackson shrugged, reached down, and switched on the microphone transmitter on his belt.

As they exited the building and headed back toward the Harley sandwiched between the two blue sedans, Jackson said, "I'm sorry we couldn't have been of more help to you, Mr. Newman." Handing Newman a business card, the Mountie added, "Here's my card. Please be in touch if we can be of any assistance in the future. Now, how are you going back to the Lower Forty-Eight? Virginia, isn't it?"

For James it was another subtle reminder about how much others knew about him. Before zipping up his jacket he said, "Yes, Chief Inspector, Virginia. I guess I'll head east on Route 1 and cross back into the states at Detroit. Fuel is cheaper here in Canada."

"One of the advantages to living up here, eh?" replied the Canadian lawman.

"I suppose," James said, then added, "Please do what you can to look after Dr. Templeton."

Jackson scowled and asked, "Do you think he's in danger?"

Newman paused a second and responded: "I don't know, but I didn't think Dr. Long would be dead today, either."

The chief inspector simply nodded and held out his hand. The two men shook hands and without further ceremony, Newman put on his helmet, fired up the Harley, put up the kickstand, stepped the big bike into gear, and eased out on the clutch. Jackson watched Newman head north on Fowler toward the Trans Canada Highway.

As the motorcycle turned right, onto the eastbound lanes of the highway, the inspector turned to his driver and said, "Morton, send a message to our office in Medicine Hat. Inform them that James Stuart Newman, a person of interest to our superiors in Ottawa, is headed east on the Trans Can and should make it there in five hours, more or less. Give them the motorcycle's GPS ident code and Newman's PERT data."

"Yes, sir," Officer Morton replied. Then he added, "But of course, you know, sir, if he's riding that motorcycle it will take him less than three hours to get to Medicine Hat."

"Thank you, Morton. Very astute," Inspector Jackson replied, looking closely at his subordinate. Then Jackson continued: "Wait ten minutes to file that report. Our colleagues in Medicine Hat apparently intend to track him with a UAV. Tell them I don't want them to interfere with him until he crosses into Saskatchewan. I don't want him stopped in Alberta. It creates too many reports. I hate filing reports."

*    *    *    *

James Newman never made it to the Alberta-Saskatchewan provincial border. Just a mile east of the institute he turned right on Centre Street and into a truck stop full of twenty-four-wheelers. Interspersed among the big intracontinental rigs were a handful of motorcycles—but no cars. He went inside, selected a half-dozen protein bars from a shelf, took three liter-sized containers of water from a refrigerated display case, went to the counter to check out, and presented his PID.

As she swept the nine items across the sensor built into the countertop and put them in a sack labeled FULLY DEGRADABLE BIO-BAG, the clerk said, "I'm sorry, sir, but our electronic payment system inside the store is down. It still works on the fuel pumps, but in here it's cash only. That will be four-point-three gex."

Newman reached into his pocket and pulled out several bills, all U.S. The young woman smiled and said, "Oh, you must be American. Well, that's okay. We still take your currency until next year, when you switch to Global Exchange Units like the rest of us." Then she added, "That will be fifteen dollars in your money, plus one more gek—the mandatory International Monetary Transaction Fee. I'm sorry, but it's the law. That will be a total of eighteen-point-six of your dollars."

He started to protest the "rounding up," then shrugged and handed her a U.S. twenty-dollar bill. She keyed an entry into a keypad on the counter, then handed him a receipt for ¤5.3 and four small coins embossed with "¤.1 Global Exchange Unit" on one side and the United Nations seal on the other.

James said, "Thank you," picked up his purchases, and headed out the door. After stuffing the energy bars and water into the bike's right saddlebag, he wheeled the machine over to the fuel pumps.

While watching for any "followers," he topped off the Harley's 3.3-gallon tank. The fifty-fifty gasoline/ethanol mix was just ¤1.0 per liter. Newman did the math in his head: one gek per liter = 3.785 gex per gallon; 3.5 dollars per gek = $13.25 a gallon—almost $4 per gallon cheaper than in the United States.

James checked the digital display on the pump to ensure the transaction was recorded, read the cheery PAID BY PERT, THANK YOU message, then mounted the bike and pulled around to the back of the service bays. He parked between stacks of discarded tires, batteries, and vehicle parts beneath a RECYCLE HERE sign. After quickly checking to see if he could spot any surveillance cameras, he reached into the left saddlebag, removed a small gym bag, and carried it into the men's room.

After locking the door, Newman pulled some scrap paper out of the trash, spread it on the tile floor, and placed the motorcycle helmet on the paper. Then he took a small can of quick-dry flat black spray paint from the bag and coated the bright blue helmet until no sign of its original color was visible.

While the helmet dried, he removed his jeans and leather jacket and put on a pair of dark green Carhartt work trousers and a navy blue nylon parka. He then exchanged his chukka boots for a pair of foil-lined military boots. Returning to the Harley, he pulled five sheets of black lead foil from the saddlebag and used them to wrap the bike's fuel tank, securing it in place with black tape—effectively putting the GPS transponder inside the tank on "mute."

Newman checked his watch: 12:35. He sat down on the bike, reconnected his helmet to the PID device on the handlebars, keyed the button on his right wrist, and said into the helmet microphone, "Change of plans. I'm coming back on a borrowed bike. I should be at Foxtrot Charlie Alpha by 2300. I'm shutting off the GPS locater on this PID. Will key you twice when I'm an hour out of FCA so you can have one of our aircraft ready. I need to be back at your end of CONUS for breakfast."

An instant after James said the words, the PID converted his voice into an encrypted data message and transmitted it in a burst of zeroes and ones to the CSG Operations Center. Five seconds later, as he fired up the bike's engine, he heard a *ping* in the helmet's earphones, signaling his message was received.

Newman exited the truck stop on Centre Street, carefully merging into the southbound lane of trucks and motorcycles headed for the Centre Street Bridge, over the River Bow. Once across the river, he picked up MacLeod Trail and followed the four-lane highway to the intersection with Glenmore Trail. Here he cut back again to the east, moving with the traffic and following the signs to Deerfoot Trail—Alberta Route 2. At the cloverleaf, he merged onto the southbound ramp, checking the rearview mirrors for followers—and trying hard not to do anything too exciting with the bike, to avoid attracting attention on the highway traffic cameras.

Thirty minutes later he was in open country, speeding south on the highway, passing broad fields of hybrid grain and corn, dotted with natural gas wellheads and oil pumps rocking slowly up and down. At every interchange there were flatbeds loaded with "fracking pipe"—steel tubes for horizontal drilling that meant billions for Canadian oil and gas companies.

Rolling with the high-speed, international truck traffic, it took him less than an hour and a half to reach Fort MacLeod. There he cut west to hit Highway 810 south, crossing the upper and lower branches of the Belly River. At Hillspring he fueled up again, this time using gex, and then took side streets through the settlement to avoid the Provincial Vehicle Inspection station.

By the time Newman arrived at the intersection with Route 5 west of Mountain View, less than ten miles north of the U.S. border, the sun was a crimson ball, well down on his right shoulder and edging toward the peaks of the

Continental Divide. He made the uphill run into Water-ton Lakes National Park without needing his headlight, but two miles after passing the park headquarters he pulled off into a deserted campground. Newman dis-mounted and in the semidark shadow of Mount Blakis-ton, he once again delved into the bike's saddlebags.

While looking around for any surveillance cameras or ground sensors, James ate two of the protein bars and drank a liter of water. Satisfied that he was alone, he used a Leatherman tool to remove the aluminum Alberta license plate from the back of the bike, scraped off the Ca-nadian RFID tag, and tossed it into the woods. He then broke the plate into eight pieces by folding it back and forth in his hands and stuffed them into his jacket pocket to scatter one at a time up the road.

Finally, in near-total darkness, he pulled out a set of lightweight U.S. military-issue, PVS-35 thermal night-vision goggles and snapped them onto his helmet. He knew he was going to need the "night eyes" for the most dangerous part of his journey—crossing the border back into the USA.

**OVAL OFFICE**

THE WHITE HOUSE
WASHINGTON, DC
TUESDAY, 14 SEPTEMBER 2032
0915 HOURS, LOCAL

J ust tell me what you've learned about this man New-man since his name came up in this morning's DNI briefing as a person of interest in the Houston attack," the president said curtly. "And remember, I don't want any record of this inquiry or this conversation, Larry."

Standing in front of the ornately carved desk, Larry

Walsh, Counsel to the President, started to pull a piece of paper from the file in his left hand.

"Stop!" the president barked. "I told you, I don't want any paper on this matter."

The lawyer took a deep breath and said carefully, "Madam President, this is attorney-client privileged information. It's just between you and me. These are my notes. They can't be subpoenaed by Congress or anyone else. I made them to ensure accuracy. Besides, most of this is open-source data from the MESH. Anyone can get this information if they want to dig for it."

"Very well," the president snapped impatiently. "Just give me the essentials about him. I have a cabinet SVT in fifteen minutes, a fund-raising luncheon at noon, and Muneer has to be in touch with the Caliph before we take off for the West Coast campaign swing."

Walsh withdrew a single printed page from the file and began to read. "Full name, James Stuart Newman; age thirty-six, Chief Operating Officer of Centurion Solutions Group, born December 7, 1995, in Jerusalem. Only son of—"

"Jerusalem?" The president broke in. "Is he an American citizen?"

"Yes, ma'am," Walsh replied, then continued from his notes. "When this person James was born, his parents, Peter and Rachel Newman, were apparently in Jerusalem on some sort of undercover mission for our government. There isn't much in the readily available unclassified record, but—"

"Peter Newman . . . why do I know that name?" the president said, more to herself than her aide. "Is this Peter Newman still alive?"

Now Walsh pulled a PID from his shirt pocket, scrolled down the screen, and continued, "Peter Newman, age seventy-six, Major General, U.S. Marines Retired; wife, Rachel, age seventy-five. He's the chairman of Centurion Solutions Group, a company that does everything from government contract security work to telecommunications support; they even have their own little airline—"

"That's why I knew the name Newman," she exclaimed. "His company, CSG, or whatever they call it, has a contract with WHCA for some kind of communications support."

"Yes, ma'am," the lawyer replied gamely.

"Okay, what else? Get on with it."

Walsh returned to the entries on his PID: "Tax records show Mrs. Newman owns property on Pawleys Island, South Carolina, and a three-hundred-acre farm in Clarke County, Virginia. It has an airstrip and apparently the whole extended family lives there. It's on the Shenandoah, along the west slope of Mount Weather—"

"Mount Weather!" the president interrupted again. She looked stunned. "*Our* Mount Weather? The Emergency Backup Site? Who gave them permission to live *there*?"

Walsh looked pained. The conversation was veering off in directions for which he was unprepared, but after riffling quickly through his PID, he pressed on: "I believe the property has been in Rachel Newman's family for decades—long before the federal government started building the underground facility at Mount Weather in the 1950s. Evidently the Newmans turned the farm into some kind of family compound early in this century."

"So James Newman—our 'person of interest'—is the son of Peter Newman . . ." The president, leaning against the edge of the desk, was all attention. Walsh recognized the expression. He thought she looked like a cobra about to strike. "Who else lives at this 'family compound,' as you put it?" she asked.

Walsh scanned his notes and replied, "They call it Narnia Farm. Satellite and UAV imagery shows seven houses on the property and numerous outbuildings—barns, stables, equipment sheds, and the like. It's the listed address for Peter and Rachel; James and his wife, Sarah, and their four children; James's sister, Elizabeth Anne Madison, and her husband, George, and their four children; and apparently Peter Newman's widowed sister, Nancy. They all seem to live there at least—"

"That's only four houses," interjected the president, who had been listening intently. "What about the other three?"

"There's a residence for a farm manager and a guesthouse. There is also a residential-style building that is listed as the CSG corporate headquarters, though the company apparently has numerous other properties in the U.S. and leases property in several foreign countries," Walsh replied. Then, scowling at a sheet of paper he withdrew from the file, he added, "They also have eight solar collection arrays and four windmills visible in overhead imagery."

"Windmills, solar collectors? Sounds like an Anark hole," the president said. "Are all their taxes paid—local, state, federal? Do they have permits for firearms at this place?"

Walsh consulted his PID and file again and responded, "The whole family files IRS returns at that address. They seem to be current. I can't tell about their state and local returns or firearms registrations from what we have collected in this quick search."

The president grimaced and said, "Well, find out. Contact the IRS the usual way and have all the Newmans and their company—this Centurion Solutions Group—audited. See if they are up on the MESH and the power grid and if their kids are in certified schools. See what kind of political campaigns they support. What are their charitable deductions? If they are closet Anarks they won't be hooked up to the electric grid and they will be doing that homeschooling crap most states have banned. Run an ATF check to see if they have properly registered any firearms. Now, tell me more of what you know about James—our person of interest."

Walsh went back to his PID and spoke while scrolling down the illuminated screen: "James Newman graduated from the Naval Academy in the Class of 2018 with a computer science degree and was commissioned in the Marines. He has two Purple Hearts, one for wounds in action during the Sinai Operation in 2020 and another from Operation Iranian Freedom in 2025. He was the subject of a classified congressional investigation for an incident during the Shindand campaign on the Afghan-Iranian border for which he subsequently received a Navy Cross. In 2022 he married the former Sarah Cooper and they have four—"

"Enough about his love life and colorful military history, Larry. I know who James Newman is even if you don't. I know him from the congressional investigation in 2026. He humiliated my late husband. What I want to know now is what he's doing poking around in Canada stirring up questions about what happened in Houston three days ago."

There was a brief pause while Walsh scrolled down on his PID before he resumed. "After the congressional hearings in 2026 he got out of the Marine Corps and joined Centurion Solutions Group. As I mentioned, Newman's father is listed as chairman and CEO and other family members serve on the CSG board. We think the younger Newman is pretty much running the company but since it is privately held, we don't know much else except what shows up on IRS filings, in court records, and congressional testimony."

"What kind of court records?" asked the president.

Now Walsh proceeded without notes: "CSG has been sued twice in U.S. courts by the ACLU. The first lawsuit was brought against Centurion Aviation—when it was a commuter air service—because they profiled passengers so they could call themselves 'a terror-free airline.' The suit was dropped when they stopped flying scheduled routes and reorganized as an air charter service. CSG was also sued for 'computer intrusion' over their work for U.S. intelligence agencies. The company was also sued in The Hague at the World Court over the same kind of charge. They have very good lawyers at Williams & Connolly, so none of the cases ever went to trial—"

"What's Newman's connection to Marty Cohen, the scientist missing in Houston?" interrupted the president.

"The only relationship with Cohen we know of is that Dr. Cohen and Peter Newman—the father—were roommates at the Naval Academy. We don't know of any connection to the son," Walsh answered.

"Why is James Newman in Canada?"

"*Was* in Canada, Madam President. On Saturday he flew on a United Airlines flight from Dulles to Chicago and arrived in Calgary that evening on an Air Canada flight from O'Hare."

"Why didn't he just fly up there in one of his company's planes?"

"Because Centurion Aviation is banned in Canada for profiling passengers. It's contrary to Canadian human rights laws."

"So what is Newman up to?"

"Our Canadian friends tell me Newman spent

Saturday night and all day Sunday with Dr. Steven Templeton—one of the scientists working with Cohen on this natural gas/hydrogen fuel cell. According to the Canadians, yesterday morning Newman was in the office of Dr. Davis Long, the other fuel cell researcher whose death is being investigated as a possible mur—"

"Stop!" the president interrupted. "In other words you don't know *why* he went to Canada. Where is James Newman right now?"

Walsh bit his lip and said, "As of five minutes before I walked in here, we don't know exactly where he is. According to his PERT data, he was in Calgary yesterday morning at 11:51:23, when he bought groceries using cash, and four minutes later he made a PERT purchase of 2.57 gallons of motor fuel. He apparently gave the Canadian authorities the slip because they were looking for him in Saskatchewan. At about 12:30 yesterday afternoon he dropped off the MESH . . . just disappeared. At 23:33:25 last night a DHS scanner at the airport in Kalispell, Montana, reported a very brief transmission from what may have been his PERT, but they think it was an anomaly. He hasn't been detected since."

He could see the color rising in the president's cheeks. When she spoke, her voice was barely above a whisper, but full of venom: "Anomaly! You're telling me the man who runs CSG, the person described in the news as 'the world's foremost mercenary and MESH expert,' the person who humiliated my husband in 2026, has just disappeared? That he might be in Montana in some Anark hole—or maybe somewhere else between here and Canada?"

When she paused to take a breath, Walsh started to interject, "We've issued a BOLO at all airports, border cross—"

She cut him off. "Don't just look for him, find him! I

want to know what he's up to; who he's communicating with; what if any connections he has in the Caliphate; and why he's poking around the Marty Cohen disappearance. And when you locate Newman, see if you can keep track of him. We have forty-eight days until the election! Once you find him—then we'll figure out what to do with him. Do you understand me?"

His throat suddenly dry, Walsh answered, "Yes, Madam President," and headed for the Oval Office door that would allow him to exit into the Roosevelt Corridor.

As the lawyer reached the portal, the president commanded: "Larry, make sure the only people who know we're looking for Newman are you, Murad, Smith, and me. Don't share this with anyone else. Do you understand me?"

"Yes, ma'am," the lawyer answered, reaching again for the doorknob.

But before he could escape she added another warning: "And Larry, if you know what's good for you, Mr. Newman will never know we're looking for him or watching him."

# CHAPTER THREE

# IN THE SHADOW

**CENTURION SOLUTIONS GROUP OPERATIONS CENTER**

22570 RANDOLPH ROAD

DULLES, VA

TUESDAY, 14 SEPTEMBER 2032

1045 HOURS, LOCAL

"The trouble is, I don't know that we're any closer to finding Martin Cohen today than we were when I left here three days ago," said James to his father. "Professor Templeton thinks Dr. Cohen may have been kidnapped—or killed—for the research he's been doing on fuel cells and speculates it could be the Caliph, but nobody really knows. He acknowledged it could be the Russians, the Chinese, even some criminal enterprise, though he says that doesn't seem likely."

"You did all you could," said Peter. "Your mother and I have talked at length with Marty's wife, Julia. She told us he never mentioned any threats. Steven Templeton told you essentially the same thing. Perhaps the data you retrieved from Dr. Long's office will lead us somewhere after we process everything we download from your PID."

They were seated in the small, windowless conference room of the CSG Ops Center, and James Newman looked tired and very much in need of a shower and a shave. Across the oval table, U.S. senator Mack Caperton, ranking member and vice chairman of the Senate Select Committee on Intelligence, leaned back in his chair.

"James," said the senator, "tell me how you managed to get across the border and back here without being detained."

The son looked at his father, who simply nodded. James shrugged and responded, "It was fairly simple. As you know, Senator, very few of the routes through the Canadian and U.S. sides of what they call Waterton Lakes National Park and we call Glacier National Park are patrolled. I simply 'masked' my PERT, muffled the Harley's GPS transponder, turned off my PID, and followed the park road south, across the border."

"How did you get from the border to Kalispell?" asked the senator, who had hiked most of the trails in Glacier Park.

James smiled for the first time since he arrived an hour earlier and replied, "I followed that dirt track you took us on years ago, west of Mount Cleveland, south to Going-to-the-Sun Road, and took it west, over the Continental Divide, down to Lake McDonald."

"Whew! That's rough country!" exclaimed Caperton.

"Yeah," said James. "I had to dismount from the Harley a few times where the track was washed out or to get around deadfalls, but the 'night eyes' helped. And after I got to the Sun Road, I just turned on my headlight, rode all the way down to Apgar, and then took U.S. Route 2 to Columbia Falls and on to Kalispell."

"Where did you leave the motorcycle?" the senator asked.

"I put it in a storage container beside our CSG hangar at the Kalispell airport FBO, jumped on a Centurion Aviation Gulfstream, and landed at Dulles a few minutes before I walked in here to find you and my father conspiring," replied James with a grin.

The senator nodded, paused a moment, then said, "You may want to have the cycle put somewhere else. There are a lot of people on both sides of the border looking for you and that Harley right now."

"Why?" asked James.

"I explained this to your father before you arrived," Caperton said. "As you know, the SSCI gets a copy of the PDB every morning. This CSG Ops Center is one of several contractors that submit information each night to the DNI for inclusion in the PDB."

"Uh huh," James grunted.

Caperton continued, "Well, since the Houston attack on 9-11 there have been several 'supplemental reports,' all of which posit that the events there were the work of Anarks, Mexican drug cartels, or even Jewish radicals. The president said as much when she addressed the much abbreviated energy conference in Houston on Sunday—"

"But what does that have to do with me?"

"I'm getting to that," said Senator Caperton. He then added warmly, "My, you're impatient. You're just like your dad."

"Not really," replied James, without a smile.

Caperton let it pass and continued. "Yesterday, after the death of Dr. Davis Long, DNI—supposedly with the help of Interpol, the Canadian authorities, and our FBI—produced a report that said her suicide was somehow connected to the disappearance of Marty Cohen, and suggested she was despondent because his loss would delay commercially viable fuel cells for years—"

"Well," James interrupted again, "for starters, she didn't commit suicide. And I still don't get what this has to do with me."

"Patience, young fella," Caperton said, leaning forward in his chair. "The report I just referred to was recalled last night. In its place, under the heading 'New Intelligence,' the DNI now claims the Canadians have DNA evidence linking an American mercenary to Dr. Long's death—and speculates it may have been a contract killing."

"Mercenary? Who?"

"You."

"Me?"

"Yes," Caperton said. "One of the assessments even suggests a motive by claiming CSG has a fiduciary interest in preventing the new fuel cell technology from being developed."

"What would that be?" asked James, looking stunned.

The senator reached into his pocket, pulled out a single sheet of paper, and slid it across the table to James, saying, "I copied the two paragraphs from this morning's PDB because they were so unusual. Your dad has already seen this."

[TOP SECRET/NOFORN]

[U] The Department of Energy estimates that mass-produced, commercially viable, fuel-cell technology [FCT] for internal combustion engines, electrical generation, and residential/commercial heating/cooling will reduce global demand for petroleum-based hydrocarbon fuel and

atmospheric carbon emissions by up to 90 percent within
five years of introduction.

[C]　Centurion Solutions Group, Inc. [CSG] currently has
contracts with four U.S. energy companies to provide
security for personnel and equipment in eleven countries.
CSG also operates a fleet of twenty-one vessels, thirty-
seven remotely piloted aircraft, eight fixed-wing, and
fourteen rotary-winged aircraft to protect pipelines, move
energy company personnel and equipment, and conduct
counterpiracy operations for petroleum tankers operating
in international waters. Successful introduction of FCT
on a global scale will likely have severe adverse financial
consequences for hydrocarbon energy companies and result in termination of nearly all of CSG's energy-protection
services.

James shook his head, handed the sheet of paper back to
Caperton, and said, "This is nuts. And if it makes any difference, it's also wrong. We have sixteen piloted aircraft
and twenty-three seagoing vessels. Our 'energy-protection
services'—as they put it—are less than twenty percent of
our business. Who prepared this part of the PDB?"

"I don't know *who*—but it's from the DNI," said
Caperton. "In all my years on the SSCI I've never seen a
U.S. company referred to by name in the PDB. And it's
pretty clear to me the reason why Centurion is mentioned
by name is to justify what the Attorney General did this
morning."

"What's that?"

"An Interpol BOLO has been issued for your apprehension as a person of interest in the death of Dr. Davis
Long and the terror attack in Houston on the eleventh.

That's why I asked your father to meet me here. I didn't want any of this said on a phone or sent over the MESH."

James was stunned. He pondered this new information and said, "As my father knows, I went to her office—accompanied by the Royal Canadian Mounted Police. She was already dead before we got there. My DNA couldn't be there, we were wearing gloves. How could . . ."

He jumped up and went to retrieve the gym bag he dumped at the door when he entered the room an hour earlier. He pulled out the jeans he was wearing in Dr. Long's office, reached into the back pocket, and pulled out . . . a single latex glove.

James quickly pawed through the other pockets, then the bag. He finally stood erect and said, almost to himself, "The other glove is missing. It must have fallen out. That would explain the DNA. Now what do we do?"

After a moment of silence, the senator replied, "That's why I'm here. We need to get this under control—and hopefully find out what happened to Marty Cohen if we can. Let me ask, have you unmasked your PERT since you left Canada?"

"No," replied James. "My PERT transponder is embedded in my right foot. To mask it I just wear these foil-lined boots."

"Have you had those boots off since you crossed into the U.S.?"

The young man sat down and closed his eyes as he thought back. After a moment he slumped back in his chair and said slowly as he recalled the moment: "After I got on the plane, just as we took off from Kalispell, I took off my boots . . ."

The two older men looked at each other and for a moment said nothing. Then Caperton said to Peter, "Okay, that explains the report that James's PERT was detected very briefly at the Kalispell airport last night. DHS thought it was an anomalous signal, but we have to assume that whoever is trying to use him as a scapegoat will eventually cross-correlate that signal with the takeoff of the CSG jet and its subsequent landing at Dulles. That means anyone looking for him will likely come here or to the farm—or both."

Now Peter Newman spoke up for the first time in minutes: "Let's prepare for the worst, pray for the best, and settle for something in between. I'll have one of our CSG folks at the Kalispell training site take care of the motorcycle. But we need to get James out of here before the authorities come looking for him. I think Cair Paravel at Pawleys Island would be a good interim place until we can think of somewhere better, probably overseas—"

"Perfect," Caperton interjected. "Yom Kippur, the Jewish Day of Atonement, begins at sundown tonight. I have to be at the synagogue in Charleston, South Carolina, for the beginning of the observance. James can fly down with me this afternoon. No one is going to search my plane or motorcade. I can get him up to Rachel's place at Pawleys by midnight."

"Do I have anything to say about this?" asked James, still smarting at the mistakes he had made.

"Not unless you have a better idea," Peter responded.

James shrugged, turned to Senator Caperton, and said, "Why are you going to a synagogue in Charleston? You're from Montana—and you aren't Jewish . . ."

"No, I'm not, but as you may know, Montana now has the largest Jewish population in the United States. Most of the Jews there are refugees from the 2020 attack on

Israel and the imposition of Shariah law in so many European countries. And as for Charleston, it has two of the oldest synagogues in America. The rabbi at Brith Sholom Beth Israel is a close friend . . ."

"So it's all about politics?"

The senator rose from his chair before responding and then said quietly, "Sure, James, some of it is about politics. But the Jesus Christ I worship was also Jewish. I like the idea of acknowledging the traditions He kept when He was here. Now, will you be coming with me? I'm flying out of the Flight Support FBO at Leesburg Airport at two—and the U.S. Air Force doesn't like to wait—even for U.S. senators named Mackintosh Caperton."

James nodded and said, "I'll be ready. And this time I'll leave my boots on."

As they exited the room and walked down the corridor, Caperton said to James, "I will have you manifested as one of my staffers. I'll pick you up here on the way to Leesburg."

The two older men shook hands, gave each other hugs, and parted. James escorted Caperton to the exit at the back of the building. When they got to the door, the senator stopped, turned to James, and said, "You know, whether you want to admit it or not . . . you really are a lot like your father. And that's not a bad thing. You could do a lot worse."

"Thanks, I hear that a lot, Senator," James replied, "but as you have just witnessed, it isn't easy living in the shadow of someone like him. He doesn't screw up like I did on this mission. I'm not feeling sorry for myself—but I'm almost thirty-seven years old and it has been this way all my life."

"Son," Caperton said, "I've known you all your

life—and your dad for most of his. You have already shown us you have what it takes. You don't have to prove anything to me, to him, or to anyone else—except maybe yourself."

## AL 'ARISH, EGYPT

COMPANY "K," 3RD BATTALION, 8TH MARINES
24TH MARINE EXPEDITIONARY UNIT
NORTHERN SINAI DESERT
MONDAY, 9 NOVEMBER 2020
2315 HOURS, LOCAL

Some humanitarian mission, eh, Seth," James Newman whispered as he crawled up beside Kilo Company's first platoon commander, 2nd Lieutenant Seth Cooper.

"Yeah, Skipper," Cooper replied, using Marine jargon for his company commander. "And if it gets any more 'humane,' we're going to need another ammunition resupply."

The two officers were quiet for a few moments, peering into the darkness through thermal night-vision scopes, scanning across the highway intersection to their northeast and periodically east and west down the railroad tracks bisecting their position. Then Newman asked, "How bad are you hurt?"

"Two killed, four wounded. Doc Fowler bandaged 'em up. All four of the WIAs want to stay."

"I'm not talking about your platoon, I'm talking about you, Seth," Newman retorted. "Doc says you took shrapnel in that last attack."

"It wasn't from the suicide bomber or in the gunfight. I got hit in the volley of RPGs that came from those mud huts over there, just as the Osprey came in to take out our casualties," Cooper replied, pointing across the intersection they were supposed to be guarding.

"So how bad did you get hit?" Newman persisted. "Roll over, let me look at you."

The lieutenant did as ordered, revealing a flak jacket shredded from shoulders to groin. His throat and both thighs were wrapped with battle dressings soaked through with blood. Looking at him through his night-vision goggles, Newman said, "You're a mess, Cooper. We ought to get you out to the ship and have a medical officer take a look at you."

"Not tonight, Skipper," Cooper said, rolling back onto his stomach. "It's just a lot of little holes—looks worse than it is—and I don't want to be the reason we lose another V-22. Besides, tomorrow is the Marine Corps' birthday—and I'll bet ol' Ahmed is going to give us a real fireworks display for our 244th. I'd hate to miss the party."

Newman knew his subordinate was probably right. The MEU had already lost eighty-one Marines and Navy Medical Corpsmen killed and wounded, an AH-1 Super Cobra, an F-35B Strike Fighter, and two V-22 Ospreys since landing on the Mediterranean coast of the Sinai Peninsula on November 6—two days after the surprise nuclear detonation that leveled Tel Aviv.

Prior to coming ashore, detailed intelligence regarding the situation on the ground was practically nonexistent. At 0227 local on 4 November, Sixth Fleet Headquarters in Naples, Italy, sent a cursory warning order to Expeditionary Strike Group 4, alerting the Marines aboard the USS *America* (LHA-6) and USS *Makin Island* (LHD-8) that they might be going ashore:

AT 0200 04NOV20, A SINGLE LOW-YIELD NUCLEAR DEVICE WAS DETONATED WITHOUT WARNING IN DOWNTOWN TEL AVIV. CASUALTIES BELIEVED SIGNIFICANT.

NO INBOUND AERIAL THREATS DETECTED. NO CLAIM OF
RESPONSIBILITY. IDF MOBILIZING.


U.S./NATO DEFCON ONE. ESG-4 AND EMBARKED 24 MEU,
PREPARE TO CONDUCT NONCOMBATANT EVACUATION
OPERATIONS & HUMANITARIAN SUPPORT OPERATIONS, VIC
ISRAEL/EGYPT BORDER. MTF.


The "MTF"—more to follow—came in a flood of
orders and instructions about where the Marines would
land, how many would go ashore, and the Rules of
Engagement (ROE) but with precious little useful intelligence.

The Israelis blamed the attack on the Iranians. The government in Tehran denied they had anything to do with it
and said the explosion was "Allah striking the Zionist entity." Reports in the European and Arab media speculated
that the carnage was caused by the "accidental detonation
of an Israeli nuclear warhead being transported through
Tel Aviv."

But, within hours of the blast, the Syrian army was
moving toward the Golan Heights and Hezbollah forces
were attacking into northern Israel from Lebanon. In
the south, Hamas announced a "state of war now exists
between the Palestinian people and the Jewish occupiers."

By noon on the fifth, tens of thousands of civilians
were fleeing south toward the Israeli-Egyptian border. In
Cairo, the Muslim Brotherhood–dominated government
pleaded for help from the U.S. Sixth Fleet to "avert a
humanitarian disaster." Officials in Sinai claimed "several
battalions of Egyptian police, border guards, and soldiers
were in need of assistance to maintain law and order."

Aboard the USS *America* and USS *Makin Island*,
the Marines and Navy Corpsmen of 3rd Battalion, 8th

Marines were told they would be making an "unopposed landing" to conduct a "humanitarian mission"—and a "noncombatant evacuation operation" (NEO)—to extricate Israeli refugees and Palestinian Christians fleeing the carnage in Tel Aviv and fighting in the north.

"Just in case the natives aren't as friendly as advertised," the battalion commander ordered "everyone going to the beach" to take a three-day supply of ammunition, food, medical supplies, and water—or, as he put it, "bullets, beans, and bandages." They needed that and more. There were no Egyptian police, soldiers, or law and order. But there were tens of thousands of refugees—and among them, others who simply came to kill.

An hour before dawn on 6 November, 1st Lieutenant James Newman was the executive officer—or "XO"—of Kilo Company as they landed in Amphibious Combat Vehicles across the beach, two kilometers east of the small Egyptian port at Ezbet Abu Sagal, about thirty miles southeast of the border with Israel. A few minutes after sunrise, less than a hundred meters from the high-tide mark, Captain Bill Sharrod, Kilo's company commander, was killed instantly when six RPGs and a French-built, Milan IV anti-armor missile hit his ACV.

With the company in heavy contact against well-armed Hamas fighters, "defectors" from the Egyptian army, and suicidal jihadis, Newman immediately became Kilo's "Acting Company Commander"—the "skipper." They had been in a nearly nonstop series of running gun battles ever since.

It was the same for the rest of 3rd Battalion, 8th Marines. As Kilo Company came across the beach, the battalion's Weapons Company landed at the port via LCAC. India Company, with the Battalion Command Group, was airlifted by V-22 into the Arish airfield, four

kilometers south of the town. Every unit was heavily engaged within minutes of landing.

After dark on the sixth, the MEU commander ordered L Company, his only reserve, to reinforce Weapons
Company at the port in case his Marines were forced to
retrograde under fire. There were so many shoulder-fired
surface-to-air missiles being fired at the V-22s that Lima
had to be landed by LCAC from the *America*, as the LHA
circled in the Mediterranean, twenty miles off the Egyptian coastline.

Kilo's mission, to secure the main east-west highway
at the intersection of Egyptian Routes 30 and 33, proved
daunting. By nightfall on the sixth, suicide bombers
mingling with the flood of refugees had killed three of
Newman's Marines and wounded eleven more. That
night, human waves of suicide bombers attacked all three
companies, penetrated the defenses at the airfield, and
wounded the battalion commander.

By the morning of 7 November, India Company had
secured the port and Weapons Company began conducting motorized patrols in their MTVs. They promptly lost
four Marines and two of their heavily armed and armored
ACVs to suicide vehicular–borne improvised explosive devices. But that night, moving under the cover of darkness,
the Marines and U.S. Navy LCACs managed to evacuate
more than 4,500 refugees—women, children, many of
them injured—through the port to civilian ships offshore.

Throughout the eighth and ninth, pilots flying from
the decks of the *America*, *Makin Island*, and the airfield
south of Al 'Arish reported that the highways from the
Israeli border—west from Beersheba and northwest
from Nizzana—were jammed with refugees in cars,
trucks, buses, and on foot. USAF MC-17s, dispatched
from CONUS, tried to para-drop food and water to the

desperate refugees, but the humanitarian flights had to be discontinued when one of the cargo aircraft was downed by a shoulder-fired surface-to-air missile.

On the ground it was even worse. Newman's roadblock/checkpoint a kilometer east of the 30/33 road junction was repeatedly engaged, despite constant overhead surveillance provided by Marine UAVs and armed U.S. Air Force Reaper III remotely piloted aircraft (RPAs) launched from British RAF bases on Cyprus. All six of the Marines' M-1G tanks sustained damage from RPGs and anti-armor missiles.

Just prior to dark on 9 November, as Lieutenant Cooper was checking on his Marines at the roadblock, a Toyota Land Cruiser—the vehicle of choice for suicide bombers—came careening into the outpost. The ear-shattering explosion killed two of his Marines instantly and felled two others. Dust from the detonation was still hanging in the air when a civilian bus commandeered by a heavily armed group of jihadis slammed into the platoon checkpoint and disgorged more than sixty young men armed with AK-47s and RPGs.

Cooper and six survivors from his 1st Squad dragged their two wounded mates into the small courtyard of a mud-walled house and tried to call for help. His radio—a shrapnel hole clear through it—was dead.

A kilometer away, Newman was with 2nd Platoon, supervising the "search and clear" of several hundred refugees, when he heard the car bomb and saw a plume of smoke and dust. He immediately tried to raise Cooper on the Company tac-net and when he couldn't, he and Gunnery Sergeant Dan Doan headed on foot to the sound of gunfire, collecting a dozen more Kilo Company Marines on the way.

It took Newman and his ad hoc Quick Reaction Force

nearly fifteen minutes, racing through narrow alleys, to reach Cooper's little Alamo. By then it was dark and two more of Cooper's Marines were wounded—but there was also a Marine F-35 on station, waiting for clearance.

Newman quickly sized up the situation, told his Marines to "light up" any targets they could see with their rifle-mounted laser target designators, and called the aircraft on his helmet-mounted radio: "Your targets are being lazed, don't hit us."

Ten thousand feet above them, the pilot of the F-35 flipped a switch on his stick. The aircraft's sensors and computers calculated the best run-in heading and activated the guidance systems on eight of the new laser-guided, hundred-pound close-in munitions. When the pilot heard the "ready" tone in his helmet headset, he pushed the stick forward and called over the radio, "Eight Charlie India Mikes, on the way."

The weapons performed as advertised. The swish of the bombs, just a fraction of a second before they hit, left no time for the attackers to get out of the way. As soon as the eighth warhead detonated, Gunnery Sergeant Doan was on his feet, leading an old-fashioned frontal assault using night-vision goggles. Newman ordered a Marine with a radio to remain with Cooper and took off with Doan and the little band of warriors.

Twenty minutes later, the engagement ended. Unable to shoot it out with Marines in the dark, the attackers melted away. Newman, concerned his troops were pursuing an enemy that would just disappear into the horde of refugees to their east, called off the hunt. But the fight wasn't completely over.

As Newman and his counterattackers threaded their way through dark, stinking alleys back toward friendly positions, he heard Cooper's voice on the radio, talking to a V-22 cas-evac bird. In the distance, he could hear the aircraft transition from horizontal flight to vertical and begin to descend. Then, through his NVGs, he could see the infrared strobes on the rotor tips as the big plane descended about two hundred meters away.

Suddenly, off to his right, between Newman's little QRF and the landing zone, there was a rapid series of dull thuds. In the darkness Doan turned to Newman and whispered, "RPGs, four or five of 'em."

The words were barely out of the gunnery sergeant's mouth when they heard four distinct explosions from the vicinity of the Osprey's LZ. As the big bird aborted its landing and clawed for altitude, Newman, Doan, and the little patrol sprinted toward where the firing originated.

They were too late. The shooters were gone. After searching for nearly an hour, Newman called his command post on the radio, told the radio operator who answered, "Pass the word, 'friendlies' approaching from the east," and headed back to the Kilo Company perimeter. An hour later he was prone beside Lieutenant Seth Cooper, the only Marine wounded by the RPG fire during the aborted cas-evac.

"If it makes you feel any better, Seth, had I known the RPG shooters were after you, I would have kept looking for 'em," Newman said lightly.

The lieutenant looked through his NVGs at his company commander to see if he was serious—and saw Newman's grin. "Gee, thanks, Skipper," Cooper replied with a smile of his own. "I feel a lot better knowing that."

Their banter was interrupted by a radio call summoning Newman to his CP for a "secure voice conference call" with the MEU commander.

Before crawling away from Cooper's OP, James patted the lieutenant on the back and said, "You did a good job today, Seth. You're a fine officer. I've known you would be since the Academy."

"Thanks," Cooper replied, once again peering into his thermal scope, searching for enemies dying to kill him if they had another chance. Then he looked over at his friend and said, "You know, tomorrow being the Marine Corps' birthday reminds me about all that stuff we read at the Academy about naval gunfire. Sure wish we had some of *that* the last few days. The close air support has been great—but it sure would be nice to have a battleship, a cruiser, or even a destroyer out there," he added, pointing to the water a few hundred meters to their north.

"Yeah, well, our navy doesn't do that kind of stuff anymore," Newman replied. He paused a moment, patted Cooper on the shoulder, and said, "Be careful out here, Seth. Your Marines need you and so do Sarah and your son back home. When we left Lejeune I promised them I would bring you home alive."

It was a promise he shouldn't have made . . .

*    *    *    *

The 60mm mortar round that almost killed James Newman hit the Kilo Company CP at precisely 0530 on the morning of 10 November. It was the first in a salvo of five, fired from the rubble of a house to the south of the company perimeter. No one heard it coming over the noise of a V-22 dropping a sling-load of ammo, food, and water fifty meters away. As the high-explosive projectile struck, Newman was in mid-sentence, briefing his platoon commanders on the battalion op order he had received an hour earlier.

An instant before the round hit, 2nd Lieutenant Seth Cooper dove toward his friend, knocking James up against the HESCO barrier on which he had taped an aerial photograph of the battalion dispositions. Cooper's back took the brunt of the explosion, killing him instantly.

Gunnery Sergeant Doan and the other two platoon commanders were all wounded by the concussion and shrapnel—but they were conscious. Newman was not.

Even before the last of the incoming rounds "walked" across their little perimeter, Doan, with shrapnel holes in his face, arms, and legs, was on his feet yelling, "Corpsman up!"

Doc Fowler, the company senior corpsman, arrived in an instant, carrying his Unit 1 first-aid kit. As he and the gunny pulled Cooper's blasted body off Newman, one of the radio operators and another Marine began tending the two other, less grievously wounded officers.

Fowler quickly checked Cooper for a pulse, shook his head, said, "He's gone, Gunny," and turned to Newman, who was unconscious, but breathing.

Red bubbles gurgled from Newman's lips and a pool of blood was spreading beneath his right leg. The corpsman quickly examined the wounded lieutenant, found a gash on the right side of his scalp, and then tore open Newman's flak jacket, looking for torso holes. He found one below Newman's right armpit, where a piece of shrapnel had ripped through his right biceps and passed just above the flak jacket's armor plate to puncture his rib cage.

In less than five minutes, with the help of Gunnery Sergeant Doan, Fowler applied an airtight compress over the sucking chest wound, started an IV flowing into Newman's undamaged left arm, stopped the hemorrhage from his right leg with an inflatable tourniquet, and wrapped the lieutenant's head wound with a battle dressing.

As Fowler turned his attention to Gunnery Sergeant Doan and the two wounded platoon commanders, 1st Sergeant Lopez arrived with a team of litter-bearers and announced, "We have a cas-evac bird inbound. How many do we need to send out, Doc?"

"The skipper is critical," Fowler answered. "Gunny and the two lieutenants are priority." And nodding toward the shattered body of Seth Cooper, the corpsman added, "and one permanent routine."

\* \* \* \*

Within fifteen minutes of their being wounded, an MV-22 transported Newman, Gunnery Sergeant Doan, and the two injured platoon commanders to the USS *America*, where they were all X-rayed and rushed into the big ship's surgical center. The team of surgeons operating on Newman installed a ventilator in his trachea, closed the laceration in his femoral artery, inserted a small vacuum tube to help reinflate his right lung, and removed fragments of bone where shrapnel tore into his skull.

An hour after coming out of surgery, Newman and Gunny Doan were wheeled to the *America*'s flight deck along with five other seriously wounded 3/8 Marines. There they were all loaded aboard a V-22 configured for transporting shock-trauma patients.

It took the Osprey less than two hours to reach the British Royal Air Force facility at Akrotiri, Cyprus, where a USAF C-17 Nightingale was waiting on the tarmac. Four and a half hours later, the seven wounded Marines were in Germany at Landstuhl Regional Medical Center.

Two days later, another C-17 aeromedical flight carried Newman, Doan, and eleven other wounded Marines to Joint Base Andrews—the big air base south of Washington, D.C. There they were loaded aboard an "ambulance bus" and taken to the Walter Reed National Military Medical Center at Bethesda, Maryland. Newman, in a drug-induced coma, missed all this.

Until he woke on Sunday, 15 November, James was unaware doctors had removed a piece of jagged metal from his right lung or that a team of neurosurgeons operated for nearly six hours to extricate a pea-sized piece of shrapnel from the right side of his brain. He looked around, saw his parents, and tried to speak, mouthing the words "Where am I and how did I get here?" With the ventilator tube in his throat, no sound came out.

After two more tries, Rachel and Peter grasped what he was trying to say. They explained where he was, told him he was badly hurt and that they had been praying for him and he wasn't "out of the woods yet." But, on orders from the doctors, they gave him few details more than he could learn by turning on the television mounted on the wall. The next day, Gunnery Sergeant Dan Doan rolled his wheelchair into Newman's room and told him the rest of the story.

When the gunny explained how Seth Cooper saved Newman's life, tears welled up in James's eyes. Doan wasn't being cruel—he was simply relating to his commander the truth of what happened—and of his friend's last, lifesaving act of heroism.

The next day, the doctors took James off the ventilator and showed him how he could cover the port in his throat to talk. An hour later he cajoled a pretty Navy nurse to find out from the Marine Liaison Office when and where Seth Cooper's funeral took place. When she told him Cooper's memorial service was to be held at the Camp Lejeune Base Chapel on Friday, 27 November, the day after Thanksgiving, James resolved to be there. Doan said he was going, too.

A week later, on Tuesday the twenty-fourth, Newman and Doan filled out applications to take convalescent leave, promising to stay with James's parents through the Thanksgiving holiday and report back to the hospital on

Monday the thirtieth. The doctors initially rejected the request but finally relented after Peter Newman, Major General, USMC (Ret.), pledged that his wife, Rachel, a nurse, would supervise the two wounded warriors and ensure they took their medications.

James's sister, Elizabeth, picked them up at Bethesda shortly after ten on Wednesday. Both men were wearing civilian clothes, carrying overnight bags, and using canes. James had a sling on his right arm—which he promptly discarded as Elizabeth helped them load their gear and get into the vehicle. She slid behind the wheel and exited the hospital gate toward the outer loop of the Washington Beltway, headed toward Narnia. But after crossing the American Legion Bridge over the Potomac and turning onto the ramp to go west on Route 267, James told his sister, "Get in the left lane and onto the Dulles Airport access road."

"Why?" she asked. "It takes longer than the toll road."

"Because we're going to the airport," James replied. "The gunny and I have round-trip tickets to Camp Lejeune. We'll be back Friday night for leftovers of Mom's turkey."

Elizabeth shook her head and said, "James, this is not a good idea. If you do this, Mom is going to pitch a fit. And remember, Dad used to be in the business of killing people. I don't want to be the reason he comes out of retirement."

James smiled at her colorful language and said, "Just tell 'em Gunnery Sergeant Doan made you do it. It's an old tradition in the Marine Corps—always blame the gunny. Now step on it so we don't miss our flight."

*   *   *   *

Newman called home to apologize to his mother when he and Doan changed planes in Charlotte. When they arrived at the airport in Jacksonville, North Carolina, the two wounded Marines were met by one of Doan's fellow gunnery sergeants, who brought them directly to the 8th Marines Regimental Headquarters, where they were greeted by Colonel Paul Sheridan, the regimental commander.

After a quick "meet and greet" in the conference room with the regimental staff, Sheridan asked the wounded lieutenant and gunnery sergeant to describe their experience on what the White House was now calling "Operation Lend Hope." Both men criticized the lack of intelligence, praised the courage and tenacity of their Marines, and showered accolades on the corpsmen, doctors, and nurses who saved them.

Afterward, in Sheridan's office, the colonel told James, "I admire you for coming here for the memorial service on Friday. It's pretty obvious whose son you are. Your father and I served together many years ago. Have you been able to talk to the families of any of your fallen Marines?"

"Not yet, sir," Newman replied. "I visited all our WIAs at Bethesda and sent letters to the families of our KIAs, but I couldn't get next-of-kin phone numbers at the hospital."

"I'll have the adjutant get you the numbers," Sheridan said. "Captain Sharrod's widow has already gone back to Ohio to be with her family. I know she would be pleased to hear from you. You know Lieutenant Cooper's widow, Sarah, is still here?"

Newman nodded and answered, "I know she and their baby are still here. I talked to her parents. As you probably know, sir, her husband, Seth, was a year behind me at the Academy. I came up from Quantico for their wedding . . ." His voice was hoarse and faded out as he choked up.

Sheridan looked at the young officer and said quietly, "This is going to be a tough Thanksgiving for everyone.

Let's see if we can make this a little easier on all concerned. The regimental chaplain and his wife are bringing Sarah and their son to our quarters for dinner tomorrow. If you're up to it, I think you and Gunny Doan should be there—and on Friday morning at the memorial service, I think you both should say a few words."

James nodded and said, "Aye, aye, sir."

\* \* \* \*

By Thursday afternoon, Gunnery Sergeant Dan Doan had somehow managed to find a dark blue suit that fit Newman perfectly, get both their dress blue uniforms out of storage, have them pressed, and still get them a ride to the Sheridans' quarters five minutes before the appointed hour of 1700.

As the two men limped up the walk, Nancy Sheridan opened the door and said, "Marines are always so punctual. Please come in."

The aroma of roasting turkey greeted them as they entered. Their hostess escorted them to the living room and said, "Make yourselves at home. I have a few things to get ready in the kitchen. The colonel will be right down."

As she left the room, Doan turned to Newman and said quietly, "When I get married, that's the kind of wife I want."

"What do you mean, Gunny?" James whispered.

"Every Marine wife should refer to her husband by his rank."

Newman was still chuckling as Colonel Paul Sheridan entered and said, "Gentlemen, thank you for coming. Are you allowed to have a beer or a glass of wine?"

"I can, sir," replied Doan, without hesitation. Then, without missing a beat, he added, "But the lieutenant here had a head wound and I'm under strict orders that he cannot have any firewater. The doctors say it will make him act crazy."

Sheridan was still laughing when the doorbell rang.

Chaplain Jayne's wife entered first, carrying an infant safety seat—the kind designed to fit in a car. The child inside was sound asleep.

James's first sight of Sarah Cooper caused him to catch his breath. She was wearing a black dress. Her long, dark hair was pulled back in a ponytail and she was wearing no visible makeup. To James she was at once terribly sad, vulnerable—and strikingly beautiful.

Sarah was thanking Colonel and Mrs. Sheridan for their invitation when she looked across the room and noticed James staring at her. She stopped talking, put her hand to her mouth, exclaimed, "Oh, James," and rushed across the room to embrace him. In a matter of seconds, they were holding each other, tears running down both their faces.

At dinner, James and Sarah sat across from each other. Colonel Sheridan, Chaplain Jayne, and Gunnery Sergeant Doan carried the conversation—carefully avoiding the specifics of what took place in the Sinai less than three weeks earlier. But after listening to them for several minutes, Sarah quietly said, looking straight at James, "Please, tell me how my husband died."

There was an uncomfortable silence for several seconds and the chaplain said, "Sarah, there will be time for this later. I don't think that—"

"No," she interrupted. "I want to know what happened. How it happened. James and Gunnery Sergeant Doan were there. I might never have this opportunity again. Please."

There was another long silence. James, looking painfully distraught, tried twice to speak but no words came out. Then Gunnery Sergeant Doan began gently, "Ma'am, you're right, we were both there. But Lieutenant Newman doesn't really remember it all because he had a bad head wound . . ."

For more than fifteen minutes, Dan Doan held the table spellbound, quietly and dispassionately describing the events leading up to Seth Cooper's death. Without embellishment he described the landing on the beach, the death of their company commander, the terrible chaos of trying to separate refugees from terrorists, how Newman led a counterattack to save Cooper and his Marines, how her husband was wounded on the night of the ninth, and how he saved Newman's life the next day.

When he finished, tears were flowing down everyone's cheeks—even the crusty colonel's. Sarah started to thank Doan, but then came a little wail from the living room. She excused herself, saying, "Little Seth needs to be changed and I need to nurse him."

After she and Nancy Sheridan left the dining room, the colonel cleared his throat and said, "Thank you, Gunny. Well done."

\*　\*　\*　\*

The following morning the base chapel was filled to over-flowing for Seth Cooper's memorial service. Sarah and the baby were in the front pew, flanked by her mother and father and the parents of her late husband. First Lieutenant James Newman and Gunnery Sergeant Daniel Doan, in their dress blues, were seated directly behind her.

At the appointed time, Chaplain Jayne summoned Doan to the pulpit for an abbreviated version of what he had said the night before in Colonel Sheridan's quarters. Other than quiet sobs from Sarah and from Seth Cooper's mother, the tabernacle was so silent it might have been empty. Then it was Newman's turn.

James spent nearly an hour on the phone with his father the night before, seeking counsel for what he should say. His father's words, "Funerals are for the living, not the dead," rang in his mind.

But when he looked down at Sarah Cooper's red-rimmed eyes, James could hardly speak. Then, after a deep breath, he looked out into the congregation and said, "Seth Cooper is my friend. We have known each other for five years—ever since he arrived at the Naval Academy, in the class behind mine. We were in the same company then, and for the short time I commanded Company K, 3rd Battalion, 8th Marines, he was our 1st Platoon Commander.

"Seth is a magnificent Marine, far braver and more tenacious than I. He is missed by me, his Marines, by our Corps, by his parents, and certainly by his lovely wife, Sarah, and their son.

"If it wasn't for Seth Cooper, I probably would not be alive today. I am consoled by the certainty I will see him again because Seth Cooper was a man who knew where he was going—and why he was going there. He knew Jesus Christ as his Lord and Savior. And he lived by the motto of our Corps—*Semper Fidelis*—always faithful.

"From this day forward, I will think of Seth Cooper every time I hear two well-known verses. The first from the Holy Bible—Paul's second letter to his protégé, Timothy. The second from the last stanza of our Marine Corps Hymn—the verse reminding us the streets of heaven are guarded by United States Marines."

And then, looking directly at the flag-draped casket for the first time, he concluded, "Seth, dear friend and fellow Marine, you have 'fought the good fight,' you have 'finished the race.' You have 'kept the faith.' Lieutenant Cooper, take your post."

# CHAPTER FOUR

# FLIGHT DELAY

**OVAL OFFICE**
THE WHITE HOUSE
WASHINGTON, DC
TUESDAY, 14 SEPTEMBER 2032
1345 HOURS, LOCAL

"How do you know the Caliph isn't lying to us?" the president asked. She was sitting behind her desk, leaning on her forearms, scrolling through her PID, and barely glancing at the three men she had summoned.

She didn't invite them to sit, so they stood: Muneer Murad, Chief of Staff; Larry Walsh, White House Counsel; and General John Smith, National Security Advisor.

When no one answered, she glanced up and said, "Look, I have to board Marine One in fifteen minutes for the flight to Andrews so I'm on time for tonight's fundraiser in San Francisco. At the major-donor event I just left, all the questions were about whether the Caliph is telling the truth when he says the Caliphate had nothing to do with the Houston attack."

Smith, trying to be helpful, said, "NSA confirms the Caliph is doing everything in his power to find Dr. Cohen—"

"Oh please, John," she sneered. "Don't patronize me. First, you didn't answer the question. And second, you sound like my late, great husband, who would still be alive if he hadn't believed all the bunk our intelligence services fed him when he sat in this office."

Smith nodded, recalling the overwhelming wave of sympathy that swept the nation after the bombing in 2027—and how that emotional surge made her election in 2028 "inevitable."

She continued, "Let's be clear about this. I don't give a flip about Dr. Cohen. But I do want to know if the Caliph was behind the attacks in Houston."

"He wasn't," interjected Murad, who then belatedly added, "Madam President."

"And how do you know that, my dear Muneer?" She stopped scrolling through her PID and looked up at him.

"Because he does not lie to *me*," Murad responded simply. "He assures us his people are trying very hard to find out who was behind what transpired in Houston."

The president stood, turned toward the thick, green-tinted ballistic- and TEMPEST-proofed windowpanes, and looked out over the Ellipse toward the Washington Monument. Suddenly she spun and said, "That's just bull and I'm not buying it! The FBI confirms there were at least a dozen perpetrators. Listen to this . . ."

She picked up her PID, scrolled to what she had been reading, and said, "Partial human remains recovered from two males aboard benzene tanker at Exxon Mobile Bayport refinery. DNA database confirms Syrian origin. Partial human remains of two males recovered from the truck that brought down the I-610 bridge, DNA indicates Egyptian bloodlines. Partial remains of a male recovered from SUV detonated north of Bayport Boulevard bridge, genetic origin, Saudi. Partial remains of male recovered from truck explosion south of boulevard bridge, genetic origin, Yemeni. And worst of all, if these DNA traces are correct, at least five of these suicidal murderers have been living legally here in the United States for years."

She stopped to look at the three, ensuring they were paying attention, then continued as she scrolled further on her PID. "DNA tests on partial remains of four male gunmen at the NASA Hilton confirm Pakistani origin. No PERTs found on any remains, but U.S. driver's licenses were found in the clothing of two of them. All subjects appear to have been wearing bomb vests. Explosive residue chemical analysis: RDX and PETN consistent with Sudanese-origin Semtex."

Now she looked up again and said, "If these murderous, suicidal scum aren't from the Caliphate, I don't know geography."

She flipped the PID onto her desk and continued: "The only ones unaccounted for are the three who show up in the digital video from the hotel hustling Dr. Cohen out the back door and onto the 'disappearing speedboat,' which we, of course, can't find.

"Why do we have a Coast Guard, a Navy, and all these satellites, UAVs, and RPAs if we can't find one lousy speedboat?" She said these last words while looking directly at Smith.

Well aware he had no acceptable answer to the question, the National Security Advisor cleared his throat and posed one of his own. "Madam President, the information you just read from your PID wasn't in our Sit Room database a few minutes before I walked in here. Who else has access to that information?"

"How the devil do I know," she said with a shrug.

"There must be a thousand FBI agents working on this case. And there's more. According to the FBI, the three abductors visible on the hotel digi-vid appear to be Latino, but they could easily be from the Caliphate. All three of them were registered guests at the hotel. They apparently checked in and paid using Venezuelan PERTs tied to a Cayman Islands bank account that isn't in the Treasury Department's international database. And of course, their PERTs went dark during the attack at the hotel and haven't been picked up since. Do you people understand what this means?"

"Yes," replied Murad, quietly. He had worked his way up the White House food chain since her husband's two-term administration to become chief of staff by knowing what to say and when to say it. He added, "The Venezuelan PERT data and the tie to a bank in the Cayman Islands support the premise a Latin American drug cartel is involved. But if the suicide bomber DNA links to Middle Eastern bloodlines get out, our story about Houston being an Anark-cartel attack may not hold up."

"May not! May not! If this gets out, the right-wing crazies will finish me! They have been saying for years the deals my husband made with Iran, the Arabs, the UN, and the Caliph were a bad idea."

Her voice became shrill and her face flushed as she berated them. "The 'right' fought us on enforcing Fairness in Broadcasting, my Framework for Peace in the Middle East. They don't like our Better Deal for All economic plan, our universal All-American Medical Insurance, the North American Union Treaty, our Hate Speech Laws, the Spreading Fear Statute, the UN Carbon Levy, or the UN Convention on Small Arms Control. They even opposed our free childhood immunization PERT implants for newborns. They hate us for everything we have done to make this a better, safer, greener world. Now they are fighting the new Global Exchange Currency. If they get their hands on this—"

"Madam President, please," Walsh interrupted when she paused her litany to catch her breath. He continued quietly. "There are Secret Service agents right outside these doors," he said, pointing to the curved portal to the Roosevelt Corridor and the doors leading to the Rose Garden. "We have to think this through—carefully, calmly, and most of all, quietly."

She sat heavily into the leather desk chair, collected herself, and said, "You're right, Larry, and I have to leave or I'll be late getting to San Francisco."

"The people at the fund-raiser will wait for you," Walsh said quickly before she could go on. "But before you depart, the question General Smith asked a moment ago is relevant. The information you read to us from your PID is very sensitive. Did it come from the FBI?"

She leaned back in her chair, looked at the three men standing in front of her desk, and let a slight smile come to her lips. "Does it bother you that I have information you three don't give me?" she asked with a hint of the coyness that had served her so well in her younger years.

"It is not important whether it bothers me," Walsh replied. "It *is* important to know who else has access to that information. It contradicts the case we are building against the Anarks and this man Newman."

Her eyes widened. She stood and said, "Stop talking, Larry. You are my lawyer. This is between you and me— and no one else. We will deal with this when I return tomorrow morning."

With that she started toward the French doors opening to the Rose Garden and commanded, "All three of you, walk with me."

As she reached the door, a female Secret Service agent suddenly appeared outside and opened it for her, holding it for all four to exit. As they headed toward the West Colonnade and the Executive Residence, the agent spoke into a wireless microphone mounted inconspicuously on her lapel, "Solo is en route to the Lima Zulu."

Murad, Walsh, and Smith fell into step behind the president as she said, "Here's what I want done while I'm gone. M&M, get your friend the Caliph on the phone—not one of his minions. Tell him I want a very public statement to the effect that no one in the Caliphate had anything to do with what happened in Houston—and that he has ordered his representatives around the world to fully cooperate with U.S. authorities on dealing with what appears to be an internal matter. See if you can get him to issue another of his famous fatwas."

Turning to her national security advisor she said, "John, by the time I get back here in the morning I want you to find every national security and U.S. government contract held by Centurion Solutions Group—classified and unclassified—so you and I can go through them."

At the entrance to the residence they were met by another Secret Service agent, who preceded the presidential party down the narrow staff stairway to the ground floor. As they reached the Center Hall, they could hear the crowd of staffers and campaign workers gathered in the Diplomatic Reception Room to see the president fly off the South Lawn.

The president nodded to the Secret Service agent leading their little procession to indicate that she was going into the Map Room; then she motioned for Walsh to follow and for Murad and Smith to wait outside. They watched as she pulled Walsh close by the lapels on his coat and stuck a finger in his chest. They couldn't hear her say,

"Listen, Larry, you and I have known each other too long for that kind of thing to happen again."

"What do you—" Walsh started.

"The business up in the Oval Office about Newman," she said. "He is our best suspect. Tell the Attorney General I want him found, locked up, and held incommunicado until after the election. Tell the AG I said to throw the book at him, use the old Bush regime antiterror statutes if necessary. Newman has motive for kidnapping Cohen and killing that scientist in Canada. His family makes millions providing services to oil and gas companies. Cohen's fuel cell would hurt them. Their Centurion Aviation and security operations make millions more every time there is a terrorist attack. They have the means—this CSG company and their hired thugs. He was or is in Canada, where Cohen's cohort was murdered. From what you have already given me, the whole family appears to have Anark tendencies. They homeschool out there in the Blue Ridge, don't they? It's like a primitive tribe. Find a way to get to them."

"We're doing our best."

"Well, dear," she replied, suddenly sweet, "do better. And while I'm gone, hold M&M's hand and make sure he doesn't let his pal in Jerusalem off the hook. The same goes for our tin-hat soldier. Keep Smith focused on the problem at hand—telling everyone Anarks and the cartels are the big threat."

Walsh nodded and then said, "The problem with that approach is the FBI report you read to us up in the Oval Office. Smith and M&M heard it. Smith understands that whoever sent it to you may have shared it with others. That's why he asked."

The president thought about it for a moment and then said, "It was sent to me 'Eyes Only' by the director. Go over to the Hoover Building and see him this afternoon. Tell him I want any dissemination of that information recalled. Let me know how he responds. As you know, my husband appointed him. It would be a shame if something happened to such an old friend."

With that, she spun on her heel, put on her brightest campaign smile, and walked out of the Map Room into the throng gathered in the Diplomatic Reception Room. A handful of aides and Secret Service agents formed a phalanx to get her out to the lawn. Murad, Walsh, and Smith followed in their wake and watched from beneath the canvas awning at the doorway.

As she boarded the glistening, white-topped VH-192 Sikorsky helicopter with UNITED STATES OF AMERICA painted on its tail, a U.S. Marine sergeant held a rigid salute. From the top step, she turned and waved to the cameras and the carefully coached crowd behind the rope line.

Immediately after the big bird lifted, the three men turned and entered the green door into the now empty Diplomatic Reception Room. As they turned left at the Center Hall and past the Map Room, Smith noticed the Secret Service agent standing in the doorway—the same one who escorted them from the Oval Office.

Their eyes met for an instant. And suddenly Smith recalled where he had seen her before. As he ascended the staff stairs to the State Floor, he pulled out his PID and scrolled to the message he received from the Secret Service Operations Center three days earlier:

110345ZSEP32:
FM:  USSS OPS CTR SWO
TO:  WHSR 1
SUBJ:  POTUS RES. PSD

SIR, IN RESPONSE TO YR INQUIRY, THE USSS AGENT
POSTED OUTSIDE THE TREATY ROOM THIS MORN-
ING WAS SPECIAL AGENT FRANCES JAMES. IF THERE
ARE ANY ISSUES, PLS CONTACT ME AT EXT 9157, SAIC
BAKER KATZ AT EXT 9122 OR USSS DIR BILL PETER-
SON AT EXT 3333.


V/R, GEORGE SANDERS, USSS SWO


As they walked back toward the West Wing, Murad
watched Smith put his PID back in his pocket and asked,
"Anything new?"

"No," the retired general responded, deep in thought.
"Just another loose end that needs to be tied up."

**USAF CODEL SAM FLIGHT #MC09–14A**
EN ROUTE LEESBURG, VA–CHARLESTON, SC
TUESDAY, 14 SEPTEMBER 2032
1525 HOURS, LOCAL


James Newman wasn't surprised U.S. senator Mackintosh Caperton arrived at 22570 Randolph Road
precisely at one thirty. The senator, as everyone knew, had
a near-legendary repute for being punctual. James *was*
surprised the senator was driving his own car and he was
even more astonished to see his wife, Angela, seated beside
him.

Once in the car, the senator reached around to James,
handed him a small but heavier than expected envelope,
and said, "Inside you will find a U.S. Senate Staff ID
badge and a PID. Both have embedded PERTs identifying
you as James Lehnert, a staff member of the Senate Select
Committee on Intelligence."

Newman pulled the contents out of the envelope and

was amazed to see his own digital image staring back at him from the SSCI ID.

As they drove west on the Greenway, the senator continued: "The envelope is TEMPEST-shielded. Put your own PID in it and use the one I just gave you for the next few days. In theory, the rest of our government isn't allowed to monitor direct communications to or from a U.S. senator or member of Congress. At least that's how we wrote the law. Do you still have the PERT embedded in your right foot wrapped in foil?"

"Yes, sir," James replied. "These are the same kind of shielded boots we were issued by Special Operations Command when I was in MARSOC."

Caperton nodded and said, "Good. Keep 'em on until we can figure out something better."

It took them less than a quarter hour to reach the Leesburg Flight Support FBO, where James and the senator got out of the car, each retrieving flat-panel computer cases and small travel bags from the trunk. Before entering the terminal, Caperton opened the door for his wife, walked her around to the driver's side, embraced her, and closed the door for her after she slid behind the wheel.

As Caperton and Newman watched her pull away, two blue and white U.S. Capitol Police sedans with a white van sandwiched between them pulled up in front of the small terminal. Newman felt a rush of adrenaline as eight people disgorged from the van and said, "Uh, Senator . . ."

Caperton, realizing James might well think he was about to be detained, quickly said, "Four of 'em are from my congressional staff, the two big guys are plainclothes Capitol Police officers, and the last two are aides to South Carolina senator John Haley. They're just along for the ride."

He introduced them to James "Lehnert," a "new SSCI 'staffer,'" and they all entered the small terminal to be greeted by a USAF technical sergeant who presented himself as their crew chief. He quickly scanned their IDs to his PID, hit SEND, and said, "We're all manifested, Senator. Please place all bags on the conveyor. No need to stop or remove any clothing or metal objects before passing through the body scanner. This FBO has the most recent upgraded detector, so just keep walking through at a normal pace. The two law officers packing heat, please come through after the senator. Once everyone is through, grab your bags off the conveyor and we'll go out to the flight line."

James Lehnert's bags and body failed to set off any alarms and the tech sergeant led them all out to a gleaming white and blue C-37C—a military variant of the venerable Gulfstream 560. As they boarded, the senator motioned for James to sit opposite him at the table in the front of the aircraft. The staff and security team spread out in seats farther aft.

They no sooner fastened their seat belts than a USAF major in a flight suit came out of the cockpit, approached Newman and Caperton, and said, "Senator, I'm sorry to inform you we have just been given a ground hold for Air Force One to transit the airspace en route west. As soon as I am told how long it will be, I'll let you know."

The senator shrugged and said, "She outranks us. So much for Mack Caperton's ego. Thank you, Major." They waited nearly an hour past their scheduled departure. He and Newman talked quietly during the delay and subsequent flight.

Caperton began the conversation by saying, "The next few days are likely to be tough on you, Sarah, and the boys. How can I help you?"

James was taken aback by the question. He held up the SSCI ID and the PID that Caperton gave him, gestured toward the top of the aircraft cabin, and replied, "Seems like you already have, Senator."

"I'm not talking about *this* James," Caperton responded, pointing to the Lehnert PID. "I'm talking about you and Sarah and the boys. I'm talking about you and your mom and dad. I'm talking about the things that *really* matter, not the stuff going on around us. And don't be calling me 'Senator.' When it's just the two of us, or with our families, it's *Mack*, just like it has always been."

James nodded but said nothing.

Mack Caperton had a well-earned reputation in Montana and Washington for straight talk. And persistence. He tried again. "Look, I've changed your diapers, James Newman. I was there when you were baptized, when you made Eagle Scout—back when this country still had Scouting. I was there when you were commissioned at the Boat School, when you got married, and I'm the godfather of your son, Joshua. I've hiked and hunted hundreds of miles with you, from the Blue Ridge to the Rockies, and we have fished most of the streams and rivers in between. I can read you like a sunrise at sea—and we've seen more than a few of those together. What's eating at you?"

James shrugged and said, "I don't know, everything seems to be turning out differently than I expected or hoped. Friday is Sarah's and my tenth anniversary and Saturday is Seth's twelfth birthday and I'm going to miss both, like too many others."

Mack nodded and asked, "So who *are* you feeling sorry for, you or them?"

Newman looked out the window for a moment then replied, "Good question." He paused and then continued: "I guess I feel sorry for all of us, but things haven't worked out the way they were supposed to. Maybe I just wasn't supposed to be married and have a family—"

"Well, you *are* married and you *do* have a family, so that's water over the dam," Caperton interjected. "And I'm not sure anything that happens in this life has a 'supposed to' attached to it—except we're supposed to use our God-given gifts and talents to play the hand we've been dealt the best way we can. Never play the game of 'should-a, would-a, could-a,' because there are no winners in that contest. More importantly, what I hear you saying is the real problem is with you and Sarah."

When the younger man nodded, wistfully looking out the aircraft window, Caperton resumed. "Tell me again how you two met and came to be married. If I recall correctly, Sarah was the widow of one of your friends from the Academy who was killed when you were wounded in the Sinai back in 2020."

James reflected for a few seconds, then leaned over the table and said, "Her husband, Seth, was a year behind me at the Academy. I first met Sarah when I was a firsty and she and Seth were dating. They got married when he graduated. I came up from Quantico to be in their wedding. Arch of swords and all that."

"Then what?"

"Before we deployed to the Med in 2020, I saw a good bit of them at Lejeune. He was in my rifle company and they used to entertain all the bachelors. She was pregnant when we deployed. By the time I saw her again at Seth's memorial service, their son was a couple of months old and she was a beautiful young widow whose husband was killed saving my life."

"When was the next time you saw her after that?"

Newman continued, "She moved back to Woodbridge,

Virginia, to be near her parents, and the Marine Corps got her a job with a defense contractor at Quantico. She came to see me while I was still in the hospital at Bethesda. When I was well enough and on 'light duty' at Quantico, we went out on a few coffee dates and did lunch on a few weekends. But it was nothing more than friendship. She was lonely, and I was a good shoulder to cry on. When she could find a sitter for Seth, she and I would go out with a group of other singles to the Kennedy Center or Wolf Trap. But we were just friends."

Mack nodded and added, "And she's pretty and despite the tears, she's fun to be around."

"Yeah," James replied, smiling as he recalled. "It was like that for almost a year, and then one weekend in the fall of 2021, I brought her out to Narnia to ride one of my sister Elizabeth's horses. Sarah, Mom, and Lizzie hit it off right away. Sarah bought a horse and Mom would babysit little Seth while Sarah and Lizzie went off competing at local events—you know, dressage, stadium jumping, cross-country . . ."

"Uh huh."

"I didn't see much of Sarah that fall because I recovered enough to go back to full duty and I got orders back to Camp Lejeune. You remember, that was the fall when the UN concocted the idea of a Caliph to get control of things in the Middle East and we pulled all our troops out of Egypt?"

"Oh, I remember the autumn of 2021 very well," Caperton replied. "But the turmoil created by the UN's 'Caliphate Plan' didn't have anything to do with you and Sarah getting married."

"No," James agreed. "That had more to do with my coming home on leave at Christmas. Mom invited Sarah and her parents to the Narnia Christmas party." Then as he thought about it he added, "In fact, you and Angela were there when it happened."

"When *what* happened?"

James smiled at the memory and said, "You know the mistletoe my mom hangs from that light in the kitchen every year?"

Caperton nodded and said, "Yes."

"Well, that's where and when Sarah and I kissed for the first time. And *you* were there!"

"And you proposed *then*, with a hundred people milling about, singing Christmas carols, and drinking your father's eggnog?"

"No," James chuckled. "But that *was* the first time we kissed. Before I left for Lejeune after New Year's, we took some long walks together and spent a lot of time talking in front of the fire," James replied, serious again. "Then, in February, when our whole family went skiing in West Virginia, Lizzie invited Sarah along. I took a long weekend from Lejeune and met them at Snowshoe. Sarah and I skied together, while Mom looked after Seth."

Caperton leaned forward and said, "Look, James, I'm not trying to be prurient here, but while you were there did you two—"

"No, we didn't," James interrupted. "Let me spare you the discomfort of asking, Mack. It's worse than you can imagine. From February on, the only time Sarah and I saw each other was when I could get a weekend off and drive up from Lejeune. And that was always at Narnia— she spent almost every weekend there that spring and early summer."

"How is that worse?"

"Well, here's how," James said. "You may remember the Fourth of July in 2022 was a Monday . . ."

"No," Caperton said, shaking his head. "I don't recall what day of the week it was that year."

"Well, there are some days a man ought to never forget," Newman replied. "I know I won't. Since it was a long weekend, I drove up from Lejeune and got to Narnia late Friday night. Sarah came out early Saturday morning to go eventing with Lizzie. On Sunday we went to church and spent the afternoon around the swimming pool. We engaged in a little horseplay in the pool but nothing else."

The senator shrugged and said, "Ah, youth. Sounds tempting but innocent enough so far."

James continued: "On Monday, the Fourth, Mom offered to look after Seth while Sarah and I took the canoe down to the Shenandoah to paddle around for a while. When we got back, it was so hot we decided to join Mom, Dad, Lizzie, and one of her med school boyfriends in the pool. Just as we got in, Danny, the farm manager, comes down the hill to tell Lizzie her horse has colic. Mom, Dad, Lizzie, and her boyfriend all jump out of the water and race up to the stable."

"And you two stayed in the pool?"

"Not for long," James answered. "Sarah said she had to go into the house to check on Seth, who was taking a nap. I went in with her. When we entered the house, the air-conditioning gave her goose bumps all over her body. I put my arms around her to warm her up. Not smart for a guy who pledged to remain a virgin until his wedding night."

Mack closed his eyes tightly as though he was trying to squeeze the word picture out of his head. James continued. "We made love for the first time in my parents' bedroom so we wouldn't wake Seth."

Caperton's eyes sprang open as though he had touched a live wire. "Do your mom and dad know this?" he asked.

"Not the part about their bedroom, but they must know the consequences," James said ruefully. "I drove up from Lejeune the next two weekends, but instead of meeting Sarah at the farm, I stayed with her at her condo in Woodbridge. When I came up the weekend of August sixth, while she was fixing dinner at her place, she told me she was pregnant."

"What did you say when she told you that?"

"Sarah might remember it differently, but I recall telling her I loved her and wanted her to marry me."

"And she said?"

"She didn't say anything, initially," James said. "She just put her arms around my neck and cried. Then while we were standing there holding on to each other she said, 'Okay.' That's how I proposed and she accepted."

"And that's how Angela and I got invited to that lovely wedding at the Quantico Base Chapel on September 17, 2022," Mack said with a smile. "I'm glad we were with the lovely couple on the day they shared their first kiss—even though we missed it—and got to witness the one they made at the altar that day."

Newman simply nodded but said nothing. Both men were silent for a moment and then Mack said, "If it matters, I believe you did the right thing by marrying Sarah. But I'm trying to figure out what has happened to the happy couple, since that has turned you into the unhappy man I see sitting across from me now. Do you mind answering a few questions?"

"No."

"Good. How much of what you just told me do your mom and dad know?"

"Well," James replied with a shrug, "nobody but Sarah and I—and now you—know the intimate details. Mom, Dad, Lizzie, Sarah's parents, and anyone else who cares to can do the math. Joshua was born six months and two weeks after we were married. Nobody has ever mentioned it to me, but I'm sure they all know he wasn't *that* early."

"Do you think Sarah lured you into marrying her?"

Newman thought before answering, "It's more complicated than that. She is a beautiful woman. She was lonely. I succumbed to temptation at a time when I felt terrible guilt that her husband, my friend, was killed and not me. I don't think she got pregnant on purpose and I'm pretty sure neither of us was thinking about the consequences when it happened. To answer your question: No. I don't think she *lured* me."

"Okay, let's try to simplify this a little. On the night she told you she was pregnant, did you mean it when you said you loved her?"

"Yes," James replied without hesitation.

"Do you believe she loved you then?"

"Yes."

"Do you love her now?"

Newman was slower to respond this time. After a moment he said, "Yes, I do still love her. But there are a lot of things between us now and it's more than having four kids to wrangle and homeschool."

"Besides having four kids, what else changed, James?"

Newman groped for words, then spoke quietly. "It was hard on Sarah that I was deployed when Joshua was born in March 2023. But within a few months of my getting home, everything seemed to be working out. I guess the train started coming off the tracks when I started deploying to Afghanistan with MARSOC in 2024. Our first two deployments went okay—there were no gunfights. But the third one, in 2025, when I got wounded again during the big fight at Shindand, knocked Sarah for a loop."

"You can see why, can't you?"

"Yeah, it was too close to what happened to her first husband," James answered. "When I got out of the hospital, Sarah told me she wanted me to get out of the Marines. But I was doing well in the Corps and didn't want to leave. We went to marriage counseling a few times and she stopped talking about it. I thought she was over it. Then there was the big congressional investigation into what happened at Shindand and the jihadist death threats and all. While we were at the safe house, surrounded by federal agents twenty-four seven, somehow she got pregnant with the twins."

"*Somehow* she got pregnant?" Caperton echoed with a smile. "Surely by that point in your marriage you guys figured out what was causing her to get pregnant."

"Yeah, we know," Newman replied, smiling. Then more seriously, he added, "But by the time the twins were born, I think Sarah had just given up on me. That's why I got out of the Marine Corps in 2026. Now we have *this*, and I am going to be gone again for Lord knows how long."

Caperton leaned back in his seat, thinking. As he was about to speak, the tech sergeant came out of the cockpit and said, "Senator, we're about ten minutes out of Charleston. Please fasten your seat belts."

They did as asked and when the crew chief moved aft to tell the other passengers, Caperton said, "James, I want to help any way I can. You, Sarah, and your boys mean a lot to me. When we land, instead of you going to the synagogue with me, I'm going to have Officer Carter drive you straight to Pawleys. Let me think about what you told me and tomorrow night I'll come up there and we can talk some more. Okay?"

"Okay."

Caperton reached into his briefcase, pulled out a gray baseball hat, handed it to James, and said, "Please wear this and your sunglasses on the way to Pawleys. When you get there, try to stay out of sight. We don't need you showing up on any surveillance cameras. The island is too small for you to hide there for long. The summer crowds are gone and Cair Paravel is fairly private, but we don't need tongues wagging. If you need to pick up anything, get it on the way—in Charleston or Mount Pleasant. Use cash or the PID I gave you to pay for any purchases. Make sure you use the Lehnert PID for all communications. The law says no government agency is allowed to monitor congressional comms, but don't contact anyone at CSG or Narnia until I arrive—even Sarah. I should get there tomorrow night, probably around nine. And be sure to keep your implanted PERT masked, even in the house."

"Anything else?" Newman asked, amazed the old man had thought of all this.

Caperton thought for a moment and said, "What kind of PERT implant do you have in your foot?"

"It's a second generation, the 2-GenB model everyone in the military had to get," James replied. "It's about the size of a grain of rice. I can just feel it between my toes with my fingers."

"Is it the kind that has to be recharged every so often?"

"Yeah. It's supposed to be recharged at least once a month by putting your foot on a magnetic induction pad. I have one in the car and under my desk at the office. We even have one of them under the sheets at the foot of our bed. Maybe that's why Sarah gets pregnant so easily."

Caperton smiled and said, "I doubt it. But tell me, do Sarah and the boys all have implanted PERTs?"

"Yes, all military dependents had to get them in case we were assigned overseas, because our PERTs serve as our passports. And of course the twins were born after the government made it mandatory for all newborns because the baby PERTs contain time-release nano-particles for early childhood immunizations."

"Right."

"Why? Does it matter?" asked James.

"Well, it's good to know. Your sister Elizabeth and her husband George are both physicians and they still live at Narnia, right?"

James leaned forward and said, "I think I know where this is heading, Mack, but Lizzie could lose her license for removing Sarah's and the boys' PERTs and I don't want Sarah and the kids to be considered Anarks."

"And you think being considered an Anark would be a bad thing?"

"Doesn't everyone think that way?" James replied as the plane touched down.

"Perhaps not everyone," mused the senator. "Hold that thought. It will give us something else to talk about tomorrow night." Then he added, "While you are waiting for me to get there, let me suggest something for you to do—so you don't get bored."

"What's that?"

"Between tonight and tomorrow night when I arrive, make two lists for me. Use two sheets of paper—don't use the PID or your computer."

"Shopping lists?"

"Kind of. On one sheet make a list of every possible positive attribute you possess, no matter how great or trivial. Use the other sheet for the same thing about Sarah. No negatives, just the positive. You get what I'm saying?"

As the plane taxied to the Air Force terminal, James nodded and said, "Uh huh. I guess that will keep me from getting cabin fever. Since there won't be anyone else there, I suppose there won't be much else to do."

Caperton rose from his seat to exit the aircraft, turned to Newman, and said, "James, let's pray you are right about what you just said."

*  *  *  *

U.S. Capitol Police Officer Mark Carter and "SSCI Staff member James Lehnert" rode side by side in the plain vanilla, standard, government-issue Chevrolet hybrid all the way to Pawleys Island. Like most men trying to avoid speaking about what was really on their minds, they talked about sports.

They stopped at a Piggly Wiggly in Mount Pleasant. Officer Carter waited in the car while James bought a half gallon of irradiated milk, some "USDA-Certified Humane" irradiated chicken, a bag of "Sanitary, Salmonella-Free Lettuce," and a box of cereal "Guaranteed Union-Grown and Made." As he placed each item in his shopping basket, the price automatically tallied in both U.S. dollars and Global Exchange Currency Units on the PID Caperton gave him. At the store exit, a "Task-Bot," its face-panel twisted into a mechanical smile, said, "Thank you for shopping with us, Mr. Lehnert. Your purchases come to 10.1 gex, or $35.24. Shall we put this on your card?"

James held up the PID and said, "Put it on this—in gex."

"Smart move," replied the machine-generated voice. "We never know what the dollar will be worth tomorrow. Please note an electronic receipt has been sent to your Personal Interface Device. Come in again the next time you are visiting from Washington, D.C."

As James entered the car, Carter asked, "Find everything you need?"

"The produce wasn't very fresh. We can check at a roadside stand on the way to Pawleys."

"I suppose," said Carter, "as long as you don't mind eating stuff not government-certified." But seven miles farther north on Route 17, they pulled over at a roadside fruit and vegetable stand.

Overshadowing the little stand was a large electronic, LED-lighted billboard emblazoned with a 15'x25' moving image of the American flag and eight-foot-high lettering:

REAL PATRIOTS IMPLANT PERTs!

At the entrance to the fruit and vegetable stand was an official sign bearing the seal of the Department of Homeland Security:

WARNING

PRODUCE SOLD HERE IS NOT USDA INSPECTED.

DISEASES CONTRACTED BY HUMAN CONSUMPTION ARE
NOT COVERED BY ALL-AMERICAN MEDICAL INSURANCE.

As James started to get out of the car, Officer Carter pointed to the steel-encased national surveillance network camera beneath the billboard and said, "I think I'll wait in the car. If they have any peaches, please get me a few."

Newman pulled the baseball hat down over his forehead, put on his sunglasses, got out, and walked into the little stand. He picked out a dozen apples, four onions, a bunch of carrots, six ears of sweet corn, a basket of fresh green beans, and a dozen peaches. The old black woman at an ancient cash register said, "That comes to eighteen dollars and twenty-five cents, sir. I'm sorry but we're not allowed to accept electronic payments and we don't take those new gex. Do you have American cash?"

James reached into his pocket, took four fives out, handed the bills to the old woman, and said, "Keep the change." Then, pointing to the warning sign at the entrance, he asked, "Does that sign scare off any customers?"

"Well, sir," she replied, "we're required to have that posted there just to stay open. I'm told South Carolina is one of the few states where people are even allowed to sell produce not prepackaged and government inspected. It doesn't keep our regular customers away, but tourists don't stop here anymore like they did when I was a little girl. But of course there are a lot fewer cars on the road nowadays."

"I see," said James. "Thank you."

As he turned to leave, the old woman said to his back, "God bless you, sir."

He turned back to her but before he could reply she said, "Oh, dear sir, I didn't mean any offense by that. Please don't report me to the authorities for offensive speech. I'm just an old lady with old habits. And you know, old habits die hard."

James nodded and said, "Yes, ma'am, they do. But some old habits are worth keeping. God bless you, too."

*   *   *   *

When Carter and Newman arrived at the Pawleys Island North Causeway security gate, it was seven thirty and getting dark. The guard stepped out of the little booth and asked for identification. Carter gave him his U.S. Capitol Police ID and Newman handed over James Lehnert's Senate staff badge.

The security guard held each one up to a scanner screen in the booth, nodded as the machine read their embedded data, handed the IDs back to Carter, and asked, "And who are you gentlemen going over to the island to see?

I'm sorry to have to ask, but we don't seem to have this vehicle or either of you in our database."

"That's because this is a government car," Carter replied gruffly. "We're on official U.S. government business, as you can see from our PERT data."

"Well, I'm sure you are, sir," said the guard politely. "And I don't mean to delay you, but unless you are an invited, preregistered guest, or you have one of the owners' ident codes, you will just have to wait here for an escort. I can have one here in a few minutes."

Over the years, James had traversed this route thousands of times, and hundreds of times since the security gates were installed on the causeways in 2020. But he always came and went with his own car or in a vehicle his parents precleared and using his real identity. Then he recalled one of their family friends and their memorable identification code. He leaned over Carter and said, "Officer, we're going to the McElveens'. The ident code is 1776."

The security guard entered the name and number on the plastic touchscreen inside the booth. As the gate in front of the car swung up, the guard said, "Well, that must be right. These computer things are really something."

"Yeah, aren't they though," Carter said under his breath as he swiped the dashboard touch panel to put the car in gear and headed east across the causeway. Then, turning to James, he said, "I don't mean to be rude, Mr. Lehnert, but that guy *isn't* an officer. *I'm* a sworn officer. He's just a gate guard."

James, immensely relieved the situation was resolved without attracting any more attention, meekly replied, "You're right, Officer Carter. My mistake. Sorry."

Five minutes later they were at the gate to Cair Paravel

on the north end of Atlantic Avenue. Newman jumped out and punched a code into the security box. As the gate swung open, the police officer pulled the vehicle in and parked beneath the house.

Carter popped the trunk. James unloaded the groceries and his small bag and asked, "Want to come up and use the head? I can rustle up a cup of coffee."

The policeman got out of the car, stretched, and said, "That would be good." Then, looking around in the twilight, he added, "Man, some digs. You been here before?"

"Yeah," James replied, "a few times. They are real nice folks."

As they mounted the stairs and Newman punched yet another code into the home security system, Carter said, admiringly, "Well, if I had the kind of money these people have to afford a place like this, I would be real nice, too."

James pointed Carter to the guest bathroom and went into the kitchen to make a pot of coffee. As the aroma of the fresh brew filled the air, Carter entered the kitchen and said, "Say, there is a picture of you with some hot chick on the wall in the bathroom."

Newman was suddenly glad he hadn't turned on any more lights. His mother's idea of decorating was to put family photographs on every available wall and bookshelf. There were pictures of James, Elizabeth, their mates, and their children throughout the place, but he couldn't recall which particular image was in the bathroom. So he said, "Yeah, I know the owner's daughter."

Carter shrugged and said, "Well, she's eye candy. If I was her old man she wouldn't be allowed to wear a bikini like that."

James realized it had to be a photo of him and Sarah taken several years ago. He chuckled and said, "I don't think I'll tell him you said so."

Newman poured two mugs of steaming coffee and asked, "Take anything in it?"

"Just the way it comes, thanks. Hate to take the mug. In the old days they used to make paper cups for this kind of thing, but not anymore."

"Don't worry about it," James answered, trying to get the lawman out the door before he made further discoveries. "Just give it to the senator. He's going to be here tomorrow night."

"Yeah, that's right. Well, I have to run. I'll probably come back with the senator tomorrow." At the door he said, "I sent my number to your PID. Contact me if you have any problems."

As he watched the security gate open and the car pull out onto Atlantic Avenue, James breathed a sigh of relief. He then looked down at the SSCI PID that Senator Caperton gave him and noticed there were two unopened messages. One was the phone number Carter sent. The second message, from Mackintosh Caperton, was marked "URGENT."

CHAPTER FIVE

# STORM WARNING

<u>CAIR PARAVEL</u>
ATLANTIC AVENUE
PAWLEYS ISLAND, SC
WEDNESDAY, 15 SEPTEMBER 2032
0305 HOURS, LOCAL

In low-level flight, a V-22 Osprey tilt-rotor makes a sound unlike anything else in the air. Part helicopter and part fixed-wing aircraft, the plane has twin Rolls-Royce Allison turboshaft engines and thirty-eight-foot-diameter rotors that create a deep and distinctive growl. As the craft clips along at an altitude of one hundred feet and speed of 275 knots, the roar comes and goes so swiftly it can be utterly terrifying to someone on the ground not expecting it. In combat, the effect on the enemy is an attribute. In peacetime it is sure to arouse complaints. The Marines dismiss the noise as "the sound of freedom."

James Newman was asleep for less than an hour

when two MV-22Cs from VMM-263, on a low-level, night training flight out of New River Marine Corps Air Station, North Carolina, swept south, past Cair Paravel. Awakened by the sudden reverberation just a hundred yards off the beach, his heart racing, James instinctively rolled off the bed onto the floor. In one fluid motion he grabbed the old shoulder-holstered Colt .45 automatic from the nightstand and bolted for the door. He chambered a round, thumbed the safety on, and was halfway downstairs when the noise faded as fast as it started.

He stopped, holding his breath to listen. Hearing nothing but the thumping of his own pulse, he crept slowly downstairs—the aluminum foil, wrapped around his right foot, crinkling against his skin. Reaching the first floor without turning on any lights, James picked up a set of binoculars off the mantel, slowly opened the door to the beach, and scanned the water, looking for swimmers. Seeing nothing, he finally went outside, sat down in a rocking chair, and listened to the sound of the surf breaking on the sand.

The regular rhythm of waves rolling ashore and the scent of salt air were soporific for everyone in the Newman family. But tonight, after sitting in the dark for a half hour, James accepted that his mind was racing too fast for sleep to return. He finally rose, went into the house, picked up the PID that Mack Caperton had given him the previous afternoon, and reread the communications he and the senator had exchanged since eight fifteen that evening.

The first electronic missive from the vice chairman of the Senate Select Committee on Intelligence once again prompted a rush of adrenaline in James Newman's gut.

U.S. SENATE PRIVILEGED COMMUNICATION
PRECEDENCE: FLASH
150115ZSEP32
FM: SSCIMC001
TO: SSCIJL001
CC: SSCIPJ001
SUBJ: URGENT UPDATE

1. CANADIAN SCIENTIST STEVEN TEMPLETON, COL-
LEAGUE OF DR. MARTIN COHEN, HOSPITALIZED IN
CALGARY. HE AND WIFE JANE APPARENTLY DISCOV-
ERED NEARLY ASPHYXIATED BY CARBON MONOXIDE
FM FAULTY HOME HEATING SYSTEM. CONDITION
CRITICAL. PROGNOSIS UNCERTAIN.

2. FBI DIR. VIC FOSTER WILL RESIGN ON WEDNESDAY,
15 SEP. HE INTENDS TO INFORM POTUS IN MORNING
WHEN SHE RETURNS FM CALIFORNIA. FOSTER APPAR-
ENTLY IRATE OVER WHITE HOUSE INTERFERENCE IN
INVESTIGATION OF HOUSTON ATTACK ON 11 SEP 32.

3. DRAFT FBI REPORT TO SSCI RE HOUSTON ATTACK
HAS BEEN RECALLED BY DNI AT WHITE HOUSE DIREC-
TION. DRAFT REPORT CONCLUDES ATTACK IN HOUSTON
WAS PERPETRATED BY TERROR CELL DISPATCHED FROM
CALIPHATE TO PREVENT COHEN/TEMPLETON/DAVIS DE-
VICE FROM REACHING COMMERCIAL MARKETPLACE.

4. DOJ APPARENTLY DRAFTING A WARRANT FOR AP-
PREHENSION OF JAMES STUART NEWMAN FOR "AID-
ING AND/OR ABETTING AN ACT OF TERROR." U.S.
ATTORNEY IN D.C. PLANS TO PRESENT INFORMATION
TO A GRAND JURY ON FRIDAY 17 SEP AND OBTAIN A
SEALED INDICTMENT.

5. WX: NOAA REPORTS EYE OF HURRICANE LUCY NOW 80 MI NE OF MONTEGO BAY, JAMAICA, WITH MAX WINDS OF 104 MPH. CURRENT STORM TRACK 290° AT 25 MPH WILL TAKE LUCY INTO GULF OF MEXICO IN NEXT 24–36 HOURS. NO ANTICIPATED RISK TO U.S. MAINLAND, USCG HAS ISSUED NOTICE TO MARINERS TRANSITING PATH OF STORM AND ORDERED EVACUA-TION OF OFFSHORE OIL & GAS RIGS.

6. JL: HOLD CURRENT POSITION. MAINTAIN COVER, CONCEALMENT, AND SITUATIONAL AWARENESS. MAIN-TAIN DATA COMMS, NO VOICE, THRU THIS PRIVILEGED CHANNEL ONLY. I WILL ARRIVE YOUR POS NLT NOON, 15 SEP.

7. PJ: AM LOOKING FWD TO SEEING U & YRS @ CP WHEN I ARRIVE.

CAPERTON

James resisted the urge to use his father's desktop com-puter or either of the two PIDs in his possession to check for information on the MESH. Instead he turned on the HD radio in the kitchen and listened for any news about a hospitalized Canadian scientist, the pending resignation of the FBI director, or potential indictments resulting from the attack in Houston. He heard nothing about any of these things. The only "breaking news" stories were about the U.S. presidential campaign and Hurricane Lucy in the Gulf of Mexico. He ignored them.

Newman's focus was on the first four paragraphs of the senator's message. It was only after he carefully reread the communiqué that James realized Caperton had carefully avoided mentioning any locations or real names other than his own. He also noted the senator addressed his message to "JL001"—the Intelligence Committee designator for James Lehnert's PID—and a copy was forwarded to another SSCI addressee: "PJ001."

It took a third read-through for James to grasp Caperton's clever "brevity code" and what it all meant: "PJ" was the moniker Peter J. Newman's parents gave him as a child. It stuck through his days at the Academy and with close friends and family ever since. "CP," military shorthand for "Command Post," was how his father referred to Cair Paravel—another nickname known to few outside the Newman family.

James smiled as he realized his father must also have an SSCI PID and that the senator intended to meet with father and son at Pawleys Island on Wednesday the fifteenth. It also occurred to James that Caperton would not be using code and military jargon if he knew for certain that the "Privileged" SSCI PID channel really was completely secure.

Newman hit REPLY and tapped out a terse response:

U.S. SENATE PRIVILEGED COMMUNICATION
PRECEDENCE: FLASH
150137ZSEP32
FM:  SSCIJL001
TO:  SSCIMC001
SUBJ:  RESPONSE TO YR URGENT UPDATE

SENATOR CAPERTON:

ROGER YR LAST. WILCO. PLS ADVISE WHO WILL AC-
COMPANY YOU TO CP. MAY HAVE TO CLEAN UP.

V/R, LEHNERT

Newman's "clean up" reference had nothing to do with dust on the floor or the garbage container beneath the kitchen sink. His concern was that the senator would be accompanied by U.S. Capitol Police Officer Mark Carter and others. Receiving no immediate response from his PID message to Caperton, James spent the next hour "sanitizing" the premises by removing photos of himself from walls and shelves throughout the house. By the time he was finished, he had more than thirty framed pictures carefully stacked in a locked closet beneath the stairs. The only one left in place was the one in the bathroom that Officer Carter had already seen.

It was nearly eleven forty-five when "Lehnert" received another PID message from Caperton. This one had a classification heading the previous message did not contain:

```
SECRET
U.S. SENATE PRIVILEGED COMMUNICATION
PRECEDENCE: FLASH
150443ZSEP32
FM:   SSCIMC001
TO:   SSCIJL001
CC:   SSCIPJ001
SUBJ:  LATEST SSCI INFO [S]


1. IRT YR LAST, OUR A/C DISPLACING FM CHS TO MYR
AT 0800 EDT. WILL ARRIVE CP APPROX 0830 EDT AC-
COMP BY OFFICER ALREADY KNOWN TO YOU. REQ. YOU
PROVIDE CLEARANCE THRU FRIENDLY LINES TO CP. NEW
INFO FOLLOWS IN ORDER OF RECEIPT:


2. NOAA-MIAMI WEATHER SERVICE UNIT: STORM-TRACK
SATELLITE REPORTS HURRICANE LUCY LIKELY TO COME
```

ASHORE VIC CANCUN ON YUCATAN PENINSULA ON OR ABOUT 0400 EDT 16 SEP.

3. NGIA–FORT BELVOIR, VA: SATELLITE IMAGERY SHOWS 31 VESSELS ATTEMPTING TO AVOID STORM TRACK AND MAKE PORT IN CARIBBEAN OR GULF OF MEXICO. TWO COASTAL TANKERS, *ILEANA ROSARIO* AND *ORFEO,* ARE APPARENTLY IN DISTRESS. INTERCEPTED VOICE & DATA COMMS INDICATE *ILEANA ROSARIO* IS REPORTING INCORRECT/FALSE IMO REGISTRATION NUMBER. USCG SUSPECTS VESSEL MAY HAVE CONTRABAND ABOARD.

4. FBI–WASH. DC: FBI DIRECTOR VIC FOSTER RUSHED TO GW MED CENTER WITH APPARENT SELF-INFLICTED GUNSHOT WOUND TO HEAD. WIFE TOLD REPORTER AT HOSPITAL THAT HER HUSBAND "HAD BECOME DESPONDENT AND HAS BEEN SUFFERING FROM EXHAUSTION AND DEPRESSION SINCE 9-11-32 ATTACK BUT REFUSED TO TAKE HIS MEDICINE."

5. DNI–WASH. DC: NEW DRAFT "INTERAGENCY REPORT" INDICATES HOUSTON ATTACK "LIKELY PERPETRATED BY PREVIOUSLY UNKNOWN ANARK/CARTEL ENTITY WITH ASSISTANCE OF 'SLEEPERS' FROM JEWISH TERROR ORGANIZATIONS OPERATING IN THE U.S."

CAPERTON

"Lehnert" replied to this message with a brief PID transmission to Caperton, instructing him to use the "McElveen 1776" ident code when he arrived at the Pawleys Island North Causeway security gate. He then made one final sweep through the house, looking for any other photographs in which he appeared. Finally, he sat down at the kitchen table with two sheets of paper to make the lists of "positive attributes" Caperton had asked him to compile earlier in the day.

By one thirty in the morning his list held twenty-one items on the sheet titled "Sarah" and thirteen on the one labeled "James." Exhausted, he turned out the lights, went upstairs, brushed his teeth, and slipped into a lightweight running suit—his normal sleeping attire.

In the bedroom, he opened a front window so he could hear the sound of the surf, removed an ancient Colt .45 model 1911A1 pistol and shoulder holster from a locked case in the closet, placed the weapon on the nightstand, and slipped between the sheets of the bed he and Sarah shared when together at Cair Paravel. He tossed and turned for more than an hour before getting to sleep, only to be startled awake shortly after 0300 by the low-flying MV-22s.

\* \* \* \*

Newman glanced at the digital display on the PID: 0415. He shook his head, picked up the .45, a pen, and the two lists he worked on before going to bed, walked into the living room, and sat down on the couch. That's where he was—sleeping soundly at six thirty in the morning—when the slam of a car door beneath the house and the sound of footsteps on the back stairs startled him awake. He sat up and reached for the .45 automatic.

## ABOARD *ILEANA ROSARIO*

NORTHWEST OF YUCATAN CHANNEL

22°42'55"N, 88°11'14"W

WEDNESDAY, 15 SEPTEMBER 2032

0615 HOURS, LOCAL

From the time they boarded the *Ileana Rosario* in the hours just before dawn on September 11, almost everything had gone wrong for "Vargas" and his five comrades. Since that morning, nothing had gone as planned by the kidnappers or those who sent them on their mission.

For Cohen, bound like a foil-covered mummy, the experience was less terrifying than his captors might have expected. Once he determined he did not have the ability to free himself, Cohen resolved—as he had with so many other things in his life—to learn as much as he could. In this situation he set out to discover who seized him and why.

Deprived of mobility and sight, he listened carefully to everything going on around him, noting movement, smells, even changes of temperature. By the time the speedboat pulled alongside the *Ileana Rosario*, Cohen had discerned the smaller vessel was gasoline powered, had two engines—hydro-jets instead of screws—and was capable of very high speeds in open seas.

Though he initially didn't know the larger vessel's name, he knew immediately after being hoisted aboard that the *Ileana Rosario* was powered by an old-fashioned diesel engine and had a single screw. He also caught the distinctive scent of heavy petroleum and correctly deduced it was a tanker. By the way it rolled on the swells he figured it was not fully loaded or ballasted and it was probably about 150 feet long. The scraping and squeaking he heard from the tackle, hoists, and hinges convinced him the vessel was in poor repair.

As his captors conversed with each other, Cohen also cataloged their voices and quickly determined the ringleader's name wasn't Vargas but in fact Ahmad. He also concluded the man who piloted the speedboat was named Ebi; he sounded older than the rest and was probably the number two in the kidnappers' chain of command. The other four were apparently named Hassan, Karim, Massoud, and Rostam.

From his decades of service all over the world in the U.S. Navy and teaching at MIT afterward, Cohen recognized the first five names to be of Arabic origin and that those individuals could be from anywhere in the Middle East. But he also knew that Rostam, a name from the mythic, epic poem *Shahnameh*, was uniquely Persian. By listening carefully to their conversations he realized his captors were speaking a mixture of Arabic and Farsi—Persian—languages he briefly studied at the Naval Academy in 1975. With nothing else to do, he probed his memory for phrases and vocabulary he had memorized a half century earlier.

Within an hour of being carried aboard the larger vessel it was clear to Cohen the captain of the dilapidated coastal oiler spoke no Arabic or Farsi and apparently little English. Of the kidnappers, only Ahmad appeared to speak any Spanish. Communications—such as they were—between the six captors and the five-man crew of the *Ileana Rosario* were conducted in broken "Spanglish"—with Ahmad acting as translator.

By listening carefully, Cohen learned that billeting space aboard the 145-foot vessel was at a premium because two of the boat's seven "staterooms" were packed full of plastic-wrapped cartons of cocaine—apparently the tanker's most frequent and profitable cargo. The captain apparently reserved only one cabin—just above the engine room—for Ahmad, his five accomplices, and their aluminum-foil-wrapped cargo. After a multilingual screaming match between Ahmad and the captain, two of the surly crewmen were ordered out of their compartment directly below the bridge and into other spaces so the kidnappers could have more room.

Four of the terrorists carried Dr. Cohen into the filthy rat's nest the two crewmen vacated. There Ahmad ordered them to hold their captive upright and begin unwrapping him from the top down. As they peeled the tape and aluminum foil off his face, Cohen momentarily saw Ahmad for the first time since he was bound on the speedboat. In the seconds before a foul-smelling cloth bag was pulled down over his head, he saw the terror chief was holding a radio-signal scanner.

As they began removing the foil from Cohen's right foot, the device emitted a telltale series of beeps and then a steady, high-pitched tone as the scanner centered over the PERT implanted there. The kidnappers hastily re-covered his leg to his knee in aluminum foil until the scanner stopped making noise. He felt them wrap the foil boot with layers of duct tape and then reattach the shackle to his left ankle. They sat him on a metal chair handcuffed, his mouth taped, and left him there until he urinated in his exercise suit trousers a half hour later. Only then did one of his captors guide him, like a Seeing Eye dog, to a head on the starboard side of the cabin.

With his cloth blindfold and his mouth still covered with heavy tape, Cohen was placed on one of the bunks, where he remained throughout most of the first day. Just before nightfall, several of his captors—he wasn't sure how many from the sound—arrived with what smelled like hot food. One of them unsnapped the cuffs from his left wrist and ankle, attached the free ends to the metal bunk, and pulled the scientist to a sitting position on the bunk.

Cohen heard Ahmad mutter "raftan"—the command *go* in Farsi—and the cabin hatch opened and slammed shut. Suddenly he felt fingers reaching up beneath the bag covering his head. Instinctively the scientist pulled back as the duct tape was ripped painfully off his face. Then, just as suddenly, the bag was lifted off his head.

Squinting into the dim light, Cohen could make out Ahmad and one of the men who had seized him in Houston. On the table beside the bunk was a metal tray with rice, beans, and a piece of what appeared to be baked fish on it. Beside the tray was a liter bottle of water. As he picked it up to quench his thirst, Cohen noted it was labeled "Bottled in Caracas, Venezuela." Ahmad pointed to the tray and said, "Eat, Jew." He did.

Late that night, after he was told, "Sleep now," Cohen was awakened by a verbal altercation from the bridge directly above his bunk. Someone—it sounded like the ship's captain—was insisting to Ahmad that the vessel had to make a "short stop" off the Yucatan Peninsula to offload some cargo for a previously scheduled customer before proceeding to their intended destination.

There ensued ten minutes of captain and kidnapper shouting almost unintelligibly at each other while Cohen strained to listen. As the argument became more heated, he heard the voice he assumed to be the captain's assure Ahmad that he and his charter passengers would be in Puerto Cabezas, Nicaragua, in plenty of time for the plane that was to meet them on September 17.

It didn't happen. Well before then, almost everything that hadn't already gone wrong eventually did.

* * * *

Shortly after dawn on the fourteenth, Cohen felt the steady throb of the ancient six-cylinder Yanmar marine

diesel, three decks and twenty-five feet below him, begin
to miss badly, then start to chug and finally buck to a
stop. Immediately afterward, he heard Ahmad jump off
the top bunk on the other side of the cabin, shout something to Hassan, and rush out the hatch.

Seconds later Cohen could hear the captain and
Ahmad yelling at each other above him, on the bridge.
A half hour later there was the sound of a smaller engine
cranking—and refusing to start—in the machinery spaces
below. From long experience at sea, Cohen assumed this
was the auxiliary engine—likely a small 50–60 horse-
power diesel to power a generator.

By listening to the captain bellow commands in Spanish to his churlish crewmen, Cohen figured out their
problem. The main fuel tanks were apparently contami-
nated with seawater. He guessed that neither the main nor
auxiliary engine fuel filters had been changed and now the
injectors in both diesels were probably clogged.

With the *Ileana Rosario* wallowing dead in the water,
it took the incompetent crew—aided in the end by Ebi—
nearly six hours to change the fuel filters, replace the damaged injectors on the auxiliary engine, drain the water out
of one diesel fuel tank, and bleed air out of the fuel lines.
Cohen listened with relief as the auxiliary engine finally
fired on the last gasp of the ship's dying batteries.

The crew-kidnapper celebration was short-lived.
Though the four-cylinder auxiliary diesel was charging the
batteries and powering the ship's radios, radar, GPS, and
navigation lights, it could produce enough electricity to
rotate the propeller only at a mere 40 rpm—moving the
vessel at less than 2 knots per hour through the water.

At midnight, Cohen heard the NOAA weather forecast
from a radio speaker on the bridge: "Over the last four
hours, Tropical Storm Lucy has intensified and is now a

Category Three hurricane with sustained winds in excess of one hundred ten miles per hour. The eye of the storm is located in the Yucatan Channel at twenty degrees, twenty-one minutes north; eighty-three degrees, eleven minutes west. The storm is tracking two-nine-zero degrees at fifteen miles per hour. At present heading, expected landfall, vicinity of Cancun, Mexico, between eleven hundred and twelve hundred hours local."

Though never a "worrier," Cohen hoped the ship's lifeboat or boats were in better shape than the engines.

*    *    *    *

They never did get the main diesel plant to light off. After replacing three of the six fuel injectors in the Yanmar 6M-UT engine and cranking it for several hours, the electric starter motor caught fire. Smoke rising from the machinery spaces was accompanied by alarm bells, colorful curses in Spanish and Persian, and much profane shouting from the bridge.

Over the rising wind, Cohen could hear the captain in the wheelhouse above him make several radio calls to another vessel he called *Orfeo*. As best Cohen could tell, there was no response. On one occasion, he heard a call from the Mexican Coast Guard inquiring if the vessel calling was in distress. By then the fire was out and the *Ileana Rosario*'s captain didn't answer.

Well before dawn on 15 September, everyone aboard the *Ileana Rosario* knew they were in serious trouble. The wind and seas were building heavily in advance of the storm and Cohen could feel the vessel barely maintaining steering way. Four of the kidnappers were too seasick to get out of their bunks except for an occasional retching rush to the head. Clothing, bedding, and the contents of two wall lockers were sliding back and forth on the pitching deck.

Ahmad and Ebi seemed to adapt better than the other kidnappers to the deteriorating sea state. Though Cohen couldn't understand most of their conversations, he could hear the concern in their voices. The two words they said most often were ones the scientist remembered: *bâd* and *âb*—Persian for wind and water.

Just before sunrise, Ahmad escorted Cohen to the head at the end of their stateroom, but when the captive came out, the kidnapper-in-chief didn't put the hood back on Cohen's head. After reconnecting the captive's leg shackle to the bunk, Ahmad placed a metal chair next to Cohen's bunk, sat down, and over the wind screaming outside the bulkhead asked, "You were in American Navy, yes?"

Cohen nodded but said nothing.

"You know many secrets, yes?"

"Some, I suppose."

Picking up Cohen's slim leather-encased computer off the debris on the deck, Ahmad asked, "Your secrets are in here?"

Uncertain where the conversation was going, Cohen shrugged and replied, "Some." Then, pointing to his head with his free hand he added, "But most are in here."

Ahmad stared at his captive for a moment and then said, "You have been in sea storms before?"

"Many," Cohen answered.

"You are not afraid?"

Before he could answer, there was a banging on the hatch. Ahmad jumped up and unbolted the door. Cohen recognized the voice and for the first time since coming aboard he got a glimpse of the vessel's captain. He was bigger and younger than Cohen imagined him and his words were alarming: "Señor Vargas, tell your men. Pumps do not work. *Rosario* taking on water."

# CHAPTER SIX

# HIDEOUT

**CAIR PARAVEL**
ATLANTIC AVENUE
PAWLEYS ISLAND, SC
WEDNESDAY, 15 SEPTEMBER 2032
0633 HOURS, LOCAL

The footfalls on the street-side stairs were fast and light. Newman knew from long experience, if there were several people coming for him, at least one would be coming up the front stairs as well. To avoid being silhouetted by the gray dawn spilling through the ocean-side windows, he raced for the windowless guest bathroom, pulling the .45 out of the shoulder holster as he moved.

Once inside the room, James tossed the holster to the floor, "took a knee" in front of the sink to reduce his target profile, and pushed the door partway closed. Anyone entering the house from the street-side doorway would have to pass his ambush.

He crouched in the dark, gripping the weapon with both hands at the ready, the muzzle resting on his upraised knee, anticipating it would take the intruders several minutes to deal with the lock. Seconds later he was surprised to hear the electronic dead bolt click open and thought, *They must have our access code in a PID.*

James immediately brought the .45 up, stretched out his arms, thumbed off the safety, and prepared to fire as the first interloper passed the bathroom doorway. His right forefinger was gently taking up the slack on the trigger when he heard, "Dad?"

As he silently flipped up the safety and took a breath, he saw his nine-and-a-half-year-old son, Joshua, pass the doorway, followed closely by Seth. When he heard both boys tear upstairs heading toward the bedrooms—clearly not under any duress—he arose, popped the magazine out of the weapon, cleared the round out of the chamber, and was putting the pistol back in the holster when the overhead light suddenly came on.

Newman spun around to see Sarah, wide-eyed and clearly shocked. She recovered more quickly than her husband and said, looking at the gun: "James? What are you hunting for in the bathroom?"

He took a deep breath and said, "I wasn't expecting *you*. What are you doing here? Where are the twins?"

"David and Daniel are asleep in the car beneath the house. Your dad is down there with them."

"Is he asleep?"

"No, but he should be," she answered. "He drove nonstop all the way from Narnia. Even with the car on autopilot he was awake all the way—all six hours."

"When did you leave? I had no idea you were coming."

"It was after midnight when we left the farm. It was all very sudden because of a message Mack Caperton sent your dad. We didn't stop or communicate with anyone the whole way down."

"Did Mom come?"

"No, she is going to fly down this weekend. Elizabeth came with us. She was a big help getting the kids ready and on the way down in the van. I'm just glad we're here," Sarah added.

James shook his head, placed the holstered weapon on the sink, put his arms around his wife, pulled her close, and said, "I'm glad you're here, too."

"Good," she replied. "Now go help your father with the twins so I can use the bathroom."

\*     \*     \*     \*

Fifteen minutes later, Peter, James, Sarah, and Elizabeth were seated at the kitchen table over mugs of coffee. As Peter explained their unexpected arrival to James, the four Newman boys played with toy soldiers on the front porch.

"I would have let you know we were coming," the general said. "But Mack Caperton insisted we communicate only with him using PID-Text."

"That's the same instruction he gave me," James said. "When did you get the SSCI PID?"

The general pulled the little device out of his shirt pocket, put it on the table, and replied, "Mack gave it to me yesterday at the CSG Ops Center while we were waiting for you to come in from Dulles."

"Are these things as secure as Mack thinks they are?"

"I don't know. They're probably pretty good against foreign penetration but not from someone in our own government who may not care it's against the law to intercept communications to or from a U.S. senator. Mack was adamant about not using voice communications of any kind, but you understand this technology better than I do."

Holding the SSCI PID Caperton gave him, James

shrugged and said, "The innards and technology are complicated, but the principle is pretty simple. When we turn on a PID, the device accesses the nearest open MESH portal much like an old-fashioned Wi-Fi Local Area Network, only PIDs work on a global scale at much higher transmit/receive rates. When we make a call or send data, the PID transmits its distinct identification code and GPS location, the electronic address of the recipient—whether it's a phone or a computer—and then passes an encrypted digital stream of either voice or data through the MESH. On a government-issued PID, the encryption algorithms are very sophisticated—less so for the commercial versions."

"How about when I use my PID to pay for something at the store?" Elizabeth asked.

"A PID being used for payment uses NFC—Near Field Communications—or magnetic field induction technology—just like old-fashioned credit cards or products with embedded RFID—radio frequency identification tags. You just wave the device near the magnetic induction coil at the checkout counter where it says 'Pay Here by PID.' Of course, a PID transmits a whole lot more data into the MESH than just your payment amount and your bank account."

"What do you mean by 'a whole lot more data'?" Sarah interjected.

"Every time a PID is used, it sends out who you are, where you are, what you bought, and tells your bank whom to pay. It also transmits all the personal information you gave to your MESH service provider when you applied for the device. At a store, your digitized image pops up on the clerk's screen so he or she can see you're not using a stolen PID. The same information—and a whole lot more—gets sent when you pay by PERT. Those things even transmit your biometric data—practically your whole medical record."

"Now wait a minute, big brother," Elizabeth interrupted. "I'm a doctor. All this information isn't available to just *anybody*. That data is supposed to be protected by HIPAA—the Health Insurance Portability and Accountability Act—and the new All-American Medical Plan."

"Well," James said with a shrug, "whatever a PID or a PERT transmits can be intercepted as a radio signal where it originates or as a data stream when it passes through a MESH node. On a commercial-version PID the data has some very basic encryption, but nothing that can't be broken with enough time and a good computer."

"What makes the PIDs Mack gave you and Dad different from the ones Sarah and I have?"

"The SSCI PIDs are government-issue so they have higher-level, multilayered encryption, better transmission and download speeds, longer range and battery life, and are a little more durable. The real security advantage with these comes from a very small circle knowing the real identities of the people using SSCI PIDs with the addresses JL001 or PJ001. That's why Mack insisted we use only data mode and communicate only with him."

Elizabeth shook her head and said, "I don't understand. How is voice different from data, and why did Mack tell Dad to send data only to him and no one else, not even you?"

"It was actually very clever on his part," James responded. "First, because every PID transmits its GPS location, Mack didn't want two SSCI-issued PIDs—one at Narnia and the other here—communicating directly with each other. He's also counting on the law Dad mentioned that forbids intercepting communications to or from a member of Congress. Third, data is much faster—and therefore harder to detect in all the other electronic noise than a voice transmission. And last, even encrypted, every voice can be run through vocal identification software that can match an intercepted voice with a known individual."

"Got it," said Elizabeth. "As long as you and Dad never speak over those PIDs nobody knows for sure who is using the device, even if they know its address and where it is."

"You're very smart, sis."

"So are you, big brother. Where did you learn all this stuff?"

"At the 'small boat and barge school' when I was a mere midshipman. We got more of it in the Marines. Most of what I know about the hardware and software is just OJT from the MESH and communications security work we do at CSG. The youngsters we employ to do this work are just phenomenal. What amazes me is Mack Caperton thought of all these precautions. They weren't teaching this stuff at Annapolis when he and Dad were there."

"No, they weren't," Peter responded. "Back then, most of this 'stuff,' as you kids call things like PIDs and PERTs, hadn't even been invented. My guess is Mack picked up a lot of this on the Senate Armed Services and Intelligence committees."

"Well, we can ask him when he gets here. What time is he arriving?" Sarah asked as she rose to quell a small riot erupting on the porch.

"His last message before we left Narnia was he would be here at eight thirty," Peter replied. "We also need to ask who else, other than Mack, knows about these two PIDs and how confident he is everyone is abiding by the law that prohibits intercepting communications with a U.S. senator."

"What do you think, Dad?" asked James.

The father looked at the son, shook his head, and said, "I hope so. But I doubt it."

**OVAL OFFICE**

THE WHITE HOUSE

WASHINGTON, DC

WEDNESDAY, 15 SEPTEMBER 2032

0800 HOURS, LOCAL

The rotor brake had barely stopped the revolving carbon-composite blades of Marine One before the president was out of the helicopter and on her way up the South Lawn toward the White House. After smiling and waving to the throng of assembled admirers on the rope line and ignoring calls from reporters relegated to the camera platform behind the crowd, she entered the South Portico. As soon as she passed through the green doors into the building, the smile disappeared and she snapped to her Secret Service PSD team leader, "Straight to the Oval Office."

White House Chief of Staff Murad Muneer, National Security Advisor John Smith, and White House Counsel Larry Walsh rose as she entered the curve-walled room. As usual, she didn't invite them to sit, so they stood in a semicircle in front of the Resolute Desk as she sat, placed her purse on the carpet, pulled out her PID, and started giving orders.

"M&M, we need to update the statement I issued last night from California about Vic Foster's attempted suicide. Put something in it about prayer. Say that we're all praying for his full recovery and his return to leading the FBI."

Murad nodded and used a small stylus to scribble a note on the screen of his PID as she continued. "John, where do we stand on the new DNI assessment of what happened in Houston?"

"The latest draft is in circulation for agency comment," Smith replied, scrolling down on his PID. "It concludes that the attack was likely perpetrated by a previously unknown Anark-cartel entity with the involvement of sleeper cells from Jewish terror organizations operating in the United States."

"Good. When will it be out?"

"We are requiring that principals clear the executive summary by close of business this afternoon. I will transmit a copy as soon as we reconcile any objections or discrepancies."

"Who is objecting?"

Smith grimaced and said, "Let me work on this for a few hours. I told department secretaries and agency heads we need to get this out quickly and we aren't going to settle for a lot of tinkering here."

"Very well, make it clear to everyone I want the report on my desk tonight and we plan to announce the findings tomorrow. Now, where do we stand on getting another statement out of the Caliph?"

When no one spoke, she said, "Murad, what does your friend in Jerusalem have to say?"

"It isn't what we wanted to hear," the chief of staff responded.

"What does that mean? Is the Caliph going to issue another one of his famous fatwas or not?"

"There will be no new fatwa. The Caliph has said all he is going to say about the attack in Houston. He asks that you try to understand his predicament."

"*His* predicament! *He's* not running for reelection, I am! What's his problem? Doesn't he realize I'm the best friend he has? If his people weren't behind this, why can't he just issue another statement along the lines I suggested?"

Smith quietly intervened to stop the tirade. "Because he disagrees with our conclusions about who was behind it."

"And what does the Caliph, sitting in his royal robes in Jerusalem, know about who killed a hundred and forty-seven Americans and wounded nearly two hundred more in Houston, Texas, on Saturday?" the president asked.

Smith tried to take Murad off the hook. "Madam President, the Caliph has many sources of information. His embassy here has been feeding him every press report and MESH blog since the attack. He is convinced the Iranians did it—to show that he is just a false figurehead for Muslims and to undermine his credibility with the West."

"Well, all the more reason why he ought to come out with a statement that nobody in the Caliphate had anything to do with what happened in Houston."

"Unfortunately, the Caliph is very much of the mind-set that he is more vulnerable to unrest within the Caliphate and from the Iranians than he is from us," Smith answered.

"The Iranians?" She sounded confused. "There is nothing in any of the intelligence or the DNA analysis implicating a single Iranian in the Houston attack. How would they pull it off? It's been seven years since we put them in their box. They haven't had the means to do anything except kill their own people since my husband took out their military capability."

At this Murad interjected. "Please remember, Madam President, the Iranians tried to assassinate the Caliph when he was in Paris last year."

"Hunff. Didn't we decide the Paris attack was carried out by a group of disgruntled Syrians?"

"That's what DNI and British intelligence concluded," Smith answered. "The French eventually came around to that view, but the Caliph has always believed the suicide bombers were recruited, trained, and dispatched by Tehran."

"Are you telling me the UN's global DNA bloodline database is wrong about the matches found in Paris and now in Houston?"

"No, ma'am," said Smith. "The global bloodline analysis is pretty accurate. As you know, nowadays we can track a DNA sample practically back to a hometown anywhere on the planet if there are enough matches in the UN registry. In the cases like Paris or Houston, DNA can tell us with near certainty who an individual is—if his or her family or tribal bloodline is in the database. If he isn't in the registry we can usually tell where he is from. But DNA won't tell us whether a Saudi, an Egyptian, or a Somali suicide bomber was working for a Sunni or Iranian jihadist."

The president shook her head and said, "So what am I to take from this? Give me the short form. I need to get ready for the noon fund-raiser in Baltimore."

Murad tried again. "The Caliph is convinced the Houston attack was the work of the Iranians, who—because they are Shiite—will never accept a Sunni as Caliph. He thinks Tehran pulled the Houston attack to throw us off track and they are preparing a much larger strike against the West in an effort to drive up oil prices."

She stood and said, "No doubt a major attack would drive the cost of oil out of sight. But how does he think the Iranians could launch any kind of significant assault against us or our friends in Europe or China? We took out Tehran's nuclear sites and long-range missile facilities back in 2025. The Saudis and OPEC are taking their price and production cues from the Caliph, and he has promised not to let oil prices go up until after November."

Murad said nothing, so Smith spoke up. "Very privately, the Caliph claims to have information the Iranians still have several nuclear weapons and the Russians or the Chinese have secretly provided them with some kind of mobile missiles or rockets capable of delivering a nuclear warhead."

"Why haven't I seen any intelligence on this?"

"We hadn't heard any of this until Murad's 'hotline' conversation with the Caliph last night," Smith replied. "I immediately asked DNI for an all-source intelligence analysis of what we know about Iranian nuclear and missile capabilities. As of ten minutes ago, I still don't have the DNI report."

She paused for a few seconds, then said, "Very well, get it to me when it comes in. Murad, make sure you get that statement out about Vic Foster. John, have you collected the information I asked you to get about this CSG outfit?"

Amazed at her ability to shift gears so quickly, the National Security Advisor simply said, "Yes."

"Good. Get the contracts to Larry so he can figure out which ones we can get out of fastest."

"Yes, ma'am."

"When the new report on Houston and this Iranian nuclear weapons intelligence estimate come in, limit distribution to the four of us and make sure none of this gets circulated to the Hill until I say so. When I return from Baltimore, I want to see all of you about this CSG matter. Murad, John, that will be all for now. Larry, stay here for a minute."

When the other two men departed, she sat again and gestured for Walsh to sit in an armchair beside the desk. "How was your meeting with the AG about this Newman person?"

"The Attorney General has drafted a warrant to arrest James Newman, but he doesn't want to proceed with it until the U.S. attorney here in D.C. gets a sealed indictment from the special grand jury. That's supposed to happen on Friday."

"How can he be sure?"

"It's a D.C. grand jury. They will indict a ham sandwich for stealing mustard. It will happen."

"Then what?"

"Then the FBI arrests him and puts him in a military brig. Under the statutes we're using, we can hold him without bond or access to anyone for ninety days."

"Good. Where is this Newman character now?"

Walsh's Adam's apple bobbed as he swallowed. "We haven't found him yet, but we have DNI, DHS, INS, the FBI, and now the FAA looking for him."

"The FAA?"

"When I briefed you on Monday, I told you a DHS scanner at the Kalispell, Montana, airport picked up what was thought to be a brief transmission from Newman's PERT."

"Yes. Go on."

"Well, it turns out the PERT signal apparently coincides with the takeoff time of a CSG aircraft."

"Where did it land?"

"Dulles International Airport, at ten sixteen yesterday morning. The FAA is checking the flight records and will get the passenger, cargo, and crew manifests. I told them to hold off on interviewing the pilots so we don't tip them off we're looking for Newman."

"What else?"

"We have entered an electronic BOLO with Newman's digital image in the National Surveillance Network. If any NSN camera images him, the Fugitive Desk at the DOJ Ops Center will get an alert and notify me. I've also told them to do a rollback on every image they have from the Canadians, Kalispell, and Dulles since he disappeared in Calgary. Interpol and the Canadians will post the BOLO as soon as the AG tells them."

"We need to get this guy locked up so we can show we're making progress."

Walsh paused before responding, "There isn't much more we can do without tipping our hand we're looking for him—or creating some kind of back-blast. We've committed a lot of resources to this hunt. People inside these agencies are liable to start asking questions. As your lawyer and your friend, I want to make sure you understand the vulnerabilities here."

"Like what?"

"Well, if Vic Foster recovers, he may want to talk about being pressured to change the FBI report on Houston. If Newman surfaces somewhere and can prove he had nothing to do with Houston, we would have a problem. If the stuff the Caliph told Murad—with Smith listening in—about the Iranians turns out to be true, it *is* a problem."

She shook her head, reached out, touched his hand on the armchair, and said, "Larry, you worry too much. We're smarter than any of these fools. Foster isn't going to recover. I know Murad is in bed with the Caliph—probably in more ways than one. I know Smith would sell me out in a minute. But now they can't. Neither can the AG, or the DNI or anyone else. They are all in this now. Their futures are tied to my reelection. All we have to do is keep the lid on this for forty-seven more days."

"What if this Newman character calls a press conference or holds one of those MESH Meets like you hold with your supporters?"

"He wouldn't dare. He is wanted in Calgary as a suspect in the murder of a scientist who was working with our disappearing Dr. Cohen. If Newman's back here, he illegally left Canada and entered the United States—violating Canada's laws, ours, and the North American Union Treaty. His family has oil and gas holdings and security contracts with a half-dozen companies in the industry that would be hurt by Cohen's fuel cell technology. They run this CSG outfit full of former military extremist goons. He has motive and means. Moreover, if all that stuff in the 2026 congressional hearings about what he did in Afghanistan is true, he's deranged and dangerous. Find him and lock him away."

**CAIR PARAVEL**

ATLANTIC AVENUE
PAWLEYS ISLAND, SC
WEDNESDAY, 15 SEPTEMBER 2032
0900 HOURS, LOCAL

U.S. senator Mack Caperton arrived at the Cair Paravel gate precisely at 0830, just as he said he would. He was accompanied by U.S. Capitol Police Officer Mark Carter, as he said he would be.

As Peter punched a button in the kitchen to open the gate, James, Sarah, and the two oldest boys quickly retreated upstairs to avoid being seen by Carter. Ten minutes later, Elizabeth knocked on their door and said, "Okay, you guys, the coast is clear."

When they came downstairs and entered the living room, Peter and Mack were laughing uproariously. After giving the senator a hug, Sarah asked, "What's so funny—and what did you do with your security man?"

"Oh my," Caperton chortled. "Peter made a quick phone call and got Officer Carter a room at the Sea View Inn so he will be near enough if I need protection from you crazy people." At that the two burst into laughter again, this time with Elizabeth joining in.

Bewildered, James said, "Okay, are you going to let us in on the joke?"

"Now, you have to understand Officer Carter takes his job very seriously," Caperton began. "As we were driving here from the airport, I asked him how he and our new SSCI staff member got along on the drive from Charleston. He went on at some length about how James Lehnert was a nice enough young fellow, but he was apparently carrying on with the owner's beautiful daughter and mentioned there is a picture of them in the bathroom."

Sarah darted into the bathroom and returned looking perplexed. "What's so funny about that? I looked pretty good before I had twins."

"Well," Mack continued, "whatever James told him last night challenged Officer Carter's sense of propriety. So when we came in, Peter and Elizabeth were here with the twins and Carter concluded 'the owner' has a trophy wife and two young children."

"I still don't get it," said Sarah.

"Mark Carter travels with me a lot. He's often heard me tell young staffers to avoid compromising situations. When I went back down to the car with him to get my bag, he turns to me very seriously and says, 'Senator, I'm not sure about these folks. Don't let your morals slip while you're staying here with that old goat and his young honey.' When I told Peter and Elizabeth what he said, they noticed all the pictures missing off the walls."

Sarah looked around, noticed the missing photographs for the first time since arriving, and said to her husband, "It's a good thing your mother isn't here to see this or to hear what Officer Carter thinks."

\* \* \* \*

With strict instructions to "stay out of the water," Seth and Josh headed out with the twins, David and Daniel, in tow to explore the dunes for loggerhead turtle nests and feed the seagulls. The four adults gathered around a table on the ocean-side porch with steaming cups of coffee.

"Let's go through what we know for certain," Mack began. "We have no new verifiable intelligence about the whereabouts of Marty Cohen. His PERT has not been picked up since Saturday night, when he was put aboard that speedboat in Houston. My source in Coast Guard Intel says the Galveston VTC tracked a high-speed boat headed down Galveston Bay and out into the Gulf of Mexico immediately after the Houston attack."

"Coast Guard Intel? VTC?" asked Elizabeth.

"Few people know the U.S. Coast Guard has a major intelligence operation for port security, counternarcotics, and the like," Mack responded. "VTC is Vessel Traffic Center. The Coast Guard operates twelve of them around the country using cameras, radar, radio reports, aerostats, RPA sensors, and satellites to keep track of shipping entering and leaving U.S. ports and off our coasts."

"Does the Coast Guard know where this high-speed boat went once it headed out into the Gulf?" asked Peter.

"Not for certain. Satellite imagery from NGA at Belvoir doesn't show it to be in any ports, but they found several vessels in the Gulf it could have come alongside—or even hoisted the speedboat aboard. I told them to narrow the search to vessels that have not entered U.S. ports to escape Hurricane Lucy. They have isolated two they regard to be suspicious—both are coastal service tankers—the *Orfeo* and the *Ileana Rosario*. Unfortunately, both are off the Yucatan Peninsula and seem to be invisible beneath the cloud cover of Hurricane Lucy."

"So bottom line, do we stand up our Hostage Recovery Unit or not?" asked Peter.

"I think you put them on standby near an airport or airfield where they can be moved quickly, once we have some idea where Marty is. I'm convinced whoever has him knows he is more valuable alive than dead."

Peter pondered this a moment and said, "Maybe we ought to move the HRU out of CONUS, just in case the White House moves to shut CSG down."

Nodding, Mack responded, "That might not be a bad idea. The question is, where?"

"Whoa," James broke in. "What's this about shutting CSG down?"

Caperton paused for a moment, then said, "I told your dad about this yesterday and don't want any traffic on this over the MESH, a phone, or a PID. I have an informant in the White House who tells me they have called for all the USG contracts with CSG and are looking for another company or companies to perform what CSG currently does for the government."

James shook his head and said, "How would they do it?"

"As a legal matter, the Department of Justice can allege that any company doing business with the government has failed to comply with some provision of a contract. But as a practical matter, the services CSG provides for DoD, DHS, State, CIA, DNI, and WHCA can't be replicated—at least not in a time frame that matters," Caperton replied. "Here in the States, CSG provides communications support, intelligence analysis, sensitive-site security, and a half-dozen other services. Overseas, you guys are doing everything our military used to do: intel collection, comms, security, log support, PSDs, facility protection, and conducting what we used to call Special Operations."

"So who would do all CSG does if we are shut down?" asked James.

"Well," Mack said with a shrug, "rightly or wrongly, they don't have a lot of options. We don't have the infrastructure in our military anymore. There are a few other contractors who can do some of what CSG does, but not all of it—and it would still take months for them to gear up. At least for now, CSG is the only company able to operate overseas, thanks to the UN Treaty on Small Arms."

"Why do you say 'for now'? Is that about to change?"

"I don't know. My guess is they could challenge CSG's exclusive license with TASER, but all this 'contract review' stuff is speculation and I want to stick to what we know for certain."

"Okay," said James. "What do we know for certain about my situation?"

"We know the president ordered DOJ to open an investigation on you. We know their premise is you were involved in what happened in Houston, in Marty Cohen's disappearance, and had something to do with the death of Dr. Davis Long in Calgary. We know they have prepared an international BOLO for you; they intend to get a sealed indictment for your arrest and detention; they don't know where you are and if they find you, they will come to get you."

Caperton's matter-of-fact recitation stunned Sarah and Elizabeth. Peter, trying to relieve the tension, patted James on the shoulder and said lightly, "That's my boy."

Sarah was not amused and asked, "But doesn't that make us all accessories—even you?"

"Don't worry about me, Sarah," Caperton said with a smile. "I have a great lawyer at Williams & Connolly. More importantly, none of us—James included—has done anything wrong. That doesn't mean this crowd in Washington won't use all their power to crush whoever gets in their way. We just need to be smart about what we do, how we do it, and—if we can—try to rescue Marty Cohen."

"Why are they doing this?" Sarah asked.

"I don't know and I don't like to hypothesize, but a friend at the FBI told me the White House is desperate to find a scapegoat for the carnage in Houston and they don't want the Caliph blamed for it."

"But why James?"

"He's a convenient target of opportunity. They know he was in Calgary when Dr. Long was killed. They know the Newman family has a long history of support for conservative causes and their political opponents. And everyone knows James's congressional testimony in 2026 was a major embarrassment for the last administration—meaning this president's now-deceased husband."

"That was six years ago, Mack," Sarah said. "What's wrong with these people?"

Caperton shrugged and said quietly, "We also know our president has a well-earned reputation for vengeance against her late husband's detractors. She is apparently willing to do anything necessary to get reelected. The Newman family is a thorn in her side, and if the terrible attack in Houston can be pinned on James, you're all at risk. That's why I suggested we get James to a safe place out of the country as soon as feasible and Elizabeth should remove all your PERTs—to make you harder to find."

James sat bolt upright. "Mack, we talked about this yesterday. Lizzie can't do that. If she's caught, she'll lose her medical license."

"I've already done it for everyone here but you, brother dear," Elizabeth said quietly. "And you're next. I brought the necessary instruments, the topical anesthetic, and a vial of ECM powder. It won't hurt at all."

"What's ECM?"

"Extracellular matrix. It's commonly called regenerative tissue repair compound. It's what they used on your wounds from Egypt and Afghanistan to expedite healing without scar tissue. That's why you and so many others recover so quickly nowadays. ECM is genetically engineered from pig bladders. How much do you want to know about this?"

"That's enough," said James, waving his sister off. "But isn't removing a PERT against the law?"

"No," replied the senator. "Your children are all old enough to have received maximum benefit from the time-release nano-material in their baby PERTs, so it's not contrary to the mandatory immunization statute. Removing an implanted PERT is a medical license issue, but we can deal with that if it ever comes up. And you're not destroying your PERTs—that *would* be a violation of law."

Caperton reached into his pocket and pulled out a small black leather pouch, then slid it across the table in front of James, saying, "We're all keeping our PERTs with us as the law requires. And we're storing them in things like these, just in case they are needed. They just happen to be lined with lead. Here's one for you."

"Yeah, I know what this is. It's called an 'Anark Amulet' or a 'PERT pouch.' A lot of Anarks hang these things around their necks on a chain. So are we all Anarks now?"

"That's up to you, James, but that's how I keep from losing my PERT," the senator replied, reaching under his shirt and pulling out a silver chain. Attached to it were a tiny metal fish and a small, metal, tube-shaped pendant less than a half inch long.

"Dad?" asked James, appealing for support. Peter reached beneath his shirt and pulled out his dog-tag chain with the same tiny fish and an identical pendant. Sarah and Elizabeth did so as well, except their chains were gold, with tiny jeweled lockets attached.

"We can get you one like this, if it makes you feel better, dear," said Sarah.

"Okay, I give up," said James, raising his hands in mock surrender. "At least I won't have to walk around with this foil wrapped around my foot. But once my PERT is out, then what do we do?"

"Well, it is ultimately up to you, Sarah, and your dad," Caperton replied. "I recommend we wait quietly for a while and see what else we can learn. I will head back to Washington tomorrow evening and keep my ear to the ground. Anything I learn, I will pass to you."

"Mack, how secure are these SSCI PIDs?" James asked, holding his up.

"Only as secure as our government wants them to be. Criminal organizations and foreign governments have tried to break the encryption. Chinese hackers give it a go several times every day. To our knowledge they have never succeeded. But our own government is another matter. If someone high enough in our government decides to break the law and intercept communications from or to a member of the U.S. Congress, they can do it because they have the codes. If this crowd in Washington is desperate enough, they will."

"Then how will we communicate?"

"While I'm here, we're going to work out what you Marines call a backup plan. We'll figure that out tonight."

Peter had been silent for several minutes. He stretched and said, "Before we take a walk down the beach: Mack, tell the others what you told me about who may be holding Marty Cohen."

"There are only four logical suspects: a criminal enterprise holding him for ransom, a criminal enterprise attempting to steal his fuel cell secrets, a foreign entity trying to keep his fuel cell from coming to market, or our own government for some nefarious purpose."

James shook his head and said, "That covers just about everybody."

"Perhaps, but we can probably eliminate some," Caperton replied. "It's not likely Marty is being held by an agency or individuals from inside our government, because an operation that big would have leaked by now. If it was simply an entity or a group trying to keep Marty's secret from coming to market, he would have been killed in Houston—just as Dr. Long was murdered in Calgary. If it was for money, somebody—likely his wife, Julia—would have had a ransom demand by now."

"So did the Caliph in Jerusalem commit the atrocity in Houston just to get Marty's fuel cell secret?"

"I don't know, James. I initially thought this had to be an operation launched out of the Caliphate—with or without the support of the Caliph—based on the DNA traces of the perpetrators, the number of suicide terrorists involved, the geographic reach, the brutality, and duration of it. After Houston we had the death of Dr. Long and then yesterday, also in Calgary, Steven Templeton was incapacitated and may not recover. They were Marty's principal partners in the fuel cell project."

"Do you have any new word on how our old classmate is doing and how this happened?" Peter asked.

"Officially, the Canadians are saying it was carbon monoxide poisoning from a faulty furnace flue. They say his wife Jane is expected to recover, but Steven is still in a coma and his condition is 'guarded.' I have also been told by a person I trust—a member of 'the Fellowship'—that the Templetons' chimney was stuffed with fiberglass insulation."

"If that's true," said James, "whoever is behind this has a lot of assets in place and it certainly seems to be bigger than anything the Latin American drug cartels could pull off. They spend most of their time shooting at each other and vying for the privilege of overthrowing the governments of Mexico, Guatemala, and Honduras."

"Well, they have nearly succeeded in that," Caperton replied. "The cartels are practically running everything south of the Rio Grande. But I agree, this is beyond their capabilities. However, I no longer think this operation was launched by the Caliph."

"Why? Everything seems to point in the direction of Jerusalem."

"For that very reason. It's too neat. As you said, everything points to the Caliphate: perpetrator DNA traces, multiple suicide bombers, international reach, and a motive—keeping the Cohen-Templeton-Long fuel cell out of production."

"But why grab Admiral Cohen?" Elizabeth asked. "Whoever did this could have just killed him, Professor Templeton, and Dr. Long and kept the fuel cell off the market."

"True," said Caperton, nodding. "But you have to remember, the Cohen-Templeton-Long research team was committed to making their fuel cell technology available to anyone who wanted it—for free. They called it 'North America's Gift to the World,' if I recall correctly. Now, who has the most to lose if that happens?"

"Every hydrocarbon fuel company on the planet—and every country relying on petrodollars to support their domestic economy," Elizabeth replied.

"Right," said Mack. "And that includes most of the countries in the Caliphate. But it's pretty common knowledge 'inside Washington' that the administration cut a deal with the Caliph—no terror attacks or oil price hikes until after the elections. He has no reason to reverse course and risk all the funding he pockets from the U.S., the UN, the IMF, the EU, and the World Bank."

"So who's left that would or could do this?" asked Sarah.

Caperton continued. "There's Russia, Iran, Venezuela, even Canada, Brazil, and Mexico. So now ask which of those places hates America the most—and has the most to gain from *selling* such a device."

There was a moment of silence around the table and then Peter said, "Iran—and perhaps the Russians."

"Right," said Mack, nodding to his old roommate. "This is too big an operation to be run by one of the 'evil capitalist companies' the White House despises. It has to be run by a well-funded government entity—like the Islamic Revolutionary Guard Corps."

"The IRGC?" Sarah asked, sitting bolt upright in her chair. "Isn't that the group that sent people to kill James, our children, and me after those congressional hearings in 2026?"

"Yes," said Peter. "The six individuals were officially in the U.S. as staff members of the Persian Students Committee in Maclean, Virginia. But the FBI Counterterrorism Division was convinced they were all part of an IRGC Quds Force sleeper cell. Since they got away, the connection was never—"

James interrupted his father. "Where does all this leave us, Mack?"

"Bottom line?" Caperton said. "My gut tells me this whole thing is an IRGC operation. But I can't prove it. What we do know is, tomorrow the White House will announce the Houston attack and the Cohen kidnapping are part of an Anark-cartel cabal. What they won't announce is last night the NSC sent out what's called an all-source request for any new intelligence on Iran.

Meanwhile, we seem to be the only people looking for Marty Cohen."

"And after all this," added Peter, "we still don't know where he is and can only guess at who has him and why they took him."

Caperton shook his head and said, "Right. We don't know much for certain. I just hope our old Boat School roommate is not floating around in the Gulf of Mexico in the path of Hurricane Lucy."

# CHAPTER SEVEN

# THOSE IN PERIL ON THE SEA

**ABOARD *ILEANA ROSARIO***

CAMPECHE BANK

21°24'06"N, 88°55'04"W

WEDNESDAY, 15 SEPTEMBER 2032

1500 HOURS, LOCAL

International law requires that every oceangoing vessel be equipped with a sufficient number of lifeboats and/ or inflatable life rafts to accommodate all passengers and crew members. It's been that way ever since the sinking of the RMS *Titanic* in 1912.

The International Convention for the Safety of Life at Sea (SOLAS) and the International Life-Saving Appliance (LSA) Code specify the emergency equipment required to be carried on lifeboats and the schedule for how often the lifeboat and its equipment should be inspected or replaced. Enforcement of these rules is the responsibility of each signatory nation. The U.S. Coast Guard routinely inspects American and foreign-flagged vessels operating in U.S. ports and territorial waters to ensure compliance with SOLAS and LSA Code regulations.

A ship with the size and crew/passenger capacity of MV *Ileana Rosario*, operating in open ocean coastal zones, should be equipped with at least two six-person, self-inflatable lifeboats, packed in weatherproof, fiberglass containers. Lifeboats of this type are designed to be manually launched overboard by the crew or automatically deployed by a hydrostatic pressure-release mechanism if the vessel sinks. Regulations for inflatable emergency equipment require the crew to visually inspect all such gear weekly, send it to a certified inspection facility annually, and deployment-test it every six years.

In May 2015, the *Ileana Rosario* was detained in Key West, Florida, suspected of transporting cocaine from Cuba. The case was dismissed by a federal judge because the crew managed to dispose of the evidence in heavily weighted containers at sea before U.S. Coast Guardsmen boarded the ship. But the Coast Guard did cite the Venezuelan owners and hold the vessel for failing to comply with safety regulations. Before being granted permission to depart Key West, the ship was required to be outfitted with serviceable lifesaving equipment.

On 11 July 2015, a USCG officer duly reported, "All rescue equipment aboard *Ileana Rosario* has been inspected. Twenty-four new, USCG-certified, inflatable life vests are operable and correctly stowed. Three new, USCG-certified, six-man inflatable lifeboats are properly cradled in fiberglass containers, aft on the port and starboard rails and atop the bridge housing." Since then, the *Ileana Rosario* avoided entering U.S. waters and undergoing inspections of any kind.

\* \* \* \*

Even before the captain's breathless announcement that *Ileana Rosario*'s pumps had quit, Marty Cohen knew they were in serious trouble. From the sound of the howling wind, he estimated it was a steady 40 knots with gusts to 50 or more. From the way the vessel was being tossed about, he sensed the seas were building. Though he could hear and feel the auxiliary engine still chugging away in the machinery space below, it was also evident from the way the vessel was wallowing through the crests and troughs of the waves that if they took on too much water, they were in danger of foundering.

About an hour after Ahmad-Vargas departed with the captain, Cohen was startled by the noise and tremor of a dreadful crash that reverberated through the entire ship. He thought for a few seconds they might have run aground or collided with another vessel but noticed they continued to pitch and yaw through the roiling sea.

Less than ten minutes after the terrible noise, Ahmad-Vargas reappeared in the cabin accompanied by one of his fellow kidnappers. Both were soaking wet from the wind-driven spray and rain that followed them through the hatch. Standing in front of Cohen, and bracing himself against the bulkhead, Ahmad said, "You told me you were in many storms in your navy. That was true?"

"Yes."

"You know what to do in a storm?"

Cohen shrugged and said, "Yes."

"Then you come with me now."

Ahmad instructed his accomplice to unlock the shackles holding Cohen's arm and leg. As this was being done, the kidnapper-in-chief said, "We are going to the bridge. The captain is afraid we are going to sink. Are you afraid?"

"No. But we may sink anyway," Cohen replied as he stood, unfettered for the first time in four days. Suddenly the deck dropped away beneath them and all three men collapsed in a heap as the ship pitched into a trough.

Ahmad scrambled to his feet, grabbed Cohen by the collar of his filthy exercise suit, and hoisted him, saying, "Be careful, Jew."

The kidnapper then reached into one of the metal lockers secured to the bulkhead, pulled out a rubber foul-weather jacket and an inflatable life vest, handed them to Cohen, and ordered, "Put these on and follow me."

When Ahmad opened the hatch, Cohen got his first glimpse of the *Ileana Rosario*'s exterior. They were one level above the weather deck, and his worst thoughts about the condition of the vessel were immediately confirmed. There was rust everywhere—to include the violently pitching steel catwalk on which they were standing—about eight feet above and fifteen feet forward of the stern rail.

In the lee of the wheelhouse, clinging to a rusty metal handrail welded to the superstructure, Cohen tried to get his bearings. Peering from beneath the hood of his jacket, he saw what caused the horrendous crash he heard and felt. The ship's thirty-foot mast, bent and twisted, had crushed the starboard rail when it fell. The shrouds—four steel cables that once held the mast in place atop the pilothouse—were lethal whips thrashing wildly in the wind.

It took them nearly five minutes, sliding hand over hand along the rusty metal handrail, to make their way to the starboard side of the vessel, beneath the mangled mast, forward and up the open stairway to the enclosed pilothouse. There, to Cohen's dismay, they found only the captain, seated in an antique, deck-mounted leather bridge chair, and a terrified helmsman standing behind the wheel.

Looking forward through the canted bridge windows,

Cohen could catch only brief glimpses of the bow through the sheets of wind-driven rain as the ship plunged into the raging swells. Off to the port side he could see low, scudding clouds of an approaching line squall. He braced himself as a roiling wave crashed against the weather rail and green water cascaded down the length of the ship.

When Ahmad entered the enclosed bridge he secured the hatch, pointed to the captain, and said to Cohen, "Tell him what to do. I have told him you are an admiral in the American Navy."

Cohen, holding on to the chart table, looked at the disheveled captain and his helmsman and asked in Spanish the only questions that made sense at the moment: "Where are we and what's our heading?"

The captain struggled out of his chair and staggered to the chart table. Gripping a handhold with his left hand, he flipped back the soaking-wet canvas cover to reveal an ancient navigational chart of the Gulf of Mexico. Pointing to a penciled tick mark west of Cuba and north of the Yucatan Peninsula, he said, "I think we are here."

The distinct odor of alcohol on the captain's breath was unmistakable. Looking around the bridge at the aging navigation and communications equipment, Cohen asked, "Where does your GPS say we are?"

"The antenna was on the mast. It is gone," the captain slurred.

"Do you have any other satellite navigation equipment aboard?"

"Nothing is working."

"Radar?"

"Gone. It was on the mast."

"Satellite data link for NOAA?"

"Don't you understand? All of the antennas are gone! Nothing is working. Even the autopilot is disabled."

"Where is your first officer, your exec—or whatever you call him?"

"He and one of my men were swept over the side trying to secure the mast after it tore loose."

Cohen, bracing himself against the binnacle, glanced down at the compass, noted that the course being steered was roughly 100 degrees magnetic—a little south of due east—and asked, "Where is your radio equipment?"

The captain pointed to a curtain aft of the hatch they had entered. But as Cohen headed for the little compartment, Ahmad stopped him, saying, "You cannot transmit on the radio."

"It is not to transmit, it is to receive. I need to know where we are and where the storm is if we are to survive."

"Do not deceive me, Jew. If you communicate with anyone I will kill you."

Cohen shrugged and grappled his way into the little compartment. Bracing himself against the rack holding the electronic equipment, he examined their available resources. There wasn't much.

The antique Axion weather satellite receiver was dead. He tried the equally old Motorola maritime GPS, single-sideband radio transceiver, VHF radio, and standard digital radio receiver—none worked. The electronic wind gauge was frozen at 47.5 knots. When he pressed the reset button, the screen went dark. He guessed the anemometer—likely mounted atop the mast—was also gone.

On the bulkhead he found the only piece of working equipment, an old-fashioned aneroid barometer showing the barometric pressure was just 1001 millibars. He tapped the face of the device and the needle dropped to 998 mb.

With Ahmad watching him closely, Cohen turned on the VHF radio and punched into the keypad

162.400—the frequency for WXJ95—hoping he could pick up the signal from the NOAA weather broadcast station on Sugarloaf Key, more than three hundred miles to their northeast. All he could hear was static. He got the same result on the other six NOAA frequencies.

Cohen had no better results with any of the other equipment. None of the vessel's electronic gear was working. As he rummaged through drawers, cubbyholes, and lockers searching for something he could use to rig a makeshift antenna, one of the *Ileana Rosario* crewmen burst into the pilothouse and shouted, "The water in the engine room is getting deeper!"

"I need to go below and see how much water we are taking aboard," Cohen said to his captor.

"No. You cannot leave. The captain is drunk. You just said you needed to find out where we are. Do that first."

"It is more important to stop us from sinking."

Ahmad was pondering this when the squall line hit and the vessel abruptly rolled heavily to starboard. As the wind rose to a scream, their list increased dramatically. Cohen struggled to crab his way across the canted deck, moving from handhold to handhold into the pilothouse. Outside, everything had gone white—the rain pelting so hard it was impossible to see more than a foot or two in any direction. Water was cascading through holes ripped in the overhead when the mast collapsed.

"We're going to capsize! Turn right to two-five-zero degrees!" he shouted. The man at the helm was frozen in place.

Cohen lurched forward, up the canted deck, fell into the helmsman, pushed him aside, and spun the wheel hard to the right.

Slowly, as the *Ileana Rosario* fell off the wind, the list began to subside. Cohen, still gripping the wheel, said,

"We must hold this course. It is more difficult to steer in a following sea, but it will be safer. Come, take the wheel."

As the displaced helmsman resumed his station, Cohen said to the captain, "I need to go below and see if we can get the pumps running."

The captain motioned to the seaman who delivered the bad news and said, "Take him."

Led by the reluctant sailor, Cohen, Ahmad, and his accomplice headed back into the violence of the storm, carefully making their way down to a hatch at the base of the stairs. Timing their entry to avoid the towering waves racing up behind them, the four men piled breathlessly through the hatch, slammed it closed, and stood panting in the small compartment above the engine room.

"Does anyone have a flashlight?" Cohen shouted over the howling wind and the hammering of the auxiliary engine as he peered into the darkness below.

"*Sí,*" said the seaman, who then tugged a small light, suspended by a leather lanyard, from around his neck.

As he took the light and draped the cord over his head, Cohen noticed that the man who gave it to him was just a boy—certainly younger than the sailors he once commanded on nuclear submarines. He asked, "*Gracias. ¿Cómo se llama usted?*"

"*Me llamo Tico.*"

"How old are you, Tico?"

"Eighteen."

Cohen turned to his chief captor and said, "I know your name is Ahmad. What is the name of your friend?"

"His name is Karim. What do you care, Jew?"

"I like to know the people with whom I go to sea, Ahmad. It's an old habit." With that, Cohen switched on the light hanging around his neck and started to descend the ladder, bracing himself as the ship pitched forward, careening down the slope of a wave like a toboggan on a steep hill.

"I will come with you!" shouted Ahmad over the din.

"Okay, just don't step on my Jewish hands."

Hanging on to the bottom of the ladder with one hand, Cohen was swinging the light around the engine compartment assessing the situation when Ahmad arrived beside him. Even in the dim glow of the flashlight, Cohen spotted something he had not yet seen in the terrorist's eyes: fear.

The old admiral concluded it was a reasonable reaction to their current predicament. They were five feet below the waterline of a decrepit rust bucket, tossed about in the chaos of a major storm with little to no power. Though the effect of the vessel's pitching and yawing was diminished by being lower, the slamming of the hull and the noise of the diesel-powered generator were unnerving to the uninitiated.

He moved the flashlight beam from the fire-damaged main engine over to the slowly rotating shaft, then shifted the ball of light aft and shook his head at the amount of seawater seeping in from the bearing seals. He was about to check on the small diesel engine powering the generator when Ahmad grabbed his sleeve and pointed down.

Immediately below the grate on which they were standing, several feet of oily water sloshed back and forth, forward and back, as the sea pounded the *Ileana Rosario*'s outer hull. From the sewage plant stench, Cohen concluded a wastewater line or tank had ruptured somewhere.

He located the circuit board on the bulkhead aft of the generator and found the switches labeled MOTOR DE LA BOMBA. The breakers on all four were tripped. Several attempts to reset them produced no results. As he traced one of the lines forward and down seeking a short circuit, he heard Ahmad retch. Cohen smiled. In the sodden, fetid air, even he—never seasick—felt nauseous.

Moving back to the ladder, Cohen shouted up to the crewman waiting at the top, *"¿Tico, dónde está el electricista?"* Where is the electrician?

The response, *"Ricardo está muerto,"* meant the pumps weren't going to get restarted anytime soon, and the old admiral grimaced in frustration. Any of his U.S. Navy crews, well trained in damage control, would have quickly rerouted cables from the generator to get the pumps working and save their vessel.

While he was considering what else they could do, Ahmad grabbed his arm and pointed down, shouting, "Look, the water is getting higher!"

Cohen nodded. The putrid fluid had been several inches below the floor grates when they arrived in the engine compartment. Now it was sloshing on their shoes. He turned to Ahmad and shouted, "Let's go! There is nothing we can do here!"

"What do you mean? You cannot fix the pump?"

"It's not just one pump—it's four pumps—and none of them are working."

"What will happen?"

"The way we're taking on water, this ship is going to sink. We need to get off before it does."

* * * *

After he and Ahmad climbed out of the engine room, Cohen told them all—in English and Spanish—they must time their sprint out the hatch, forward beneath the broken mast, then up the stairs and into the pilothouse to avoid being caught on deck by one of the towering waves chasing them. He thought they all understood. Perhaps they did. But none of them saw it coming.

Ahmad, at the top of the stairs, had just opened the bridge hatch. Cohen was right on his heels when it hit them from behind. The monstrous wave first pitched the bow down, deep into the foam, and then thousands of tons of water came crashing over the stern. Ahmad and Cohen were catapulted into the pilothouse, sliding on their backs across the deck and into a painful pileup against the port bulkhead. Tico, Karim, and the broken mast disappeared.

For an interminable moment, the *Ileana Rosario* seemed to wallow, half under and half above the water. Cohen said to himself, *She's going to founder.* But then, somehow, the bow rose, the water started draining off the midship tank covers, and the dilapidated vessel remained upright.

The torrent of water that delivered Ahmad and Cohen into the pilothouse momentarily roused the captain to action. He scrambled out of his chair to secure the hatch and dogged it down before the next deluge. Noticing his crewman was missing, he shouted, "Where is Tico?"

"Gone. Washed overboard," Cohen replied as he crawled to the binnacle and pulled himself up to check their heading. He marveled that the compass was swinging back and forth plus or minus 10 degrees of the 250-degree course he ordered.

"*¿Cómo se llama usted?*" he shouted at the helmsman, who was working hard, especially given their slow speed, to hold the vessel on a steady course.

"Rikki," said the boy, barely taking his eyes off the compass.

The old admiral pointed to the binnacle, patted the boy on the shoulder, and shouted over the screaming wind and rain, "*¡Muy bien, Rikki!*"

The captain, until now seemingly oblivious to the

catastrophe happening around him, returned to his pilot's chair and proceeded to wail, "Oh, Tico, Tico . . ."

Cohen made his way over to the chair, grabbed the morose figure by the arm, and shouted over the wind howling outside the thick Plexiglas window, "Get hold of yourself, man. He's gone. The pumps cannot be fixed. We are sinking. What is your name?"

"Roberto."

"Good. Now, Roberto, where are your life rafts?"

The question seemed to drag the captain from his stupor and he replied, "There are three six-man inflatable lifeboats. One is cradled on the rail at each stern quarter and there's another up there," he said, pointing to the overhead.

"The one on the starboard side is gone."

"Gone?" asked Roberto.

"When the mast came down it took out the rail. Where are more of these?" asked Cohen, pointing to his life belt and its self-contained inflatable life jacket.

Roberto pointed to a locker beneath the chart table.

The old admiral turned to his captor, who was bracing himself against the chart table, and shouted, "Ahmad, get the life belts out of that locker and make sure everyone has one on!"

The kidnapper looked as though he was about to vomit. "Don't give me orders, Jew!" he snarled, but then got down on his knees and removed ten life belts like the one Cohen was wearing. He slid two of them across the sopping-wet deck.

Cohen handed one to the captain, then crabbed his way to the helmsman and proceeded to fasten it around his waist so the young man would not have to take his hands from the wheel. Turning to Ahmad again, he shouted, "Make sure all your men have life belts on and bring them up here! We don't have long!"

Ahmad put on a life belt, looped four more over his arm, and grappled his way to the hatch, prepared to confront the elements once again. As he started lifting the handle to undog the hatch, Cohen felt the fantail begin to rise and yelled, "Wait! Hold on!"

An instant later the bow dug into the water as another enormous wave lifted the stern, sending the ship careening at a sickening angle deep into a trough. Seconds later, the peak of the wave broke over the pilothouse and forward across the tank covers. The *Ileana Rosario* shuddered and, for a moment, seemed to be dead in the water.

"She won't take much more of this," Roberto said as the vessel's bow slowly appeared, barely visible through the sheets of rain and the deepening gloom.

"You're right," replied Cohen. He turned to Ahmad, frozen at the portal. "Go now. I'll secure the hatch behind you. Be careful bringing your men back up. Don't get caught by one of those big waves."

For a split second it looked as though the Iranian was going to say something. But then he lifted the handle, pushed open the heavy door, and charged down the stairs. Cohen slammed the hatch behind him, dogged it down, turned to the captain, and asked, "Roberto, do all three of your lifeboats have EPIRBs?"

"Yes."

"Do you know which type? Are they automatic?"

"I do not know. I just know they are certified by your Coast Guard. The paperwork is in a drawer in the communications compartment."

Cohen half slid, half crawled back into the comm shack and started pulling damp and moldy paperwork from the desk until he found what he was looking for. He tore open the plastic envelope, quickly scanned the documents, and shoved it all beneath a pile of other paper

as he heard feet pounding up the metal stairs outside the
bulkhead. By the time the five kidnappers piled into the
pilothouse, he was braced against the equipment rack,
looking at the barometer. Seeing him near the radio sets,
Ahmad burst into the cramped space and shouted, "Get
away from the radios, Jew!"

Cohen looked at him, noticed he was now armed with
a small submachine gun slung over his shoulder, and said,
"The radios don't work, Ahmad. I am checking the barometric pressure. And my name is Martin."

"I don't care about your name, Jew," he spat through a
twisted sneer. "What does this barometer tell you?"

Cohen tapped the glass and watched the needle drop
to 981 mb. Turning back to his captor he said, "It tells
me, Ahmad, the atmospheric pressure is still dropping and
the worst is yet to come."

*  *  *  *

Over the next half hour, as the storm intensified and the
sky darkened, Cohen prepared the five terrorists and the
two surviving members of the *Ileana Rosario* crew for
abandoning ship. First, he went out on the port bridge
wing and confirmed the life raft canister on that side was
still intact. He then sent the two crewmen up the ladder
welded to the starboard side of the pilothouse to ensure
the raft canister mounted above them was not damaged
by the falling mast. Having verified they did indeed have
the means to escape, he told them all to sit on the deck
with their backpacks against a bulkhead. Roberto remained planted in his chair and Rikki stayed at the helm.

With Ahmad translating, the old admiral first asked
them their names, explained the tanker was sinking, and
warned it could happen very suddenly. Cohen then demonstrated—much like a flight attendant—how to open the

pouch on their life belts and pull the life vests over their heads, how to activate the nitrogen canisters for inflation, and how to use their whistles and chemical lights if they found themselves separated in the wind-tossed waves.

He then assigned them to their lifeboats: Ahmad, Cohen, Rikki, and Ebi to the boat on the port-side aft; Roberto, Hassan, Massoud, and Rostam to the boat on top of the pilothouse. His explanation on how to activate the life raft was as precise as possible under the circumstances, but he assured them that both he and Roberto would be able to initiate inflation, erect the canopy, and deploy the sea anchor. The only detail he omitted was the purpose and function of the EPIRB.

When he finished his "lecture" he asked if there were any questions. With Ahmad translating, Ebi asked the one most pertinent to a mariner in distress: "Where is the nearest land?"

Cohen pulled himself to his feet, lurched across the pitching deck to the chart table, grabbed the soggy sheet, and sat down in the slop on the deck. Pointing to the tick mark on the chart, he said, "If we were here when we changed course to run downwind, we are probably seventy-five to one hundred miles northeast of Telchac Puerto on the Yucatan Peninsula. The storm will continue to blow us toward land until the eye passes—then the wind will shift and blow us back out to sea."

Roberto, leaning attentively from his chair, interjected anxiously, "Martin, we have less than two feet of freeboard over the tank deck. Without pumps we will not stay afloat through the night. It is already getting very dark. If we broach and capsize we may not make it out. We should go while we still can."

Cohen stood, looked out into the gloom, and asked, "Do we have any lights?"

"Only this," Roberto replied, reaching up and twisting a switch on the panel above his right shoulder. A high-intensity lamp mounted atop the pilothouse lit up the area in front of them like the headlights of a car in a snowstorm.

"It's better than nothing; leave it on. Pull up your life vests. Don't inflate them until you go over the side or into the water. Let's get ready to go."

Ahmad repeated the order in Persian and the two lifeboat teams lined up as instructed at the port and starboard hatches, awaiting Cohen's signal. Rikki stayed at the wheel, attempting to hold the sinking vessel straight downwind until the last second.

"We go after the next wave!" Cohen shouted. As soon as he felt the bow begin to pitch up he yelled, "Now!"

Ahmad, Cohen, and Ebi bolted out the port-side hatch and headed aft into the wind. Rikki, as instructed, remained on the bridge long enough to crank the helm lock down as hard as he could to hold the rudder centered. The other four were already out the starboard hatch and headed up the ladder to the top of the pilothouse by the time Rikki caught up to Cohen and his crew at their lifeboat station. They almost made it.

Cohen had just hit the hydrostatic release button to pop open the fiberglass container when another towering wave hit, knocking all four men down and washing them forward along the safety rail. In the five seconds it took Cohen and the others to get back on their feet, the rolled-up lifeboat floated out of its container and washed over the side. As the package reached the end of its forty-foot tether, the raft inflated as advertised.

Blown forward and alongside the ship by the wind, the lifeboat was now in danger of being cut to pieces as it battered the rusty hull. Grabbing the line holding the raft to the *Ileana Rosario*, Cohen popped the inflation canister on his life vest, shouted, "Follow me!" and started working his way forward to where the raft was being buffeted against the vessel.

They were all knocked down again by another wave before they made their way to the raft. No one let go of his grip on the line, but both Ahmad and Ebi lost the submachine guns that had been slung over their shoulders. In the glow of the light atop the pilothouse they crawled one by one over the rail and flung themselves into the inflated orange oval. Cohen was the last one in, landing square on top of Ebi. As soon as they were untangled he shouted, *"¡Rikki, corte la cuerda!"*

The helmsman-turned-deckhand promptly pulled a knife out of his pocket, flicked it open, severed the line, and pushed them away from the sinking tanker. In a matter of seconds the beam emanating from the pilothouse was all but invisible. Rocking wildly in the wind, nearly blinded by the spray, Cohen grasped his chem-light, held it out in front of himself, cracked the plastic tube to activate it, and shouted to the others, "Turn on your lights!"

In the dim illumination of the four chemical lights fastened to their life vests he located the lifeboat's survival kit, canopy, sea anchor, and collapsible canvas buckets. With Ahmad and Ebi busy bailing, he and Rikki deployed the sea anchor and set up the canopy to protect them from the driving spray. Then, with everyone else occupied, he felt around the exterior of the inflated raft until he found what he was looking for.

The little buoy, about the size and shape of a liter-sized soda bottle with a pencil sticking from the top, was floating behind them, tethered to the raft by a nylon cord. A tiny, blinking LED indicated its water-activated battery was working.

Leaning far over the side of the raft, he pulled the apparatus close and flipped it over so he could see the number on the bottom. Holding Tico's light in his teeth and wiping the blinding spray from his eyes, he read the tiny print: MMSI #775-425791C; CAT I 406MHz/121.5MHz.

Satisfied he had done everything possible to save their lives, Cohen let the device slip into the water, pulled himself into the life raft, rolled onto his back, closed his eyes, and recalled the hymn he first heard at the Naval Academy fifty-eight years before:

> *Eternal Father, strong to save,*
> *Whose arm hath bound the restless wave,*
> *Who bidd'st the mighty ocean deep*
> *Its own appointed limits keep:*
> *O hear us when we cry to thee*
> *For those in peril on the sea . . .*

To which he added, *Father, cause someone who cares to hear our EPIRB.*

### CAIR PARAVEL

ATLANTIC AVENUE
PAWLEYS ISLAND, SC
WEDNESDAY, 15 SEPTEMBER 2032
2100 HOURS, LOCAL

As usual at the beach, the kids ate dinner before the grown-ups. Afterward, as Peter and Elizabeth prepared a meal for the adults, Sarah gave the twins a bath while James read a chapter of Robert Louis Stevenson's *Kidnapped* to Seth and Josh. Pirate stories were always better at the beach. There followed a protracted negotiation between Josh and Seth over who would have the top or bottom bunk in "the boy cousins' bedroom."

James successfully arbitrated an agreement that they would—as usual—take turns and the order—as usual—would be decided by tossing a coin. Seth won. Joshua grumbled, "As usual," and snuggled beneath the covers of the bottom bunk. They were asleep in minutes.

When Peter, James, Sarah, Elizabeth, and Mack Caperton assembled around the table, Peter—as usual—began by asking God's blessing for the meal. After that, almost nothing about the evening went "as usual."

Dinner conversation, normally light and filled with family chatter about the day's activities, was instead consumed with planning their next steps. The only levity revolved around the surgical removal of James's PERT earlier in the day.

*   *   *   *

Peter and Sarah took all four boys on an expedition down the nearly deserted beach, ostensibly on a quest for starfish, interesting shells, sharks' teeth, or the most impressive finds possible at Pawleys—intact sand dollars and sea urchins. Back at the house, Elizabeth, Mack, and James took over Peter's small office and turned it into a surreal surgical suite.

They closed the blinds, taped aluminum foil over the windows, and erected a small aluminum-foil tent on Peter's desk. Elizabeth assembled her surgical instruments and told her brother to sit down in the desk chair and rest his right foot beneath the "tent." She and Mack pulled on latex gloves and with Mack holding a desk lamp in one hand and passing instruments to her with the other, it took her less than five minutes to extract the PERT from between James's toes, wash it in alcohol, deposit the tiny device in the lead-lined leather pouch, and close up the incision.

* * * *

"So what kind of patient was he?" Peter asked as they passed the salad around the table.

"It's not dinner conversation, Dad," Elizabeth replied.

"Why?"

"Because his foot smelled really bad. Nurse Caperton can confirm that."

"All true," the senator chimed in with a laugh.

"Aw, give me a break," James said. "If your foot had been wrapped in aluminum foil for days, your foot would smell, too."

"James," Elizabeth replied, "a lady's feet never smell—right, Sarah?"

"Absolutely. And James, I must tell you—after being married to you for ten years on Friday, your feet often smell."

"Okay, okay, so give me some foot powder for our anniversary."

"Sorry I started this," said Peter. "I was really trying to find out what kind of doctor your sister is. Did it hurt?"

"No. I really never felt a thing. Whatever that stuff is you sprayed on it, sis, it completely numbs all sensation."

"It's actually a fast-acting neuron blocker that stops the transmission of all sensation from the site where it is applied. In the dosage I used, the effects last for a few hours, but by applying the ECM material immediately after extracting the PERT, it's unlikely you will have any discomfort. Barring an infection, the site should be completely healed in a day or two. I checked all the cuts I made yesterday and they all look fine."

"Did you do Sarah, Dad, and the kids the same way you did me?"

"Uh huh. Except I did all theirs in the sick bay at the CSG Ops Center with better light in a TEMPEST-hardened facility, so I didn't have to operate under aluminum foil or work so fast. And of course, they didn't cry and their feet didn't smell."

\* \* \* \*

There was no more laughter at the table. Shortly after the good-natured sibling rivalry, Mack Caperton reached into his pocket, pulled out his PID, excused himself, and went into the living room to take a call.

The others heard him say, "Caperton." Then a few moments later, "Okay, go ahead and send it. I'll get back to you if I need more. Thank you."

There was silence for a minute or so. When Mack returned to the table, holding the PID, he said, "That was my lieutenant commander friend at the U.S. Coast Guard Ops Center. He just came on duty and forwarded a message they transmitted about two hours ago." He handed his PID to Peter so he could read the text:

1. USMCC AUTOMATED SARSAT ALERT SYSTEM REPORTS TWO EPIRBS REGISTERED TO LIFEBOATS ABD MV *ILEANA ROSARIO,* IMO#775-425791 ARE TRANSMITTING DISTRESS/RESCUE SIGNALS ON 406.0MHZ/121.5MHZ.

2. VESSEL IS CONTRABAND SUSPECT AND DNR TO RADIO OR DATA COMMS. NGA, FT. BELVOIR NOTIFIED.

3. MEOSAR/DASS INDICATES POSITIONS AS FOLLOWS:

IMO#775-425791A: 22°16'44.2"N; 88°28'2.7"W
IMO#775-425791C: 22°10'28.9"N; 88°33'58.6"W

1. NO VIZ/IR SAT/UAV COVERAGE AVAIL DUE TO HUR-
RICANE LUCY.

2. USN PROV P-8B AND HSV SUPPORT FOR SAR ASST.

3. CDR USCG DIST. EIGHT DESIG. RCC OIC/POC.

4. SECDEF CONCURS.

BT

After reading the message, Peter passed the PID to James, who in turn handed it to Sarah. Elizabeth, reading over Sarah's shoulder, said, "Mack, you guys may get all this but it's Greek to me. How about a translation?"

Taking the PID back, Caperton scrolled to the top of the message and said, "Okay, here's the short form of what it means. USMCC is the U.S. Satellite Mission Control Center in Suitland, Maryland, run by NOAA. Their automated SARSAT alert system is reporting that two EPIRBs from lifeboats on the *Ileana Rosario* have been activated—"

"Back up," Sarah interrupted. "SARSAT? EPIRB?"

"Sorry," said Mack, "lots of acronyms. SARSAT—Search and Rescue Satellite-Aided Tracking. EPIRB is Emergency Position-Indicating Radio Beacon—every ship and lifeboat is required to carry them."

"What are all the numbers?"

"The ship's International Maritime Organization

registration number. The first three digits tell us it is registered in Venezuela. The last six identify it as the *Ileana Rosario*—a contraband suspect. The A and C tell us that it has likely deployed two of at least three lifeboats. DNR is short for 'does not respond.' NGA is the National Geospatial-Intelligence Agency."

"What's MEOSAR/DASS and all those numbers in the third paragraph?"

"Medium Earth Orbit Search and Rescue—Distress-Alerting Satellite System—and all those numbers are the latitude and longitude of those two EPIRBs. It works with GPS—Global Positioning System—satellites, just like a PERT."

"Like a PERT?" Sarah exclaimed, grabbing the locket suspended around her neck.

"Yes," Peter interjected, "but with different data. Unshielded, your PERT identifies who you are and where you are—just like an EPIRB."

"Let me guess," said Sarah, "the 'no viz/ir sat/uav coverage avail' means that there is no visual or infrared satellite or unmanned aerial vehicle coverage available because of Hurricane Lucy."

"Well done!" said James. "How did you know that?"

"I've heard you talk for a decade. You didn't think I was listening?"

"Okay, Mack," Elizabeth said, "what's P-8B and HSV support?"

"A P-8B is a U.S. Navy patrol aircraft, twin-engine jet—jammed full of sensors. The ones flying over the Caribbean and Gulf of Mexico do a lot of surveillance, pinpointing Russian and Venezuelan submarines, chasing drug runners, and ever since climate change became a 'major threat,' tracking storms like Hurricane Lucy.

HSVs—high-speed vessels—are those big water-jet-propelled multi-mission catamarans the Navy uses for special warfare operations."

"And the stuff at the end?"

"It tells everyone Coast Guard District Eight Headquarters in New Orleans is the Rescue Coordination Center for this mission. The message doesn't have his name in it, but that's Rear Admiral Jeb Livingood. He's designated as officer in charge and point of contact, and last, the Secretary of Defense has approved the Navy aircraft and surface support."

Peter waited until everyone had their questions answered and then asked one of his own: "Mack, how sure are we Marty Cohen ever made it to the *Ileana Rosario*?"

"We're not. My young friend in Coast Guard Intel and I are about the only ones who seem to have drawn that conclusion."

"Tell me again how you arrived at it."

"We know the time he was taken aboard that black speedboat—we have that on visual. We know the time the boat passed the sea buoy at the mouth of Galveston Bay and it does not show up in any port covered by our satellites or UAVs. Computer models show there were two possible link-ups in the Gulf—the *Ileana Rosario* and the *Orfeo*. Both vessels are coastal tankers and both are suspected drug runners."

"What do we know about where the *Orfeo* is now?"

"Nothing. It's disappeared. It may have gone down in the hurricane."

"Then we have to hope Marty is either safely ashore somewhere or he's in one of those lifeboats. Let's take a look at where that message says they are. I have a chart book in my office."

All five got up from the table and gathered around the

desk Elizabeth had used as a surgical table for her brother. Peter grabbed a book of nautical charts, flipped it open to one showing the Gulf of Mexico, and said, "You were the swabbie, Mack, but it looks to me like those two EPIRBs are just north of the Yucatan Peninsula."

Mack checked the lat/long on his PID, bent over the chart, and said, "Well, if the hurricane holds its present course, it will blow them ashore right in the Federation Cartel's home turf."

"The Federation Cartel, what's that?" Elizabeth asked.

"It's the biggest criminal enterprise in the world," Mack responded. "The 'Federation' is the ruling drug cartel in Mexico. They won a bloody, twenty-year-long turf war against six other cartels—and the government of Mexico—to control the shipment of cocaine and heroin into the U.S. and Europe."

"Wasn't 'legalization' supposed to stop all that?"

Caperton put away his PID, stood upright, and said, "That's what people said when Congress voted to legalize and tax marijuana and then hashish. Remember, it was supposed to produce revenue for local, state, and of course the federal government. And of course legalization was going to make the hard stuff—cocaine, meth, heroin, and the like—less desirable. It didn't work. If the classified HHS data is right, there are nearly forty million people in our country who routinely use cocaine, heroin, or some other opiate—"

"Wait a minute, Mack," Elizabeth interrupted. "That's nearly ten percent of the U.S. population. And what's this about the Department of Health and Human Services having classified data?"

"HHS has lots of classified information nowadays—on pathogens being developed in bioengineering labs, naturally occurring communicable diseases, our supplies of various vaccines—even records on who travels to places where outbreaks of certain diseases occur. And yes, the number of users is staggering, but it's twice as bad in Europe. The Federation lets the other cartels deal the soft stuff—marijuana, hash, and meth—and the Fed Cartel controls the distribution of the hard stuff—cocaine from the Andean basin and heroin out of Afghanistan. Unfortunately, the Fed also runs most of Mexico today, and the Yucatan Peninsula is their private domain."

"What's that mean for Dr. Cohen?" asked Sarah.

"Well," said Mack, pointing at the chart, "if Marty is ashore there, he's gone from the frying pan into the fire. The Fed's enforcers are very well armed and absolutely vicious. They're the ones who overran that National Guard outpost on the Arizona-Mexico border back in '27."

"I remember," Sarah interjected. "The newsies called it 'the Massacre at Fort McCain.' But it was like a one-day story and then it disappeared."

The senator nodded and said, "You're correct. Over two hundred Federation enforcers crossed into the U.S. through the Tohono O'odham Autonomous Territory in armored vehicles and overran a National Guard border checkpoint using mortars, RPGs, and heavy machine guns. They killed and beheaded all twelve Guardsmen before escaping across the border."

"But why didn't we hear more about it? Wasn't there supposed to be a congressional investigation?"

"The president declared the event to be a classified national security matter and then had the Attorney General lock up the two reporters who tried to dig into the attack. Two days later 'big media' dropped the story like a hot rock. That pretty much finished independent journalism in the U.S. I was on the Senate Homeland Security Committee and called for an investigation but the Progressives spiked it. They're the majority on every committee and control whether we can subpoena records from the executive branch."

Peter remained silent through this exchange, but as he put away the chart book he said, "I think we ought to move the CSG HRU to Mexico City before Hurricane Lucy makes landfall. If we get the team on the ground before the storm hits, they will be in position to move if we get any info on Marty's whereabouts." He turned to his son and asked, "James, what do you think?"

"If it's likely or even possible Dr. Cohen is in one of those life rafts, we ought to do it soon. According to what I've heard on the radio, Cancun is already closed. Mexico City is closer to the Yucatan than Texas. Depending on the track of the storm, Lucy could shut down all flights into Mexico within the next forty-eight hours. But if we send in our shooters we're going to need a cover plan."

Peter nodded and said, "We can deploy the HRU with our Humanitarian/Medical Relief Team that's packing up now. We'll just speed up the clock and tell our friends in the Mexican government that due to the severity of the storm, we need to pre-position our assets."

"Whoa," said Elizabeth. "George is at Narnia with our kids. He's tagged to head the Med Team on this trip. If he goes out before I get back there, Mom is going to have her hands full."

Sarah, the only other mother in the room, instantly said, "Why doesn't Elizabeth fly back to Virginia with Senator Caperton tomorrow?"

"Is that even legal?" asked James.

"Sure," the senator replied. "Getting Elizabeth to Virginia tomorrow at government expense is essential to carrying out a humanitarian relief mission that is in U.S. national interests. Good idea, Sarah."

"Wait a minute," James said. "A few hours ago we decided I had to get out of the country. How do I link up with the HRU if they are heading out now to hunt for Dr. Cohen? And how are we going to communicate if we can't use our PIDs?"

"I'm working on that. I think we'll have it all figured out shortly after I get to Washington tomorrow," said Mack. "Now, I don't know about the rest of you, but I'm ready for a good night's sleep."

Peter, Sarah, and Elizabeth left to clear the table and clean up in the kitchen. Mack and James were given the assignment of picking up the toys and seashells spread over the ocean-side porch, turning out the lights, and locking up.

In the kitchen, Sarah asked Peter, "I know that you, Mack, and Dr. Cohen were roommates at the Naval Academy—and I know what you and Dr. Cohen did after graduation. What did Mack do?"

Peter smiled and said, "I call Mack a swabbie, but when I was in the Marines, he was a Navy SEAL."

\* \* \* \*

After they cleaned up the children's debris on the porch, Mack sat down in one of the rockers and said, "James, sit down here next to me for a moment, would you please?"

As he did, Caperton said, "When we were still at the table and I was translating the message on my PID, Sarah jumped in at the definition of *viz, IR, sat,* and *UAV.* Do you remember that?"

"Yeah, and I was impressed."

"Right. And do you recall what she said in response to your question?"

"No."

"She said, 'I've been listening to you talk for ten years. You didn't think I was listening?'"

"Okay. Why is that so important?"

After a moment's silence Caperton said, "I am truly sorry we're not going to have more time together on this trip. Things are happening very fast and we all have a lot on our minds. With all that's been happening, did you have time to make up those lists we talked about?"

"Yep," James replied, pulling two sheets of folded paper out of the back pocket of his jeans and handing them to the senator. "Two lists, just like you wanted."

"Good. Thank you. Now, before I look at these, tell me, did you hear Sarah remind you twice at the table that you have been married for ten years and once that Friday is your anniversary?"

"I recall suggesting she give me foot powder for our anniversary."

"On the list of your positive qualities did you mention that you are a good listener?"

"Yeah, something like that."

"And did you list as one of Sarah's attributes 'good listener'?"

The two men were standing now. James paused for a moment and said, "No."

Mack smiled, put his arm around the younger man's shoulder, and said, "You should have. Tomorrow morning at oh-six-thirty let's go for a walk on the beach. That will give us a chance to talk about you and Sarah and some other important things before I have to leave here with your sister."

"Okay."

It was a good plan. But it didn't work out.

# CHAPTER EIGHT

# FATAL ERROR

**SITUATION ROOM**
THE WHITE HOUSE
WASHINGTON, DC
THURSDAY, 16 SEPTEMBER 2032
0430 HOURS, LOCAL

There is a well-established protocol for contacting the President of the United States after-hours. All calls to POTUS—even from a family member—are routed through the White House Situation Room's senior watch officer.

Even though he was in his West Wing office, less than fifty yards from where the president was sleeping, General John Smith picked up the secure phone on his desk. It rang once and he heard, "Sir, this is Senior Watch Officer Ferris."

Smith said into the ancient mouthpiece, "Put me through to the president."

"Sir, she has given us instructions not to awaken her unless it is a national emergency."

The National Security Advisor pondered this information for a moment. He knew from the White House physician, an Army major, that she had prescribed a fast-acting inhalant sleep aid for the president—medication apparently being used with increasing frequency on the campaign trail as the president's poll numbers plummeted. "Put me through to her on the secure line."

Smith counted seven rings before he heard the receiver pick up and the president's voice say, "What is it, John."

She sounded alert enough, so the National Security Advisor continued. "Madam President, I'm sorry to wake you but I have been informed by NSA that the Caliph has dispatched two aircraft en route to Mexico City with the intention of having them arrive before the hurricane makes landfall."

"You woke me up to tell me this? The Caliph and a couple dozen other heads of state have all pledged humanitarian support for those affected by this hurricane. That was in the evening brief—along with a reminder from our inept Secretary of State that the sixteenth is Mexican Independence Day."

"Yes, ma'am," the National Security Advisor replied, surprised she recalled this tiny detail. "But I was just informed there is a sizable military contingent from the Caliphate on at least one of the aircraft."

"Is there some kind of Independence Day parade in Mexico City?"

"Yes, but there is no contingent of troops from the Caliphate invited to march in the parade."

"How do you know this information about the troops is true?"

"We don't know how much of this is true. Global Flight Watch at the UN Air Traffic Control Center in Geneva has confirmed two Caliphate-registered transport aircraft are en route from Jerusalem to Mexico City. The rest—about the commandos and military equipment aboard—is an NSA assessment based on communications intercepts. Some of this information has been verified by our military attaché in Jerusalem and—"

"Then why did you wake me?"

Smith took a deep breath and pressed on. "Madam President, the NSA decrypts indicate the Caliph has personally ordered as many as forty commandos to Mexico. Included in their 'package' are mobility assets—vehicles—and perhaps even two small helicopters. You told me to immediately inform you of any developments regarding Dr. Martin Cohen."

"What else do we know?"

"We know the Caliphate has not informed us or the Mexican government about anything other than a humanitarian shipment—nothing about commandos, military personnel, or equipment. And we know the Caliph's intelligence service began inquiring about Dr. Cohen with their Hezbollah counterparts in Venezuela and Mexico about twenty-two hundred, our time, tonight."

"What the devil is the Caliph up to? Does this mean the Caliph was behind the attack in Houston and the kidnapping of our mad scientist, Dr. Cohen? Why else would he be sending military personnel to Mexico?"

"Let me try to answer those three questions in order. First, we really don't know what the Caliph is up to. Second, we have no new information on who perpetrated the Houston attacks or who kidnapped Dr. Cohen. As you know, we're on record saying the attack was carried out by an Anark-cartel conspiracy. Third, as to why the Caliph is sending military personnel to Mexico, it may well have to do with Dr. Cohen's PERT signal being picked up on the north coast of the Yucatan Peninsula—the second item in my 'evening brief' last night."

There was a moment of silence and then the president said, "Remind me: what's the latest we have on Cohen?"

Smith touched his computer screen, scrolled through his logs, and replied, "As of twenty-two hundred hours, when I sent the brief to you, we had a confirmed signal on Dr. Cohen's PERT from a DEA listening site in Merida, Mexico. The PERT GPS coordinates were identical to the location of an EPIRB signal from a lifeboat apparently washed ashore on the north coast of the Yucatan Peninsula . . ."

"All right, enough of the military acronyms, John, I remember now. Is there anything new on this?"

"Only that the EPIRB is still stationary on the beach and Dr. Cohen's PERT has moved about a mile south—inland. It now appears the Caliph has the same information. NSA believes the decision to dispatch Caliphate commandos to Mexico is directly connected to the Cohen location data."

"The 'Caliph's commandos'—isn't that a unit we trained and equipped? Don't we have U.S. advisors with them?"

"Yes, it is U.S. trained and equipped. But no U.S. advisors are on the aircraft from Jerusalem. The Pentagon has been in communication with Colonel Stan MacAskill, our senior advisor to the Caliphate commando unit. He says he was ordered off the base at midnight our time. He promptly sent a message through to CENTCOM, AFRICOM, and Special Operations Command. That's how we found out about this and started tracking what was going on."

"How are they flying out of Jerusalem? The new airport isn't finished, is it? The Caliph promised me he was going to hold off opening it until after our elections. Everybody knows opening the New Jerusalem International Airport is going to infuriate the Jews."

"Well, Madam President, the airport may not be officially opened but it's apparently finished enough for two of the Caliph's Russian-built IL-90s to fly in from Egypt, land at the new Jerusalem airport, and take off for Mexico loaded with commandos and equipment."

"Dammit, John, why the devil don't we know about these things? Why do we even have all these so-called intelligence agencies—CIA, NSA, DNI, DIA, and all the rest of this stupid alphabet soup—if they can't even tell us an airport is open for business?"

Smith reflected for a second on his response and then plunged on. "Madam President, satellite imagery and intercepts can only tell us so much. When we opened our embassy in Jerusalem three years ago, you made an agreement with the Caliph that neither of us would use our diplomatic missions for intelligence collection or covert operations. We have kept our end of the deal. Right now, I'm much more concerned about how the Caliph knows what we know about Dr. Cohen's possible whereabouts."

"What are you getting at, John—are you insinuating I told him?"

"No, ma'am. But someone inside our government had to have told him or his minions."

"Who do you think it is?"

"I don't know, and I don't want to speculate. But we need to find out. I've talked it over with Admiral Turner at DNI and we want to start intercepting the communications coming into and out of the Caliph's embassy here in Washington. He also urges you to approve putting some HUMINT collectors on the ground in Jerusalem—probably contractors. He's preparing a presidential finding to implement these recommendations. I'll have it for your signature later this morning."

"What do you mean, contractors? What do we have a CIA for? Isn't that what they are supposed to do—collect intelligence?"

"Ma'am, I'm not sure we ought to have this discussion at this hour of the morning, because you have a very busy day coming up, but the bottom line is the CIA's Clandestine Service—what they used to call the Operations Directorate—hasn't done a job like this for years. They outsource all these kinds of taskings to contractors—but they still require a presidential finding to fund the mission."

"Fine, fine. Just bring it straight to me and we'll talk about it, but I don't want this finding circulated."

"Yes, ma'am. I'll also be bringing a DAO directing SOCOM to prepare a unit for covert deployment to Mexico."

"A what?"

"A Deployment Authorization Order. We haven't had to do this since you have been president, but you must personally approve, in writing, the dispatch of military forces outside the United States—overtly or covertly—if there is the prospect of armed combat. We need to do this if we're going to rescue Dr. Cohen."

"Hold on, John! Have you lost your mind? Do you really think we could pull off a covert deployment of a U.S. military unit? If we send an armed posse into Mexico without the permission of the Mexican government we'll get nailed for a clear violation of the North American Union Treaty—and I will lose every Hispanic vote in November. Come up with something better in the morning. Do you understand me?"

Smith's sigh was audible over the secure link, but "Yes, ma'am" was all he said.

The president hung up the phone and grabbed her PID from the nightstand. In the dark she tapped the screen, then spoke into the device: "Muneer: Meet me in the Treaty Room at seven a.m. Bring the Secretary of State with you. No assistants. I have an idea."

**CAIR PARAVEL**

ATLANTIC AVENUE
PAWLEYS ISLAND, SC
THURSDAY, 16 SEPTEMBER 2032
0630 HOURS, LOCAL

The senator, garbed in a blue polo shirt and khaki shorts, was already on the walkway to the beach, sipping from a mug of coffee and watching the sunrise, when James bounded off the porch. "Good morning, Mack," he said as he came up beside the older man.

Caperton smiled and said, "Let's walk and talk. I need the exercise—and the sound of the surf will ensure no one else can hear what we have to say."

They kicked off their sandals and headed south on the beach toward the long pier jutting into the Atlantic, the wind to their backs. A gaggle of long-legged Black-bellied Plovers and short, little sanderlings and sandpipers skittered back and forth in front of them along the edge of the surf as the senator continued. "Before we talk about you and Sarah and those lists you made for me, let me fill you in on some new developments. I already talked to your dad about this, but we will only do what we have in mind if you agree."

"Do you and my father ever sleep?"

"Sometimes, but not much in times like these. I've

never been much of a believer in those expressions like 'sleep is a crutch' or 'I'll sleep when I'm dead,' but what's happening right now to our country generally and particularly to my dear friends named Cohen and Newman doesn't lend itself to many restful nights."

James felt his adrenal cortex react and asked, "What's new?"

"Last night the Coast Guard informed me the lifeboat EPIRB transmitters they have been tracking in the Gulf of Mexico have come ashore about a mile apart on the northern coast of the Yucatan Peninsula. A short while later, a DEA signals intelligence site in Merida—the capital city of Yucatan state—picked up Dr. Cohen's PERT in the same vicinity as one of the EPIRBs. As of a few minutes ago his PERT signal was still being received intermittently—and had moved south, inland from the coastline."

"That's good news," said James. "What's the bad news?"

"Well, as usual, there is some. Apparently the Caliph has dispatched a military unit to Mexico. CENTCOM, AFRICOM, and SOCOM are all aware—as is the White House. Evidently our 'friend in Jerusalem'—as the president refers to the Caliph—didn't bother to tell anyone in Washington or Mexico City about this."

"Caliphate troops headed to Mexico? What for?"

"Don't know. It could be the Caliph intends to get Dr. Cohen. Whether that's to get credit for saving him or to grab him for his fuel cell secrets, I can only guess."

James probed further. "What do you know about the relationship between the Caliph and our president?"

Caperton shrugged and said, "There are a lot of us who believe the Caliph is funding her reelection campaign. And as I said last night, there are many rumors the Caliph and the president have cut some kind of deal regarding post-election oil purchases in exchange for no

Islamic terror attacks. It's pretty clear to me the Caliph has a source or sources of information at a very high level inside our government—and he is being very well informed about what our government knows about Marty Cohen."

James shook his head and said, "A few years ago the Caliph was nothing but a disgruntled Egyptian imam in the Muslim Brotherhood. Now he's a world leader with a military force and funding the election of an American president. So what are *we* going to do about rescuing Dr. Cohen?"

"By 'we' do you mean the U.S. government or CSG?"

"Either or both."

"My guess is the White House and Pentagon will get all wrapped around the axle of the North American Union Treaty and do nothing militarily. After a few weeks of diplomatic dithering and diddling they may end up sending the FBI HRT out of Quantico—which of course will accomplish nothing because the Yucatan Peninsula is a no-go zone for the Mexican government—and therefore for the FBI."

"So what do you think *we* should do?"

"Here's what your dad and I think we ought to do at this point—and again, much of this depends on your decision, and what the weather permits. We ought to get the CSG Humanitarian Relief Team—including some members of the CSG Hostage Recovery Unit—on the ground in Mexico today."

"Why the rush? We don't even know precisely where Marty is or who has him."

"True. But today is Mexico's two hundred and twenty-second Independence Day—and the entire country is celebrating, even as they're about to get hit by a major hurricane. Nobody is going to notice a few extra humanitarian aid workers or containers of relief supplies coming in for at least a few days. By the time everyone sobers up, hopefully Marty Cohen will be on the way home."

"Okay, but how do just a handful of our Hostage Recovery guys find Dr. Cohen, then get him away from whoever is holding him in—what did you call the Yucatan Peninsula last night, 'the Federation Cartel's private domain'—and do all this in two or three days?"

"James, you know what a DEA Foreign-deployed Advisory and Support Team does, right?"

"Sure, despite the benign name, they're the direct-action arm of the DEA overseas. My MARSOC unit was with FAST-ALPHA when I got whacked in Afghanistan back in '25. As you probably know, CSG now provides logs, aviation, and training support for them."

"Right. Well, it just happens that DEA FAST-KILO has dip-clearance to dispatch a six-agent survey unit to Mexico. They are slated to deploy as soon as possible after this hurricane passes. A friend of mine at DEA agreed I can send an Intelligence Committee staffer with them to assess their work for our upcoming budget decisions."

"I thought FAST teams were supposed to be ten or twelve agents."

"Usually they are, but they often task-organize for specific mission requirements. Since CSG will already have highly trained, Spanish-speaking HRU specialists on the ground, a small FAST unit, supplemented by CSG specialists and an able-bodied SSCI staffer, sounded about right."

The pair arrived at the pier and turned beneath the massive structure to head back into the wind, toward Cair Paravel. James walked in silence for a few steps, then, looking at the older man as though he were seeing him for the first time, said with a faint smile, "You know, Mack, you never cease to amaze me. You came up with all this since we talked last night?"

"Actually, no. Your dad came up with the idea two days ago. It took a day to push it through the DEA Special Operations Division. I got the green light from a friend at DEA at about oh-four-hundred this morning."

"You have a lot of amazing friends."

"No. I have many relationships—among them are a fair number of people who claim friendship, but only a very small handful of truly reliable, *good* friends. You and your family are in that little group of steadfast, 'I would die for you' good friends."

"Well then, you have some amazing relationships."

"That's true. And in this case, all those you have heard me refer to as 'friends'—at the White House, in the military, our intelligence services, such as they are, in the DEA—are all people who have put themselves at risk for the benefit of our country and one another, not just me. We all share a common belief that our country is in serious trouble right now and we all agree this is a time when we must stand up and do what is right—regardless of the risks."

"So you think I should go with DEA FAST-KILO to Mexico as James Lehnert, SSCI staff member."

"Well, it's one way to get you out of the country and out of the clutches of the people in this White House who are trying to make you a scapegoat for Houston. If DEA's FAST Team finds Marty Cohen, you could also be crucial to identifying him, since only his captors—whoever they are—and you know exactly what he looks like."

"His PERT will do that."

"Only if his captors haven't removed it—or it hasn't gone dead from not being charged."

"Oh yeah . . ."

"James, the decision is yours. I also know this is going to be a hardship for Sarah and your boys. I recommend you talk it over with her before you decide. You can let me know on the PID I gave you."

"Okay."

"And if memory serves me correctly, you have some other important matters to deal with in the next two days."

"What's that?"

"Well, since tomorrow is your tenth wedding anniversary—and you shouldn't be seen wandering around off this island—I suggest you take the kids off Sarah's hands for a while tomorrow so she can go to that nice spa up toward Litchfield. And on the flight down here you mentioned Saturday is Seth's twelfth birthday. Do you have a present for him?"

"You're right, it is his birthday. And no, I don't have a present for him. I need to talk to Sarah and ask her to run out to get him something."

"I recall what you received from your dad on your twelfth birthday. Do you?"

"Uh huh," James replied with a half grin. "A twenty-gauge shotgun, a compass, and a Bible."

"Do you remember what your dad said when he gave them to you?"

"Oh yeah, because I was embarrassed in front of all the other boys at the birthday party. He said if I learned to use all three of those presents—the compass, the shotgun, and the Bible—I would never get lost, never go hungry, and never need to fear anything."

"He was right, you know."

"I suppose . . ."

"No, you don't suppose. You know he was right. That

kind of gift makes a pretty good tradition for a Newman boy turning twelve. You might want to think about it."

"Well, that's not going to happen for Seth's twelfth birthday. Even if Sarah had a federal permit to purchase a firearm, we're a little late on the six-month waiting period to buy a shotgun. Maybe next year."

"Well now, if it's something you and Sarah think is a good idea, I just happen to have picked up a very nice little twenty-gauge from a friend in Charleston. It's right now keeping a Capitol Police sergeant company over at the Sea View Inn. He also has the required paperwork to make the gift legal with the new federal firearms registration laws. And as for a compass and a Bible, I don't think either of them require a six-month federal waiting period—at least not yet."

Newman smiled and said, "How do you keep all this straight in your head?"

"Because it isn't just in my head—it's also in my heart. And that's a good segue to the other topic we're supposed to talk about this morning—the two lists you prepared for me."

Mack was reaching into the cargo pocket of his shorts for the two sheets of paper when he suddenly said, "What now?" and fished his PID out of another pocket. He touched the screen, held the card up to his ear, and said, "Caperton. Go ahead, William."

As the two men walked along the edge of the incoming tide, Caperton listened for a while, then asked, "When?" He listened some more and then said, "It will take me three hours to get from here to Washington. Tell the chairman I'll be there before noon and not to start without me. I'm on the way."

Putting the PID back in his pocket, Mack said, "I'm sorry, James. That was the SSCI chief of staff. I must go straight to Washington. Something about a new presidential finding. We're going to have to postpone our discussion of those lists."

Newman nodded and said, "I understand," then the two men walked in silence for the last few hundred yards, enjoying the light breeze and the glow of the sunlight on the sea.

As they reached Cair Paravel's long wooden walkway over the dunes, James tapped the senator on the arm and pointed to an American osprey coasting into the wind twenty yards offshore. They watched in silence as the bird folded its wings and dove, feetfirst, into the shallow water. In seconds the raptor reappeared, extended its wings, shook the salt water off its feathers, and took off into the breeze, banking hard left over the island—a small fish firmly gripped in its talons.

Pointing toward the bird, Caperton turned to James and said, "Mission accomplished. You know, ospreys are migratory—and that one will probably leave here soon. Do you know where many of them go for the winter?"

"No."

Mack put his arm around James's shoulder and said, "Mexico."

## LA COSTA ESMERALDA

55 MILES NE OF MERIDA, CAPITAL OF YUCATAN STATE,
MEXICO
THURSDAY, 16 SEPTEMBER 2032
1210 HOURS, LOCAL

No matter where on the globe he was, Marty Cohen always kept the ancient chronograph on his left wrist set to the Eastern U.S. time zone. It was a habit he began in the Navy decades before so he wouldn't have to figure out whether he was going to awaken his wife and children with a call home.

According to the admiral's battered old timepiece, they washed ashore just before 9 p.m. EDT on Wednesday, 15 September. Seconds before the lifeboat flipped over, he heard the ominous sound of crashing surf over the roar of the wind and rain and glanced at the watch. He was surprised they could be near any shore. The storm surge literally tossed the inflatable raft, upside down, onto the beach—spilling all four men hard into the sand.

Though the life vest prevented serious injury to his upper body, the fall knocked the air out of the old admiral's lungs and he struggled to crawl out of the waves and catch his breath. For nearly half an hour he simply lay there in the sand, barely above the surf, his arms wrapped around the trunk of a toppled tree as the howling wind shredded their inflatable lifeboat, scattering the survivors' few possessions.

Shivering in near-total darkness, Cohen took stock. He could feel a cut on his chin and scrapes on his knees and hands from being pounded into the sand by the surf. The temperature had dropped at least ten degrees since they went over the side of the sinking *Ileana Rosario* and he was feeling the effects of prolonged exposure to the elements.

He still had his chem-light and the little compass from the lifeboat survival kit—both tethered to his life vest. But the plastic signal mirror, small folding knife, waterproof matches, and can of water he took from the kit were all gone. His only shoe was lost when the raft capsized. His warm-up shirt and jogging pants were both torn but still serviceable enough to afford some protection.

Just a few yards away the admiral could see the dim glow of a chem-light and the outline of a dark form clinging to another fallen tree. He had no idea who it was or where they were, but he was glad to be alive and ashore—and knew that no matter how battered or fatigued he was, this was very likely his best opportunity for escape.

Jamming the chem-light beneath his life vest to hide its glow, he pulled out the little compass, stuck its luminous dial in front of his face, and started crawling away from the roaring surf, heading due south, into the jungle.

Less than fifty yards off the beach he found himself enmeshed in a tangle of saw grass, thick weeds, fat vines, and downed trees flattened and compacted by the driving wind and rain. His tattered shirt and pants caught on invisible, sharp snags with every movement. After thirty minutes of attempting to paw his way through the impenetrable thicket, he was completely exhausted.

Desperate to evade his captors and survive the furious storm, Cohen burrowed deep as he could into the sodden mass, rolled onto his side, pulled his legs up into a fetal position to conserve body heat, and resolved to live until dawn.

Though he could not remember dozing off, he awakened with a start as the first tendrils of gray light penetrated his hiding place. Rotating his wrist, he first confirmed the time—0610—and then checked the wind direction with the compass.

He noted the gale was still driving sheets of rain almost horizontal, but the wind seemed to have dropped a few miles per hour. It was also somewhat warmer and gusting more from the east than the north. From long experience at sea, Cohen knew that unless it veered back to the south, the worst of the storm had passed.

Pulling himself from the little burrow where he had taken shelter in the dead of night, the old admiral carefully peered around, looking for any signs of the other seven men who cast themselves over the side of the *Ileana Rosario* the night before. Seeing no one, he stood—then sat down abruptly to extract a sand burr from the sole of his bare left foot.

In less than a half hour, Marty Cohen demonstrated his reputation for a rare combination of brilliance, resilience, and common sense. When he stood again he wore a pair of "shoes" he'd fashioned from palm fronds, fabric torn from the T-shirt beneath his jogging suit jacket, and aluminum foil and soggy duct tape from the boot his kidnappers applied aboard the *Ileana Rosario* to block his PERT signal.

Arming himself with a sturdy stick pulled from the detritus washed up by the storm, he set out to get on higher ground, which he could see a mile to the south. It took him more than two hours to make his way through tangled, uprooted vegetation and a foot-sucking swamp deepened by the deluge. Along the way he saw a piece of the orange canopy from a life raft, flapping in the wind on a broken branch. It was too high to reach or tear down so he kept moving, hoping that somewhere nearby, the raft's EPIRB was still transmitting and the orange panel would be spotted by a SAR flight after the storm passed.

When the admiral topped the gentle rise, he stopped and looked to see if he was being pursued. To the north he could see low, scudding clouds—squall lines—over the Gulf of Mexico. While still gusting hard, the wind seemed to be hauling somewhat and he judged the eye of the hurricane had passed over them during the night. He estimated the storm was changing course toward the northwest.

Through gaps in the rain bands he could see for a mile

or so along the coast to the east and west. Though he was standing on what would have been prime, seafront property in the United States, there wasn't a single dwelling, structure, or person in sight.

He sat, his back to a fallen tree, picked up a large leaf, curled it into a gutter, placed one end between his lips, and let rainwater drain into his mouth. In a matter of minutes the downpour slaked his thirst. Refreshed, he rose, took out the compass, and headed due south again.

After another half hour of "breaking brush" he came to a muddy, deeply rutted dirt track about seven feet wide, running generally east–west. Before venturing forth, he looked carefully left and right for any signs of recent vehicle or foot traffic. Whatever clues there might have been before the storm, none could be seen now.

Cohen thought for a moment, then decided to go right—west—since it was slightly uphill. He reasoned the high ground was the most likely place to find human habitation, shelter from the storm, and protection from any of the terrorists who survived their shipwreck.

Just before noon his spirits were further buoyed when he came upon a small clearing—about twice the size of a football field. Near the center of the open space were four single-story structures of varying size. Several rows of corn and a small vegetable garden—all flattened by the storm—could be seen on the south side of the clearing.

Resisting the impulse to race across the clearing to the buildings, he stepped back into the wind-whipped foliage and hunkered down next to a tree, where he could scan the area for any signs of life. From his vantage point Cohen could see that three of the buildings were constructed of wood and one—apparently a house—was built of concrete block.

He could see no power lines, vehicles, or machinery.

No dogs or livestock were visible. The largest of the buildings, apparently a barn, had lost part of its metal roof—whether from the storm or prior to it, he could not tell. What looked to be the house had no glass in the windows he could see, but it appeared otherwise undamaged and, more importantly, unoccupied.

He watched the place for nearly an hour, weighing whether it would be best to approach the dwelling during daylight or wait until after dark. Finally, the absence of any visible human activity—and hunger pangs gnawing in his stomach—won over patience. He stepped out of the vegetation and walked straight toward the doorway on the small porch.

It took Cohen less than two minutes to cross the wind- and rain-swept clearing and step onto the weather-beaten boards of the porch. The front door was open and banging with each gust. From the doorway he took it in: a rough wooden floor, not dirt, soaked by storm-driven rain; an upturned wooden table; two crude wooden chairs; three small benches along the wall; and a short corridor leading to a kitchen—with two interior doors to his right. He shouted *"¡Hola!"* twice. Receiving no response, he entered.

The blow to the back of the admiral's head knocked him to his knees. For an instant, just before he was struck again, the thought *Fatal error* flashed through his mind.

# CHAPTER NINE

# OPERATION COYOTE

**CAIR PARAVEL**
ATLANTIC AVENUE
PAWLEYS ISLAND, SC
THURSDAY, 16 SEPTEMBER 2032
1815 HOURS, LOCAL

"Well, we finally have some good news," Peter Newman said with a smile, tossing James and Sarah an
armload of towels as they came up to the porch from a
swim with their boys.

"Thanks," said James as they wrapped the twins in terry
cloth and Seth and Josh raced for the shower. They had
been out of the house fishing, tossing Frisbees, searching
for loggerhead turtle nests along the dunes, and generally
playing on the edge of the ocean since Senator Caperton's hurried departure with James's sister, Elizabeth, that
morning.

Their late-day swim was the result of a dare by Josh.
Since the afternoon air was considerably cooler than
the Atlantic water, everyone arrived on the porch with

a serious case of goose bumps. As he rubbed the towel through his hair, James asked, "So what's the good news?"

"Two positive reports while you guys were getting some time together. First, our Ops Center sent out a Sit-Rep that the CSG Humanitarian/Med Support Team is on the ground in Mexico City. Second, Mack was right about the Independence Day holiday. Nobody at the airport even noticed our HRU add-ons to the Humanitarian/Med package."

As Sarah nudged the twins up the stairs and into the house, James looked at his father, suddenly concerned. "The Ops Center didn't put the stuff about our HRU in the Sit-Rep for the whole government to see, did they?"

"No. Our report simply provided a head count and informed the usual list of agencies that 'need to know' about the team's arrival with nine containers of medical gear, humanitarian relief supplies, and essential life-support, communications, and mobility equipment. It's all in the proper format—and it has the additional merit of being the truth. We just added Dan Doan and his operators to the Med Team list."

The two men moved into the house and Sarah, now wrapped in a robe, rejoined them as James asked, "So how do we know the Mexican authorities didn't take notice of Doan and his HRU shooters?"

"That came directly from Mack on the SSCI PID, shortly after the CSG flight from Dulles landed in Mexico City."

"Have we heard from Dan? Who did he take on such short notice?"

"Dan and his HRU are on radio silence—listen-only mode until we tell him otherwise. He has Ken Connor, Zane Felton, Dan Smith, Ken Knapp and Steve McNaughton with him. If it turns out they need another medic for their mission, George will give up his deputy, your former Navy corpsman, Doc Fowler."

James nodded and said, "Well, I'm living proof Jack Fowler is the best field trauma doc around if he has the right equipment."

"We can be pretty sure he has everything he needs," Peter said. "Before I left to come down here, I told Sergeant Major Doan to give Don Gabbard a list of whatever he wanted. They added a few items to the fly-away kit and were waiting at IAD when George arrived with the Med Team. Mack's plane flew directly from Myrtle Beach to Dulles so Elizabeth could say good-bye to George before his Med Team left for Mexico. Mack personally briefed Doan and the HRU on what was going on and about our new comms procedures."

"Do we have a fix on who knows what about the HRU and the rest of what we're doing in Mexico outside of medical and humanitarian support? Is there a bigot list for this operation?"

Before Peter could answer, Sarah asked, "What's a bigot list?"

Peter smiled and replied, "It's an old-fashioned term that goes back to World War II and the OSS. When Wild Bill Donovan, the head of OSS, sent American officers to Gibraltar for training with the British, their orders were stamped 'TO GIB.' Those who passed the test and were cleared for covert missions in Nazi-held Europe had their orders stamped with the letters reversed—'BIG OT.' Ever since, the term *bigot list* has referred to those who are cleared for information about a particular classified operation or activity."

Sarah said playfully, "Well, I'm glad it's not the kind of bigot I was thinking of . . ."

"So let's move beyond the history lesson," James

interjected, clearly annoyed at his wife's interruption. "Who is on the bigot list for this operation—whatever it's being called?"

Peter watched with concern as Sarah's cheerful demeanor disappeared instantly and she turned and walked away, heading back upstairs. He took a deep breath and said to his son, "That wasn't necessary."

"Look, Dad, I have a lot on my mind. Let's get on with the important things here . . ."

After a long pause, Peter said, "We're calling the Marty Cohen rescue effort 'Operation Coyote.' It was Doan's idea, partly because McNaughton, the great coyote hunter, is on the op and because the DEA and Border Patrol routinely catch Mexican drug smugglers who are also human traffickers—called coyotes."

"So back to my original question, who's on the bigot list for Operation Coyote?"

"Outside our immediate family, only Senator Caperton, Master Gunnery Sergeant Gabbard at the CSG Ops Center, and of course Dan Doan and the rest of the HRU. Mack knows everything you and I know. He is also communicating with some others—in the DEA and elsewhere we don't know—who feed him information. They probably know some of what we know—but not everything."

"If we're going to do this right and maintain some control over op-sec, we need to know who those others are at some point."

"You're right, James, and I'm sure Mack will inform us who else knows what, when the time is right. He won't hold anything back if it's a matter of your safety or Marty Cohen's."

"So what are the communications procedures you mentioned?"

"Very simple, really. After talking with Mack, Don

Gabbard and Dan Doan pulled one of your overseas communications plans out of the files at the Ops Center and modified it for this deployment. They set up the Comm Plan for Mexico based on what you worked out last year for the relief operation after the typhoon hit the southern Philippines. Both George and Dan deployed with a lightweight, broadband CSG sat-comm suite. Don packed out four solar-powered portable cell towers with satellite uplink capability for interface with the Mexican commercial G6 HTM systems for PID service. He also sent enough PRC-5722 waveform-compatible, encrypted radios for short-range comms and sufficient multispectrum IFF transponders for everyone in both teams plus the DEA FAST unit when it arrives."

"I can't argue with that. What about fail-safe procedures?"

"For last-resort backup, Don also shipped twenty-five 9855 Iridium handsets registered to AvecVous SA, one of our unactivated, Swiss-based proprietary companies. Every team member has a call sign, one-time pad, and an emergency comms number through our CSG comm site in Australia. Mack also has the name and contact information for one of his trusted agents already in place."

"In Mexico?"

"That's what he told me. His code name is 'Travel Agent.' He gave the info to Don Gabbard but doesn't want it passed electronically by anyone. Mack said he will give you the name and contact info when he sees you in person before you deploy with the DEA FAST."

James took all this in, nodded, and said, "Yeah, I still have to talk to Sarah about me going to Mexico . . . So what's our next step?"

"I'm not entirely certain. We're really on hold here until we find out when the DEA FAST unit you are accompanying will deploy. Until a half hour ago, Mack was fairly certain they would be heading out this weekend, but that may slip."

"Why?"

"Well, shortly after we got the word our CSG teams were safely on the ground at Juarez International, a suicide bomber blew himself up at the airport, killing at least forty and wounding more than a hundred."

"Were any of our CSG people among the casualties?"

"No."

"Any claim of responsibility?"

"Not yet, but the State Department's response was to issue a Travel Warning Notice, telling U.S. citizens to get out of Mexico."

"That kind of event and response had to go over like a lead balloon in Mexico on their Independence Day. Aren't warnings like that for business travelers and tourists? This doesn't apply to official missions like the DEA, does it?"

"I don't know what it means for the DEA FAST, but a lot of other U.S. government employees are being ordered out of the country. Come on in and read what the fools at Foggy Bottom have posted on the MESH. I logged on with your SSCI Lehnert alias password."

They walked into Peter's office. James sat down at the desk, touched the clear plastic pane, and read the notice:

U.S. Department of State Foreign Travel Warning

The Department of State warns all U.S. citizens of the dangers of travel to Mexico. The security situation in Mexico continues to deteriorate as violence perpetrated by narco-terrorists affects rural and urban areas. The potential for violence by terrorists and other criminal elements exists in all parts of the country. This Travel Warning replaces the Travel Advisory for Mexico issued on February 7, 2032, provides new information on recent security incidents, and gives instructions for contacting and registering for evacuation with the U.S. Embassy in Mexico City.

The Independence Day suicide attack at Mexico City's Juarez International Airport on September 16 was intended to inflict maximum casualties on humanitarian relief organization personnel. It is apparent from this attack and the lack of cooperation from the Government of Mexico (GOM) in investigating the September 11 Anark-cartel attack in Houston, TX, that the GOM is unable to provide protection for U.S. citizens living and traveling in Mexico.

The threat of serious criminal violence throughout Mexico remains very high and travel in the countryside can be extremely dangerous due to the presence of narco-terrorists. Common crime remains a significant problem in many urban and rural areas. For additional details about the general criminal threat, please see the Department of State's Country Specific Information for Mexico.

A series of cartel-related bombings have occurred recently in Mexico City, Merida, Acapulco, Chihuahua, Ciudad Juarez, and several smaller cities. On April 27, 2032, an explosion in a commercial building in Mexico City resulted in two fatalities and a dozen injuries. A hand grenade bombing of a restaurant on July 8, 2032, injured twenty students, including seven Americans. On August 12, 2032, a bomb detonated in Monterrey injuring eighteen persons, including one American. Many expatriates live in and frequent the neighborhoods where these explosions occurred.

The incidence of kidnapping in Mexico has increased significantly since the DOS issued its last Travel Advisory. The

Federation Cartel and other criminal organizations continue to kidnap and hold civilians for ransom or as political bargaining chips. No one is immune from kidnapping on the basis of occupation, nationality, or other factors. Kidnapping in rural areas is of particular concern. On August 19, 2032, fifteen hostages, including three Americans, were killed when the Government of Mexico attempted to rescue them from the narco-terrorists who were holding them for ransom. Although the U.S. government places the highest priority on the safe recovery of kidnapped Americans, it is U.S. policy not to make concessions to or strike deals with kidnappers. Consequently, the U.S. government's ability to assist kidnapping victims is limited.

All nonessential U.S. government officials in Mexico are hereby ordered to depart the country immediately for assigned safe-haven locations. All U.S. government employees are instructed to repatriate family members to the United States and are urged to do so only via USG-certified air carriers. U.S. government employees and family members may not use inter- or intra-city public transportation, or travel by road outside urban areas at night. All nonofficial American citizens in Mexico are urged to follow these precautions.

Effective immediately, all U.S.-Mexico land Ports of Entry [POE] are closed to nonofficial and noncommercial transportation except to U.S. citizens with valid passports/PERTs returning to the United States from Mexico. Restrictions on air travel from Mexico are contained in DHS Circular No. 2032-09-16B.

Private American citizens currently living or traveling in Mexico should immediately register with the U.S. Embassy through the State Department's travel registration website

(MESH://travelregistration.state.gov/ibrs/home.asp) to obtain updated information on travel and security within Mexico.

The U.S. Embassy is located at Paseo de la Reforma 305, Col. Cuauhtemoc, 06500 Mexico, D.F. In case of a serious emergency that jeopardizes the health or safety of an American citizen in Mexico, call the U.S. Embassy at [52] (744) 484-0300 or contact Consular Service at [52] (744) 484-1566. The Embassy's American Citizens Services office provides routine information at MESH://mexico.usembassy.gov. For questions not answered there, inquiries may be sent by MESH-mail to ACSMexico@state.gov.

U.S. Consulates and Consular Agency offices in Acapulco, Ciudad Juarez, Guadalajara, Hermosillo, Matamoros, Merida, Monterrey, Nogales, and Nuevo Laredo will remain open with limited staffing until close of business on Friday, September 24, to process passport applications, provide PERT validation, and perform notarial services for U.S. citizens. Thereafter, these offices will be closed until further notice. Consulates and Consular Agency offices are not staffed to respond to after-hours emergencies. U.S. citizens requiring emergency services should contact the U.S. Embassy in Mexico City at [52] (744) 484-0300.

As the Department develops information on potential security threats to U.S. citizens overseas, it shares credible threats through its Consular Information Program documents, available at MESH://travel.state.gov. U.S. citizens should consult warden messages for Mexico at MESH://mexico.usembassy.gov/acswardenmsg, as well as the Department of State's Country Specific Information for Mexico and the latest Worldwide Caution at MESH://travelwarn.state.gov.

U.S. citizens may obtain up-to-date information on security conditions by calling 1-999-407-4747 toll-free in the U.S. and Canada or, for overseas callers, on a regular toll line at 1-202-500-4444. U.S. citizens calling via landline service must provide their PERT ID number to be connected. Persons placing PID voice calls may be required to provide a PERT code for verification purposes.

Office of State Department Public Communication Division, 202-647-6575

James scrolled quickly through the message twice, leaned back in the chair, and said to his father, "This is stunning! They buried the info about shutting down the U.S.-Mexican border in the middle of the notice! What are they thinking? Has this kind of thing ever happened before?"

"Sure, but it was reserved for places like Lebanon, Somalia, Sudan, and Yemen back in the years before the Caliphate. It has certainly never happened with Mexico."

"I don't get it. Who came up with this less than two months before a presidential election? The political left in this country will go nuts. It could cost her the election."

"That's what I said to Mack when I first read it. But he thinks this is part of a very shrewd political plan on her part to take advantage of events that might otherwise finish her."

"So how does closing the U.S.-Mexican border help her get reelected—when she and her Progressive Party have done nothing but encourage illegal immigration for decades?"

"Here's what Mack says: Most American voters are now independents and don't belong to any political party. They vote on issues. In the aftermath of the Houston attack, security is certainly the hottest political issue. The president knows no Anark is going to vote for her—so she blames the attack on a previously unknown cabal of Anarks and Mexican drug cartels. Shutting down the U.S.-Mexican border makes her look tough on terror. It also defangs conservatives who claim she is soft on illegal immigration and distracts everyone from focusing on radical Islamist oil producers who are probably financing her reelection."

"Man, that's pretty cynical," said James, shaking his head.

"Well, if Mack is right, it's even worse than anyone might think. Look at the 'kidnap-hostage language' and the succeeding passage about ordering U.S. government personnel to leave the country."

James scrolled to the fifth and sixth paragraphs of the notice. When his son nodded, Peter continued, "If Mack is correct—and he knows Washington politics better than you or I—those two paragraphs give them a perfect excuse for not trying to rescue Marty Cohen anytime soon."

"Mack may be right. This notice is certainly a rationale for doing nothing. It definitely reinforces what the world is being told about Houston being an Anark-cartel operation. Maybe I'm just paranoid, Dad, but this notice reads like it was put together well before the attack at the Mexico City airport."

"That's exactly what I thought when I read it," Peter replied. "It's all very strange. According to our Ops Center, there were no leaks to the media about this until the warning notice was posted just before this afternoon's State Department press briefing. As you might expect, Centurion Aviation is overwhelmed with calls and MESH messages from American citizens looking for a safe way home."

"Okay, I understand all that, Dad. But none of this explains why the administration wouldn't do everything in their power to get Dr. Cohen back safely, as soon as possible."

"Consider for a moment that Mack has it figured out: they really did fabricate the whole thing about Houston being perpetrated by some Anark-cartel conspiracy—and the president's reelection campaign really is being financed by the Caliph. If that's correct, the last thing the White House wants is Marty Cohen suddenly appearing before the election with the truth about his kidnappers—and a workable fuel cell design."

"That's just plain evil."

"You're right," Peter said, nodding to his son. "It also complicates our planning for Operation Coyote. I just hope Mack's trusted agent isn't one of the Americans being told to get out of Mexico."

---

**U.S. CONSULATE**

CALLE 60 NO. 338, COL. ALCALÁ MARTIN

MERIDA, YUCATAN STATE, MEXICO

THURSDAY, 16 SEPTEMBER 2032

2145 HOURS, LOCAL

Arthur James Jones Jr. really intended to retire from intelligence work. In fact, he officially retired twice— the first time from the National Security Agency and a second time after ten years as a consultant with a Washington, D.C., defense contractor. When Jones turned in his credentials, access badge, and cipher codes in May 2029, he told everyone he was going to do charity work with his church in Gainesville, Virginia. And he meant it.

But then, in July 2030, the DEA called asking him for advice on its wires operation in Mexico. His first response was "I'm too old for the cloak-and-dagger stuff." But Frankie Moyer, DEA's Director of Overseas Intelligence

Operations, did his homework and knew the right buttons to push.

"A.J.," Moyer said, "we came to you first because you are a patriot. You know this business inside and out. You know how to keep your mouth shut. And your country needs your help. You will be home in Virginia in two months. Ninety days max."

That was more than two years ago. As in his previous employment, A. J. Jones quickly became an MVP in DEA's Mexican counternarcotics intelligence operations. They gave him a black diplomatic passport wrapped in foil and hidden in the sole of his right shoe, a new PERT, a "non-official cover," and a little office next door to the U.S. Consulate in Merida, capital of Yucatan state. Above his door was a sign: GLOBAL FINANCIAL SERVICES. To enhance his cover as he traveled around the Yucatan, his new employers created a legend that A. J. Jones was also an amateur archeologist fascinated by ancient Mayan culture. To answer calls and distract visitors, the DEA Special Operations Division gave him a gorgeous "receptionist" named Marcia Quintero.

Señora Quintero was one of the very few people in Mexico who knew A. J. Jones's real job. Marcia was the person who ran next door to the U.S. Consulate to pick up and drop off "items" being shipped via diplomatic pouch. She was actually a DEA special agent from San Diego, a former member of DEA FAST-CHARLIE, and the wife of a Marine major.

Before joining DEA, Quintero was a San Diego narcotics officer. As a martial-arts instructor at the DEA Academy in Quantico, Virginia, she used to tell her students, "Killing an armed assailant with your bare hands is better than having him kill you, but if you maintain situational awareness you shouldn't have to. I am your hand-to-hand combat trainer and an expert pistol shot. I carry a forty-five—because they don't make a forty-six."

An attractive, gun-toting receptionist wasn't the only perk A. J. Jones enjoyed in Merida. Through a cutout corporation in Guatemala, his new employers paid the lease on a delightfully refurbished old downtown residence on Paseo de Montejo. From his upstairs sitting room he could see the steeples of the cathedral on Plaza Mayor, the oldest church in the Western Hemisphere.

Two months into A.J.'s current assignment he updated the cathedral's sixteenth-century architecture by covertly installing half a dozen miniature, solar-powered, omni-directional, broad-spectrum, multiband receivers and tiny microwave relay transmitters in the bell towers for his real line of work. Two flat-plane microwave antennas hidden atop the cathedral beamed every signal intercepted by forty-seven receivers in northern Yucatan to the equipment A.J. installed in his attic.

A tiny uplink antenna barely visible on the roof of his house on Paseo de Montejo broadcast the intercepted signals on a dedicated Ku-band "pathway" to the Ameri-Star 77 satellite in geosynchronous orbit over Puerto Rico. Four milliseconds later the intercepts were received in the DEA Special Operations Division (SOD) "wires room" in Sterling, Virginia.

At SOD they claimed, "Our man in Merida knows what every drug lord in the Federation Cartel has for breakfast, how much cocaine they ship before lunch and who they will kill after dinner." There was some hyperbole in that—but the intercept equipment A.J. placed in Merida and along the Yucatan coast, from Sisal in the west to Cerrito in the east, provided a near-constant stream of valuable, real-time intelligence on drug shipments, who was making them, and where they were destined. The fact that many of the Federation Cartel kingpins used Global Financial Services to move money served as added value for the raw information being fed to SOD—and afforded A.J. a certain degree of protection from mindless Mexican mayhem.

Even in this lawless region of Mexico, Jones knew his dangerous job became genuinely life-threatening if he fell while installing a piece of intercept equipment—or if the targets of his surveillance somehow discovered his actual line of work. To guard against those possibilities he had a mountain climber's obsessive attention to detail and planned each step of an installation as though he were making a solo ascent at fifteen thousand feet. He knew his physical limits, nearly always worked alone, and was careful to the point of being described as aloof, a recluse, type A, even anal.

To prevent being identified and targeted by the Federation Cartel's enforcers, he zealously avoided talking about his undercover work with others, shunned the expatriate social circuit, and carefully maintained his cover "legend." On the few occasions when A.J. was cornered in conversation, his interlocutor was presented with a staggering array of incredibly wearisome macro- and micro-economic statistics and exchange rates befitting the manager of a financial services office. When pressed, he could also lapse into a mind-numbing soliloquy on ancient Mayan culture.

A.J. usually managed to avoid festivities like the nationwide Independence Day celebration. He would gladly have stayed home this year but for encrypted instructions he received from SOD, directing him to report certain signals on specific frequencies along the Yucatan's Emerald Coast.

He initially intended to wait until after Hurricane Lucy passed, anticipating the storm would likely damage some equipment he'd already installed along the Gulf. But less than an hour after the message from SOD hit his computer, he received an inquiry posted at MESH:// mayandigs.org, the MESH site for an amateur archeology club he had joined to enhance his cover.

Transmitted in the clear, the communication looked like a simple request for information on Mayan maritime artifacts from a fellow club member. In fact it was a coded message from Senator Mackintosh Caperton, asking A.J. to do all he could to pick up any signals from the MV *Ileana Rosario*, the vessel's lifeboat EPIRBs, and a PERT registered to Dr. Martin Cohen.

* * * *

Mack and A.J. first met nearly two decades earlier, when Caperton was a junior senator on the Armed Services Committee and Jones was working for NSA at Fort Meade, Maryland. They became close friends, shared a fascination with signals intelligence, and learned they both carried identical tiny metal fish on thin chains around their necks. Like most "People of the Book," they trusted each other implicitly, regarded the words "How can I help you?" to be a pledge, not just a question, and found ways of staying in touch with each other over the years.

Acting on the SOD's orders and Senator Caperton's "archeology message" required A.J. to drive through high winds and a monsoon-like downpour to his installations in Progreso, Telchac Puerto, and Cerrito. He took Marcia Quintero with him to ride "shotgun" and provide security while he was occupied recalibrating the equipment for intercepting and relaying emissions on the frequencies and bands requested.

Returning to Merida after dark in the driving rain, A.J.

dropped Quintero off at her apartment and went home to adjust the equipment in his attic so he would get a computer-generated alert if any of the three sites picked up EPIRB or PERT signals. A few minutes before 9 p.m. on Wednesday, 15 September, he hit pay dirt.

The first intercepted signals came almost simultaneously through his Cerrito and Telchac Puerto facilities—a data stream SOS/Mayday on 406MHz and 121.5MHz from a CAT 1 EPIRB, MMSI #775-425921C. A few minutes later, the same two sites detected emissions from a second EPIRB and then both sites picked up the faint signal from an encrypted, Type B, military-series PERT, transmitting Dr. Martin Cohen's ID and biometric data.

Without waiting for the Semantic Fusion Framework software on the computer in his attic to decipher and analyze what was likely a fragmentary PERT algorithm, A.J. pulled a 1:100,000 scale chart of the Yucatan's north coast out of a drawer, spread it out on his desk, and quickly calculated the azimuth from each of his intercept stations to the EPIRBs and the PERT emitters on the beach. He estimated they were within a few hundred yards of each other, about midway between Dzilam de Bravo and Cerrito. Jones immediately transmitted this news over an encrypted data link to SOD. Five minutes later he posted a manually encoded missive with the same information in a "draft" message on the "Mayan Digs" MESH message board and sent a two-word message to Mack Caperton: "NBA DRAFT."

Over the next twenty-four hours, A.J. used the separate channels to send a half-dozen updates to both SOD and Caperton. He reported the two EPIRBs to be stationary on the beach, the torturously slow inland movement of "the Cohen PERT," and later, the fact the Cohen PERT had not moved since shortly after noon today.

A.J. would still have been at home monitoring the signals for any changes but for a phone call he received from Marcia Quintero at 2030. She told him the legal attaché at the U.S. Embassy in Mexico City sent her a MESH-mail ordering her home ASAP in compliance with the State Department's travel warning. She wanted to talk, so A.J. agreed to meet her at the consulate.

Quintero was there waiting when the security guard admitted A.J. through the back door of the building and into the counsel general's small conference room. His loyal receptionist was clearly agitated.

"I've been ordered to depart on the next available flight to the U.S. from Rejon International," she complained bitterly. "The only reason I don't have to leave on tomorrow morning's Delta flight to Miami is the airport is shut down because of the hurricane. Nobody has ever told me before I'm 'nonessential.' This will finish my future at DEA. I need your help getting these orders canceled, A.J."

"Do you have a copy of the MESH-mail you received?"

She handed him a four-page printout from her office computer. The first sheet had a State Department seal in the upper left corner and was full of the usual bureaucratic travel jargon citing this and that appropriation authority. The final sentence instructed, "U.S. government employees covered by this order must retain PID receipts and file for reimbursement of out-of-pocket expenses from their respective departments or agencies." The remaining three pages were an alphabetical list of more than four hundred Americans being ordered home. Under "Q" he found "Quintero, Marcia D."

A.J. shook his head and said, "Marcia, you have to realize this is not personal. It's compiled by some mindless clerk at our embassy in Mexico City."

"No, A.J., that's not the case. There are no other DEA

agents' names on that list but mine. And I know why. The legal attaché is a worthless DOJ slug. He's tried to get me into the sack every time I'm in Mexico City on DEA business. Because my husband and I believe the Marine motto, *Semper Fidelis*, is a way of life, not just a slogan, this useless toad is paying me back for turning him down."

A.J. sat down in one of the chairs and shook his head. This all sounded very much like one of the reasons he didn't miss "new age" government duty. He asked, "Did you contact DEA HQ at Army Navy Drive about this?"

"Not about the legal attaché trying to bed me, but I did talk to the Ops Center watch officer about being ordered home. He told me the administrator is out of Washington and will have to talk personally with the Attorney General about this on Monday, when they are both back in Washington. Well, if the weather forecast is right and this hurricane spins north or blows itself out, I could be either home or in violation of my orders by tomorrow night if you can't get this turned around."

When he nodded in understanding, she continued, "Besides all that, you need my help, A.J. If I'm reading the official message traffic right—and the little trip we just made up north to the coast means what I think it means—things are about to pop here in the Yucatan."

Her comment elicited no visual or audible response from Jones, so she pressed on. "Look, no offense, A.J., but you're no spring chicken anymore. I marvel at how inscrutable you are and what great shape you're in. I couldn't begin to understand all you can do with electronics. But I watched you climb that lighthouse in Progreso with all that wind and rain yesterday. When you got back to the car, you were bushed."

A faint smile appeared on A.J.'s lips and he said, "You

weren't supposed to be *watching* me, you were supposed to be looking away from the lighthouse and *warning* me if anyone was coming. But I take your point. I'll contact some people in Washington to see what can be done."

After seeing Quintero out the door, Jones made two phone calls from the consulate's communications center. The first was to Frankie Moyer's government-issued PID. It didn't answer, so he left a message. The second call was to the home phone of Senator Mackintosh Caperton. They spoke for less than five minutes about having Quintero's travel orders rescinded.

When it was all over, those who survived agreed that trying to help his loyal assistant was the only serious mistake Arthur J. Jones Jr. ever made in his long career.

# CHAPTER TEN

# LOYALTY TEST

**OFFICE OF THE CHIEF OF STAFF**
THE WHITE HOUSE
1600 PENNSYLVANIA AVENUE
WASHINGTON, DC
FRIDAY, 17 SEPTEMBER 2032
0625 HOURS, LOCAL

Muneer Murad was proud of being described as "the most tech-savvy White House chief of staff in history." He was secretly pleased when his detractors labeled him a "techno-geek." His office, on the southwest corner of the West Wing, was crammed with the latest electronic gadgets, courtesy of WHCA—the White House Communications Agency.

Along the wall where predecessors in the chief of staff's office once had a bookcase, Murad mounted a four-foot-high, six-foot-long, quarter-inch-thick sheet of flat ceramic plastic serving as his "A-Viz"—the audiovisual device that replaced televisions a decade before. Powered by magnetic-coil resonators, it had no visible power supply, wires, or speakers. The device could be switched on and off and the volume adjusted using a PID, voice commands, or a card-sized remote. Sound was produced by invisible ceramic piezo-actuators that caused the plastic panel to act as a diaphragm.

No paintings on loan from the Smithsonian or the Corcoran Gallery graced his walls. Instead, a half-dozen black ceramic-plastic sheets—digital image panels—displayed a constantly changing series of landscapes, photo portraits, and modern art. Many of the "digi-pix" images showed Murad with the president and her deceased husband-predecessor.

Murad's telephone—the latest voice-activated, wireless "tele-cube," five inches high, wide, and deep—had no handset. The plastic box served as a speakerphone or allowed him to speak and listen through an earpiece. When he wanted to place a call, he simply said "call-clear" or "call-secure" and the name of the person he wanted to contact, and the six-sided device connected him—glowing red for an encrypted call and green for an unclassified conversation. If the party he was calling had the capability, Murad could activate the tele-cube's embedded cameras, and with a wave of his hand, the device would display the person with whom he was speaking.

\* \* \* \*

At 0615 Murad turned to the tele-cube and said, "Call-secure, Jon Keker." He listened as the phone he was calling rang once and a voice said, "Acting Director Keker is unavailable. If this is an emergency, please contact the FBI switchboard. Please leave a message."

In reply, he said to the box, "Jon, Muneer Murad, call me immediately."

The chief of staff stood behind his desk, impatiently waiting for the return call. Through the windows of his office facing the Washington Monument, he watched the streetlights around the Ellipse turn off as the first hint of dawn tripped a photo-cell somewhere on Constitution Avenue.

Shaking his head to clear away fatigue and cobwebs, he sat down at his desk and scrolled again through the brief message from the Acting Director of the FBI displayed on his wireless, flat-panel computer screen:

```
TOP SECRET/NOFORN/SIGINT
EYES ONLY FOR POTUS & WHCOS
  DTG:    171120ZSEP32
   FM:    ACTING DIR, FBI
   TO:    POTUS/WHCOS
 SUBJ:    ELECTRONIC SURVEILLANCE OF DIPLOMATIC
          MISSION
  REF:    [A] TITLE 50, U.S.C., PUBLIC LAW 95-511,
          "FISA"
          [B] PRESIDENTIAL FINDING #2032-09-16A
```

1. IAW REFS [A] AND [B], FBI SIGINT FACILITY, WASH DC [SIG-FAC DC] COMMENCED INTERCEPTING VOICE, VISUAL & DATA COMMUNICATIONS TO/FROM THE EMBASSY OF THE ISLAMIC CALIPHATE [CAL-EMB] ON MASS. AVE. AT 0001 EDT 17 SEP.

2. IAW REFS [A] AND [B], SIG-FAC DC IS ALSO INTERCEPTING PERSONAL VOICE & DATA COMMUNICATIONS TO/FROM CAL-EMB INDIVIDUALS LISTED IN APPENDIX 1 OF REF [B].

3. UNODIR, SIG-FAC DC WILL PERMANENTLY RETAIN DIGITAL ELECTRONIC TRANSCRIPTS OF ALL INTER-CEPTED COMMUNICATIONS SPECIFIED IN PARA 1 AND 2 ABOVE.

4. IAW REF [B], SIG-FAC DC WILL PROV. A DAILY SYN-OPSIS OF INTERCEPTED COMMUNICATIONS SPECIFIED IN PARA 1 & 2 ABOVE, EYES ONLY TO POTUS, NLT 1900 HOURS EDT/EST.

5. ACTING DIR FBI HAS REQUESTED SSCI/HPSCI CLARI-FICATION RE POSSIBLE INTERCEPTS THAT COULD BE PERCEIVED VIOLATIONS OF CONGRESSIONAL COMMU-NICATIONS PRIVACY PROTECTION ACT [CCPPA].

RESPECTFULLY,
JON KEKER, ACTING DIR, FBI
BT

The tele-cube on the corner of Murad's desk beeped once and glowed red, indicating an incoming secure call. The chief of staff glanced at the little six-sided device, saw "JON KEKER/FBI/HOOVER-WHCA SECURE VOICE," touched the top of the cube with his right index finger, and said as calmly as he could, "Jon, are you alone?"

"Yes," came the voice—radiating from the plastic cube. "I'm in my new office here at the Hoover Building." Then he added gratuitously, "You're the first person I've talked to on this phone since moving into my new office."

"Good. I hope you get to stay there," Murad replied sarcastically. "I'm looking at your message regarding yesterday's presidential FISA finding. What the hell are you thinking?"

There was a pause. Then the voice emanating from the cube said uncertainly, "What do you mean?"

"What do I mean?" Murad responded, his voice rising. "Paragraph five. Look at paragraph five. You have to be more brain-dead than Vic Foster to go to the congressional committees asking for 'clarification.' You're creating an audit trail about this that the press and our political opponents will salivate over."

There was another long moment before the Acting FBI Director responded, "According to our counsel here, we're required to put that paragraph in every FISA notification just in case we inadvertently intercept a call being made by or to a member of Congress. As you know, we're not allowed to—"

"Jon, I don't need you to lecture me about what we're allowed to do and not allowed to do." Murad was standing now, practically shouting at the tele-cube. "The president named you as Acting FBI Director while Vic Foster is incapacitated because she thought you were smart enough to thread the needle over there."

Keker, playing defense, tried to justify the content of his message. "Well, you have to understand, mistakes sometimes happen in this business. This finding requires us to tap hundreds of phones and data ports. Last night when our SIGINT techs were setting this up, they inadvertently intercepted a phone call being made from Mexico to a U.S. senator. They were talking about the missing Dr. Cohen."

Now it was Muneer Murad who was silent for a moment before asking, quietly, "U.S. senator? What U.S. senator?"

"That's the kind of thing we're not supposed to listen in on, even by accident," Keker continued, oblivious to the chief of staff's sudden angst. "We have to be very careful not to keep any—"

"Jon! Shut up!" Murad shouted at the tele-cube. "If you want to stay as Acting Director of the FBI long enough to unpack your pictures from home and hang them on the walls of Vic Foster's office, listen to me!"

Hearing nothing back, Murad continued, his voice loud enough to echo down the West Wing corridor to the Oval Office. "Jon, I want to know—no, let me rephrase that—the president wants to know which U.S. senator is interfering in the foreign policy decisions of the executive branch. I—no, she—she wants to know who the senator is, who the senator was talking to in Mexico, and what was said. And don't send me any messages about it. I want you to call me—on this secure voice circuit—and I want answers before our oh-eight-hundred brief with the president. Do you understand me?"

There was another long pause before the voice on the tele-cube said, "I'll see what I can do."

"Don't see what you can do, Mr. Acting Director. Just get it done." With that Murad touched the top of the cube and the glow faded from the little box. He turned away from the window toward the hallway and was stunned to see a female Secret Service agent reaching to close his office door.

Their eyes met and she said, "Excuse me, sir. I'm just making my rounds before going on Oval Office duty and heard voices. I was just closing your door to give you some privacy."

Murad nodded and said, "Yes. Good. Thank you. What's your name?"

"Special Agent Frances James, sir."

THE WHITE HOUSE
1600 PENNSYLVANIA AVENUE
WASHINGTON, DC
FRIDAY, 17 SEPTEMBER 2032
0815 HOURS, LOCAL

Admiral Stanley Turner, U.S. Navy (Ret.), now in his seventh year as Director of National Intelligence, liked the job, the perks that came with it, and his carefully cultivated reputation as nonpartisan. He had just completed his morning briefing for the president when the chief of staff knocked twice on the curved Roosevelt Corridor door and entered the chamber.

Turner, flanked by General John Smith, the National Security Advisor, and White House Counsel Larry Walsh, stood in front of the Resolute Desk. The president, as usual, was seated. She glanced up at Muneer and said to Turner, "Go on."

The retired admiral, looking suddenly uncomfortable, said, "Perhaps we should continue this conversation later."

"No, I want him"—she nodded toward Murad—"to hear this."

As the chief of staff moved to stand beside Walsh, Turner shrugged his expensively tailored shoulders and continued. "Muneer, I just told the president this information is not included in the PDB. We have concluded the suicide bomber who blew himself up yesterday at Mexico City's Benito Juarez International Airport was actually one of the individuals in the contingent of commandos dispatched by the Caliph."

"How do you know that?" asked Murad.

"We don't *know* it. But our liaison with the MPN—the Mexican National Police—has given us at least some of the imagery from the scene, their preliminary investigation results, and transcripts of eyewitness accounts and interviews with survivors. All of it supports the conclusion that the bomb went off inside one of the two buses ferrying the Caliph's Humanitarian Support Team from their aircraft to a hangar on the other side of the field."

"So why is that such a big secret? Bombs go off in Mexico all the time."

"Because *this* bomb was apparently being worn or carried by one of the people dispatched by the Caliph. The detonation and fire caused at least eleven secondary explosions on the bus—evidently from munitions in the baggage accompanying the Caliph's personnel."

"The PDB has thirty-nine dead and a hundred and five injured. Do we know what caused all the casualties?"

"All but two aboard the first bus, including the Mexican bus driver, seem to have been killed by the primary detonation. Everyone else was hurt or killed by the secondary explosions and fire while trying to rescue those on the lead bus. Though they have not announced it, the MPN claim to have evidence the entire contingent sent by the Caliph was heavily armed."

"I realize I just walked in here—but I don't get it," said Murad. "Why is that a problem for us?"

"Because of the imagery," Turner said, pointing to the eight-by-ten-inch DigiVu digital viewer in the president's hands. "It's very graphic stuff—lots of charred bodies—but several frames show the tail fins of a U.S. AT-8 anti-armor rocket. The manufacturer's ordnance registration codes are clearly visible. Our analysts enlarged the frames and traced the serial number to a shipment from Redstone Arsenal delivered to the Caliph's military warehouse outside Jerusalem six months ago."

"Look, you two, I'm busy," the president said. "Stanley,

cut to the chase. When Murad walked in here, you were about to tell us what else is likely to blow up."

Turner nodded and pressed on. "The Mexicans were already upset with us for saying the Houston attack was an Anark-cartel conspiracy. When we blamed the Federation Cartel for yesterday's airport bombing and closed the border, they went ballistic. Mexican president Domingo Rodriguez is considering whether to announce the airport explosion was caused by the accidental detonation of a Caliphate weapon provided by the U.S.—and accuse the Caliph of exporting terrorism, with our help."

Murad shook his head and asked, "But didn't you just say the explosion on the airport bus was a suicide bomber?"

"That's *our* conclusion—because the DigiVu imagery shows the effects it had on the person closest to where it went off. He was literally blown to pieces. From years of documenting jihadi suicide bombs, we think it looks like he was wrapped in multiple layers of Semtex—probably as much as fifteen or twenty pounds of it. Some of those digi-pix show the blast blew out the entire side of the bus, starting in the third row of seats."

"Couldn't the bomb have been planted beneath the seat by someone else, before the Caliph's people ever got aboard?"

"Perhaps, but one of the two survivors on the bus that blew up told Mexican investigators one of his teammates jumped up and yelled, *'Allahu akbar!'* just before the explosion."

"Can we confirm any of this?" asked Murad.

"Not really. A lot of evidence was destroyed in the subsequent fire and they won't let our forensics experts near the scene to do any testing. The Mexicans have detained all the surviving members of the Caliph's supposed Humanitarian Support contingent and MPN investigators are interrogating each of them individually. If our liaison contact is telling us the truth, the police have found all kinds of weapons, munitions, and military equipment in the Caliph's 'medical supplies' shipment."

"Have any of the survivors said what a military unit was doing on a humanitarian aid mission?" asked Muneer.

"According to our liaison source, they claim they were along to protect their medical and relief personnel. The Mexicans think that's a cover story and aren't buying it. Rodriguez seems prepared to tell the world the Caliph sent jihadists to Mexico to overthrow his government—at our direction."

The president stood, handed Turner the digital viewing device, looked at the four men in front of her desk, and said, "I can't figure out what Rodriguez stands to gain from any of this."

When no one else spoke, Smith said, "Here's the short form: Fifteen percent of Mexico's entire gross domestic product comes from Federation Cartel cocaine shipments. They deliver across the border into the U.S. and into Europe through West Africa. The Federation is essentially running Mexico. They killed the last two Mexican presidents, and Rodriguez knows he is alive today because the Federation Cartel lets him live. They can't buy him, so they rent him and much of his government. Now they have reason to kill him."

"And the reason?" Muneer asked.

Smith: "The thugs running the Federation are furious we fingered them for terrorism because it cuts their international travel and banking options. Being placed on the UN's International Terror Watch List effectively limits them to Caracas, La Paz, Quito, Managua, and Havana. Unless Rodriguez can show the world the cartel isn't committing terrorism, he's expendable."

"I got it," said the chief of staff. "Rodriguez proves his loyalty to the Federation by accusing the Caliph of terrorism—aided and abetted by Yankee imperialists—and the cartel lets him live. That could hurt us."

"Could hurt?" the president said, leaning over her desk. "The Mexican president, who is also former head of the OAS and former UN Secretary-General, accusing the U.S. government of helping the Caliph commit terrorism will finish my campaign. Think, gentlemen. How do we convince Rodriguez to keep a lid on all this until after the election?"

Once again the four were silent, until Turner spoke very quietly. "According to his psychological profile, Rodriguez is very pragmatic. He responds to carrots and sticks. We have some of each."

"Such as?"

"Rodriguez is vulnerable. He and the Federation Cartel bankers have done a good job of hiding whatever he is getting from the cocaine trade. But we know he also does business with the junior cartels that move meth, hash, marijuana, and people across the border."

"People? What people?" she asked.

Turner grimaced and said, "The Gulf, Juarez, and Tijuana cartels move a lot of people into the U.S. through their family networks. Not all the people they move are sex slaves, domestic servants, farm laborers, and construction workers. Some of those they move—for a price, a portion of which goes into Rodriguez's hidden bank accounts—are Hezbollah and Hamas agents coming in from Venezuela. If we very privately let Rodriguez know what we know about his profiting from moving people, particularly children for the sex trade, we will probably lose some valuable intelligence assets—but it could be enough of a stick to keep him quiet for six weeks or more.

Allegations about profiting from human trafficking would end his hopes for a Nobel Peace Prize."

"And the carrots?"

"The Strategic Petroleum Reserve. We tell Rodriguez, again very privately, that we will replenish the SPR with Mexican crude at world-market price plus, after you are reelected. He gets to pocket the 'plus.'"

"Wait. We can't do that," Murad interrupted. "We've already privately told the Caliph we're going to buy Caliphate oil for the SPR after the election at whatever price OPEC—"

"Shut up, Muneer!" she snapped. "John, how much oil do we need to top off the SPR?"

Smith, already consulting his PID, replied, "Since imposing the ban on domestic and offshore drilling, we have drawn the SPR down to 149 million barrels. To 'top it off,' as you put it, we would have to add 851 million barrels. With winter coming on, we will have to replenish supplies for heating oil from foreign sources starting in mid-November. Those numbers are of course classified."

The president pondered this information for a moment, looked at Turner, and asked, "So how do we let Mr. Rodriguez know about these carrots and sticks and advise him it's in his best interest to keep his mouth shut about the Caliph's commandos and the U.S.-made ordnance in those digi-pix?"

"If that is the message you want passed, I can arrange it," Admiral Turner replied. "But I will have to make a quick, quiet trip to Mexico City as soon as Hurricane Lucy is clear."

"And then what do we tell the Caliph when the SPR 'carrot' leaks from Mexico?" asked the chief of staff, still stinging from her rebuke.

"Look, if it comes out before the election, have one of

our pet reporters deny the story," she replied firmly. "Prosecute anyone who tries to report it under our Fairness in Media laws, and if someone posts it on one of those MESH sites, lock them up as a national security risk. If it leaks after November second, it won't matter. We'll just cut a new deal with Rodriguez and the Caliph. As long as nobody outside this room knows how much crude we need to replenish the SPR we can just get half from each of them," she said decisively.

Then, turning to the DNI, she continued, "Stanley, as soon as this hurricane is past, get to Mexico and make sure my good friend President Rodriguez keeps all this business about the Caliph's commandos under his sombrero until after the election. Now, I have other work to do. Muneer, you and Larry stay here for a moment."

As the door closed behind Smith and Turner, the president sat back down and said, "Muneer, did you and Larry have a chance to discuss what you told me earlier this morning about this Senator Caperton's caper?"

"Only what I finally learned from Keker about the bureau's Signals Intelligence technicians inadvertently overhearing a conversation between Senator Mackintosh Caperton and an individual in Mexico. During the call they discussed a person named Marcia Quintero and her importance in locating Dr. Martin Cohen."

"Have we determined where Cohen is?"

"Not for certain. His PERT signals were being picked up intermittently from a location three or four miles inland from the north coast of the Yucatan until shortly after noon yesterday, but they haven't been heard since."

"What do we know about Caperton?"

"More than we know about Cohen. I sent his official bio to your PID. In addition, we know he has Anark tendencies—just like most of his crazy right-wing constituents in Montana. He's also been to a bunch of those Freedom Congress rallies and—"

"So Caperton is an Anark and a 'Free-Cong.' Who was he talking to in Mexico?"

"We don't know yet. Keker finally told me the call to Caperton was placed from the U.S. Consulate in Merida, Mexico, by a male who referred to himself as 'A-Jay.' We have no USG employees there with that name, nick-name, or initials. He could be a contractor with access. State is going to quietly inquire with the consul general later today to see what he knows, but I think we need to find out more about what Caperton is up to. Larry disagrees."

She looked at her lawyer. Walsh had not uttered a word since the meeting commenced. He began. "Madam President, I'm *your* lawyer—not Muneer's. Any advice I give *you* privately is privileged. Anything I say to you in the presence of others is not. I strongly recommend—"

"Larry, I don't have time for this legal crap!" she exclaimed, cutting him off. "I want to know what Caperton is up to, who he is talking to, what laws he may be break-ing. As you may have noticed in the information Muneer collected on him, Caperton is a Naval Academy classmate of Peter Newman—father of the fugitive James Newman. And in case you haven't made the connections, this is the same James Newman who is suspected of having illegally entered the United States from Canada across the border into Montana."

"Yes." Walsh nodded meekly in her wrath. "I realize Senator Caperton is from Montana, but—"

"Good, I'm glad you realize all this. So let's get to the point. If a member of Congress is suspected of commit-ting a crime by aiding a fugitive suspected of involvement in terrorism, isn't that sufficient cause to overcome the restrictions of the Congressional Communications Privacy Protection Act?"

"It's not settled law. Back in 2026, your husband ordered the Attorney General to tap the phones of several of the congressmen and senators on the special committee investigating what happened on the Iran-Afghan border during Operation Protect Freedom. As you recall, the evidence collected then was never used, because all charges were eventually dropped and—"

"Larry, stop! Answer my question. If Senator Mackintosh Caperton is suspected of breaking the law, can we intercept his communications or not?"

Walsh shrugged and said, "I don't know. I suppose if the Attorney General agrees it is warranted, he can direct the FBI to do it as a Criminal Intelligence Surveillance activity."

"Good. Stop talking. Go write up an order for the AG to sign, directing the FBI to intercept all of Senator Caperton's communications between now and November first in order to assist in the apprehension of a federal fugitive. Muneer will deliver it to the Attorney General."

Muneer and Walsh were headed out the door to the Roosevelt Corridor when the lawyer turned and said, "It may be a fine point, Madam President, but technically James Newman won't be a federal fugitive until such time as we have a warrant for his arrest. That won't be until later today, when we get a sealed indictment from the grand jury."

"That will do," she said. "Maybe we can apprehend both Newman and Caperton at the same time."

As Murad pulled the heavy door closed, he nearly collided with the same Secret Service agent he spoke with outside his own office little more than two hours earlier. Proud of his photographic memory he said, "Hello again, Frances."

## PARKSIDE COMMUNITY CHURCH

DULLES, VA
FRIDAY, 17 SEPTEMBER 2032
1230 HOURS, LOCAL

The old sanctuary of Parkside Community Church was a special place for Rachel Newman. It was here, on the evening of March 3, 1995, that Rachel began what she called her "joyful walk beside our Lord and Savior." That journey began when Lucy Brooks, the pastor's wife, glimpsed the anguish in Rachel's face, sat down beside her, and said, "I saw you sitting here and you looked like your heart was breaking. Would you like me to pray with you?"

Now, more than thirty-seven years later, there was a new, larger sanctuary; Lucy and Rachel were the closest of friends; and the old sanctuary was used for outreach ministries, homeschooling events, and choir rehearsals. And every once in a while, the two women adjourned there after a church leadership meeting or a Bible study to just pray quietly for a few minutes and savor the blessing of their long friendship.

When Peter and Rachel moved to Narnia in 2010, they made Parkside Community their church home. On Sabbath mornings, between services, Peter started teaching a Sunday school class and Rachel began leading a women's Bible study for the spouses of Soldiers, Sailors, Airmen, Guardsmen, and Marines deployed around the world in the war against radical Islam.

Though Rachel welcomed the challenge of preparing her weekly lessons, coping with the questions of anxious wives and consoling grief-stricken widows was an emotional roller coaster, taxing all her experience as the mate of a Marine since 1980. To assist in helping her "students" through their difficulties, Rachel often called on her husband, Peter, for his practical wisdom and her friend Lucy for spiritual counsel.

Five years earlier, Rachel started a second study group—called "God, Women, and Government." The class—composed of professional women, most of them single, convened on Thursday evenings at seven in a Sunday school classroom. After this week's lesson, one of her students asked Rachel for a private appointment at her earliest convenience. They agreed to meet in the old sanctuary at twelve thirty the following day.

* * * *

Rachel arrived at the church a half hour early—driving quickly without traffic from Narnia, east on Virginia Route 7 to the Greenway at Leesburg, and exiting at Route 606 for the church. She spent a few minutes talking to Lucy, told her about the appointment, and went to wait. She sat in her favorite spot—the pew where she first encountered Lucy and Jesus in 1995.

Uncertain of the purpose of the meeting, Rachel prayed for wisdom. She had just finished reading Solomon's advice on the matter—in Proverbs 9—when the door opened behind her.

The young woman, silhouetted in the doorway, peered cautiously into the dimly lit auditorium, seemingly hesitant until Rachel waved and said, "Over here, dear."

Frances James entered, and when Rachel motioned to the space beside her in the pew, she sat beside the older woman and said, "Thank you for agreeing to meet with me on such short notice, Mrs. Newman."

Smiling, she replied, "Please, Frances, call me Rachel. I'm glad it worked out. How can I help you?"

Without preamble, the younger woman began. "Rachel, I am a Secret Service agent at the White House. I very badly need some good advice from someone who knows the Lord, a person I can trust, one who will not divulge what I am about to say, and a person who can help me discern the right thing to do."

"Well, Frances, I certainly meet the first requirement. Hopefully, I have the remaining qualities. Before you begin, let me ask you a few questions. Is that okay?"

"Certainly."

"How old are you, Frances?"

"Thirty-three."

"How long have *you* known Jesus as your Lord?"

"Since April 2029, my second week coming here to church. I attended General Newman's Sunday school class. He was explaining the plan of salvation. It changed my life."

"It's evident from your participation in our class that you prepare. Do you read the Word regularly?"

"Yes. Sometimes it's the only way I could get through the day. I would be at your class more often but my duty shift changes every month. And now with the campaign, we do a lot more traveling."

"What is it that brought you here today?"

"The lesson you gave us for this week was the first chapter of Paul's letter to the church in Rome. When I read verse twenty-five—'They exchanged the truth of God for a lie, and worshipped and served something created instead of the Creator, who is blessed forever'—I finally realized, I'm surrounded by people like that every day I go to work."

Rachel was surprised at the young woman's vehemence and was concerned about whether she might even be unstable. Trying to assess the origin of the young Secret Service agent's anger, she said, "You know, Frances, Paul didn't write that as a political statement."

"Oh, I understand that. But I'm not talking about politics. I'm talking about right versus wrong—good versus evil. Where I work there is very little good, a great deal of evil, and I do not know whom—if anyone—I can trust. I'm not supposed to share any of what I see or hear on the job with anyone but my Supervisory Special Agent. And worst of all, some of what I have heard in the last few days affects your family."

Rachel looked intently at the younger woman for what seemed an eternity. Then, making up her mind, she said, very quietly, "Tell me what you have heard."

\* \* \* \*

It took nearly an hour for Secret Service Agent Frances James to tell Rachel Newman everything: about White House meetings in which the president, her chief of staff, National Security Advisor, and lawyer plotted whom to blame for the 9-11-32 attacks in Houston; about secret "no-terror-now" deals with the Caliph; about phony FBI reports and doctored intelligence; and about plots to ensure Dr. Martin Cohen did not materialize before the election.

The young Secret Service agent delivered the information in a straightforward, businesslike manner, chronologically, in the sequence in which she heard it over the course of the last week. She did it without referring to her PID or any notes. Through most of it, Rachel simply nodded and uttered an occasional "uh huh."

But when Frances described the progression of false charges against her son James, Rachel probed for more information. "Did you hear any of them say the name of anyone in Canada who thinks James had anything to do with the death of Dr. Long?"

"No."

"You said they talked about James and evidence being presented to a grand jury. Did they say when they might indict him?"

"This afternoon."

"When you heard the chief of staff yelling at the Acting FBI Director this morning, did you hear the name of the senator they want to wiretap?"

"Yes. His name is Caperton. Senator Mackintosh Caperton."

"Did you hear when they were going to start intercepting his communications?"

"I think it may have already started."

When Rachel ran out of questions, she said, "Frances, I am grateful you shared this information with me. I don't know what advice to give you right now other than to pray. That may sound very glib—maybe even inadequate right now—but it works for me. And I have been in some pretty tough spots more than once."

"I understand, Mrs. Newman. I didn't expect you to tell me exactly what to do today. I can't go to the FBI. I don't really trust my supervisor. I will have to decide what to do before the fifteenth of October, when I have my quarterly polygraph. One of the questions they always ask is 'Have you talked to anyone outside the Secret Service about what you have seen or heard on duty?'"

"Well, I certainly understand now why you are alarmed. If you don't mind, I will talk to my husband about this. I won't tell anyone else. And I feel led to suggest you shouldn't either, until we see each other again. Will you be here for our Bible study next Thursday?"

Frances nodded and said, "Unless something happens and they change the duty roster, I'll be here. I won't talk to anyone else about this until we see each other again. And I would appreciate you telling me then what General

Newman thinks as well. But I am concerned he might think I'm a nut case or perhaps even a provocation from the people who are out to do harm to your family. I'm not."

"I don't think you're nuts—nor do I believe you are in league with those who have apparently forgotten their oath of office."

"Well, I just want you to know I'm here because I really do care about you and what happens to your family. You see, I knew you before I ever met you."

Confused, Rachel asked, "What do you mean?"

"Full disclosure here, Rachel. You see, 'James' isn't my maiden name. My husband, Bill James, was a Navy SEAL. He was killed four years ago in Yemen. My maiden name was Vecchio. My father, Mitch, was a TWA pilot. He was apparently a pretty good pilot but not much of a dad and certainly no model husband. But he carried a picture of you until the day he died—drunk, as it turns out."

Rachel was stunned, but tried hard not to show it. She hoped the dim lights would not reveal the color rising in her cheeks. After a moment of silence Rachel said, "Your father carried a picture of me?"

"Yes. It was you, my father, another pilot, and two other TWA flight attendants in an airport somewhere. I found it in his wallet, years after he walked out on my mother. I was spending one of those 'parent exchange weekends' the kids of divorced parents have to endure."

Rachel shook her head and asked, "Why would he do that?"

"Carry your picture? I actually asked him once—when he came to see me while I was in college. He got drunk at a frat party and I had to take him to a motel off campus. The next day I asked him why he had the picture and he rambled on at length about you being the most wonderful woman he ever met."

"I have to admit, Frances, I'm astounded."

"Well, I'm not. Since starting your Bible study here, I've spent a lot more time with you than I did with him. You are an amazing person, Rachel. Everyone in this church who knows you says the same thing. My father didn't elaborate about your relationship, but I gathered from the way he said it that there was more between you two than just time in an airplane. He was married three times that I know of and he never spoke of his wives—not even my mother—the way he talked about you."

"Did he come to know the Lord before he died?"

"I don't know, because at the time, I didn't either, and it never occurred to me to ask. But I do have a question for you."

"Go ahead."

"If this is none of my business, just say so, but I would like to know how you and General Newman handled the business of my father in your lives."

Rachel thought for a moment, then said, "Your father wasn't really part of my husband's life. He was part of my old life. And as Paul wrote to the church in Corinth two thousand years ago, '. . . if anyone is in Christ, there is a new creation; old things have passed away, and look, new things have come.' Those of us who are new creations have no need to bring up old things."

# CHAPTER ELEVEN

## QUEST FOR FREEDOM . . .

**4 MILES EAST OF DZILAM DE BRAVO**

YUCATAN STATE, MEXICO

FRIDAY, 17 SEPTEMBER 2032

1330 HOURS, LOCAL

His first sensation was acute pain. It radiated from the back of his head, down his neck, into his shoulders. He briefly opened his eyes but they would not focus, and light intensified the severe ache pulsing in his skull—so he closed them. In minutes he was asleep once more.

When he awoke the next time, the throbbing he felt earlier was less intense, so he opened his eyes again. This time he could see nothing and for a moment he thought he might be blind. Then he realized it was completely dark.

Deprived of sight, the old admiral checked his other senses like a ship's captain running down a checklist before setting out to sea. He could hear wind and heavy rain beating on a metal roof—but didn't feel it hitting him, so he assumed his hearing was unimpaired and he was inside a structure. He recognized his own body odor—and the scent of others—apparently nearby, though he couldn't see or hear anyone. His tongue, dry as sandpaper, denied him any taste—but reminded him of his intense thirst.

He could tell he was on his back, loosely tied to a mattress or a bed, his hands bound to his sides. From the dampness of his clothing and the smell, he knew he had lost control of his bladder while unconscious. When he tried to raise his legs, he realized they too were tethered by fetters he could not see and barely feel except when he moved. To shoo away flies lighting on his face, he shook his head from side to side and experienced vertigo and mild nausea—and concluded he had sustained a head injury, perhaps a concussion.

After conducting his own corporeal diagnosis, he tried to determine how he came to be in this situation. Though it aggravated the dull headache, he forced himself to re-call details of how he was kidnapped in Houston, events aboard the *Ileana Rosario*, abandoning the sinking vessel in the midst of a hurricane—and being cast ashore by the storm on what he assumed was the north coast of the Yucatan Peninsula.

Cohen remembered fleeing his captors on the beach and the long trek through howling wind and rain to an apparently abandoned farmhouse. He had no awareness of what transpired after he arrived on the porch of the dwelling. Nor did he know where he was now, how long he had been unconscious, or who had tied him down.

Feeling somewhat encouraged by his physical and mental assessment, he decided it was time to discover who else was here with him. He cleared his throat and called out a raspy *"¡Hola!"*

Almost immediately, a voice he recognized bellowed in English, "Silence, Jew, or I will cut off your head."

In the dark, despite being thirsty, hungry, dirty, and unable to move more than a few inches in any direction, Marty Cohen smiled. His head throbbed from an injury he hoped wasn't a fractured skull. Yet he was strangely comforted by the voice of his "captor-in-chief."

"Ahmad," the old admiral shouted hoarsely above the noise of rain pelting on the metal roof and the howling wind outside, "you are proof the devil I know is better than the one I don't! I need a drink of water."

"Too bad, you filthy Jew. You tried to escape. You will have to wait until morning. Shut up or I will kill you now."

The exertion of shouting over the raging maelstrom aggravated the pain in his head and for several moments Cohen heard nothing but the noise of the storm. Suddenly he felt, rather than saw or heard, the presence of someone very near. A hand touched his face and he instinctively flinched as adrenaline raced in his abdomen. Then a voice very close to his ear whispered, *"Agua, para usted."*

*"¿Quién es?"* he croaked, barely audible. Who is it?

The whisperer replied, *"Beba esto."* Here, drink.

Cohen felt something round, smooth, and hard being pressed lightly to his lips and realized it was the top of a bottle. As it was tipped up, water flowed over his parched lips and he swallowed until the container was empty. His thirst quelled if not quenched, the old man muttered *"Mil gracias"* to his unknown benefactor. In a matter of minutes he was asleep once more.

* * * *

The sound of Ahmad's voice awakened him. Dim, gray daylight illuminated his surroundings but for several moments Cohen was disoriented and did not grasp he was hearing voices from another room. Rain was still falling steadily on the metal roof, but the wind had died and it was apparent the hurricane was finally blowing itself out.

Immobilized, except for his head, Cohen surveyed his surroundings. He realized he was tied to a low, narrow cot in a small, ten-by-ten-foot room with sand-colored, stucco walls unadorned by paint or decoration. Above him, there were rough-hewn beams and rafters and a corrugated sheet metal roof. Though he did not recall any signs of an electric line running to the house, there was a bare light fixture with a pull-cord attached to a beam over the center of the room. Behind him, a window provided the only source of illumination. To his left was an interior door, through which he could hear two, perhaps three male voices—one of them Ahmad's—speaking what sounded to the old man like Farsi.

He arched his neck, striving to see out the window behind him, and instantly felt a spasm of pain from a large lump on the back of his head. As he stopped straining, a quiet voice from that direction whispered, *"¿Quiéres mas agua, señor?"* Do you want more water?

*"Sí,"* Cohen replied, and without another sound, a young boy holding a beer bottle appeared beside him. The youth knelt beside the cot, held the bottle to the old man's lips, and gently tipped it up, pouring the liquid into the admiral's mouth.

When the bottle was drained, the admiral whispered, *"Gracias. ¿Cuál es su nombre?"*

He was surprised when the boy answered in a low voice with a strangely British accent, "My name is Felipe. What is your name, *señor?*"

"My name is Martin."

"You speak English, Señor Martin?"

"Yes, Felipe, I do. Thank you for the water."

"You are welcome, Señor Martin."

"Was it you who gave me water before?"

"Yes. Last night."

"That was very kind of you, Felipe. I was very thirsty."

"I was afraid you were going to die, like Jorge. You slept for many hours after the man hit you with the club. I am glad you did not die, Señor Martin."

"So am I, Felipe. Tell me, what are you doing here?"

"I live here."

"Alone? How old are you?"

"I am eleven. My father and mother and my two younger sisters went to Merida two days ago to celebrate Independence Day with my cousins. My sixteen-year-old brother Jorge and I stayed here to protect our *finca* from the *cartelistos* who burn places that are not occupied." Tears suddenly welled up in the boy's big brown eyes and his lower lip trembled as he continued. "We did not do a very good job."

"Where is your brother?"

At this the tears overflowed and ran down Felipe's face. "Yesterday morning when the storm was very fierce, we went to the barn to make sure our two cows were safe. The wind blew part of the roof down on Jorge and killed him."

"Dear God. Are you sure he is dead?"

"Yes. I could not move the heavy wood that was on top of him. I was running to Señor Macklin's to get help when the four men who hit you caught me. I took them to where Jorge was under the barn but he had no breath. They made me come into the house with them and then you came and they hit you and they tied you up and put us together in this room."

"Is that door," Cohen asked, gesturing with his head, "the only way out of here?"

"Yes. The windows all have bars. And I heard them put a chain on the door. I tried to open it, but I cannot."

"You said there are four of them. What do they look like?"

"Two of them have very black beards. They look like *cartelistos* or pirates. The old one and the one who is *el jefe* do not have beards."

Cohen thought back to the terrorists he assigned to lifeboats on the *Ileana Rosario*. Ebi matched the "old one" description. Ahmad was certainly *el jefe*. And the two he recalled having black beards were Massoud and Rostam. He asked, "Do they have weapons?"

"They found the trapdoor beneath the kitchen floor where my father keeps his guns."

"What kind of guns?"

"Two AK rifles and a pistol. My father taught Jorge and me how to shoot them."

Cohen chose not to inquire why a poor farmer might need two military rifles in his house but asked instead, "Where did you learn to speak English so well, Felipe?"

"Our neighbor, Señor Macklin, has been teaching me English since I was a little boy. He was once a British soldier and he is a very kind man. He has a large *finca*. My father and mother work for him. He gave them this house and this land."

"How far is Señor Macklin's house from here?"

The boy shrugged, thought for a few seconds, and said, "Perhaps two kilometers."

"What direction?"

"Toward Dzilam de Bravo."

"Is that south, east, or west of here?"

"I am sorry, Señor Martin, I do not know directions. It is that way," he added, pointing to the wall opposite the window, "toward the sunset."

Cohen nodded and continued. "Do any of the four men who tied me up know you speak English?"

"No. *El jefe* is the only one who has said anything in English. He and the others speak a language I do not understand, but I heard him say he was going to cut off your head. That is what the *cartelistos* do to their enemies. Why does he want to kill you?"

"He is a very bad man, Felipe. Try to make sure he does not know you can understand or speak English. It may help us both."

The boy nodded and then asked, "Why did *el jefe* call you a 'filthy Jew'? Are you a Jew?"

"Yes."

"Señor Macklin used his Bible to teach Jorge and me how to read. He told us the Jews are God's chosen people and they are hated by those who do not know the One True God. Is that true?"

"Yes, I suppose it is," Cohen replied, thinking it surreal to be having a theological discussion with an eleven-year-old boy while chained to a bed in Mexico.

Felipe went on. "Señor Macklin is a very wise man with many books. One of his books has pictures of people called Nazis who killed many, many Jews. Are the four men who hit you and tied you up Nazis?"

The old man pondered the question for a moment, then said, "Yes, Felipe, they are like the Nazis in Señor Macklin's book. They have no respect for human life. Do you understand what I mean?"

"Yes, I think so. Does that mean they will kill me, too?"

"I hope they will not kill either one of us."

"Moses led the Jews to freedom. Can you lead us to freedom?"

Cohen was about to answer when they heard a chain

rattling on the door. By the time Ahmad swung the door open and stomped into the room, Felipe was again hunkered in the corner wrapped in a cotton blanket and the admiral was feigning sleep.

"Wake up, you stinking Jew!" Ahmad shouted as he poked his trussed-up captive in the side with the muzzle of an ancient but lethal-looking AK-47.

"You thought you could escape? If I had not been ordered to keep you alive, I would kill you now, Jew. How long has your PERT been uncovered?" Ahmad demanded, pointing at Marty Cohen's feet.

The old admiral raised his head to look at the tattered remains of the aluminum foil, foliage, and duct-tape boots he fashioned from the shielding his kidnappers wrapped around his foot before they abandoned the *Ileana Rosario*. He stared at his captor, shrugged, and said, "I do not know."

Ahmad doubled up his fist and snarled, "How long has your PERT been open like this, Jew?"

"The foil you wrapped around my leg started coming apart when the storm flipped us over the first time—while I was pulling you back into the life raft and saving your life."

"You are a fool, Jew. If you were not a Kaffir you would know better than to thwart Allah's will. I should have cut off your foot containing the PERT."

"There is no need to cut off my foot. My PERT has not been charged in more than six days. The battery is surely dead."

"You had better hope so, Jew. Because if your PERT is transmitting our location and we are caught, I will cut off your head."

Cohen looked at him for a long moment, shook his head, and said, "How can you speak this way? You are an educated man. While we were on the life raft you told me you were born in the United States and didn't go to Iran until you were a teenage boy. I saved your life more than once in the last few days. Why do you hate me?"

"Because you are a Kaffir. You practice *fitna*. You oppose the will of Allah as told to us by Muhammad. That is enough." Then, reaching into his pocket, Ahmad withdrew the knife Rikki used to cut their life raft free from the *Ileana Rosario*.

As the terrorist flicked open the blade, Cohen's reaction was instinctive but futile as he strained against his bonds to defend himself.

Standing over the old man, brandishing the knife in his right hand, the Iranian chuckled mirthlessly and said, "Hold still, Jew, I am going to cut you loose." As he severed the ropes holding the old man's wrists and ankles, Ahmad gestured toward Felipe with the rifle and said, "I am untying you, Jew, so you can talk to this boy in his infidel tongue."

**CAIR PARAVEL**
PAWLEYS ISLAND, SC
FRIDAY, 17 SEPTEMBER 2032
1930 HOURS, LOCAL

She arrived just as they were sitting down to dinner. They had all just joined hands around the table to offer a blessing over the food when the security system chimed, signaling the gate in front of the house was unlocking. A moment later the living room door opened and she walked in. Peter's salient observation, "You never cease to amaze me," was echoed by everyone at the table.

After hugs and kisses all around, she said, as though her surprise arrival should have been anticipated, "I just couldn't miss tonight's tenth wedding anniversary celebration and tomorrow's birthday party for Seth."

"Yeah," said James with a smile, "Sarah and I were concerned our anniversary just wouldn't be complete without you being with us, Mom—and here you are. How did you get here, on your broom?"

Rachel gave her son a withering look—the kind he came to know as a child—and said, "Heed the Fifth Commandment, James, and watch your mouth. Words some people think are funny don't sound that way when they come from the lips of your own offspring. And by the way, you need a shave."

In an effort to avert the sudden friction, Peter said, "James is growing a beard. I'm glad you're here. I missed you." As the four boys clambered for their grandmother's attention, he set another place at the table and added, "James and Sarah decided to celebrate their anniversary here at Cair Paravel. We have a delightful dinner this evening, catered by the nice people at Chive Blossom Cafe. Let's thank God for this good food, your safe, if unexpected, arrival, and eat."

They did. And during the meal the four adults tried to refrain from discussing anything but the most lighthearted topics. Seth prompted the closest thing to a serious exchange when he asked, "How did you get here, Nan?"

"I flew from Winchester to Myrtle Beach with Henry Simmons, CSG's chief pilot, in the Beech King Air 450. You boys have flown in that plane before. Remember the trip we made to the air show in Oshkosh, Wisconsin, a few years ago?"

"Oh yeah," Josh interjected with a grin. "That was where Seth got lost in an old airplane."

"I wasn't lost. And it wasn't just an old airplane, it was a World War II B-17 and I was in the cockpit."

James joined in. "And how did we find you?"

"My PERT."

"Right. And now that none of our PERTs are transmitting anymore, what's the new rule?"

The two older boys answered in unison, "Stay with Mom and Dad and keep an eye on our little brothers."

"Right, again," James replied. Then, looking at his mother, he said, "I'm sorry for my mean comment when you arrived. Did Henry bring you from the airport to Cair Paravel?"

"You're forgiven. Yes. Henry rented a car at Myrtle, dropped me here, and is staying at the Sea View Inn. The DEA has chartered the 450 and he's flying it on to Fort Worth when they call for it."

James glanced at his father, caught Peter's quick shake of his head no, and let the matter drop. For the remainder of the meal, conversation focused on an enormous horseshoe crab that washed up on the beach and the best techniques for coaxing seagulls into snatching bread crusts from a boy's upraised hand.

After James and Sarah took the children upstairs to read stories and put them to bed, Peter and Rachel began clearing the table. They were no sooner alone than Rachel said quietly, "I'm sorry for the unexpected arrival, but I needed a way to tell you what I learned this afternoon from a Secret Service agent. James is in great jeopardy. So is Mack Caperton—perhaps more than any of us anticipated. I didn't want to call."

Peter stopped placing items in the dishwasher, turned to his wife, and said, "That was very smart. Let's go for a walk on the beach."

They took off their shoes on the porch and headed out into the dim light of a waning crescent moon. The temperature had dropped and the light breeze shifted offshore. Peter draped his light cotton sweater over Rachel's shoulders as they walked slowly south on the deserted white sand.

The sliver of moon set and the couple passed the pier jutting into the Atlantic before Rachel completed her summary of all she had learned that afternoon. The only thing she omitted was the part about Frances's father. When she finished her account, Rachel asked, "Is there any way to find out if our son was secretly indicted this afternoon?"

Peter had not spoken since they began their walk and now he said, "I don't know. But let me ask a few questions first. Do you trust this woman?"

"Yes. After meeting with her, I went to the CSG Ops Center. Don Gabbard helped me verify her background information. It all matched what she told me."

"You don't think she was sent by someone at the White House to see how we would respond to the information—what we call a provocation?"

"It occurred to me but as Don pointed out, we weren't being targeted by the government when she joined the church and started attending your Sunday school class or my Bible study for women in government. She may be a great actress, but she seems genuinely concerned and straightforward about what she overheard and relayed to me."

Peter nodded in the dark and said, "That's good enough for me. You have always had greater gifts of perception and discernment than I. For as long as I've known you, people have been willing to share the most amazing things with you they wouldn't tell others under torture."

Rachel snickered, "I think that's a compliment." After a moment of silence, she asked, "So if we believe Frances's story, where does that leave us with finding out about whether our only boy has been indicted by these creeps?"

"I'm not sure. Certainly the U.S. attorney for the District of Columbia would know if a sealed indictment was handed down by a grand jury. I would normally just call Mack or Judge Hodson in Richmond, but given what you told me about the communications intercepts, we have to be very careful how we go about inquiring."

"Do we have any way to warn Mack Caperton that his communications are being monitored?"

"Yes. But we're going to have to start exchanging information the way criminals do to avoid being detected on the MESH. Back at the house, in the safe hidden behind the fireplace, we have a thousand disposable, prepaid MESH interface devices—just like our PIDs—only unregistered."

"A thousand? Why so many?"

"Because we never want to use the same one more than once or twice. Unlike a PID, or a registered MESH phone, these don't have an integral GPS chip and they can't be recharged. They really are meant to be disposable."

"Where did you get them?"

"From Mack. He brought them with him when he came here on Wednesday. I don't know precisely how he got them."

"Are those the things the government calls Anark MESH links? They're illegal, aren't they?"

"Yes to both. But the Chinese still manufacture them by the millions and sell them all over the world on the black market. And according to Mack, there are Anark workshops in places like Montana, Wyoming, Idaho, and Texas that produce them as well. We just have to be very careful how we use them."

"What do you mean by careful?"

"Every device that accesses the MESH—whether it's a

PERT, a PID, a telephone, a computer, even an Au-Vid camera—has a unique electronic interface code that identifies what it is and who owns it. It's called a device recognition signal—DRS for short. By international treaty and U.S. law, every DRS has to be registered to a business or an individual's Personal Identification Number. Here in the U.S. that's a business tax-ID number or an individual Social Security number. The Anark MESH link devices in the safe at the house each have a DRS—otherwise they wouldn't work—but their registrations are all phony."

"Will we be breaking the law if we use them?"

"Yes. It's illegal to send or receive information over the MESH from an unregistered device—even though it happens all the time. The UN and national governments can't collect their MESH user fees—what the Anarks call MESH Taxes—from unregistered devices. Anyone caught using an unregistered MESH interface device can be prosecuted for violating international, federal, and state laws—and the IRS code."

"Why would anyone take such a chance?"

"Some people use unregistered devices to avoid paying the MESH Tax. Others use them for privacy or secrecy. That's certainly why criminals and terrorists use them. The fact is, very few people actually get caught—and when they do it's usually while they are in the process of committing some other crime."

"So can we just call Mack on one of these unregistered devices to warn him about being intercepted and find out about whether a secret warrant has been issued to arrest our son?"

"We can't call him directly. Based on what your Secret Service agent told you, we should assume Mack's communications are being monitored twenty-four seven in real time—and the people doing the intercepts will be able to determine the DRS of the device originating the contact almost instantly. If it's a voice call, they will be able to run a voice pattern analysis—and identify the caller from his or her audible fingerprint in an hour or so."

"How about just sending him a text message?"

"A data or text message sent on one of the Anark MESH link devices is safer for the originator because the people intercepting the communication can't do a voice ID. They may eventually be able to decrypt the message—but the greater concern is they will know the sender's location within seconds even though they won't know who it is."

"How do they know the location of the sender? I thought you said these unregistered devices don't have a GPS chip in them."

"That's correct. But the FBI or any other government agency intercepting messages being sent to Mack can backtrack to the portal where the device with the unregistered DRS entered the MESH. They would know the message originated on or near Pawleys Island, South Carolina, in less than half a minute."

"Then what good are they if we can't use them?"

"We can use them, but we have to go through a series of cutouts. It takes a little longer to get a message through, but it's much safer and it helps protect the recipient—in this case, Mack."

"What do you mean by cutouts?"

"It works like this. We use one of the unregistered Anark MESH link devices to send an encrypted message to another unregistered device in some other place—"

"You mean to another Anark?"

"Some of them probably are Anarks. According to Mack, many are former SEALs, soldiers, and Marines. He calls them his 'trusted MESH addressees'—and describes

them as 'People of the Book who know bullets and ballots.' We send our text message for Mack to one of those
unregistered MESH addresses. The recipient scrapes off
our DRS data and relays the message over a private fiber-
optic line to a person with a registered PID in a third
location. The encrypted message is then sent to Mack via
a properly registered PID from this third relay station."

"How long does all this take?"

"According to Mack, it all happens in less than ten
minutes."

They arrived at Cair Paravel's wooden walkway over
the dunes. As Rachel stepped onto the stair she stopped,
turned to her husband, now at eye level, and said, "Before
we go back in the house, just a few more questions. How
do you know all this stuff about MESH devices—from
Mack?"

"No. Most of it I learned from our son. He knows
more about electronics and the MESH than I ever will."

"So are we going to go inside and deliver all this bad
news to James and Sarah on their tenth wedding anniversary?"

"I don't want to—because we really need to know
more. Until we contact Mack and determine a course
of action, all the information you received from your
young Secret Service agent is just one more thing to worry
about."

"What if FBI or Homeland Security agents come here
looking for James?"

"I think we have to assume they eventually will. But
right now they have no reason to come looking here. Our
PERTs are all masked. We used Sarah's ID code to log
into the MESH from the computer in the house. All of
our other communications have been with Mack using
the SSCI PIDs that have false names assigned. The FBI or

Homeland Security goons will eventually figure out those SSCI PIDs are bogus, but that will take a while. All this means we need to come up with a plan in the next forty-eight hours or so. And that's why I need to communicate with Mack tonight."

"Oh dear, dear Peter, how did we come to this point in this country?" she asked. Though he couldn't see them in the darkness, he knew from her voice that tears were welling up in her eyes.

"We gave it all away," he replied quietly. "In exchange for the promise of comfort and security, 'We the People' surrendered our freedoms to our government—and the 'international community,' whatever that is. Our liberty has been ebbing away for decades and we just let it go. When our economy fell apart, we turned to elites in Washington for handouts and bailouts and did nothing when they took over our banks, industries, hospitals, doctors, even the press. Our government surrendered our right to keep and bear arms to the UN, but did nothing to stop the Iranians and half a dozen others from building nuclear weapons. We legalized the use of illicit drugs, opened our borders to armed enemies, and offered amnesty to millions of people who came here illegally—because they would vote the right way. We abandoned allies like Israel and agreed to the creation of the Caliphate so we could buy cheap oil from people who hate us—while we turned our military into a laboratory for social engineering. And when a handful of good men like Mack warned us years ago we were on a path that would forfeit the future, 'We the People' ignored them—and handed the government even more power over our lives."

Rachel's face was now so close to his, he could sense the warmth of her breath when she said, "So you have decided to consciously break the law. How do you and Mack reconcile this with the oath you each took to support and defend the Constitution of the United States and what you teach in Sunday school about 'rendering unto Caesar what is Caesar's'?"

Peter reached out in the darkness and put his arms around his wife. She felt him take a deep breath and then reply, barely above a whisper, "I anguish over all this, Rachel, just as our founders did when all thirteen colonies organized secret Committees of Correspondence in 1774. Good God-fearing men like Patrick Henry, George Washington, and John Adams eventually concluded that the monarch and Parliament had become intolerably tyrannical. Fifty-six of these patriots pledged their lives, their fortunes, and their sacred honor to declare independence. A Newman ancestor marched with Daniel Morgan in the American Revolution and was wounded at the battle of Cowpens. Mack, our daughter, our son, and I all took an oath to support and defend the Constitution from all enemies foreign *and* domestic. I pray that what we do in the days ahead will restore rather than usurp that Constitution for the benefit of our children and grandchildren."

She pulled him closer and gave him a long kiss on the lips, and then said, "Good. I'm with you, Peter Newman—wherever this takes us."

# CHAPTER TWELVE

# COMMITTEES OF CORRESPONDENCE

## RESIDENCE OF U.S. SEN. MACKINTOSH CAPERTON

305 MARYLAND AVE. NE, WASHINGTON, DC
SATURDAY, 18 SEPTEMBER 2032
0125 HOURS, LOCAL

Senator Mackintosh Caperton's colleagues on both sides of the aisle knew him to be ethical, diligent, possessed of extraordinary foresight, and incorruptible. Though not celebrated for lengthy oratory, when he rose to speak even his opponents listened. The Navy Cross, Silver Star, and three Purple Hearts he was awarded for action as a U.S. Navy SEAL during Operation Just Cause in Panama, Operation Desert Storm in Iraq, and a dozen more classified missions all speak to his courage.

Although Caperton was the most decorated member of the U.S. Senate, few had ever seen the classified citations for his bravery under fire and he never spoke publicly about those events. A slight limp from the prosthesis replacing his right leg below the knee was the only visual clue to the injuries that eventually forced him to retire from the service. When asked about the tiny blue and white device he wore on his lapel he replied simply, "I wear it to remember those with whom I served who did not make it home alive."

Now, two-thirds of the way through his third term as Montana's senior senator, even his political rivals described him as "three steps ahead of the rest of us." Caperton's most frequent response when presented with a "we must do this now" legislative issue was "John Paul Jones once said, 'In matters of principle, be deaf to expediency.' Jones was right." When pressed, he invariably insisted, "I understand your sense of urgency, but before we rush this through, we must ask ourselves, 'What will the American people say about us five, ten, twenty, or even a hundred years from now?'"

One of his detractors, intending to insult him, once told a reporter, "Never tell Caperton what you intend to do. By the time you finish a sentence, he has thought through the options and figured out something he thinks is better. That's probably how he picked his wife." When the accusation was published, Mack commented, "He's right. SEALs always 'think ahead.' Angela was the best option I was ever going to get. As every SEAL should be, I was 'good-to-go.' I'm glad she was, too."

Despite Caperton's reluctance to engage in unwarranted legislative activity, those who served with him on the Senate Armed Services Committee and the Senate Select Committee on Intelligence also knew that when it came to issues affecting the nation's security or the safety of U.S. troops, he could be swift and decisive. His legendary foresight led him to prepare backup communications plans with Peter Newman and scores of others around the United States and overseas.

* * * *

The "Flash Precedence" message pinged Senator Mack Caperton's government-issued Personal Interface Device exactly eight minutes after Peter Newman hit SEND on his unregistered PID. Despite the hour, Caperton immediately arose from the bed he normally shared with his wife, Angela, went to his small office next to their bedroom, and turned on an ancient desk lamp.

He placed his PID next to a DigiVu on his desk so the two devices could "talk" to each other through their short-range infrared transceivers and pinched the top right corner of the DigiVu screen with his right thumb and index finger to turn it on. The text of the PID MESH-mail message instantly appeared on the thin plastic sheet.

CONFIDENTIAL

U.S. SENATE PRIVILEGED COMMUNICATION
PRECEDENCE: FLASH VIA PID
180617ZSEP32
FM:  TCALPJ
TO:  SSCIMC001
SUBJ: CRITICAL MATERIALS PRICE PROJECTIONS
J17A3TR29 [C]

PER YOUR REQUEST, PROJECTED PRICES FOR THE RARE EARTH MINERALS & SHORT SUPPLY ELEMENTS IN THE HIGH-DEMAND TIME-FRAME YOU SPECIFIED ARE LISTED BELOW IN GLOBAL EXCHANGE CURRENCY [GEX] PER GRAM OR PER MILLILITER AS APPROPRIATE:

La = ¤2.3; Ce = ¤2.4; Pr = ¤27.1; Nd = ¤27.8; Es = ¤13.14;
Pm = ¤5.2;
Sm = ¤12.9; Eu = ¤28.10; Gd = ¤36.1; Tb = ¤20.5; Dy = ¤3.11;
Ho = ¤22.11;
Er = ¤4.6; Tm = ¤37.3; Yb = ¤23.3. Md = ¤27.1; Ac = ¤31.4;
Th = ¤35.7;
Pa = ¤18.5; U = ¤14.4; Np = ¤21.10. Pu = ¤10.5 ; Am = ¤19.4;
Cm = ¤26.4?


MY BEST TO ANGELA,
SEMPER FIDELIS, TOM


All PIDs issued by the U.S. government come equipped
with basic encryption algorithms built into their software.
PIDs used by individuals doing classified work have a
more complicated level of encryption—though even this
can eventually be broken by code crackers using sophisticated computers. But anyone intercepting this transmission, even if they broke the PID encryption, would see
only a listing of elements from the periodic table and their
expected "prices" in gex—Global Exchange Currency
units. That's what Caperton intended when he set up the
system.

The first thing Mack checked was the routing—who
sent and relayed the message. Reading backward on the
"From" line, Caperton could see that PJ—Peter J. Newman—was the originator. Newman sent it to AL—Alvin
Loomis—a former Navy SEAL living in Oklahoma. If all
the protocols Caperton established were being followed,
Loomis then sent the message over an Anark-controlled
fiber-optic cable to TC—Tom Cooper—a retired U.S.
Marine sergeant major in Texas. Cooper used his registered PID to send the message to Caperton, rendering

the originator—Newman—and the first relay station—
Loomis—invisible. Anyone intercepting and decrypting
the transmission would think Cooper originated the
message.

Next, Mack checked which "one-time pad" Peter
used to encode his message. Though slow and primitive
compared to modern electronic encryption systems, a
frequently changed pad is an effective cipher system—
providing an adversary does not know the key being used
to convert letters, words, symbols, or numbers from one
meaning to another.

Caperton devised a very simple system using articles
appearing in four of the few surviving, readily available,
daily U.S. newspapers: the *Wall Street Journal, Financial
Times, Washington Times,* and *Washington Enquirer.* The
entry on the message subject line—J17A3TR29—told
Mack all he needed to know: Newman used the *Wall
Street Journal* of 17 September. The article Peter used was
in Section A, page 3, on the top right of the page and it
was twenty-nine lines long. He fetched the previous day's
edition of the *Journal* from the far side of his desk, opened
the paper, and found the referenced article:


## THE WALL STREET JOURNAL
### Texas Businesses Hit Hard by Mexican Border Closure

*Austin, TX, Sep. 15, 2032*—Texas Governor David Charles
says the White House decision to close the U.S.-Mexican
border will likely cost his state a million jobs between now
and the November election. "We all need to ask if this is
the best way to conduct foreign policy," Mr. Charles told
reporters at a news conference in Austin.

"We've been the target of international terrorism and now we are being targeted by our own government," the governor said in a prepared statement. Responding to a reporter's question he insisted, "Can you think of a worse way to handle a crisis than the way Washington is handling this? We won't have any jobs or a friend left in the world if they keep this up. If this is the best they can do, make my twelve-year-old son Secretary of State. He could certainly do a better job."

Asked about progress in investigating the 9-11-32 terror bombings in Houston, the governor was blunt in criticizing the administration: "We had our best people working on this. But as you all know, the entire investigation has been taken over by the FBI and the Department of Homeland Security. We know that no one has yet been indicted for these crimes. To the extent we are able, we are monitoring the investigation but communications with the crowd running the show from Washington are marginal at best. I know there are a lot of rumors floating around out there but we're not allowed to confirm or deny any of them. If you have a source in Washington, let them know I told you 'We the People' have a right to know what they know, today, not after the election. We need to know who did this to us."

Governor Charles, who considered running for president this fall, has also been outspoken about what he says is an inadequate federal response to the environmental consequences of the Houston attack. "It has been slow coming and poorly coordinated," he said on a national radio interview on Wednesday. "What this says to me, is that the elites in Washington just don't care about the rest of us. Your job is to tell 'em that."

Placing the newspaper column beside the DigiVu, Caperton used a pencil to number the lines of text in the paper, 1 through 29, confirming he was using the appropriate pad. He then quickly matched each of the twenty-four line and word number combinations in Newman's PID message with the appropriate lines and words in the newspaper's text:

| | |
|---|---|
| Line 2, 3rd word: | *White* |
| Line 2, 4th word: | *House* |
| Line 27, 1st word: | *source* |
| Line 27, 8th word: | *told* |
| Line 13, 14th word: | *my* |
| Line 5, 2nd word: | *best* |
| Line 12, 9th word: | *friend* |
| Line 28, 10th word: | *today* |
| Line 36, 1st word: | *that* |
| Line 20, 5th word: | *FBI* |
| Line 3, 11th word: | *now* |
| Line 22, 11th word: | *monitoring* |
| Line 4, 6th word: | *all* |
| Line 37, 3rd word: | *Your* |
| Line 23, 3rd word: | *communications* |
| Line 27, 1st word: | *source* |
| Line 31, 4th word: | *also* |

Line 35, 7th word:                    *says*

Line 18, 5th word:                    *our*

Line 14, 4th word:                    *son*

Line 21, 10th word:                   *indicted*

Line 10, 5th word:                    *Can*

Line 19, 4th word:                    *you*

Line 26, 4th word:                    *confirm*


With the punctuation Newman subtly inserted among the "prices" in his message, the brief missive was both a warning and a plea for help:

White House source told my best friend today that FBI now monitoring all your communications. Source also says our son indicted. Can you confirm?


Though the first sentence would alarm almost anyone, instead of becoming agitated, Caperton smiled as he re-read the brief communiqué. In using the phrase "my best friend" he realized Peter was referring to his wife. Rachel had somehow developed a "White House source" as good or better than anything the vice chairman of the Senate Select Committee on Intelligence was able to recruit.

Second, Caperton anticipated he might eventually come under suspicion and planned accordingly. Over a year before, he obtained ten thousand unregistered, "throwaway" PIDs from contraband seized during a counternarcotics operation in Nigeria carried out by the Drug Enforcement Administration.

In the course of his travels, he and Angela delivered

hundreds of these unregistered devices to trusted individuals who shared his concerns about where the West in general and the United States in particular were heading. Mack called the others in his network "Committees of Correspondence." With Peter Newman now in, that brought the number of "trusted messengers" to fifty-six. He smiled again at the historical significance of the number. In July 1776, just fifty-six patriots signed the Declaration of Independence.

Knowing he was under surveillance was also a great advantage. His SEAL experience, long tenure on the SSCI, and close connections with DEA undercover operations were invaluable. He knew he would have to maintain a pattern of life that would appear routine to his watchers and listeners.

To that end, Mack first deleted Newman's encrypted message from his PID and put the annotated newspaper story and his notes into the Organic Chemical-bath, Certified-green Shredder beneath his desk and listened while the documents were ground into compost mulch. He then activated the DigiVu's MESH connection and placed a Vid-Call to a number in Montana.

Angela picked up on the third ring. "Oh, Mack, you should be here," she said as her image appeared on his plastic screen—before he could even say hello. "The cottonwoods are turning early this year. The slopes above the river are covered with gold leaves. On the way here from the airport I saw a half-dozen mountain sheep, a herd of mule deer, and a pair of elk grazing in our yard when I pulled up the drive."

\* \* \* \*

Caperton smiled at his wife's effervescent enthusiasm for their ranch. Twenty-five miles west of Great Falls and across the Sun River from Fort Shaw, it had been in his family for four generations. His great-grandfather built the original ranch house in 1907 with river stone hauled up from the Sun River on a horse-drawn wagon. The roof beams were hand-hewn lodgepole pines that Mack's namesake cut in the foothills of the Rockies nearly forty miles upstream and floated down the river in the fast-flowing spring melt.

There the Caperton clan thrived, raising kids, wheat, soybeans, corn, and cows, gradually expanding the original 1,500-acre parcel to more than 20,000 acres. Mack's dad, born in the midst of the Great Depression, used to tell how his father was famous for helping neighbors with interest-free loans when failing banks tried to foreclose on ranchers late on their mortgages. In 2016, during the Great Double-Dip Recession and a tidal wave of new fore-closures and government bank seizures, the descendants of the families Grandfather Caperton aided in the 1930s were the ones who convinced Mack to run for the U.S. Senate. For reasons of her own, Angela readily agreed and Mack won handily.

Much of Mack's political success was Angela's doing. They grew up on neighboring ranches and as youngsters, Mack and Angela were high school sweethearts. Her family was also renowned in Montana. Angela's grandmother, Mabel, was the oldest World War II–era Women Airforce Service Pilot—a WASP. She flew P-39 Airacobra fighters and B-25 Mitchell bombers from Great Falls Army Airfield—now Malmstrom Air Force Base—to Fairbanks, Alaska, for deliv-ery to Russian pilots under the Lend-Lease program.

On a midwinter flight in 1943, an engine fire in the P-39 that Mabel was piloting forced her to bail out of the aircraft and parachute into the snow-covered, trackless wastes of northern Canada. The story of her perilous, six-day hike to civilization is still part of Montana folklore.

When Mack became the first graduate of tiny Fort Shaw High School to attend the Naval Academy, Angela pledged to wait for him and went to study business at the University of Montana in Missoula. They married in 1978 at the Naval Academy Chapel with Marine 2nd Lieutenant Peter Newman and Ensign Marty Cohen leading six other classmates in forming an arch of swords for the new bride and groom.

Mack and Angela instantly became what she called "military migrant workers," as they moved first to California, then Virginia, Florida, Hawaii, and finally back to Virginia. Their son John was born in 1980 while Mack was assigned to Naval Special Warfare Group One in Coronado, California. Daughter Beth came along three years later while they lived at the naval base in Little Creek, Virginia. Mack learned of her birth while he was deployed with SEAL Team Four to Beirut, Lebanon.

In 1991, Mack was badly wounded on a classified SEAL mission in Iraq during Operation Desert Storm. After months of life-threatening infections and painful attempts to save his right leg, Navy surgeons finally removed the shattered limb and fitted the SEAL with a prosthetic replacement. Confronted with the prospect of a protracted period of desk duty, he opted to be "surveyed out" of the service in 1992.

Undaunted by an unwanted and unexpected career change, he polled Angela, John, and Beth about where they wanted to live. The answer was unanimous: "the Ranch."

Angela started homeschooling their children while Mack was still in the SEALs, and when they moved to Montana, she converted the old bunkhouse at the ranch into a classroom. John and Beth mastered their *Libertas* textbooks—and the use of hunting rifles, shotguns, pistols, and fishing rods. They rode fence lines, rounded up stray calves on horseback, shot rattlesnakes, coyotes, and prairie dogs from the saddle, and hiked the peaks of the Lewis & Clark National Forest, visible from the living room windows, to the west of their home. A portion of every winter was spent on skis at Big Sky, Moonlight Basin, Bridger Bowl, and Whitefish.

The children tracked their parents' footsteps into adulthood. John went to the Naval Academy and, upon graduation in 2002, became a SEAL. Beth followed her mom to the University of Montana as a business major and then on to law school. That's where she was in 2006 when her family was devastated by news that John had been killed in Ramadi, Iraq.

Beth immediately drove the 160 miles from Missoula to the ranch to wait in anguish for her brother's flag-draped, gunmetal transfer case, borne by eight of his fellow SEALs, to arrive on a USAF C-17 "Angel Flight" at Malmstrom AFB. Two weeks later, at Arlington National Cemetery, every member of the forty-man SEAL honor guard embedded his golden SEAL Trident in the lid of John's casket after Angela was presented with the flag once covering her only son's remains.

It took ten more years for their friends and neighbors in Montana to finally convince Mack Caperton to run for the U.S. Senate. Though neither woman told him so at the time, Beth—by then married and the mother of three boys—agreed with her mother: "Being a senator will help Dad stop blaming himself for John's decision to become a SEAL."

\* \* \* \*

Caperton won in a landslide. For the entirety of his first term, Mack and Angela rented a tiny apartment on C Street, on Capitol Hill, a brief walk through Stanton Park to Mack's office in the Dirksen Senate Office Building.

Then one afternoon in February 2023, shortly after Mack was sworn in for his second term, Angela noticed a brick town house on Maryland Avenue. It had been the property of the U.S. Episcopal Church before the denomination disintegrated in acrimonious schism over the ordination of lesbians and homosexuals and the decision of church leaders to perform same-sex marriages.

A sign in front of the building announced FORECLOSURE— nothing unusual in the long-depressed real estate market. Angela called the phone number on the sign and the agent listing the property was only too glad to show her the three-story residence that had been partitioned into office space. After a single walk-through—and an inspector's certification the building was sound—Mack agreed with his wife's plan to turn the town house into their "home away from home."

It took Angela almost ninety days to push the paperwork through the city's foundering bureaucracy and another six months to make the place, in her word, livable. She converted the basement into a comfortable apartment for one of Mack's single staffers and transformed the third floor into a guest suite for their frequent visitors from "out west." Mack and Angela lived on the first and second floors—space she decorated as tastefully as their "real home" in Montana. It was her idea to turn the small bedroom next to theirs into the home office from which Mack sent two text messages—one to United Airlines and the second to Capitol Police Officer Mark Carter, the head of his PSD. Then he placed a Vid-Call.

\* \* \* \*

"It's after eleven out here. Why are you up so late?" she asked.

"I was in bed when my PID went off. After reading the

message, I missed you and remembered we hadn't spoken since you flew out this morning. Did you have any trouble making the connection from Denver to Great Falls?"

"No, but both flights were almost empty. I don't know how either airline manages to survive in this economy. I suppose they are next for a government takeover."

"Let's hope they stay in business. I don't want us to have to drive back and forth between here and Montana. How many of our constituents have you talked to since you arrived?"

There was a long pause and he could see her purse her lips. "Mack, I'm concerned. Just a couple of miles from the airport, at the I-15 intersection with U.S. 89, there is a large billboard that says, 'Join the Tax Revolt—Just Say "No" to Federal Taxes.' Is that kind of thing showing up elsewhere?"

"I'm told there are similar signs in Wyoming, the Dakotas, Idaho, Utah, Texas, Oklahoma, Arizona, Nevada, and all over the South. I'll look in South Carolina when I go down there tomorrow to see Peter and Rachel. I hope to be on the oh-nine-twenty flight from Reagan."

Angela didn't miss a beat. She and Mack had talked at length about what he was doing to help protect James Newman. She also knew that as of her noon departure from Reagan Airport, Mack had not planned a return to Pawleys Island. She assumed something urgent had come up, and simply replied, "I'll confirm your reservations and send the boarding pass to your PID from here so you can get some sleep. You're not going alone, are you?"

"No," Mack replied. "I'm taking Officer Carter with me."

He could see Angela nod. "Good," she said. "When you get to Pawleys, give Peter and Rachel my love and remind them they are always in my prayers. Now go to bed. I love you."

"I'll do that. You, Beth, Samuel, and their boys are in my prayers. I love you, too. Good night." As he shut off his desk lamp and made his way back to bed, Mack reflected, *After fifty-four years of marriage, not everything works like it used to, but some things just get better with age.*

\* \* \* \*

At 0730 Saturday morning, Mack Caperton walked downstairs to the basement apartment of their town house and knocked on the door. Niles Martin, a twenty-eight-year-old former Navy SEAL and a member of the SSCI staff, looking somewhat the worse for wear from Friday night frivolity, opened the door, then followed the senator back to the Capertons' kitchen.

There Mack gave the young man the name of a records clerk at the federal court on Judiciary Square, an unregistered PID, the number for another unregistered PID, and precise instructions on what to do when he completed his mission. Caperton then walked back to the second floor, swung back a framed painting of a bison on the east wall of his office, and spun the dial on an old U.S.-government-issue safe built into the brick and mortar. He removed the two reports labeled TOP SECRET he had brought home from his U.S. Senate office, placed the documents in a manila folder, and stuffed the package into his briefcase.

After closing and locking the safe, Mack used the mini-cam on his SSCI PID to take digital images of the combination and the placement of the papers and articles on his desk. Satisfied the room was recorded and sanitized, he went downstairs to meet Officer Carter, who arrived at the front door precisely at 0800. They got in a dark blue government sedan behind the driver and departed for Reagan Airport and the 0920 flight to Myrtle Beach for which Angela had confirmed the reservations.

Just prior to boarding, the unregistered PID in Mack's shirt pocket pinged once, signaling an incoming text message. He glanced around to see if he could spot anyone tailing him; decided one or two of the other dozen or so passengers could be FBI or contract surveillance; and told Carter he had to use the men's room. The officer nodded to the restroom sign and said, "We're inside security. I'll wait out here."

Caperton stepped into a stall, took out the PID, and looked at the screen. There was a one-word message from the unregistered PID he gave Niles Martin: "YES."

Standing in the men's room stall, Mack bent the little ceramic-plastic card back and forth until it broke, then did so again until it was in four pieces. After wrapping each piece in several sheets of toilet paper, he flushed them down the toilet. Senator Mackintosh Caperton now knew he was en route to deliver some very bad news to some very good friends. A sealed indictment had been issued for James Newman.

## 4 MILES EAST OF DZILAM DE BRAVO

YUCATAN STATE, MEXICO
SATURDAY, 18 SEPTEMBER 2032
1030 HOURS, LOCAL

Until the burst of automatic weapons fire from behind the farmhouse, Marty Cohen was increasingly confident he was going to survive this brutal experience. That feeling ebbed like an outgoing tide with the gunfire.

\*    \*    \*    \*

After cutting the admiral free on Friday afternoon, Ahmad ordered Massoud and Rostam to help the old man to the outhouse so he could relieve himself. Then, through hand gestures and much pointing, they had Felipe use the hand pump atop the well behind the house to fill the fifty-five-gallon drum serving as the family shower and allowed Cohen to bathe. While Marty air dried in the post-hurricane sunlight, Felipe found him a shirt, a pair of trousers that almost fit, and two worn, mismatched sandals.

Later, as Ebi prepared a meal of beans and rice on the propane stove, Ahmad took the chain and lock from the door of the room Cohen was sharing with Felipe and shackled the admiral's right leg to a heavy wooden chair in the kitchen. Having completed the task, the terrorist sat across the table from the old man and said, "Now, Jew, if you try to escape again, you will have to drag the chair with you and when I catch you, I will break both your legs and leave you in the chair until insects eat you and you rot. Do you understand?"

The old admiral simply shrugged and said nothing. Ahmad continued, "Do you know where we are, Jew?"

Cohen, feeling better than he had in days, stared across the table's wooden planks at the Iranian for a moment, then said, "I believe we're just inland, on the north coast of the Yucatan Peninsula in Mexico. Exactly where, I cannot tell without a map and compass or a GPS. Where are Roberto, Hassan, and Rikki?"

"What do you care, Jew?"

"They are not here. Did they make it ashore?"

"Since you answered my question, I will answer yours," Ahmad replied without any inflection. "Roberto and Hassan were in the life raft with Massoud and Rostam. Their raft flipped over several times before coming ashore just as ours did. Hassan could not swim. Apparently Roberto could not swim, either. Rostam told me their life jackets did not work and neither one of them made it back into their raft after it tipped over the last time."

"What about Rikki?"

"I killed him."

"Killed him? Why? How?"

"He had a knife. I needed it. He would not give it to me, so I killed him with a rock while Rostam and Massoud held him."

Ahmad said all of this without the slightest hint of emotion or sign of remorse. Cohen said, "Rikki was just a boy. Hassan was not much older. Don't you feel anything about them?"

Ahmad looked at the American with undisguised disdain. "You do not understand, do you, Jew. It is Allah's will that they should die when, where, and how they did. I was simply the instrument for Allah's will."

Cohen said nothing, so Ahmad went on. "Tomorrow we must find communications so I can report to my superiors and summon assistance."

At this the old admiral leaned forward and asked, "Who are your superiors, Ahmad? Why have you kidnapped me?"

For a moment Ahmad just stared at Cohen, but then he leaned forward and responded in English, "You might as well know, Jew. I am *sarhang dovom*—a lieutenant colonel—in the Quds Force of the Islamic Revolutionary Guard Corps. Ebi, my deputy, is a *nakhoda sevom*—a lieutenant commander in our naval component. There are other Quds Force units here in Mexico, Venezuela, and Cuba. I was ordered to deliver you alive to our unit in Nicaragua."

Cohen, amazed at what he just heard, shook his head and said, "But why me?"

"I do not know why, Jew. It doesn't matter," Ahmad replied. "If it was up to me, I would have killed you with the others in Houston. What does matter now is that you get information from the Mexican boy on where we are and how I can communicate. You will translate for me or I will kill the boy. After you watch him die slowly, I will kill you. Do you understand me?"

Cohen nodded. By now Ahmad had threatened to kill him so many times it barely registered anymore. It wasn't that the old man didn't believe the terrorist's threats; rather, he believed the Good Lord kept him alive through all this for a reason. While Cohen didn't know why he had endured all the near misses since September 11, he was increasingly convinced he was going to get through this ordeal intact. But after the cold description of Rikki's murder, the admiral also knew Ahmad's threat to kill Felipe was real. It added a new dimension to what was, until now, his singular focus: personal survival.

When Ebi finished cooking, he poured the contents of the pan into six bowls he located on a shelf in the corner. He found an equal number of spoons in a drawer and placed four bowls on the table. While Ahmad, Ebi, Cohen, and Felipe ate at the kitchen table, Massoud and Rostam, each armed with an ancient AK-47, ate outside, standing watch on the front and back doors of the house.

During the meal, Ahmad probed Felipe for information, using Cohen to translate from English to Spanish, then back to English again.

"Ask him where we are."

"He says we are in Mexico."

"Yes, but where in Mexico?"

"He says we are in Yucatan."

Ahmad's patience began to wear thin. "Where in Yucatan?"

"We are on his father's farm."

"Where is his father?"

Cohen knew from his predawn, whispered conversation with Felipe that the boy's response was a facile lie, but he translated the answer: "He says his father is a policeman and went to visit his older sister."

"Where does his sister live?"

"In her house."

Exasperated, Ahmad slammed his palm on the table and said, "The boy is an infidel idiot. Ask him how his father got to his sister's place. Does he have a vehicle?"

"He says his father took their truck."

"Ask him when his father is coming back here and how far it is to the nearest telephone, radio, or someone with a PID."

As Cohen repeated the question in Spanish, the boy's big brown eyes filled with tears and he began to sob.

Ahmad became agitated. "What's he saying? Why is he crying?"

Cohen listened for a moment, amazed at how Felipe deftly avoided answering the original question, and translated the child's reply: "He says his brother Jorge is dead and must be buried or his father will be very angry with him."

Ahmad's reaction surprised Cohen. In the days since being kidnapped the admiral hadn't witnessed the slightest hint of human compassion in the Iranian. But now the Quds Force officer sat upright in his chair and said, "Yes. That is correct. We are not animals. Tell the boy we will bury his brother in the morning. After we have done that, I will ask him more questions."

Rostam was summoned to unshackle Cohen and accompany him to the privy. As the old sailor shuffled back to the house, acting more feeble than he really felt, he noticed stars already winking in the dark purple of the eastern sky. *Tomorrow will be a clear day. Good for flying. Perhaps someone will find our EPIRB.*

Darkness was filling the farmhouse as Cohen and

Felipe were escorted to the same room where they first encountered one another. On the way, the boy grabbed three rough blankets and a pillow from another room Cohen surmised to be his parents'. While Ahmad ran the chain through the rough hasp on the outside of the door, he shouted, "Remember, Jew, if I hear you and the boy talking, I will cut out his tongue while you watch!"

Cohen tapped the boy on the shoulder to gain his attention in the gloom and placed his index finger over his lips, motioning for silence. Felipe nodded and without a word, helped the old man flip over the mattress so Cohen would not have to sleep in the dampness of his own urine. For the next twenty minutes or so they sat next to each other on the edge of the cot, whispering quietly in English.

*    *    *    *

On Saturday morning, Marty Cohen awakened at the break of dawn to the sound of a cock crowing. He stretched, did a quick assessment of his bodily aches and pains, observed the knot on the back of his skull was smaller, and swung his feet to the floor. He noticed Felipe rolled in a ball beneath the window and quietly pulled the threadbare blanket over the boy's shoulder. A moment later he heard the chain being pulled through the hasp on the outside of the door.

Ahmad, speaking louder than necessary in the early morning silence, said, "Get up, Jew. Tell the boy to go out with Rostam and get us some eggs. After we have some food, we will bury his brother."

Cohen marveled that Felipe did not move a muscle until the old admiral translated Ahmad's command into Spanish. Then, as Ahmad watched, the boy arose, picked up the blankets and pillow, placed them on Cohen's bed, and headed outside to comply. Rostam traipsed along behind like a bored shepherd, toting an AK-47 over his shoulder and gripping the barrel.

It was nearly nine in the morning by the time the four terrorists and their two captives finished the breakfast of eggs, fried beans, and fresh corn Ebi prepared in a large frying pan. Though the "chef" used far too much cooking oil, the admiral judged the fare to be more than passable for fugitives on the run.

As Rostam and Massoud delivered their bowls back to the kitchen, Cohen said to Ahmad, "Please tell Ebi I thank him for two good meals. But, before we eat again, we should wash the dishes and cooking pans. Otherwise we may all get sick."

The terror chieftain, a handgun jammed into his belt, snickered and replied, "You are amazing, Jew. You are afraid we will get sick? If you want clean plates, wash them yourself."

Cohen gestured at the chain holding his ankle to the chair and Ahmad spat, "Tell the boy to get some water. Then we will go bury his brother. After that, he will lead us to a telephone or a radio so we can get out of here."

Felipe carried in a bucket of water hand-pumped from the well behind the house and placed it on the kitchen floor in front of the admiral's chair. Cohen set to work scrubbing the large iron frying pan, bowls, and utensils with a bar of soap and a rag Ebi produced from a shelf beneath the sink.

As Ahmad, Rostam, and Massoud headed out the door with Felipe to find shovels for their interment detail, Cohen said, "Ahmad, you should bring something to wrap around the body. In your faith and mine, a burial shroud is appropriate."

The Iranian looked hard at the American, started to

speak, but decided otherwise. Instead, he went into the room off the kitchen and reentered a moment later carrying a blanket. The three men followed the boy out the door, headed toward the partially collapsed barn fifty yards south of the farmhouse.

After watching his hostage for a few minutes, Ebi went to the room off the kitchen and Marty heard bedsprings creak as the terrorist stretched out. A half hour later, Ahmad returned, found the admiral alone in the kitchen, and rushed into the bedroom beside the kitchen, berating his deputy for failing in his duty to Allah. As the pair returned to the kitchen, it happened.

\* \* \* \*

The burst of three rounds from an AK-47 was followed by shouts, another single shot, and more shouts. Ahmad reacted instantly, yelling to Ebi in Farsi, "Stay here with the Jew. If I'm not back in fifteen minutes, kill him!" With that he rushed out the back door of the farmhouse toward the sound of the shooting and shouting.

Cohen, chained to the chair, watched as Ebi grabbed a large knife off the counter and warily looked out the door toward the commotion. Before the death sentence was due to be carried out, Ahmad returned, covered in sweat and cursing in his native tongue. He stormed into the kitchen, waving the pistol about, and shouted in English, "The boy is gone. It is your fault, Jew!"

"How is it my fault?"

"All your talk about burying his brother! Massoud and Rostam were digging the grave while the boy wrapped the body in the blanket. When they looked up from the hole they saw him running into the jungle. They shot at him but both their weapons jammed. I sent them to follow his trail."

"Perhaps he went to look for the missing cows," the admiral responded helpfully.

"Even you know better than that, Jew," snarled Ahmad, pointing the ancient pistol at the old man's head. "You had better hope they catch him."

Cohen was hoping not that the pursuers caught the boy, but that their bullets missed. With the exception of the gunshots, everything was going according to the plan he and Felipe had concocted the night before, when they were locked in the bedroom. Marty looked down at the floor and silently prayed, *Godspeed, Felipe*.

## FINCA DEL GANADOR

3 MILES EAST OF DZILAM DE BRAVO
YUCATAN STATE, MEXICO
SATURDAY, 18 SEPTEMBER 2032
1130 HOURS, LOCAL

The boy ran as if the devil himself were on his tail. None of the four shots fired by his pursuers even came close—but Felipe wasn't taking any chances they might catch him, so he raced the whole distance to the front door of Señor Macklin's farmhouse. As Felipe sped past the sign at the front gate, the four English words below FINCA DEL GANADOR took on a whole new meaning: *He Who Dares Wins*.

Major Bruno Macklin, Royal Army (Ret.), didn't look or act sixty-four. Though his close-cropped hair and well-maintained mustache were graying, his sharp eyes, trim build, massive shoulders, and muscled forearms suggested his life's earlier work: as an officer in "A" Squadron, 22 SAS.

For more than two decades Macklin was involved in some of the most daring special operations undertaken by

Britain's Special Air Service regiment. His 1998 citation for the George Cross cited him for "heroic action during a prolonged, sensitive assignment of vital interest to Her Majesty's government." What the award did not mention was that it covered the time frame during which he was "seconded" to a highly classified Special Operations Unit commanded by a certain Lieutenant Colonel Peter Newman, USMC.

Macklin retired from the SAS in 2007 after three additional combat deployments to Afghanistan and two more to Iraq. He intended to stay in England as a security manager for a bank but emigrated to Belize in 2013 when a British court, citing Sharia law, vacated the life sentences of six men convicted of stoning a Muslim woman to death in London. The day he departed England for good he told his brother, "I didn't fight Muslim fanatics in Mesopotamia and 'the Stans' so English-speaking Islamo-fascists could take over my country."

By 2023, Macklin had married, fathered a daughter, and become a successful cattle breeder in Belize. When he heard about ranch land being abandoned in Mexico because of narco-violence instigated by competing drug cartels, he flew to Merida and paid pennies on the peso for the two-thousand-acre property now named Finca del Ganador.

A year after he moved to Yucatan, a gang of twenty-one *cartelistos*, enforcers for the Federation Cartel, came to the ranch while Macklin was in Merida selling cattle. He returned that night to find his wife and ten-year-old daughter raped and murdered. The killers boldly MESH-mailed digital video and photographs of themselves perpetrating the heinous acts—along with a warning for the bereaved husband and father to leave Mexico immediately.

After burying his wife and child, Bruno Macklin delivered the evidence to the Yucatan state police. They did nothing. He then went to Mexico City and gave the same digital images to the chief of the Mexican National Police and the attorney general. They suggested he take the cartel's advice and leave the country.

A month after the murders—and the receipt of four more death threats from the Federation—Macklin decided to act. Instead of fleeing, he hunted down and killed all twenty-one of the rapist-killers.

It took him fifty-three days—taking them one by one with a variety of weapons. He dropped seven of them in broad daylight at five hundred yards or more with a Remington 700 M40A6 sniper rifle. Six others died at night when they were struck by bullets from a SPA-SIMRAD KN253 Mk IV–equipped 7.62mm FN-Herstal SCAR. Three were killed at very close range by projectiles fired by a suppressor-fitted .22-cal Walther P22 semiautomatic pistol. Two perished by "apparently self-inflicted multiple gunshot wounds" from their own weapons. One blew himself up when he inserted the ignition key in his car. Another was found skewered by a Gurkha kukri blade. The leader of the vicious gang was the last to die—a broken neck. An accident, the police said.

Since then neither Macklin nor any of his ranch workers had been bothered by the cartels as the latter fought each other and their government for control of Mexico's lucrative cocaine export business. When British or American diplomats asked Macklin how he managed to stay alive amid all the violence, he replied, "As long as bad people leave me alone, I leave them alone." At least that's how it was until Felipe banged on his front door.

* * * *

"Señor Macklin! *¡Ayúdame, por favor!*" the boy gasped.

"Stop, lad!" Macklin said, holding Felipe by his sweat-drenched shoulders and closing the door behind them. "Come in here. Let's get you some water and you tell me in English what's the matter."

"They are trying to kill me . . . They shot at me . . . Jorge is dead . . . They are going to kill Señor Martin . . . He is a Jew . . . They are very bad men . . ."

"Hold on, Felipe. Catch your breath and start over," the old special operator said as he guided the boy into the kitchen and filled a glass with water from the tap.

Felipe gulped it, steadied himself, and began again after saying, "Thank you, sir."

Five minutes into the child's recitation of the last forty-eight horrific hours, Macklin interrupted and asked, "Are you sure the four bad men are not *cartelistos*?"

"No, they are not. None of them speak Spanish. Only one of them, the *jefe*, speaks any English. They all speak a language I do not understand. Señor Martin says they are Iranians."

"Iranians, eh. What else does Señor Martin say?"

"Oh, I almost forgot. He made me memorize what I was to tell you."

"What did he make you memorize?"

"I am to tell you that he is Admiral Martin Cohen of the U.S. Navy and he was kidnapped by Iranian terrorists in Houston on September 11 and would you please contact Mexican authorities and ask them to call the American Embassy for help."

"A fair lot of good that will do," Macklin muttered.

"I do not understand, señor."

"Never mind," Macklin said, patting the youngster on the shoulder. "You did very well, Felipe. I'm very sorry about your brother. Jorge was a fine lad. He knew our

Lord and Savior and I am sure we will see them both together—but not today."

Felipe looked a bit confused, so Macklin continued.
"I'm glad you are all right. Our landline and wireless
phones and MESH services were knocked out by the hurricane and have not been restored, but my solar collectors
and generator are working. Perhaps we can summon some
assistance on the sat-phone. Come into my office."

Following the soldier-turned-rancher into the spacious
room, Felipe said, "This is where you taught Jorge and me
to read, write, and speak English. Now it makes me sad."

Macklin patted the youth on the shoulder, picked
up the old but reliable Iridium 9775 handset from the
docking port on his desk, and checked to ensure the roof-
mounted antenna was still connected and functioning. He
then keyed in a twelve-digit number from memory.

The instrument he called rang twice and answered with
a simple "Hello, Bruno. Did you have much damage from
the hurricane?"

"Some. Lost a few calves. We have some fences down.
A couple of buildings with roof damage. How about you?"

"No serious wreckage from the storm here in the city;
a little flooding, that's about all. It's nothing compared to
the destruction caused by Washington's new travel restrictions."

"Are you going to have to leave?"

"Don't know yet. Most of the consular staff have been
ordered out, but they can't go until the airport reopens.
Two big hangars collapsed and the runway is covered with
debris. Looks like we will all be here for a while."

"Good," Macklin replied. "While you are waiting
around doing nothing, my friend, how about checking to
see if you blokes are missing one of your navy admirals—a
fellow named Martin Cohen."

There was a long pause. For a moment, Macklin thought the connection had dropped. Then he heard the voice in the handset say, "No joking around, Bruno. What do you know about Admiral Cohen? He's been MIA from Houston, Texas, since 11 September."

"Well, I have a young man here beside me, the son of my ranch manager. He tells me your admiral is being held by four Iranians at his house not far from here. If it's important to you, I'll just go next door, kill the Iranians, and bring the admiral to you."

A. J. Jones had known Bruno Macklin for less than two years—but he was certain the retired SAS officer was capable of doing all he offered. They talked for another five minutes. By the time Macklin pushed the END CALL button on his handset, they agreed the major would do nothing except protect Felipe and try to intercept the boy's parents until he heard from A.J. again.

As things turned out, it might have been better had Macklin immediately launched his one-man hostage-rescue operation.

# CHAPTER THIRTEEN

# CHAOS THEORY

<u>U.S. NAVY EC-8; CALL SIGN: "SEEKER ONE FIVE"</u>

22.31°N; 88.95°W

36,000' OVER THE GULF OF MEXICO

SATURDAY, 18 SEPTEMBER 2032

1600 HOURS, LOCAL

They were seven hours into their ten-hour mission when Petty Officer 1st Class Sarah Hemingway detected the first, faint signals. She tweaked the digital array at her console, then came up on her wireless, helmet-mounted intercom: "I'm picking up a new nonhostile emitter on the EMF antenna. It appears stationary. It's in the right spectrum to be an EPIRB signal. Looks like it's right on the coastline . . . true bearing, one-eight-five degrees . . . looks like it's about sixty miles out, just about on our nose."

Lieutenant (jg) Duane Ward, mission SSO, spun around on his deck-mounted swivel seat and touched the button labeled STATION 7-EMS on one of the four flat-panel screens mounted over his console. Instantly a multicolored moving map appeared on the screen—the Caribbean in blue and the coastline of the Yucatan Peninsula in green. Hundreds of blinking red dots displayed precise locations for every radio, radar, cell phone, PID, PERT, or wireless device within range of the EC-8's sensitive antennas.

"Which one, Hemingway?" Ward asked into his lip mike as he stared at the busy screen.

"Bogey Six Four Five," she replied.

With the swipe of his hand across the front of the screen, Ward zoomed in on the blinking icon. He looked at it a moment and said, "Get a lock on the position." He then said the word "All!" into the mike, listened for a second to ensure he wasn't interrupting any crucial intercom or radio traffic, and announced to everyone in the aircraft, "This is the SSO. We have what may be an EPIRB distress signal. Recommend we hold course, descend to twenty thousand feet, and slew the FLIR and RDF antenna to one-eight-five degrees true. EMAC says it's emitting on two frequencies, 406 and 121.5 megahertz."

In the cockpit, Lieutenant Commander Laura Bolton, the pilot and aircraft commander, replied, "Roger. That heading is going to take us right toward the beach and we have to stay thirteen miles offshore over international waters."

"Yes, ma'am," replied Ward, rapidly scrolling through the data being displayed on his screen. "EMAC now confirms the emitter is a cat-one EPIRB. Am passing its registry number to your HUD."

In the cockpit, Bolton and her copilot saw the codec, "MMSI #775-425791C," appear on the holographic head-up displays. Over the intercom she said, "Okay, what's this mean?"

"According to EMAC," Ward replied, "it's an EPIRB

registered to a life raft on MV *Ileana Rosario*—one of the vessels we've been looking for. If this bogey is aboard the ship or on a life raft, we ought to be able to verify it with a visual on the high-res FLIR from thirteen miles out at twenty grand."

"Roger. Seat belts and shoulder harnesses on. Hang on for rapid descent. We'll level off and slow down when we reach two-zero."

Bolton pushed the yoke forward and the entire aircrew experienced a familiar roller-coaster effect in their guts as the big bird nosed down. At the bottom of the dive the twin-engine craft leveled off, pressing them all into their seats.

Ward came up on the intercom again: "We have a steady hit on the emitter signal . . . I have a solid mark on the location . . . EMAC readout reconfirms EPIRB registry number MMSI #775-425791C; CAT I 406MHz/121.5MHz. Passing data to FLIR and on data uplink to SAR HQ . . ."

Seconds later, as the aircraft raced toward the coastline at nearly 400 knots, Petty Officer Josh Smallbone, the FLIR operator, seated at the console beside Hemingway, came up on the intercom: "I've got a visual on bogey six-four-five. It appears to be an international orange panel . . . No, it looks like a torn-up life raft, about fifty meters ashore, right off the beach. No thermals on any nearby life-forms . . ."

"Roger," Bolton replied from the cockpit as she pulled back on the dual throttles. "Slowing to a hundred and fifty knots. Holding at altitude two-zero. Am coming up on sat-comm requesting permission to overfly Mexican territory to conduct a visual search for any signs of life before it gets dark and we bingo on fuel."

With airspeed dropping, the big plane was approaching the shoreline at 2.5 miles per minute when Hemingway spoke up again: "I've got a new emitter, number six-four-six. It's intermittent . . . from a fixed location about five klicks inland from the life raft. It seems to be a U.S. military PERT, but I can't hold the signal long enough to ID it on the Blue Force tracker."

Ward zoomed in on icon 646 and hit RECORD on his console as the aircraft crossed the thirty-mile warning zone off the Mexican coast. He watched as the emitter-marker blinked for a half second, then disappeared, blinked on again—and went out. It wasn't much—but it was just enough for the EMAC. The computer flashed a message on his screen:

EMITTER#646: US MIL PERT JMC#327-99-8324 NO BIODATA

He spoke into his wireless lip mike: "If EMAC is right, Hemingway may have just found Admiral Cohen's PERT. Signal is intermittent and very weak. We're not receiving any biometric data. Could be a dying battery."

"Or a dead host," replied Bolton. "SSO, go up on the data link to Nav-Sea Search and the Coast Guard. Have them notify all nearby U.S. vessels what we've found. Let 'em know I've requested an okay for an overflight of the targets."

Less than twenty-five seconds later, the USCG Search and Rescue Coordination Center in New Orleans, two dozen other U.S. military components, including the National Military Command Center and an aging Littoral Control Ship, USS *Milwaukee*, LCS-5, heading south from Galveston, received the data-link message transmitted from the aircraft:

UNCLAS

182212ZSEP32
FM:   SEEKER 15
TO:   TF 22.3
CDG 611
USCG SAR
UMG 413.2

SUBJ:   EPIRB & US PERT DETECTED NOTAM SEARCH
AREA 18-4

1. 182202ZSEP32, USN EC-8, CALL SIGN SEEKER ONE
FIVE, DETECTED & CONFIRMED CAT 1 EPIRB SIGNAL,
MMSI #775-425791C @ FREQS 406MHz AND 121.5MHz.
REGISTRY # IS CONFIRMED AS ONE [1] OF THREE [3]
INFLATABLE LIFE BOATS ABOARD MV ILEANA ROSARIO.

2. 182206ZSEP32, VISUAL IDENTIFICATION OF LIFE
BOAT ACQUIRED BY A/C MOUNTED HI-RES FLIR @ SITE
OF EPIRB SIGNAL @ NAVGRID AL2455/GW4717. NO VIS-
IBLE LIFE FORMS IN VICINITY OF DEBRIS. STREAMING
VID FROM FLIR AVAIL ON SAT CHAN 77.1.

3. 182211ZSEP32, DETECTED INTERMITTENT SIGNAL
FM US MIL PERT JMC#327-99-8324 @ VIC AN2145/
BW8862. NO BIODATA RECEIVED.

4. MSN CDR REQ PERMISSION TO OVERFLY MEXICAN
TERRITORY TO VERIFY PROOF OF LIFE.

Six minutes after the message was sent, Seeker One Five
was directed to "Abort current mission and Romeo Tango
Bravo."

Over secure voice satellite radio, LCDR Bolton protested the order: "We're just fourteen miles offshore. If we step on the gas we can overfly both targets and be back over international waters in less than ten minutes."

Thirty seconds later she was told, "Overflight permission denied. Break off mission immediately and return to base. Airspace must be cleared for unmanned sensor platforms." The crew of Seeker One Five groaned as the big bird turned and headed back toward Texas.

When the EC-8 landed at NAS Corpus Christi three hours later, the tower vectored the aircraft to a remote apron, well away from the Navy flight line. Bolton was ordered to "remain in Em-Con and await security personnel."

As soon as she shut down the engines, four men in civilian attire came aboard, confiscated the crew members' PIDs, and directed them to immediately exit the aircraft, board a waiting crew bus, and proceed to a debriefing. Only later did some of them figure out why they were interned for three days. By then it was already too late to rescue Marty Cohen.

## TREATY ROOM, THE WHITE HOUSE

1600 PENNSYLVANIA AVENUE
WASHINGTON, DC
SATURDAY, 18 SEPTEMBER 2032
1800 HOURS, LOCAL

So does this mean our missing Dr. Cohen has been found?" the president asked, looking up from the message on her PID. "Who is this 'Seeker Fifteen,' anyway?"

General John Smith, the National Security Advisor, was tired—and he knew it was beginning to show. His response was curt. "Seeker One Five is the call sign of the U.S. Navy patrol aircraft that detected the EPIRB and PERT signals in Mexico. These confirm what the DEA listening post picked up two days ago. The EC-8 is an old airframe but the electronic detection gear aboard is first-rate."

"Please, John, don't feed me another lecture on the unnecessary technological feats we have bought with billions of wasted tax dollars in our defense budget. What's the bottom line here: is Cohen alive or dead?"

At this, her chief of staff, Murad Muneer, interrupted in an attempt to refocus the discussion. "The answer, Madam President, is we don't know whether Cohen is alive or dead. That is not of immediate importance. What we do now about the message on your PID is very important."

"Why?" she asked. "Didn't you hear John just tell us the aircrew that detected the rescue beacon and Cohen's PERT has been sequestered in Texas?"

"Of course I heard that," Muneer replied, trying hard to keep his temper from showing. "But as General Smith just pointed out, these signals simply confirm what the DEA listening site already surmised. Unfortunately, the message you have on your PID was also sent to scores of U.S. military personnel. If we do not announce some kind of rescue or recovery effort in the next forty-eight hours or so, there will be speculation and rumors about—"

"Stop!" she commanded. "Are you crazy, Muneer? If Cohen is alive and he surfaces before the election, we're finished. We can't launch a rescue mission in Mexico."

"I didn't say we should launch a rescue mission right now. I said we should announce one now."

"Quiet!" she ordered, once again holding up her hand. Looking at her National Security Advisor, she asked, "John, where is Admiral Turner, the DNI, right now?"

Smith responded, "Stanley is en route to Mexico City for a meeting with President Rodriguez. Depending on the weather, he should be on the ground in the next hour or so."

"Good. As soon as we finish this meeting, get him on secure voice with me so I can talk to him privately about the problem of Dr. Cohen."

Turning to White House Counsel Larry Walsh, the president asked, "Has our Acting FBI Director—your friend Keker—any idea where young Newman is hiding?"

"Not yet. But as you directed, the FBI has acquired all the Newman family's medical records. Keker says they have four analysts going through everything in the data, looking for psychological problems, addictions, prescriptions for psychotropic medications—"

"Larry, I don't want Newman committed to a mental institution. I want him dead. Didn't you tell me just a few hours ago the special grand jury handed down a twenty-three-count sealed indictment on James Newman for acts of terrorism, attempted mass murder, crimes against humanity, and a host of other violations of U.S. criminal law?"

"Yes, but—"

"Don't give me any 'buts,' Larry. Get a copy of the indictment to the Attorney General, the DNI, and your pal Keker. Tell 'em—don't send a MESH-mail on this—tell 'em—I want a Capture/Kill finding for Newman and I want it today, without any congressional notification."

Smith, looking stunned, said quietly to no one in particular, "A death sentence finding on an American citizen? A decorated U.S. military officer is going to be executed without a trial?"

"Man up, John," the president sneered. "This has been legit since 2011, when they took out that American imam in Yemen with a couple of those high-tech Hellfire missiles you're so proud of. What was his name?"

"Anwar al-Awlaki," Muneer replied.

"Right," she continued. "The rules they wrote then still apply. All it takes is for the AG, the DNI, the National

Security Advisor, and the Director of the FBI to certify the target is an illegal enemy combatant who has committed 'crimes against humanity' and presents a 'clear and present danger' to American citizens. That suffices for due process and it certainly fits the description of James Newman. He belongs on the Capture/Kill list and needs to be taken out. Get it done. That's all for now."

As the three men started for the door she said, "Larry, you stay."

When the door closed behind Muneer and Smith, the president said to her lawyer, "What have you found out about our Senator Caperton? Is he an Anark working against our country, trying to overthrow the government?"

Walsh hesitated a moment before responding, "You know Caperton is a former Navy SEAL. Badly wounded . . . very highly decorated . . ."

"Larry, I don't give a damn what Senator Caperton did in the past. What's he doing now? What's he up to? Keker has a 'wires warrant' to monitor Caperton's communications and movements. What's the surveillance turning up? Where is Caperton now?"

"He's apparently in Pawleys Island, South Carolina, for the weekend."

"What's he doing there? Is he running around on his wife?"

"Running around on his wife? I doubt it. He's evidently a guest at the Newman family beach house."

She was silent for nearly half a minute before she said quietly, "So the 'Free-Cong' senator from Montana is at the Newmans' house on that island in Anark-infested South Carolina . . . Ask Keker how long it will take him to get a search warrant and raid the place."

"I already asked this morning as soon as I found out Caperton was headed there. Jon says both the senior

Newmans are there along with James Newman's wife and
children. He doesn't know if our target is there or not. Keker
wants to use DHS agents instead of the FBI. He's working
with the AG and Homeland Security to have all the paperwork and people in place to take the residence down. He's
certain he will be ready tomorrow. He wants to do it at night."

For the first time, the president smiled. Then, usher-
ing Walsh to the door, she said, "You do very good work,
Larry. Wouldn't it be a shame if the treasonous Senator
Mack Caperton and federal fugitive-terrorist James Newman both died while resisting a search warrant by federal
law officers?"

**CAIR PARAVEL**

PAWLEYS ISLAND, SC

SATURDAY, 18 SEPTEMBER 2032

1900 HOURS, LOCAL

Newman clan traditions hold that birthday activities
are chosen by the person celebrating the occasion.
There is only one rule—all family members must be able
to participate in all events.

Seth Newman's twelfth-birthday celebration—an all-
day affair—came off without a hitch. The weather was
a perfect 75 degrees, with classic Carolina blue skies, a
gentle surf, and a steady 10-knot breeze from the southwest. The first event, an "Around the Island Kayak Race,"
was followed by a "Three Laps Around the Island Bike
Race." This in turn was succeeded by a half-mile-long
ocean swim and a break for lunch. They were ravenously
consuming sandwiches and soup when Capitol Police Officer Carter deposited "Uncle Mack" at the Cair Paravel
gate and departed for his room at the Sea View Inn.

After the meal, Senator Caperton and Peter Newman

withdrew from the "Youngsters vs. Oldsters Body Surf-
ing Contest" and a "size matters" fishing competition to
closet themselves inside the house. Hours later, as the sun
was setting, while the older boys engaged in a "duel to the
death" kite battle and the twins built sand castles, James
noticed that his father, the senator, and one of the rental
cars were gone.

At dusk, the air temperature dropped quickly with the
offshore breeze. When it became too dark and chilly to play,
the herd straggled off the beach, rinsed the sand off their
bodies in the outdoor showers, and piled into the living
room for a series of "Round Robin Checkers" games and
fiercely contested rows of dominoes while awaiting dinner.
James had just fired up the propane grill beneath the house
when Peter and Mack pulled through the gate and parked.

The two older men sat in the car talking as James
finished preparing the birthday feast Seth ordered: homemade venison sausage, Narnia Farm beef burgers, and his
grandfather's famous "game-bird stew of pheasant, goose,
duck, and wild turkey." He didn't select any vegetables but
he got them anyway—corn, potatoes, celery, carrots, pep-
pers, and onions—all from Rachel's garden.

Their conversation concluded, Peter and Mack helped
James carry the meal upstairs to the hungry horde. On the
way, James asked, "What's got you guys acting so weird?"

"Later. After the kids are in bed" was all Peter answered.

Caperton added, "Let's enjoy the moment. There's a lot
to discuss and decisions we have to make. But it will all
keep for a few hours."

\* \* \* \*

No adult concerns were evident during the birthday party.
After the main courses, Sarah dimmed the dining room

lights and Rachel served her famous carrot cake—complete with twelve candles stuck in the white icing. As the crowd around the table sang "Happy Birthday," Seth extinguished them all with a single long breath—to the applause of his siblings.

After the cake and homemade ice cream were devoured, it was time for presents. Each one had a tag with a hint about the contents from the giver—a family tradition Rachel started many Christmases and birthdays before.

Seth was stumped right from the start. He guessed that a package labeled "Sharper than our brother" from David and Daniel was a new PID game. It turned out to be a Swiss Army knife.

Josh wrote, "This will make you look very bright." Seth speculated the box contained a new pair of glasses. Inside he found a SureFire flashlight.

The large gift from "Uncle Mack and Aunt Angela" was surprisingly light but the hint read: "For your heavy loads." The lad deduced it was a new book bag to replace his old one—the one with a failed zipper. Instead it was a top-of-the-line, feather-light, internal-frame, mountain backpack.

When there were but two presents left, the birthday boy chose the largest and heaviest—the one with a tag reading, "Seth: For the rest of your life."

"I have no idea," he said, opening the box to find a Benelli .20-gauge automatic shotgun, a lensatic compass, a copy of the Holy Bible—and another note. He read it aloud: "Seth, if you master all three—the shotgun, compass, and Bible—you will never go hungry, never be lost, and need fear nothing. Love, Mom and Dad."

"Wow!" the boy exclaimed, running his hand over the black composite stock of the shotgun. "Can I take it outside and try it tonight?"

Sarah, knowing her son was thinking only of the firearm, replied: "You can start tonight on the Bible. Since today is the eighteenth of the month, I suggest you try Proverbs, chapter eighteen. All thirty-one of them are full of good advice for a young man. Try one a day. Tomorrow you can work on nineteen. Then your dad can show you how to take apart, clean, and shoot the shotgun—and how to find your way with the compass."

Seth nodded and said, "Okay, Mom, got it." As the boy reached for his final present—one Rachel picked out at a Winchester, Virginia, hobby store—a PID in Mack Caperton's pocket pinged. Mack looked at the device, nodded at Peter, and they excused themselves to go out onto the ocean-side porch to take the call. Had either man seen what was about to happen, he would have stopped it before it was too late.

The tag on the wrapping read: "Seth: Landings must = Takeoffs. Love, Nan & Granddad." He guessed: "It's a model airplane."

He was almost right. The box contained a small, battery-powered, remote-controlled helicopter—complete with a tiny built-in camera that broadcast real-time video to the operator's PID.

With the remaining grown-ups distracted while picking up discarded gift wrapping and dessert dishes, Seth grabbed the unregistered PID his grandfather left on the table and quickly mastered the controls, launched the toy from the tabletop, flew it around the room, and hovered it above their heads. As Peter and Mack returned to the dining room, the boy flawlessly landed the miniature aircraft among the dishes without incident.

Forty-five minutes later all four children were in bed. But the little helicopter had already done its damage.

Everyone at Cair Paravel—especially James Newman—
was now in grave danger, all because of a toy.

* * * *

It was nearly 9:15 p.m. by the time the empty boxes and
toys were cleared away, all the plates, bowls, glassware,
and utensils were in the dishwasher, and the adults could
convene again around the table with mugs of coffee. On
the table in front of Mack was a manila file folder—the
one he removed from the safe in his home that morning.
The senator began by thanking Rachel for a wonderful
evening. Their discussion quickly became ominous.

"The president and her White House staff are committing criminal acts," Caperton began quietly. "All the
things we talked about here on Wednesday and Thursday
are no longer just speculation. They are all true. It's much
worse than we suspected . . . Please bear with me. There
is no way to sugarcoat what I'm about to tell you, except
to confirm Peter and I have evaluated the information
and, God willing, we have devised a plan to ensure the
safety of all here . . . James, I learned this morning the
special grand jury in Washington has delivered a sealed
indictment accusing you of acts of terror against our
country."

Sarah uttered a soft "Oh, no!" and tears welled up in
her eyes. James put an arm around his wife and pulled her
head against his shoulder. Peter, who had spent the afternoon with Mack, held Rachel's hand on the table.

For the next ten minutes, the vice chairman of the
Senate Select Committee on Intelligence spoke dispassionately and without interruption about the evidence he
had accumulated on what he called "the president's most
provable crimes and impeachable offenses":

- Withholding intelligence about those who really perpetrated the 9-11-32 terror attacks in Houston;

- Secret promises to enrich the Caliph by granting the Muslim leader exclusive "refill rights" for the U.S. Strategic Petroleum Reserve in exchange for a commitment to prevent terror attacks against the United States until after the election;

- DNI Admiral Stanley Turner's current secret trip to Mexico City, offering President Rodriguez the same "SPR refill rights" in trade for the Mexican leader's undisclosed "help" in preventing the rescue of Admiral Marty Cohen.

Mack concluded his dire presentation: "There are many other offenses harder to prove: violations of the Foreign Intelligence Act; tampering with a grand jury; campaign finance violations in accepting money from a foreign government; abuse of executive power by breaching the Congressional Communications Protection Act; presidential orders to ignore the Federal Patient Records Privacy Act in an effort to collect pejorative information about members of the Newman family. But the most important thing we can do right now is to get James and his family out of harm's way."

James's mother was the first to break silence around the table. Rachel asked quietly, "How much danger is James in right now?"

Mack pursed his lips. "The call I received on my PID while Seth was opening his presents came from my White

House source for all of this," he said, tapping the thick file before him on the table. "This person called to inform me the president had just ordered James placed on the Capture/Kill list."

Rachel gasped and the color drained from her face. As Peter hugged his wife, he said, "Mack, I think you should tell the others what you told me this afternoon about your White House source."

Caperton nodded and continued. "He's a very ambitious man, at the center of all this controversy. He has not always been trustworthy and his lifestyle is not one I can admire. He is well aware I am one of his severest critics. It turns out he is also a very brave man. He's seen firsthand how vicious this president and her closest advisors can be. He knows my communications are being monitored by a special unit at the FBI, yet he has recently found the integrity and courage to pass to me his contemporaneous notes of all that's been happening at the White House for the past twelve months. Most importantly, he made the call this evening, warning of the Capture/Kill finding for James. My source is General John Smith, the president's National Security Advisor."

"Why do you trust him now?" asked James.

"Fair question," Mack replied. "Particularly since all our lives may depend on his veracity. First, General Smith has taken enormous personal risks to get the information in this file to me—and the call he made tonight regarding the Capture/Kill list. Second, much of what I have in this file has been independently verified by other sources. Some of it is from a Secret Service agent who confided in your mother. Still other information has been confirmed by old friends in the armed services, the CIA, DEA, even the FBI."

"So what do we do now?" asked Sarah, looking at Mack through red-rimmed eyes.

"We get you, James, and your boys out of the reach of the criminal in the Oval Office."

"Where will we go?" she pleaded.

"We take James out of the country and we hide you and your boys in Montana with Angela, Beth, Sam, and their boys. That way they can't use you as bait to lure James into a trap."

"How will we get there?"

Now Peter spoke. "Mack and I spent this afternoon coming up with a plan we think will work."

"When?"

The old general shook his head and said, "We don't know exactly when. Smith will give Mack a heads-up if they figure out where James is and come for him. Based on what we know now, we need to be ready soon."

When Peter said it, he didn't know how soon "soon" would come.


**LAFAYETTE PARK**

WASHINGTON, DC
SATURDAY, 18 SEPTEMBER 2032
2330 HOURS, LOCAL

Automated WHCA records showed the National Security Advisor placed four calls from his office phone on Saturday evening. The first two calls, at 1921 and 1935, were to the White House chief of staff's office and lasted less than two minutes each. The third call, at 2005, to the Treaty Room at the Chief Executive's Residence, lasted three minutes, twenty-five seconds. In accord with current protocols, these conversations were not recorded. At 2015 a final call lasting ten minutes, twenty-three seconds was placed to an unregistered PID through a wireless MESH portal at Litchfield, South Carolina. A digital recording of this call was made on a White House Communications Agency computer in the basement of the Eisenhower Executive Office Building—the EEOB.

Secret Service logs show entry and departure times for every employee, guest, and visitor to the White House and the EEOB. All staff and visitor badges contain RFID tags. Within the eighteen-acre complex, forty-three sensors track specific locations of individual RFIDs and PERTs inside and outside the White House. Two hundred and thirty-five live-feed cameras document every movement within—and the immediate area around—the White House complex. Computers in the Secret Service Command Center cross-correlate RFID tag and PERT locations with the video record.

At 2145 General John Smith walked from his office on the ground floor of the West Wing and descended the staff stairway to the White House Situation Room. He said, "Hello, Frank" to the Secret Service agent standing watch at the desk outside the door as his PERT deactivated the electronic lock.

Inside the high-tech facility, Senior Watch Officer Ben Carver rose and said, "Good evening, General. How can I help you, sir?"

"Nothing needed, Ben. Just thought I'd check in with you before heading home. Anything new from Admiral Turner in Mexico City?"

"Nothing since the 'Everything has been arranged' message he sent to the president, you, and the chief of staff a few hours ago."

Smith nodded and said, "Okay. I'll be in my apartment and back here first thing in the morning. Notify me right away if anything pops."

"Yes, sir. Shall I notify your Secret Service PSD and driver to meet you outside on West Exec?"

"No. I need the exercise and it's a nice night. Now that the Park Police have cleared out the occupiers from Lafayette Park, I can take up my morning and evening walks again."

Carver shook his head and said, "General, I know it's not my place, but you shouldn't be out walking alone. This isn't the Truman era. Why don't I have a uniformed officer meet you at the Northwest Gate and escort you."

Smith smiled, patted Carver on the shoulder, and said, "Thanks anyway, Ben. It's a five-minute stroll from here to the Army and Navy Club. I'll be all right."

* * * *

Automated Secret Service logs and surveillance camera digi-vid records confirmed the National Security Advisor departed the personnel portal at the White House Northwest Gate at 21:58:09. Digital files from four surveillance cameras mounted atop buildings and pedestals on the EEOB, the Executive Mansion, Blair House, and Decatur House on H Street showed him walking alone across Pennsylvania Avenue into Lafayette Park.

At 22:03:47, surveillance camera #1173, pointed east from a town house on Jackson Place, recorded 4.7 seconds of video showing General Smith walking north through the park toward H Street. Beside him was an unidentified, six-foot-three individual wearing a dark blue hooded Windbreaker, black or dark blue trousers, and brown or black athletic shoes. A four-hour time-lapse scan of Lafayette Park detected no PERT emissions from any person matching this individual.

At 22:15:09, a watch officer in the Secret Service command center noted a stationary PERT signal emanating from the northeast quadrant of Lafayette Park. After slewing several video and thermal surveillance cameras, he determined the location to be in a coverage gap and sent a "Check Site ASAP" MESH message to the Park Police. The dispatcher sent the nearest K9 unit.

Sixteen minutes later, U.S. Park Police Officer Mike Manning and his dog Casey found the body of General Smith in low shrubbery just ten yards south of H Street. The officer quickly determined the National Security Advisor was shot once with a small-caliber projectile at very close range, just behind his right ear. He immediately summoned an ambulance and called for backup.

Less than an hour after the general's body found, the White House released the following statement to every U.S. and international news service:

Office of the Press Secretary

September 18, 2032: 1129 PM

At approximately 1030 PM, EDT tonight, General John A. Smith, U.S. Army (Ret.), National Security Advisor to the President of the United States, was killed by an unknown assailant in Lafayette Park, less than one block from the White House. General Smith, the first openly gay National Security Advisor, was apparently walking alone, en route to his residence, when he was attacked.

The President was notified immediately. She says, "We have lost one of the most valuable members of our national security team. The person or persons who committed this heinous act will be brought to justice whether they are for-eign terrorists, drug dealers, Anarks, or common criminals committing a hate crime." She has extended her personal condolences to Gen. Smith's parents, siblings, and loved ones.

The crime is being investigated by the U.S. Park Police, the Secret Service, the FBI, and the Washington, DC, Metropolitan Police. All media inquiries should be made to the Department of Justice.

# CHAPTER FOURTEEN

# RUN!

**TREATY ROOM, THE WHITE HOUSE**

1600 PENNSYLVANIA AVENUE

WASHINGTON, DC

SUNDAY, 19 SEPTEMBER 2032

0045 HOURS, LOCAL

She was seated behind the large desk, wearing her trademark red, white, and blue exercise suit with the presidential seal and an American flag embroidered above her left breast. She was clearly agitated. "What do you mean they can't be arrested tonight? You assured me Keker and his goons would have everything ready! We know where these criminals are. I want them taken now! This is just the kind of boost my campaign needs."

Chief of Staff Muneer Murad and White House Counsel Larry Walsh stood mutely before her. She summoned them to the Treaty Room but didn't invite them to sit. Muneer spoke quietly: "Madam President, Acting Director Keker is still moving assets into position. He's had Newman's indictment and arrest warrant for less than twenty-four hours. As I reported to you earlier, Keker wants to use Homeland Security officers for the apprehension, not FBI agents. He says he will have everything in place in eighteen hours."

She slapped her palm on the desktop and stood up. "That's not good enough! I want Newman and Caperton apprehended now. They are a threat to the security of the United States and that threat needs to be eliminated."

Walsh tried to intercede. "Please listen. Things are happening very quickly and we cannot afford to have anything go awry. Keker has his hands full right now dealing with the investigation into General Smith's untimely demise just a few hours ago. We need another day to make sure this goes right. We don't even have an arrest warrant for Caperton and we won't be able to get one until later this morning."

"Don't make excuses, Larry. We have all we need. You saw the PID-vid. James Newman is with his wife, his children, and his parents, and Senator Caperton is with them. Caperton is identifiable even in the brief seconds he appears—conspiring with a wanted terrorist. Tell the AG to draft a warrant to arrest Caperton based on what we already have from our communications surveillance and this PID-vid—and get it to one of the pet judges I appointed. We need to get on with this. Do we have a PERT track on their locations?"

Walsh shook his head and said, "There are no PERT signals from anyone in the Newman family. We have to assume they have been disabled or masked. But according to the MESH portal database, the PID-vid originated at or near the Newman house—they call it Cair Paravel—on Pawleys Island."

The president picked up the digi-vid from her desk and touched the screen to replay the twenty-three-second video. "Look!" she exclaimed. "There's even a firearm visible on

the table—in the presence of children! That's a violation of
our Federal Child Protection statute. Add child endanger-
ment to the Caperton arrest warrant and indictment. Have
you found out why there is no sound on this vid?"

"Apparently there is no audio signal," her counsel
replied. "We wouldn't even know this vid existed but
for an analyst at the MESH Surveillance Service. He
programmed Newman's image into the facial recognition
software at the DHS all-source intel-fusion center and the
system spit out the vid. The DHS analyst thinks the vid
is from some kind of flying toy being operated from an
unregistered PID . . ."

"Well, well; an unregistered PID. That's another
violation of law. What more does Keker need to take this
whole gang into custody tonight?"

Muneer sighed and said, "He says he needs another
twenty-four hours. He wants to get the right DHS people
in place—with a Schedule C agent in charge. There are
already more than sixty agents headed down there right
now, but Keker wants time to coordinate everything so
Newman can't escape. There are two causeways connecting the island to the mainland. Both have to be sealed
without creating a lot of attention. He also wants to pre-
position some armed agents offshore, cordon off Highway
17, and get an ISR platform in place."

"ISR platform. Remind me what that means," she said.

"An intelligence, surveillance, and reconnaissance aircraft—manned or unmanned. I don't know which he's planning to use. But the point is all this takes time. Keker says
we need to do all this during the hours of darkness—and the
earliest it can be put together properly is tomorrow night."

"We can't afford to wait—and we're not going to.
These people could be gone by then. We know Smith
double-crossed us and warned Caperton—"

"Stop!" Walsh said. "You have to get out of your head anything you know about Smith's call to Caperton. You must not talk about that to anyone. It gives motive to what happened to—"

"I got it, Larry," the president interrupted in return. "Now, you two get this: Newman and Caperton need to be taken down tonight. I want this to make the Sunday morning talking-head shows eight hours from now. That will give us maximum political impact. It's just what we need in the aftermath of Smith's unfortunate passing. Make it happen. And then plant a rumor we've broken the Anark ring responsible for the attack in Houston. If Newman and Caperton happen to die resisting arrest—so be it. Tell Keker I want this to go down before dawn. To-night!"

As Murad and Walsh headed for the door, she asked, "Have we heard anything new from Stanley Turner in Mexico City in the last few hours?"

They both paused as Murad responded, "Only that Mexican President Rodriguez has expressed his condolences over the murder of General Smith and 'Everything is in place to deal with the Cohen matter.' Turner should be back here by mid-morning."

She nodded and asked, "What do you two think about appointing Turner as interim National Security Advisor?"

As Murad opened the door, Walsh answered, "Turner's ambitious enough to take the job and this trip to Mexico indicates he's reliable—but we thought Smith was, too. I think you should leave Muneer in charge of the national security portfolio until after Smith's memorial service on Wednesday. That should give me time enough to see if we have anything on Turner that's not already known—to hold him in line. News of the appointment three days from now will give us something to distract the media from any dust kicked up in this Newman-Caperton operation."

She nodded her assent and the two men exited the Treaty Room, then headed for the stairs. Neither one looked back in the dimly lit corridor to acknowledge the Secret Service agent posted outside the door.

## CAIR PARAVEL

PAWLEYS ISLAND, SC
SUNDAY, 19 SEPTEMBER 2032
0211 HOURS, LOCAL

Rachel Newman was awakened by the ping of her PID. It was on a charging pad atop the nightstand beside the bed she shared with her husband. Peter barely moved as she reached for the device and pressed the corner between her thumb and forefinger to activate it. She glanced at the screen and read the nine-character text message: "IS40:31FJ."

She immediately sat bolt upright in bed, nudged her husband awake, and handed him the PID. He looked at the glowing screen, shook his head, and asked, "What's this mean?"

Rachel took the device and said, "It's Isaiah 40:31—you know, '. . . mount up with wings as eagles . . . run and not be weary . . . walk and not feel faint.' It means they are coming for our son."

"Who sent it?"

"It's from Secret Service Agent Frances James . . . a very simple signal we worked out when we met at church. It's far too complicated for you special operators and spies—but the message means we have to get Jim-Boy out of here. Now!"

Peter was suddenly energized. As he swung his legs out

of bed he whispered, "Rachel, you really are amazing. I'll wake up Mack. You get James and Sarah. Tell them not to turn on any lights or wake the kids yet."

Less than five minutes later, all five hastily dressed adults were gathered in Peter's office. He had closed the blinds and pressed the rheostat for the lights to the dimmest setting. After Rachel read the message on her PID and explained what it meant, Peter said, "Mack, can you check with General Smith to see what's up?"

Mack pulled his government-issued PID out of his shirt pocket, pressed the corner to turn it on, and grimaced when he saw the message displayed: "PID-SIG BLOCKED."

The senator frowned, quickly shut off his PID, and said, "Rachel, before we went to sleep, we agreed yours would be the only authorized PID left on. Is yours still working?"

She glanced down at her screen and said, "It was, but now it says my signal is blocked."

"That's not good," Caperton said. "Unless the whole PID system is down, which is very unlikely, it probably means someone has set up a local jammer to block any inbound or outbound PID signals to discrete devices."

"What does that mean?" asked Sarah, standing beside James, her arm around his waist.

James, a PID in each hand, looked up and answered, "Whoever is doing this doesn't want to block the whole system, because then they couldn't talk to each other except by radio or landline—so they block specific PIDs at various MESH nodes instead. My SSCI staff PID is blocked, but unregistered PIDs should still work—at least until a tech can figure out what's being transmitted. Why don't I go down the beach, away from the house, and try to send a short message to the CSG Ops Center."

"Good idea," said Peter, "but as far as we know, you're the one they're after and if they are already here, they could grab you. I'll go."

"No, Peter," Rachel said, "I'll go. I'm probably the only person in this room who isn't wanted for something. I'll walk down to the Sea View Inn, tell Henry to get to the plane right away, and see if I can contact the CSG Ops Center. You and Mack stay and help everyone get ready to get out of here."

The old Marine smiled at his wife. "Like I said, you never cease to amaze me." Then, handing her an unregistered PID, he added, "Don't turn it on until you get to the Sea View. If you have service when you get there, after contacting the Ops Center, wipe it down to remove your fingerprints, leave it on, and drop it in the dunes before coming back. It may help distract whoever is coming and buy us a few extra minutes."

"Okay, what else? Do you think I should take those night-vision things with me?"

Peter unlocked his desk, reached into a drawer, pulled out a set of PVS-42 thermal glasses, checked the battery, pressed a tiny button atop the right temple hinge, and handed them to his wife, saying, "I've turned off the transmitter, but the memory chip will record the image and range of whatever you're seeing for up to an hour. You remember how to turn them on?"

She looked for the little switch on the front of the bridge, pointed to it, and asked, "This one, right?"

"Right," Peter replied. "If you're approached by anyone out there, just slip them in your pocket. Unless someone knows what they are looking for, they will likely mistake them for a pair of old-fashioned eyeglasses with ugly frames."

Rachel slipped the thermal optics into the pocket of her fleece vest, put on a dark blue Windbreaker, and quietly exited the beach-side door. As she left, Mack pointed to an old digital radio on the shelf behind Peter's desk and said, "We need to get some news. Does that still work?"

Peter reached up, turned the radio on, and pressed a preset button for BBC.

They had to listen for only a few moments before the newsreader said:

> *And now, the latest developments from the United States. According to the U.S. Justice Department, a full-scale manhunt is under way to find the individual or persons responsible for last night's slaying of General John Smith, the National Security Advisor to the president of the United States. A Justice Ministry official speaking on background to our BBC correspondent in Washington says there is a reward of twenty-five million gex for information leading to the apprehension of the assailants who are now listed as "wanted—dead or alive." We'll have more at the top of the hour.*

"Well," said Mack, "that explains why we didn't hear from Smith. We better put our 'E-and-E plan' into effect."

James and Sarah went upstairs to complete the packing they began before bedtime and start gently waking their boys. Mack went to his room and changed into a pair of dark trousers and an old black turtleneck sweater. Then he pulled a pair of dark athletic shoes out of his bag, sat down, and put one shoe on his foot and the other on the foot of his prosthetic leg.

Rachel was gone for nearly thirty minutes. By the time she returned, James and Sarah had dressed the boys and moved them down the darkened stairway to the living room. When she let herself in, the twins, David and Daniel, were asleep on the sofa while Seth and Josh, caught up in the drama of a late-night expedition, whispered excitedly while poring over the items they were taking. The adults reassembled in the dimly lit office to hear her report.

"I didn't see anyone on the way to the Sea View. I went to Henry's room and woke him. His PID was working, so he texted the CSG Ops Center telling them to activate the flight plan he filed when we arrived at the Myrtle Beach FBO. Don Gabbard is on duty and called Henry right back."

"Could you tell if they were on a secure voice circuit?" Peter asked.

"Yes. Henry had the speaker on so I could hear and it had that garbled sound. They talked for only about fifteen seconds because Don said he was concerned about 'shouting in a crowded room'—whatever that means."

"It means Don is aware others are listening. Did he pass on any news about what's happening?"

"Yes, but he sent it by digi-text—two messages. Henry and I read them both. I was going to forward them to the PID you gave me but Henry told me not to activate it until he got off the island. Before he left for the airport he showed me how to take digital images of the two messages off his PID screen with the night glasses. He said you and James would know how to download them to a digi-screen."

"Henry's savvy," James interjected. "He was a Night Stalker pilot in the old days."

Rachel pulled the PVS-42 thermal glasses from the pocket of her Windbreaker, handed them to her husband, and said, "The first message is a Global Press MESH report about General John Smith, the National Security Advisor, being murdered earlier tonight . . ."

"We caught that from the BBC just after you left," said James, pointing to the old radio.

"Did the BBC report name a suspect?" she asked.

"No."

"Well, according to the MESH newswire Don forwarded, a Justice Department leaker says you are the prime suspect."

Sarah, long past tears, simply shook her head and hugged her husband.

As Peter took the PVS-42 glasses from her, placed them atop the viewer plate on his desk, and touched the Proximity Download icon, Rachel said, "Skip to the second item—that should be Don's second message. It's a short news flash from a Swiss MESH service, but it's very cryptic."

All five of them crowded around the eight-by-ten-inch plate to read what she copied. It was fuzzy but legible:

(EIN) Alpine Rescue—*Berne, Switzerland*—Seven hikers presumed lost on the east slope of Mount Drümännler in Berne Canton have been found and rescued according to Swiss authorities. More than 70 Alpine Lifesaving Experts were dispatched to the site. Dr. Hans Brükke, the senior Rega Rescue authority on-scene, said the normal route off the mountain was blocked by an early winter storm. "We had to find them and get them out immediately because of the likelihood of an avalanche," he said. The hiking party included Hansel and Trina Oldmund, their four young children, and 76-year-old Pieter Bernard Van Hooser, a well-known wilderness guide who lost a leg to frostbite during an Antarctic expedition.

After the successful rescue, Brükke told reporters, "We would have found them sooner if they had PERTs or wilderness transceivers but they didn't. Thankfully, we had all the right equipment and sent out a search party after dark

with Recco detectors. Otherwise they might never have
been found."

"What does it mean, Peter? Why did Don send us this?"
asked Sarah.

"It's a coded warning—made to look like a press
release. 'Alpine Rescue' is one of our CSG emergency
signals. James devised these two years ago for our teams
operating in denied areas where we couldn't use encryption equipment. Ignore the past tense, names, and places
in the message—this has nothing to do with the Swiss
Alps. Here's what it all means:

"'The seven hikers' are the targets . . . 'Seventy experts'
is the number of armed people coming . . . The 'normal
route' being 'blocked' is a warning not to use an obvious escape path. 'Winter storm' and 'avalanche' are code
words for an imminent attack. 'Immediately' is a signal to
get out now. The names are bogus. The only husband-wife
pair here with four children are James and Sarah. 'Pieter
Bernard,' the seventy-six-year-old, one-legged 'wilderness
guide' has to be Mack—and this means they are coming
for him, too. The part about PERTs and transceivers is a
warning to stay off the MESH and all other emitters."

"What about the 'Recco detectors'?" asked Sarah.

"It's a very sophisticated search device used by ski patrols to rescue avalanche victims. In this message it means
the people headed here are very well equipped. The part
about 'a search party after dark' is a warning they are coming at night. Probably right now."

"Well," said Rachel, "all that matches what I saw right
after Henry left the Sea View Inn for the airport. If I
pushed the right button on the glasses, it's the next entry
on what you just downloaded."

Peter touched the play-video icon on the screen and said, "Tell us what we're seeing here, Rachel."

She nodded and said, "As soon as Henry left, I stood on the walkway at the Sea View, facing the North Causeway, and turned on the glasses . . . You can see the old chapel there . . . Those red lights are the taillights of Henry's car, just as he passed through the security gate heading off the island. Now watch . . . Less than a minute later, all those lights . . . it's a convoy of seven big SUVs headed onto the island . . . The lead car stops . . . five men jump out . . . grab old Mr. Bergan and drag him out of the guardhouse . . ."

"It looks like they are beating him!" said Sarah.

"They are," said Rachel. "Watch . . . It's hard to see, but they throw him into the back of the last SUV . . . and it pulls sideways to block the roadway by the security gate . . . the gate opens . . . and six of the vehicles race across the causeway and onto the island . . . Now you see one of the vans headed south on Myrtle Avenue . . . toward me at the Sea View . . ."

The video suddenly stopped. "That's all I could get. I didn't want them to see me and cut me off before I could get back here. I turned on the PID you gave me, wiped it off, and dropped it on the dune as I ran back to the beach. I couldn't tell for sure, but it looked like one of the SUVs stayed at the intersection of Causeway and Myrtle—right by the police station. Just as I got back here, I could see three or four bright flashlights moving out on the pier. I didn't want to stop and put on the night glasses because I was afraid they might shoot me."

Now Peter put his arm around his wife and said, "I'm glad you are safe. You did a great job, sweetheart—as good as any MARSOC Marine . . . You got just what we need so James, his family, and Mack can get off this island."

"But how?" Rachel asked. "It looks like they have the only exits blocked and they must be headed here. They could be here any minute."

"Right." He nodded. "But while you were gone, Mack, James, and I came up with Plan B. We have to hope the person in charge of the people you saw has some kind of operational experience—meaning he's likely to try setting up a complete cordon without alerting us. There doesn't seem to be anyone this far north yet—and we have an advantage, we know about this . . ." He pointed to the tides table hanging on the wall beside his desk.

Turning to his son he said, "James, your eyes are better than mine. Check the chart and see when the next mean low tide is at Midway Inlet between Pawleys and Litchfield."

James ran his finger down the fine print and said, "Three thirty-seven a.m."

Mack looked at the dive watch on his left wrist and said, "That's eleven minutes from now. We better get going."

Peter touched the DELETE icon on the DigiVu and handed the PVS-42 glasses to his son. Then, reaching into the desk drawer, he pulled out two more pairs of the thermal optics and handed one each to Sarah and Mack, saying, "The transmit and record modes are shut off to save the batteries. They should be good for three hours or so . . . at least through sunrise. The only change in what we originally worked out is Mack will now be going all the way with you. Everyone remember the rest of the plan?"

Sarah, James, and Mack all nodded but no one spoke. "Good," said Peter. "Let's ask the Good Lord to bless this journey."

They linked arms in a huddle and bowed their heads as

Peter said, "Lord of all, we bow before You and no other. Heavenly Father, in the Thirty-Second Psalm, David prayed You would hide, protect, and deliver him from his enemies. You guided him and showed the way he should go, counseled and watched over him. Now we beg You to do the same for James, Sarah, Seth, Josh, David, Daniel, and Mack. Please deliver them to safety, Lord. We ask this in the Name of Your Son, Jesus."

Rachel added, "Amen."

"Now," said Peter, "Rachel, it's time to cook a ham and some bacon. The rest of you, get under way. Godspeed."

Four minutes later they were gone. As they slipped silently out the beach-side door and headed up the beach toward Middle Inlet, seventy-five yards north, James and Mack each carried one of the twins. Seth wore his new backpack and Josh had on his book bag. Sarah carried the .20-gauge shotgun.

At 3:40 a.m., the smoke and carbon monoxide alarms performed to specifications.

*    *    *    *

When the first two fire trucks and an ambulance, lights flashing and sirens blaring, raced up to the North Causeway roadblock, there was a brief shouting match. Three men clad in black armor emblazoned with the words FEDERAL AGENT and toting automatic weapons refused to let the emergency vehicles pass until Midway Fire-Rescue Chief Bill Potter threatened to push the agents' black SUV off the causeway and into the creek. Two additional engines, one each from the DeBordieu and Litchfield stations, arriving just minutes later, experienced no such delay.

Dark, sooty smoke was pouring from a kitchen window when the first engine and a ladder truck arrived at Cair Paravel. Peter and Rachel met them at the open gate and the firefighters immediately illuminated the house and surrounding yard with a half-dozen xenon lights. Chief Potter jumped out of the lead vehicle and shouted, "Anyone left inside?"

"No! The fire is in the kitchen!" Peter yelled over the controlled chaos of ear-piercing emergency radios, roaring diesel engines, firefighters rushing to hook hoses to a street hydrant, and ladders being raised against the porch, twenty-five feet above. As the chief shouted out orders, more sirens and flashing lights announced the approaching DeBordieu and Litchfield trucks.

Four firefighters, their reflective yellow, flameproof jackets and helmets gleaming in the bright lights, reeled a three-inch-diameter hose out of the lead truck, pulled on SCBA face masks, and charged up the stairs. Two of them carried narrow steel cylinders on straps over their shoulders and the other pair dragged the hose up and into the house. Two minutes later one of them appeared on the porch and shouted, "Fire's out! Bring up some fans to clear the smoke."

"Whew!" said the chief, checking his watch. "Four-oh-three. Twenty-three minutes from the time the alarm came in. We'll give the boys a few minutes to blow the smoke out before we go up to assess the damage. Hope it's not too bad."

"Thank you for coming so quickly," said Rachel. "I'm afraid this is all my fault, Chief. I had a ham in the oven . . . must have left it on. I guess the drippings caught fire . . . I'm getting forgetful in my old age."

"Don't you fret about it, Mrs. Newman," Potter said, removing his helmet. "We all make mistakes. Good thing your alarm worked. Smoke kills more people in their beds at night than fires. Let's go up and check for damage and I'll file a report for your insurance."

As they climbed the stairs the chief said, "We would have gotten here a few minutes sooner but some assholes, all kitted up in SWAT gear, had the causeway blocked . . . Tried to keep us from coming on the island . . . Said they were federal agents. Did they tip you off about what they're doing, General?"

"Not really," Peter replied. "Did they say why they're at Pawleys Island? This is a pretty quiet place."

"One of 'em said something about a federal law enforcement operation. Probably a drug bust like the one they did down in Georgetown Harbor last year to seize that boatload of cocaine coming up from Mexico."

When they arrived in the kitchen, the open doors, windows, and powerful fans had cleared most of the smoke from the house. A fireman with a digital camera paused from documenting the scene and introduced himself.

"I'm Lieutenant Strickler, ma'am. Sorry about tracking sand in your house on our boots and equipment. You have some smoke and soot here in the kitchen but it looks like the only fire damage is to the oven . . . and whatever you had in there."

The charred oven was sitting in the middle of the kitchen floor. Rachel peered into the blackened interior and said, "Thank you for your good work, Lieutenant. How did you put it out so fast? I don't see any water . . ."

"We didn't use the hose, ma'am. It's a gas oven . . . not electric, so we used this." He held up a steel cylinder with a long, tubular nozzle. "This is a nitrogen micro-fog bottle—we call it a NIMBLE. It sprays a fog of nitrogen gas and tiny, ionized water droplets to displace oxygen needed for combustion and cool any flammable material. The fire was out in just a few seconds. This thing eliminates the mess from water, foam, or chemicals."

"Well, I'm very impressed. You're very efficient."

"Thank you, ma'am," Strickler replied. "Just don't try to use the range. We pulled it out to shut off the gas valve and check for any hot spots on the floor, walls, and cabinets. Since all the interior doors in the house were closed, it looks like the only room with any serious smoke damage is the kitchen . . . and of course whatever you had in the oven—that's a total loss."

"Yes, it's a shame," Rachel said dryly. "General Newman and I are very grateful to all you first responders. I hope you'll allow me to come to the station some evening and prepare a meal for y'all that's less well done."

As the firemen packed up their gear, Peter and Rachel went back outside to make amends to neighbors awakened by the commotion. At 0445 Chief Potter handed Peter a digi-chip containing his report and vid-files from the firefighters' helmet cams. Before boarding his truck the chief said quietly, "Take a look at the last vid-file, General. It shows a guy in SWAT gear getting out of a black SUV pulled up behind DeBordieu engine number forty-four. The SUV is gone now, but the SWAT guy asked one of my men how many people were in the house and then left. You may want to check it out."

Peter and Rachel waved good-bye to the firefighters and went back upstairs to close and lock the doors and windows. As they stood in the kitchen she said, "Well, it cost us one stove, a seven-pound ham, four pounds of bacon, a quart of vegetable oil, and some smoke damage. Do you think it worked?"

The old Marine put his arm around his wife and said, "I hope so. We should know in a few hours. Let's hope our bedroom doesn't smell like burned bacon, and get some sleep."

**DEA AIR WING HANGAR**

DALLAS–FORT WORTH INTERNATIONAL AIRPORT (DFW)
SUNDAY, 19 SEPTEMBER 2032
0710 HOURS, LOCAL

"That's DFW, just forward of the right wing," Mack said, pointing out the window as the King Air 450 throttled back, descending out of a cloudless, cerulean sky.

Sarah sighed deeply, looked back in the cabin, where her four boys were nestled up against her husband on a sleeper seat, and asked, "Shall we wake up the rest of these refugees?"

Caperton smiled at the sight, nodded, and said, "Yeah, we better get 'em into seat belts. We'll be on the ground in a few minutes and start the next leg of this adventure."

She and the senator had been talking quietly since shortly after takeoff—reviewing the escape from Pawleys Island and plans for the days ahead. As Sarah slid out of her seat and tenderly nudged each of her boys awake, Caperton marveled at how a woman's gentle demeanor could mask courage and iron resolve.

\*  \*  \*  \*

The seven refugees had arrived at the Midway Inlet breakwater precisely at low tide. Mack checked his watch to confirm the time: 0337. As Peter had predicted, the waterway between Pawleys and Litchfield was practically dry.

James, carrying Daniel on his back, led the little band across the passage, followed by Seth, then Josh, and Mack, carrying David on his back. Sarah was last in file—with the mission of helping anyone who fell, got stuck in the soft, wet sand, or strayed off course. No one did. Four minutes after leaving the Pawleys shoreline they were all high and mostly dry on Litchfield Beach as the tide shifted and Atlantic Ocean seawater began coursing back through the inlet.

Though all three adults were wearing PVS-42 thermal optics, it took longer than expected to get to where Mack and Peter had hidden the rental car. Mack had to stop and clean the wet sand out of his prosthetic leg ankle joint. They arrived at the car, parked beneath the fifth house on Norris Drive, just as sirens and flashing lights erupted on Pawleys Island.

Mack was feeling for the car key he taped behind the license plate the previous afternoon when Seth asked, "What's happening back there?"

"That, my boy, is what's called a diversion. Let's get in and go for a ride," said Mack, checking his watch. It was just 0350. They had been on the run for less than half an hour. As they piled into the vehicle, Mack said, "Next stop, the FBO at Myrtle Beach airport."

At the intersection of Litchfield Drive and Highway 17, they saw two police cars and a Midway Fire-Rescue vehicle speeding south toward Pawleys but their drive north was fast and otherwise uneventful. They arrived at the Myrtle Beach FBO at 0430 and were greeted outside by CSG Chief Pilot Henry Simmons.

"Good morning, Senator, Mrs. Newman, James . . . and boys," Henry said, as if their arrival were a routine passenger pickup. "Senator, if you would, please pull the car through the gate and up to the left side of the plane. I've arranged for you to bypass security. The folks here at the FBO will take care of the rental car paperwork."

Mack drove through the gate onto the tarmac, right next to the aircraft, and they began to unload. "What about this?" Sarah said, pointing to the shotgun on the floor in the backseat.

"Ah," said Henry, looking about. He quickly boarded the aircraft, grabbed a blanket from a seat, and returned to the car. Reaching into the vehicle, out of sight of any of the ground personnel or surveillance cameras, he expertly disassembled the firearm, covered it with the blanket, and carried it up the steps into the cabin.

With everyone aboard, he gave a thumbs-up to the two-man ground support crew, pulled up and secured the hatch, climbed into the cockpit, and started his takeoff checklist. A few seconds later he came on the internal intercom and announced, "It's four forty. Unless the winds change or we get rerouted, we should be at DFW by seven. I'm dimming the cabin lights so you can get a little sleep."

The second turbofan engine was just spooling up when Henry got on the intercom again: "Sorry, folks, we've just been given a ground hold to keep clear of the runway."

Mack bolted out of his seat and went to the cockpit. He returned a moment later and said to James and Sarah, "The tower has been ordered to clear the runway for the takeoff of a government RPA. Look out the right side of the aircraft at that hangar over there and you may be able to see it."

While they watched, the doors opened on the nearby hangar and a small, haze-gray, saucer-shaped aircraft with tricycle landing gear rolled out onto the tarmac, turned right onto a taxiway, then left to runway 36. It paused there for a few seconds, then quickly accelerated out of sight.

Fascinated by the sight of the unusual plane, the older boys speculated about what it was doing and where it was headed. "Was that a drone looking for us, Dad?" asked Josh.

"Well, it's not really a drone—it's properly called an RPA—meaning a remotely piloted aircraft or an unmanned aerial vehicle—UAV. That looked like an

RQ-240, a surveillance and reconnaissance bird. They are sometimes used to detect drug runners and human smugglers off the coast."

"Is that the kind of UAV that can shoot missiles?"

"No. Any UAV or RPA with an 'R' designation doesn't carry weapons. They are equipped with FLIR—forward-looking infrared cameras, synthetic aperture radars, and radio intercept gear. They can stay airborne—we call it 'on station'—for many hours, some of them for days." He didn't mention that the military variant, designated MQ-70 Marauder, was capable of delivering precision-guided munitions.

Shortly after the UAV disappeared Henry announced, "We're cleared for takeoff. We should be at DFW shortly after oh-seven-hundred local."

\*　\*　\*　\*

At 0710, the King Air touched down. Guided by a follow-me truck and then a ground handler, Henry pulled the twin-engine jet up to the front of the DEA hangar and shut down the engines. As the hangar door opened, a tug pulled out, hooked up to the nose gear of the CSG aircraft, and towed it inside.

When the hangar door closed behind the plane, Henry opened the hatch and Special Agent Paul DeMelius, head of the DEA Air Wing, bounded up the stairs and said, "Senator Caperton, Mr. Lehnert, Mrs. Newman, boys . . . welcome to Texas. Anyone who wants breakfast, follow me. We'll go to my office."

While the boys washed down breakfast sandwiches with orange juice, DeMelius briefed the adults: "Senator, as soon as you, Mrs. Newman, and the children have had a bit to eat, we'll get you aboard the CSG golf-seven that's inbound from Montana. He's coming in light, so after he takes on a little fuel, we'll pull him into the hangar, get you aboard, and on your way to Malmstrom at about oh-eight-hundred. In that bird it will be a quick flight."

"How long?" Caperton asked.

"Depending on winds and flight profile, at point-nine mach you should be at Malmstrom in about two hours. Sure would like to have a couple of those horses in our DEA stable, Senator."

Mack smiled and said, "Good lobbying pitch, Paul. I'll see what I can do in next year's budget." Then, more seriously, he added, "I need to make arrangements to get picked up when we arrive. As you know, this trip was set up very quickly."

"Not a problem, sir. I'll arrange to have some of our agents from the Great Falls Field Office meet you, Mrs. Newman, and the four boys at Malmstrom and take you wherever you have to go."

Mack nodded approval and added, "It would probably be best if you don't put my name in your message traffic. Just notify your office we need space for six pax. It will be a nice surprise for my wife."

"Can do, Senator." Then, turning to James, DeMelius continued his briefing. "Mr. Lehnert, you're going to stay here with me until about nineteen-hundred tonight. When the golf-seven returns from Montana, we'll load you and some of our DEA FAST personnel and equipment aboard for a quick flight to Mexico. We're still working out a few details."

Seth, the only one of the boys who had been listening to the adults, asked, "Dad, why does he keep calling you Mr. Lehnert?"

There was a sudden silence in the room until Mack said, "It's a secret, Seth. I'll tell you all about it on our trip to Montana."

DeMelius didn't miss any of this but he simply shrugged and said, "I'm going to make sure everything is in order. If you all are ready in fifteen minutes or so, we'll head back into the hangar." Turning again to James he added, "Mr. Lehnert, I noticed you don't have any luggage. If you will just jot down your shirt, trousers, and shoe sizes, one of our DEA logs guys will put a kit together for you to wear in Mexico." Then, smiling, he asked, "Briefs or boxers?"

Fifteen minutes later they were standing in the hangar beside the gleaming Gulfstream VII, exchanging good-byes. Mack, the first to board, watched as James hugged each boy and lifted him up onto the stairs. He saw Sarah and her husband share a long embrace and a kiss. At the top of the steps she turned and said, "I love you," as the door closed.

Sarah checked each of her sons to ensure their seat belts were fastened and sat down across the table from the senator. Mack saw tears in her eyes while she waved to James until the aircraft was pushed clear of the hangar and they could no longer see each other. Then she put her head down on her arms atop the table and sobbed quietly as they taxied.

Ten minutes after they were airborne, Sarah moved to the back of the cabin to check on her sons and then stretch out beneath a blanket on the starboard-side couch. A short while later, Seth came forward and took the seat opposite Caperton his mother vacated. He began the conversation by asking, "Uncle Mack, why is my dad in so much trouble?"

The old senator looked at the boy, nodded, and said, "I guess you're old enough to know the story. Two hours is about enough time." He didn't leave anything out.

# CHAPTER FIFTEEN

# THE SENATOR'S STORY

**ABOARD CSG GULFSTREAM VII**

51,000' EN ROUTE DFW, TX, TO MALMSTROM AFB, MT
SUNDAY, 19 SEPTEMBER 2032
0830 HOURS, LOCAL

You asked why your dad was in so much trouble," Caperton began. "It's a complicated story, Seth, but since you were homeschooled you will get it. If I say something you don't understand, or have a question, interrupt me, okay?"

"Yes, sir," the boy responded, looking into Mack's eyes.

"Good. Most importantly, your dad can be sure where he is going—and why he is going there—because he knows his Lord and Savior. That's why he and your mom gave you that shotgun, Bible, and compass for your birthday."

"I understand," Seth said earnestly. "Mom carried the shotgun. The compass and Bible are in my backpack."

"Well done. Keep the note they gave you. Tuck it into your Bible. It's a great reminder about how to live the rest of your life—and part of the reason your dad is in trouble with our government.

"You also need to know your dad is a faithful husband who loves your mom, you, and your brothers. He would give his life for his family. He's also an American hero who has put himself at great risk for our country. Those are virtues not well understood in our culture today. I have known him since he was a small boy—much younger than you.

"Now, the direct answer to your question actually begins in 1979—before your dad was born. That was the year a Shiite ayatollah named Khomeini returned from exile in Europe to become the Supreme Leader of Iran and proclaim a worldwide Islamic revolution. Within months of taking power, his followers seized the U.S. Embassy in Tehran, took fifty-six American hostages, and held them for four hundred and forty-four days."

"I remember learning about that," Seth said. "The hostages were freed when President Ronald Reagan was inaugurated in 1981."

"Right. But the problem didn't go away just because we had a great president. The Shiite clerics in Iran were intent on creating a worldwide hagiocracy by every means necessary. We didn't catch on—no matter how many times they said it."

"What's a hagiocracy?"

"The dictionary defines it as a government run by a body of people esteemed as holy."

"Isn't that a theocracy?"

Mack smiled and said, "You're very well educated, Seth. To some it may be a distinction without a difference, but a theocracy could be ruled by a king or a dictator—or even an elected leader. The hagiocracy in Iran holds elections. They may be completely flawed, but they are elections. The Iranian people get to vote for their legislature—they call it a Majlis—and a president. They also elect mayors of cities and some other officials. But the candidates for these offices are all selected by a group of so-called holy men called the Spiritual Council.

"In the Iranian hagiocracy the Spiritual Council holds ultimate power. They choose a Supreme Leader from within their own ranks and they pick their own successors. The Spiritual Council and the Supreme Leader determine everything important in Iran: who has rights and who does not; what is law and what isn't; who shall live and who shall die; whether to have war or peace—all of it based on their interpretations of Islamic holy books—the Quran and the Hadith.

"Few in the West have ever bothered to read these books. When Khomeini seized power in Iran, most of the 'experts' said, 'Not to worry—he's an old man. When he dies, the Iranian regime will become more moderate, even reasonable.' But it didn't. There were some like Bernard Lewis who knew better—and tried to warn us. Our politicians ignored his advice. They didn't get it. I have Dr. Lewis's books at the ranch. You're welcome to read them."

"Why didn't our leaders 'get it,' Uncle Mack?"

"Good question. We missed the 'cause' but certainly saw the 'effects.' In the 1980s, American airplanes were bombed and hijacked, our embassy and a U.S. Marine barracks in Beirut were attacked by suicide bombers driving vehicles loaded with explosives, and American citizens were kidnapped all over Lebanon. We ascribed responsibility to terrorist organizations and gave them names like Islamic Jihad, Hezbollah, Hamas, Black September, or al-Qaeda. We even issued Capture/Kill orders for the leaders

of these organizations. I was wounded and lost some very
good friends in Beirut on one of those missions."

"In 1988, my SEAL team was sent on a mission to
rescue a U.S. Marine lieutenant colonel kidnapped in Beirut—and capture or kill the terrorists who grabbed him.
We thought we had good intelligence but it wasn't. It was
a setup and we were ambushed. I was hit by an RPG."

"What happened to the kidnapped Marine?"

"The kidnappers tortured him for over a year, then
murdered him in 1990. They sent a videotape of what he
endured to his widow. We eventually figured out the Iranians directed the whole thing. But even then we missed
the forest for the trees—we were seeing individual terror
groups but we were actually up against something much

"Was that when you lost your leg?"

"No, that was a few years later, in Iraq, during Operation Desert Storm. It was a different country—but the
enemy was the same—radical Islam. But even then, we
still couldn't name our enemies."

"Why didn't anyone in our government figure it out?"

"It wasn't just in our country—it was all of us in the
West—meaning the United States and Europe. We couldn't
grasp the idea that self-appointed leaders of a religion—not
a political system like communism or fascism, or a nation-
state like Germany or Japan in World War II—had declared
jihad against us. And so it got worse—especially as the
most radical leaders of Islam's Sunnis decided to prove they
should lead the jihad by being even more violent than the
Shiites. Do you know what *jihad* means, Seth?"

"It means 'holy war,' I think."

"Correct. The word *jihad* appears more than forty

times in the Quran—the Muslim holy book. Its literal English translation is 'struggle' or 'striving.' Some Muslims say it means an 'inner' or 'spiritual' struggle. But to many, many other Muslims, especially the Sunni and Shiite radicals who envision a global hagiocracy—jihad is a religious war against nonbelievers—infidels—those who refuse to submit to the teachings of Muhammad—particularly Christians and Jews. Unfortunately, very few of our political leaders have been willing to accept that idea—even after the terrible attack on our country on September 11, 2001, when your dad was just five years old. Do you know what happened that day, Seth?"

"Yes, sir. That's the day Islamic radicals attacked America by hijacking four airliners and killed almost three thousand people."

"You're right. But most Americans would say the attack was carried out by a particular group—al-Qaeda—led by a man named Osama bin Laden. Who told you it was 'Islamic radicals' who attacked us that day?"

"I don't know. I guess I read it somewhere or my mom or dad said it. Maybe Granddad."

"Well, that's another reason why your dad is in trouble. For decades our government told us it was wrong to refer to those who hate us as 'radical Islamists.' Our government refuses to use terms like that—in fact in 2014, they declared the phrase 'radical Islamist' to be 'hate speech' and made it unlawful to say or print the words. They describe those who attacked us then—and since—as 'violent extremists.' Our government wants us to believe those who attack us are a small group of bad people led by a particularly bad man."

"Why?"

"Several reasons. First, we abandoned our Judeo-Christian heritage and became so totally self-centered and secular in our thinking we could no longer comprehend how others regard religion to be so important they want to die for it. Therefore, we called vicious killers 'extremists' or 'al-Qaeda'—not what they really are: radical Islamists, guided by the vision of a global hagiocracy.

"Second, for more than a century we in the West have gotten most of our oil from parts of the world where Islam is the predominant religion. Our economy has long been very closely tied to the cost and availability of oil. But we refuse to acknowledge our petrodollars—I suppose we'll call them 'petro-gex' next year if the president is reelected—actually fund the jihad against us.

"Third, it's human nature to deny our own errors or acknowledge our own bad judgment. It's easier for us to believe bad outcomes are someone else's fault. In this case we convinced ourselves the problem of 'extremism' and 'unrest' in the Middle East would all just go away if Israel made peace with the Palestinians. So we abandoned Israel—our only real ally in that part of the world. What nobody understood was radical Islamists never wanted peace—they just wanted Israel to disappear. The Islamists spelled 'peace' with Israel 'p-i-e-c-e.'

"By the time your dad graduated from the Naval Academy in 2018, the United States was no longer an economic or military superpower. Our country was deeply in debt to foreign lenders—principally China and India—and in 2019, our government decided to all but eliminate the brightest, best-equipped, most competent and effective force for good the world has ever known—the U.S. military."

"Why?"

"Because the United States and most of Europe went bankrupt—morally, spiritually, and financially. For decades political leaders in Europe and America told people that government could provide for all their needs. People came to expect government to give them housing, food, electricity, health care, transportation, jobs, and a comfortable retirement. In Europe it's called 'social welfare.' Here in the United States we call them 'entitlements.' Politicians use these government programs to redistribute wealth—taking it from some and giving it to others—as 'legal bribes' to get reelected. To pay for all the promises the politicians made they kept borrowing more and more money, raising ever higher taxes on the most productive Americans and eliminating what they called 'wasteful military spending.' It was a disaster.

"By 2018, when the 'second dip' of the 'Great Recession' hit, our two-party political process—which served us well for more than two centuries—self-destructed. The Democrat Party rebranded itself as the 'Progressive Party.' The Republican Party fractured into a half-dozen splinter movements when 'Progressives' decided the best way to pay off our debts was to grant citizenship to millions of illegal aliens and encourage hyperinflation of our currency. Americans with the means to do so fled to other countries."

"Where did they go?" the boy asked.

"Australia, New Zealand, Singapore, Switzerland— some to South America—anywhere they felt safe. The 'brain drain' and 'capital flight'—that's what the press called it—resulted in those who departed being described by our government and media as 'selfish traitors.' Later, when we made it unlawful to say or write things critical about abortion or radical Islam or homosexuals—and revoked tax exemptions for churches that refused to perform same-sex marriages—there was a second wave of departures."

"But how did all this make my dad a wanted man?"

"Because families like yours, who stayed and fought back—not with bombs or bullets, but with ballots and hard work—infuriated the political elites and were branded as politically incorrect, intolerant, unpatriotic 'religious kooks.' That's where the term 'Anark' originated. It doesn't have anything to do with anarchy. It's an abbreviation for 'Anti-American Religious Kooks'—a pejorative term for describing American Jews and Christians who wanted to do more to help Israel after the nuclear attack on Tel Aviv in 2020. By the time your dad got in that terrible gunfight in Shindand, Afghanistan, in 2025, the Newman family name was already on a blacklist of people who were deemed politically incorrect."

"You know, Uncle Mack," Seth said, in a voice barely above a whisper, "my dad has never talked about what happened in Afghanistan. He and Mom have told me how my father was killed saving Dad's life in Egypt back in 2020—and about getting married two years later and how he adopted me before Josh was born. But neither of them ever mentioned anything about what happened in 2025 at Shindand or the congressional hearings the following year. All I know about those things is from reading books and articles on the MESH."

Caperton thought for a moment, then said, "Well, it's time you know more of the story. In 2024, during his reelection campaign, our president backed a United Nations plan for reestablishing a Sunni Caliphate to govern in the Middle East. Advocates of this idea thought it would help keep the price and availability of oil down and keep the Iranians in check because the mostly Sunni Arabs supposedly hate the Shiite Persians. The president won by a landslide among the Americans who bothered to vote—about twenty percent of those eligible to do so."

"Do Arabs really hate Persians?"

"When it's convenient. And Sunnis generally don't get along with Shiites. But again, only to a point. They also have an ancient axiom: 'The enemy of my enemy is my friend.' At the United Nations and in countries dependent on Arab oil—the Europeans, China, Japan, Korea, and the United States—political leaders claimed a Sunni Caliph would bring stability to the Middle East—and the price of oil—so they ignored that little piece of history."

"But I thought we have plenty of oil in America. Is that wrong?"

"No. You're correct. We have more than enough coal, oil, and natural gas to supply our own needs—and even export those products to others. But long before you were born, Seth, the 'Progressives' decided to ban any further exploitation of what they called our carbon resources, because doing so supposedly threatened the global environment. At first they claimed using hydrocarbon fuels caused temperatures to rise and would melt the polar ice caps. When 'global warming' was disproved they said fossil fuels cause climate change, hurricanes, cyclones, and tornadoes. The 'Progressive' slogan, 'Earth would be a great place to live except for the people,' resulted in a complete ban on new U.S. coal, oil, or gas exploration in 2024. That's when motor fuel went to six dollars a gallon.

"The day after his inauguration in January 2025, the president began what he called a World Changing Global Tour, pushing the UN Caliphate plan, apologizing for his predecessors who backed Israel, and pledging 'equal dialogue and fairness for all.' He even made his State of the Union address to Congress that year from Saudi Arabia—and called it his 'State of the World Report.' I was one of just twenty-three members of Congress who objected because we believe he violated Article Two, Section Three of our Constitution."

"Did anyone pay attention?"

"No. In February, when the president finally returned to Washington, first the UN and then our Congress overwhelmingly supported reestablishing a Caliphate—with Jerusalem as its capital. By then there were so few Jews remaining in what was left of Israel, putting the capital of the Islamic Caliphate in Jerusalem didn't matter to the rest of the world. And of course, nobody in Europe, the UN, or Washington paid any heed to the Shiites in Tehran and elsewhere screaming about how they would never tolerate a Sunni Caliph in Jerusalem.

"On June 6, 2025, at the end of the Muslim Hajj, the Supreme Islamic Judicial Council of Saudi Arabia, called the Majlis al-Qaeda al-a'la, selected Sheikh Yusef Al-Rahaman Shihab—an Egyptian cleric and member of the Muslim Brotherhood—as the First Modern Caliph.

"That same day, the Shiite government in Iraq announced they were allied with Tehran against the Sunni Caliph. And the next morning, June seventh, Iranian 'volunteers' from the Islamic Revolutionary Guard Corps attacked Afghanistan to seize the city of Herat, claiming they were 'liberating the region to protect the indigenous Persian population.' It was the same rationale Hitler used to occupy Austria and Czechoslovakia in the 1930s."

"Didn't Afghanistan's army fight back?" Seth asked.

"They tried. But it wasn't enough. The Afghans did the best they could, but they didn't have much to fight with."

"Why?"

"Well, when we pulled the last of our troops out of Afghanistan in 2014, we promised to continue helping them build their army, air force, and security services. But in 2019, Congress cut off all military aid to other countries. The president told us it would 'save billions for the American taxpayers.' By 2025 Afghanistan's military looked okay on paper—but they had old weapons, only a few airplanes that worked, and very little ammunition. They were a pushover for the Iranians—who declared Herat to be a 'liberated Shiite enclave' on June tenth, just four days after the invasion.

"That afternoon, the new Caliph made a big speech in Jerusalem, demanding a UN Security Council resolution authorizing an international intervention force to 'save innocent Sunni women and children from being massacred by Shiite butchers.' To the surprise of some, the Russian and Chinese UN ambassadors who had threatened to veto the resolution boycotted the meeting and the resolution passed."

"Were you surprised, Uncle Mack?"

"No. The Russians deliberately did the same thing in 1950 when their ally North Korea invaded South Korea. They could have vetoed that resolution but they boycotted the Security Council meeting then, too. The result was that we lost more than seventy-eight thousand Americans in the four-year-long Korean War. And just like that fight eighty-two years ago, we were caught flatfooted in 2025. But in the Second Afghanistan campaign, it was even worse because our military was so much smaller than it was five years after World War II.

"The only troops we had available to help Afghanistan were Special Operations units—like your dad's half-strength MARSOC detachment. That's how he ended up in Afghanistan during the long hot summer of 2025. He and his Marines deployed to Helmand Province on June eighteenth, two days after Congress passed a resolution approving the use of U.S. military force in what the president called 'Operation Protect Freedom.'"

"Did you vote in favor or against the resolution?"

"I voted no, because I believe if we're going to

war—not simply conducting a raid, or a hostage res-cue—Congress ought to declare war, just like it says in the Constitution. But it didn't matter. The president's 'Progressives' had a sixty percent majority in the House and all but thirty-one seats in the Senate. They all voted to support what the president called a 'brief overseas contingency operation led by the United Nations.'

"By the first week of August, your dad's MARSOC unit—just ninety-four Marines—had equipped and partially trained a force of more than one thousand Afghan irregulars who were willing to fight for their country—or at least their part of it. Many of them were just ten or fifteen years old when the Americans pulled out in 2014.

"Because they had to move on foot—mostly at night—it took them over a month to fight their way north to an old U.S. base near Shindand, about a hundred and twenty kilometers south of Herat. Just after dark on Wednesday, September third, he and his men broke through to allied troops defending the Shindand airstrip—a company of Canadian Rangers and two hundred seventy-five Afghan soldiers—the remnants of a regular Afghan Army battalion.

"The senior Canadian advisor—a major—was killed by an Iranian rocket, along with his Afghan counterpart. The wounded Canadian XO—a captain—told your dad they had not been resupplied for more than a week and were desperately low on ammunition, food, water, and medical supplies. Nearly half the Canadian-Afghan force was already dead or wounded by near-constant Iranian artillery and air strikes.

"On Thursday, September fourth, UN 'mediators,' meeting with Iranians in Ankara, Turkey, negotiated what they called a 'Twenty-four-Hour Sabbath-Holiday Truce' to coincide with the Muslim holiday Mawlid al-Nabi—it means 'Birthday of the Prophet.'"

"Muhammad, right?"

"Right. A message was sent out to all UN units in the field to 'cease fire unless fired upon' and 'hold in present positions.' When enemy fire stopped at around one in the morning on Friday, the fifth of September—the Muslim Sabbath, and the birthday of Muhammad—your dad made a satellite radio call requesting evacuation of their most seriously wounded and an emergency resupply. The UN Command at Bagram Air Base north of Kabul dispatched nine RH-85, remotely piloted, twin-rotor helos to deliver pallets of food, water, ammo, and medical supplies. On the way out of Shindand, they evacuated twenty-five seriously wounded American, Canadian, and Afghan casualties.

"The last bird out—with a wounded Marine, the Canadian XO, and a severely burned Afghan soldier aboard—took off just after dawn on Friday morning. About a kilometer outside the perimeter, the RH-85 was hit by a shoulder-fired surface-to-air missile and went down in a wadi east of the base. Without hesitation or waiting for UN 'permission,' your dad immediately launched a twelve-man QRF led by Sergeant Major Dan Doan in three up-armored AATVs with the mission of recovering the wounded and destroying the UAV.

"Before they reached the site of the downed bird, Doan and his little QRF were engaged by hundreds of Iranians and had to dismount from their disabled vehicles. When he heard the gunfire and the radio calls, your dad immediately authorized Marine snipers to engage any visible enemy combatants, told the four mortar crews in their pits around the base to fire in support of Doan's unit, and then personally led a second QRF—just nine Marines in four AATVs—where Doan and his men were pinned down, battling for their lives. The fight went on until well after dark.

"By the time they fought their way back inside the Shindand base just before dawn Saturday morning, every Marine had been wounded at least once. Your dad was hit twice by Iranian bullets and three times by shrapnel from Iranian RPGs, rockets, and artillery. All their vehicles were destroyed. Despite very heavy enemy fire and carrying all the casualties, they fought their way back into the base. The only ones who didn't make it out alive were the three casualties who went down on the unmanned helo. The wounded MARSOC Marines carried the bodies of the dead Marine, the Canadian officer, and the Afghan soldier all the way back to the base under fire so the bodies of the dead couldn't be desecrated by the Iranians.

"Just after sunrise on Saturday, six September, three U.S. Air Force MH-70, long-range rescue choppers flew from Bagram all the way to Shindand. Though the Shindand base was being plastered by Iranian artillery and rocket fire, the Air Force 'Pedros' and 'PJs' succeeded in evacuating eighteen of the most seriously wounded Marine, Canadian, and Afghan casualties—including a wounded Afghan civilian woman about to give birth.

"By then, your dad was unconscious from loss of blood, so his XO, Captain Paul Goodwin, put your dad on the last cas-evac bird. Three days later—September ninth—he arrived at Walter Reed National Military Medical Center, Bethesda, Maryland. I went with your mom, granddad, and grandmother to see him. He was still unconscious."

Seth shook his head and said, "Uncle Mack, I've never heard any of this before. But I don't understand, how did anything you just told me get my dad in trouble?"

"Well, son, that should have been the end of the story—but it wasn't. The day your dad arrived more dead than alive at Bethesda, the Iranians claimed the Shindand incident was a violation of a UN-negotiated Sabbath-Holiday Truce. They said the resupply/cas-evac RH-85s at Shindand were delivering reinforcements in violation of a UN-sponsored cease-fire and insisted 'American Marines and other foreign warmongers'—meaning the Canadian Rangers—assassinated an Iranian diplomat. Turns out the last allegation was almost true. A Marine sniper—armed with a Barrett .50-cal sniper rifle—shot and killed the commander of the IRGC Quds Force early in the gunfight on the fifth. The Quds Force commander was apparently the only son of a very senior ayatollah on the Spiritual Council in Tehran.

"Iran's ambassador to the UN charged 'American invaders' in Afghanistan with assassinating a diplomat and precipitating a wider war. That afternoon IRGC maritime units, using corvettes they bought from Spain and a flotilla of speedboats, dropped mines in the Hormuz Strait as an 'act of self-defense' under the UN Charter. On the night of September ten, a high-altitude Global Search RPA caught imagery of the Iranians putting what looked like warheads on five ICBMs at their Nantez Space Research Site. The next morning our UN ambassador showed the imagery at an emergency meeting of the Security Council and everyone at the UN and the White House panicked."

"Why?"

"Mostly because of oil. The price had already jumped from $195 per barrel before the Caliphate was declared to $315 per barrel. On September 11, 2025, it went to $550 per barrel—and we were already draining our Strategic Petroleum Reserves. So, at our request, the British introduced a resolution authorizing NATO and the Caliphate to use military force under the UN Charter to take out Iran's missile sites and nuclear facilities."

"Could NATO and the Caliph do that?"

"No. Only the U.S. had the means—but the president wanted to have the cover of a UN resolution because he was a big proponent of 'collective security.' It didn't matter anyway because the Russians and Chinese vetoed the resolution. So that night the president finally issued orders for unilateral U.S. strikes using nonnuclear, AHW munitions against all known Islamic Revolutionary Guard Corps nuclear weapons and long-range missile installations."

"What are AHW munitions?"

"Air-, ground-, and sea-launched Advanced Hypersonic Weapons. They are precision-guided missiles with extremely high-explosive—called EHE—conventional warheads. AHWs hit their targets at better than mach twenty—about sixteen thousand miles per hour. The fuses can be set for an airburst over the target, to explode on impact, or to penetrate up to four hundred feet underground before detonating. The president ordered more than thirteen hundred air-, sea-, and ground-launched AWHs fired in less than an hour on the night of September 11, 2025. They hit every confirmed missile assembly complex and nuclear weapons site in Iran—most of them multiple times."

"If our military was so small, how did we fire so many at once?"

"Well, the attack required nearly half our entire inventory of AHW weapons. The sea-launched missiles came from our submarines and surface vessels in the Persian Gulf, Red Sea, and the Indian Ocean. Ground-based missiles were fired from Kuwait, Turkey, the United Arab Emirates, Kenya, Uganda, and Somalia—and some from as far away as Sicily and Diego Garcia. The air-launched missiles were launched from USAF flights scrambled from Kuwait, Turkey, and Diego Garcia and carrier-based Navy and Marine attack aircraft in the Indian Ocean."

Seth, wide-eyed, asked, "Did they knock out all the Iranian nuclear weapons?"

"We thought so at the time. But we were wrong. All the Iranian missile assembly sites were destroyed—but not their nuclear weapons facilities. We just didn't have enough AWH weapons to go after other locations deemed to be suspicious. As it turned out, at least five of their most advanced nuclear installations were untouched."

The boy shook his head and said, "So what did the Iranians do then?"

"The morning after the AHW attack, Iran's Supreme Leader called for an immediate cease-fire in Afghanistan and direct peace talks with the United States. Against the advice of the Joint Chiefs of Staff, the Director of National Intelligence, and some of us in Congress, the president refused to back a covert plan for supporting an armed opposition movement to overthrow the regime in Tehran. Instead he agreed to the cease-fire and direct talks in Berlin with the ayatollahs. That's what created the problem for your dad."

"How?"

"The so-called peace talks began on October first. During the first meeting, the Iranians handed the president a long list of grievances against us. At the top of their list was a demand to immediately lift all economic sanctions. The second item was a requirement to apologize and punish all responsible for 'violating the UN's Sabbath-Holiday Truce' at Shindand on September fifth. In what he called 'a show of good faith,' the president agreed to these terms. That afternoon, 'Progressives' in Congress introduced a resolution lifting all economic sanctions against Iran and announced formation of a 'special, nonpartisan, Joint House-Senate Committee to immediately investigate and punish all responsible' for what they called the Tragic Incident at Shindand."

"Did they mean the one where my dad was wounded?"

"That's what they meant—but they didn't know then your dad was the senior American officer at the Shindand base during the gunfight. That didn't come out until about three weeks later, when congressional investigators leaked his name to reporters and blamed him for breaking the Holiday-Sabbath Truce. On the morning of October nineteenth, every newspaper, television, and MESH news outlet on the planet had pictures of Major James Stuart Newman in news stories about 'the renegade Marine' who started a war . . ."

"I remember that," Seth said. "I was only five years old, but I recall Mom taking us to see Dad in the hospital. There were a lot of reporters with cameras waiting for us at Bethesda that morning. They chased us all the way from the parking garage into the hospital shouting questions at her about being married to the man who caused a war. Josh was crying and so was she . . ."

Caperton patted Seth on the shoulder as tears welled up in the boy's eyes. After a moment the senator quietly asked, "Do you remember what happened next?"

The boy frowned and said, "Not much. I remember when we left the hospital after seeing Dad, reporters on motorcycles followed us all the way to the hotel where we were staying. It was scary—they raced up beside our car and pointed cameras at us as Mom was driving . . . I think it was that night there was a fire at the hotel and there were a lot of firemen and policemen . . . and then Grand-dad Newman came . . . He and a big group of policemen in SWAT gear took Mom, Josh, and me in a helicopter to an airport, where we got on an airplane and flew back to Camp Lejeune . . .

"It all kind of runs together . . . I try not to think about those times very much 'cause Mom was really sad until Dad came home and we had Thanksgiving and Christmas together. He and Mom don't talk about any of that around us kids, so we don't know much of what really went on. There's a lot of really bad stuff about Dad being charged with committing 'war crimes' and 'crimes against humanity' on MESH links I've seen, but nothing much about our family. Do you know what was happening back then, Uncle Mack?"

"Yes," the senator replied, nodding. He paused and continued. "At some point, your mom and dad will tell you more, but here's what I know: The fire at the hotel on the night of October nineteenth was caused by a bomb that detonated prematurely as it was being planted under your mother's car by an Iranian terrorist. Your granddad—and a team of CSG security agents—took you, your mom, and Josh to Joint Base Andrews for a flight to Camp Lejeune on a Marine jet. A few weeks later, when your dad was well enough, the Marines took him on a V-22 directly from Bethesda to Camp Lejeune.

"Just after Christmas, even before he could walk without crutches, your dad was served with a subpoena ordering him to testify before the Special Congressional Committee—the same people who spread all the lies about him you have seen in those MESH reports. The hearings began on January twentieth. They were supposed to be open to the press and the public, but then one of the 'Progressives' remembered what happened when they forced another Marine officer to testify publicly in the 1980s . . ."

"Was that Oliver North?" Seth asked.

"Yes. He's an old friend of mine and your granddad's. His public testimony in 1987 really embarrassed a lot of liberal congressmen and senators back then, so when your dad was forced to testify in January of '26, the 'Progressives' decided to hold the hearings in closed session."

"In secret?"

"That's what they hoped. But it didn't work out that way. Over the course of the four days of your dad's testimony, more than a dozen congressional staffers and even some members of the special committee carried hidden digi-cams into the hearings and then posted what transpired on the MESH."

"Were you on the special committee, Uncle Mack?"

"Yes."

"Did you make any recordings of my dad's testimony?"

"Yes. And I still have them. You can watch them when we get to the ranch if your mom agrees."

"Did you post your vids on the MESH?"

"No. I didn't have to. Others did and it was all very embarrassing to both the 'Progressives' in Congress and the president. That was the big difference between what happened in 1987 and 2026. Lieutenant Colonel North's testimony supported what President Reagan was doing to bring down the Soviet Union's evil empire. Your dad was very critical of how our whole government appeased radical Islamists, abandoned Israel, created the Caliphate, and surrendered to Iran. The 'Progressives' in the White House and Congress tried to make your dad the scapegoat for their own failed policies—and he made fools of them all."

"Was he wrong to do that?"

"No, he was absolutely right. From what they saw posted on the MESH, most Americans admired your dad for telling the truth—but he infuriated the president and his Progressive Party pals and they vowed to get him. They said your dad was 'mentally unstable' and 'deranged.' When our current president's husband was assassinated by a suicide bomber in 2027, she and some prominent 'Progressives' claimed it was because your dad's testimony the year before created a 'climate of hatred among Muslims.' None of that is true, but that doesn't keep them from saying so."

"Is that why they are after my dad now?"

"What happened in Afghanistan in 2025 and his testimony in '26 started the Progressives' vendetta against him. They were outraged when the Supreme Court dismissed all charges against him—and even more so when he took a medical retirement and the Marines awarded him the Navy Cross for what he did at Shindand. Now they need a scapegoat for the terror attack on Houston. They don't want it known the perpetrators were really radical Islamists. So they concocted a story about the attack and the kidnapping of Dr. Cohen being carried out by Anarks—and your dad. The government has indicted him. That's why he has to get out of the country until after the election—and why I gave him a PERT, a PID, and a government ID card identifying him as James Lehnert."

"Doesn't that make you a criminal, too?"

"Criminal? No. Your dad isn't a criminal, either. We have done no harm to our country or our fellow Americans, nor do we pose a threat to either. We do have information that is dangerous to the president's reelection—but we're not criminals, even though they may describe us as such. If the president was abiding by the Constitution and the laws of our land, she would have nothing to fear. But that's not the case today, and that's why it is so important you and your family survive this experience—so what's happening now will never happen again in our country."

*   *   *   *

Ten minutes after the old senator finished his story, the CSG jet landed at Malmstrom Air Force Base and a tug towed the aircraft into the DEA-leased hangar on the northwest end of runway 03. When the hangar door closed, Caperton, Sarah, and her four boys disembarked from the jet.

While Mack introduced his travel companions to DEA Special Agent in Charge Danny Shroyer, a team of techs in blue coveralls lowered the tail ramp of the special-design Gulfstream and began offloading the leather passenger seats and installing standard military web benches on the sides of the cabin. By the time Sarah and the boys returned from the restrooms and grabbed some snacks from the table in the ready room, the senator and the DEA chief had finished a quiet conversation and the aircraft tail ramp was already buttoned up. They all piled into a black GMC Suburban with dark-tinted windows.

As the CSG jet was being pushed out of the hangar to take on fuel and head back to Fort Worth, Shroyer, seated in the right front seat of the Suburban, leaned back and said, "Senator, if you're in a hurry to get to the ranch, I can have the Suburban behind pull in front and hit the blue lights."

Caperton smiled and said, "Thanks anyway, Danny. I'm sure the boys would enjoy that, but let's make this trip as low-key as possible."

"Roger that, sir."

The two-vehicle caravan headed off the base and west on old U.S. Route 89, en route to Interstate 15 and Fort

Shaw. As they got under way and the boys were dozing again, Sarah quietly asked Mack, "So what were you and Seth talking about all the way up from Texas?"

"He wanted to know why his dad was in trouble with the government. So I told him."

"Everything?"

"Pretty much. He's very smart and you have taught him well. Most importantly, he knows his dad is a hero, not a criminal. And no matter what happens to the rest of us, he will be able to tell the story."

Sarah looked out the windshield toward the mountains in the distance and said, in a voice barely above a whisper, "I know James is in great danger. Will my boys be safe out here?"

Mack, looking directly into her eyes, replied, "I hope so."

# CHAPTER SIXTEEN

## GOOD TO GO

**FINCA DEL GANADOR**
3 MILES EAST OF DZILAM DE BRAVO
YUCATAN STATE, MEXICO
SUNDAY, 19 SEPTEMBER 2032
1930 HOURS, LOCAL

Bruno Macklin was never known to waste time. Immediately after his Saturday afternoon sat-phone conversation with A. J. Jones, the retired SAS officer began preparing in case the Iranians occupying Felipe's house a little over a mile away decided to pay him a visit. Unlocking the spacious gun room behind his office, he removed a formidable array of weapons and ammunition that he staged at key locations inside the thick adobe walls of Finca del Ganador.

Then, as soon as it was dark, Macklin turned off all the interior and exterior lights and he and the boy donned thermal night-vision glasses. It took them six hours to place ten well-concealed, radio-controlled claymore mines beside the road and along likely avenues of approach to their refuge.

On Sunday morning, after a few hours of sleep, Macklin fixed them both bowls of hot oatmeal with honey and fresh milk. As they consumed the meal in his spacious kitchen, he and the boy read the Twenty-Third Psalm aloud. Then they commenced re-aiming and adjusting the focus of six hi-res digi-cams mounted on the roof of the two-story house so the location of every mine could be seen on a portable wireless flat-panel monitor from anywhere inside the house. By sunset the old soldier was satisfied they had done everything possible to convert his home into a well-defended fortress.

They had just finished an evening meal of tortillas filled with beef, vegetables, and rice when the sat-phone behind his desk began to chirp. Macklin picked up the handset, looked at the number on the screen, pressed OK on the instrument's keypad, and said, "Go ahead, A.J."

"Bruno, I shouldn't be doing this in the clear but there is no other way and almost no time."

"Right. What's up?"

"At least six SUVs with heavily armed Federation Cartel enforcers are headed your way right now from Merida. The Federal Police Headquarters in Mexico City has issued a 'do not interfere' directive to all units in the Yucatan. According to one of our intercepts, the hands-off order came directly from President Rodriguez himself."

"So how many of these thugs are en route? Do they all want to die tonight?" Macklin asked as he reached for the old, night-scope, suppressor-equipped, 7.62mm SCAR on the shelf behind his desk.

"I don't know yet how many there are—but they aren't coming for you. They are en route to get our MIA admiral."

"Well, to get to where he is by vehicle, they have to come right past here. Where are they going to take him?"

"They aren't going to take him anywhere. They're coming to kill him."

"So your missing admiral is about to go from the Iranian frying pan into the Mexican fire. What's this chap done to make so many enemies?"

"Not sure, Bruno, but I have been asked to see if we can save him."

"Right. How much time do I have and how much help can I get from you fellows?"

"The Federation *cartelistos* have been chattering away on handheld radios because so many PID nodes were knocked out by the hurricane. They are trying to round up as many shooters as possible for a hit at midnight—and they seem to know right where to go. There is a seven-man DEA unit en route from Fort Worth aboard a modified Gulfstream VII, but both runways here at Rejon International are still closed with hurricane debris. According to the message I just received, the DEA team can parachute in at or about twenty-one thirty if you can mark a drop zone—"

"Not so fast, mate," Macklin interrupted. "One can't parachute from a Gulfstream."

"The person who sent the message informs me this aircraft has a tail ramp. I trust him. He's one of us."

Bruno shrugged, glanced at Felipe asleep on the couch on the other side of his office, and said, "Well, a Gulfstream has to have a very narrow ramp—meaning they will have to come out one at a time. Unless they really know what they are doing, they will land miles apart, spread out all over the Yucatan. Do your pilots and paras have night-vision equipment?"

"Let me check the gear list." There was a pause while A.J. consulted the message from Caperton and then replied, "It says here the ground team is equipped with automatic rifles, personal sidearms, TASER rounds; ball, armor-piercing, and incendiary ammo; six grenades apiece; seven AT-9s; NVGs; PRC-5722; encrypted, helmet-mounted, short-range tactical radios; a portable PID terminal; sat-comm radio transceivers; and four hand-launched Hummingbird micro-UAVs. The aircraft is equipped with a FLIR pod, six Hellfire VII rack-mounted missiles, sufficient fuel to remain on station for two-plus hours, and—"

"That's enough, A.J.," Macklin interrupted. "I don't need to know their brand of underwear. Tell me, do you have any contact with the aircraft?"

"Not directly. They are already in the air. I have to relay through two other stations to get messages to or from the aircraft."

"Okay, let's get this done," Macklin replied. "We will use my southwest pasture for a drop zone—it's about seven hundred meters long by four hundred meters wide running north to south. There are no cows, trees, or power poles in it. Since I won't have any comms with the aircraft, tell 'em I'll light the four corners of the Delta Zulu with infrared strobes set on one-second intervals and place a T with steady infrared chem-lights in the center to mark wind direction. As soon as I get out there with my GPS, I'll send you the lat-long coordinates for the center of the zone so you can relay that to the aircraft. You got all that?"

"Got it," A.J. replied.

"Good. Also let your lads with the parachutes know I won't have any comms with them until we link up on the ground. The PID nodes out here are still down from the hurricane and I don't have their tac-set crypto settings. I'll meet them on the DZ. There will be two of us. We will both have infrared chem-lights in the shape of the ancient sign as a recognition signal so they don't shoot us. If you can, see if they can give us a challenge and password so we can prevent a blue-on-blue gunfight. Tell 'em I'm armed. I'll keep this sat-phone with me so you can pass any updates."

"I'll relay all you said and call you to confirm they got the message."

"One last question. What's your exfil plan?" Bruno asked. "Once we get your admiral out of the hands of the Iranians, how do we get him and your lads with the parachutes out of here?"

"The original plan was to have them land at Merida and convoy over to the coast in SUVs with dip-plates I 'rented' from the consulate motor pool. Now I'm hoping you can spare a couple of your vehicles and bring 'em all back here."

"Well, that will cost you extra, given the cost of motor fuel these days, but your credit is good with me."

"Thank you, Bruno. I owe you. Godspeed."

"Think nothing of it, mate. Sir Winston said it was a 'special relationship.' Just make sure your boys don't shoot their 'tour guide' on arrival. That's why we have all these nonmigratory geese down here."

There was a brief pause before A.J. said, "What's this have to do with nonmigratory geese?"

"It's simple," Macklin responded, smiling in the near-dark room. "The reason we have so many Canada geese on our fields year-round is because hunters shot the tour guides. The rest of 'em don't know how to get home."

\* \* \* \*

It took the retired SAS officer less than fifteen minutes to assemble the equipment he needed from shelves in the gun room, place it all in a rucksack, and throw the pack straps over his shoulders. He then returned to the dimly lit office, grabbed the SCAR, gently awakened Felipe, and said, "Sorry to have to get you up, son, but you need to come with me."

"Where are we going, Señor Macklin?"

Handing the boy the same dark sweater and night-vision goggles he wore the previous night while they placed the claymore mines, Macklin responded, "Some soldiers are coming here to rescue the admiral being held at your house. They are going to come down from an airplane using parachutes. We're going to help them."

Felipe was suddenly wide awake and excited. He pulled on the sweater, placed the night-vision glasses over his forehead, and followed the SAS officer down the hallway to the kitchen. Macklin poured them each a glass of water and said, "We're going out to the pasture that you, your father, and brother helped me clear last year. We're going to place some lights on the field so the soldiers can see them from the air. When we get outside, stay close to me. Okay?"

"Yes, Señor Macklin."

"Good. Now I'm going to turn out the light. Put on your glasses and turn them on like I showed you last night. I recharged the batteries, so they should work okay."

The boy did as ordered. Macklin adjusted the head strap so the phosphor glow from the lenses would not leak around the rubber edges and said, "There, you should be good to go."

The boy looked up at his mentor and said, "I can see you but I do not understand 'good to go,' Señor Macklin."

The old soldier smiled and said, "That means you are ready for anything, Felipe."

* * * *

Though it was completely dark, it took Macklin and the boy less than an hour to walk the half mile from the house and install four infrared strobes at the corners of the pasture. When they finished placing and activating the last six chem-lights in a T pattern at the center of the field, Macklin and Felipe moved twenty paces upwind of the marker and Bruno motioned for the boy to sit beside him. He then pulled a GPS device and the sat-phone out of his pockets, inserted the foam-covered earpiece into his right ear, extended the Iridium's antenna, and pushed OK on the phone keypad.

Two rings and ten seconds later, he heard "A.J. here" in his right ear.

"Right, mate. I'm at the center of the DZ. It's lit as I described earlier. Are you ready to copy the coordinates?"

"Don't send it!" A.J. ordered. "Others are listening in. I have the GPS coordinates from your Iridium and will make sure the aircraft has them. They know your visual recognition signal and have confirmed an audible challenge and countersign. It's the first name of the 'special relationship' fellow. The password is his last name."

Macklin nodded in the darkness, replied, "Got it, mate," and ended the call with the push of a button. He then pulled four more of the infrared chemical lights out of his jacket pocket and fashioned them into two of the agreed-upon recognition signals using pieces of tape to se-cure the plastic tubes. Preparations complete, the old sol-dier pulled an SAS poncho liner from his pack, wrapped himself and the boy in it, placed the SCAR across his chest, and leaned back on the rucksack to look at the star-lit sky and await help from the heavens.

**TREATY ROOM, THE WHITE HOUSE**

1600 PENNSYLVANIA AVENUE
WASHINGTON, DC
SUNDAY, 19 SEPTEMBER 2032
2100 HOURS, LOCAL

In all his years around the president and her late husband, Chief of Staff and Acting National Security Advisor Muneer Azzam Murad never saw her so agitated. He and White House Counsel Larry Walsh were persona non grata in her presence since Acting FBI Director Jon Keker awakened her at 0500 to tell her James Newman had somehow escaped from Pawleys Island. The day went downhill from there.

For all of them it was sixteen hours of information overload. It wasn't just the bad poll numbers—they had that covered. It was everything else. At the White House they knew so much—and yet they still could not control events.

After Murad rebuked Keker for calling the president directly without going through the chief of staff, the Acting FBI Director began calling on the secure digi-cube with updates almost hourly. At 2030, Keker called again, asking for an "urgent, private meeting with the president." Murad knew it couldn't be good news.

She had just returned from an evening campaign fundraising event at the Ritz-Carlton hotel when the chief of staff called her in the residence. The president was curt: "Tell Keker to meet me in the Treaty Room at nine p.m. You and Walsh be here ten minutes early."

Murad mentally noted the "Walsh" instead of "Larry," but instantly did as bid, summoning the White House counsel by secure PID message and voice-mail. Walsh raced to 1600 Pennsylvania Avenue in a staff car and arrived in the chief of staff's West Wing office at 2047.

With no time to compare notes or share any new information, the pair practically double-timed across the colonnade, into the residence, and took the stairs two at a time to arrive at the Treaty Room door out of breath at 2055. The female Secret Service agent at the portal admitted them without challenge.

The president was seated at her desk, clad in a blue warm-up suit bearing the presidential seal, looking tousled. She didn't rise and instead looked at the time on her PID and said, "You're late."

Muneer started to say, "We got here just as soon . . ."

She cut him off. "Shut up, M&M. Don't make excuses. I'm sick and tired of excuses. What does Keker want this time?"

Before either man could tell her they didn't know, there was a knock on the door and Secret Service Agent Frances James stuck her head in and said, "Excuse me, ma'am. Acting FBI Director Keker is here. Should I send him in or ask him to wait?"

"Send him in."

As Keker entered the office the president motioned to four chairs in a semicircle in front of the desk and said, "You three sit over there. I don't want to catch stupid from any of you and I have to get up early in the morning to get to Chicago. I'm taking the vice president with me on Air Force One. That means I won't be able to get anything done on this until I get back here tomorrow night."

Murad shook his head and asked, "Does the Secret Service know he's going with you? They howl every time you're in the same city—much less the same airplane."

"Let 'em howl. It's Air Force One. It's the veep's

hometown and he's agreed to make the money pitch."
Turning to the Acting FBI Director she said, "Now, Jon,
tell me what the hell is going on with the Newman family
fugitives and our sinister Senator Caperton."

Without prelude, Keker began: "Since my call early
this morning, I have tried to keep all three of you up to
speed on all I know, but—"

She slammed her palm down hard on the desk and
snarled, "Stop! I don't give a damn what you tried to do. I
just want to know what's going on and get advice on what
to do about it. I don't want explanations, excuses, or em-
bellishments. Do all of you understand?"

They nodded in unison. Keker began again. "Since this
morning we have determined the following: Last night
there was a fire at the Newman residence at Pawleys Island,
South Carolina. In the confusion, James Newman somehow escaped and disappeared again. The place at Pawleys
Island and the Newman home in Virginia were searched
by DHS counterterrorism agents with warrants at thirteen
hundred this afternoon. The agents seized computers, financial records, and multiple unregistered firearms at both
locations but little else. There were no family members at either location and we presently do not know where they are."

"Why don't we know?" she asked. "Last night you told
me James Newman, a federal fugitive, was at Pawleys
Island with his wife, four children, two parents, and the
traitor Caperton. All of them are former military personnel or military dependents. They all must have PERTs and
PIDs. They can't simply disappear. With all the expensive
high-resolution cameras and technology the government
owns, why the hell can't you find them?"

Clearly uncomfortable, Keker continued: "As I told
you all this afternoon, the Newman family members
have apparently disabled or masked their PERTs, which

makes them very hard to trace. We have fed their images and PERT biometric data into the DHS and UN global tracking systems, but none of them have shown up on any facial, fingerprint, or DNA recognition checkpoints in CONUS or overseas."

She shook her head and said, "Your report at seven tonight said you located Caperton. How did you find him?"

"Our Signals Intercept Unit told me their voice pattern computers have high certainty Senator Caperton is at his ranch, west of Great Falls, Montana. The communications analysts believe he has been there since this morning."

"In Montana? Last night he was in South Carolina with his friends the Newmans. How the devil did he get to Montana?"

"We don't know yet. But our SIU experts say Caperton is communicating with others in Mexico about an unknown aircraft headed from Texas to Mexico. That's why I asked to meet with you on such short notice tonight."

The president shook her head and said, "I don't understand what you're telling me. Explain."

Keker took a deep breath, consulted his PID, and went on. "Our SIU has been attempting to monitor all communications to and from Senator Caperton in real time. That's not always possible because he is apparently using multiple unregistered PIDs, so SIU has to rely on voice pattern analysis. Our techs say Caperton is apparently communicating via satellite voice and data interface with a person named A-Jay in Merida, Mexico. This A-Jay person is in voice sat-phone contact with a third suspect named Bruno—also in Mexico. They have been talking about an aircraft headed to Mexico from Texas. According to one of our analysts, Caperton, A-Jay, and Bruno are apparently part of some strange international organization called the Fellowship of Believers. It's—"

"The Fellowship of *what*?" she interrupted.

"Believers."

"Who is in this 'Fellowship of Believers'? How many of them are there?"

"We don't really know. We've done all the usual crime stat, Interpol, and MESH searches but there is next to nothing about them. The members of this group don't seem to communicate through normal channels."

"Who is in charge of this group? Where is their headquarters? What do they believe in? Are they Anarks?"

"We don't know any of that, either. One of our analysts says it's a weird, international Christian group. They apparently use some kind of ancient symbols to identify each other. That's how we figured out—"

"Madam President," Murad interjected, "we're getting very far off track. Can we go back to what Jon was telling us about an aircraft heading to Mexico?"

She nodded and Keker continued. "Caperton and the two in Mexico—the suspects we're referring to as A-Jay and Bruno—have been exchanging information about an unknown aircraft en route from Texas to somewhere in Mexico. In voice sat-phone conversations between these A-Jay and Bruno suspects, we have heard them refer to the 'MIA admiral.' Our analysts believe that's likely to be Admiral Cohen."

What little color that wasn't a cosmetically applied, added attraction drained from the president's face. She turned to Murad and Walsh and said, "Cohen? I thought Stan Turner took care of our Cohen problem with Rodriguez in Mexico City. What's going on here?"

The two men glanced quickly at each other before the White House counsel said quietly, "I'm speaking as your lawyer. Jon and the FBI don't have a 'need to know' about

Stanley Turner's conversations with President Rodriguez. That's a diplomatic matter. It's not part of this discussion about domestic law enforcement."

To change the subject, Murad asked, "Jon, what more can you tell us about this unknown aircraft?"

Keker, clearly confused by the exchange he just heard, again consulted his PID and replied, "We know it's a modified Gulfstream VII and it's not a USG aircraft. It's apparently registered to a company in Switzerland named AvecVous SA but it's not showing up as currently on charter by any U.S. government agency. I've asked the FAA to pull all the records on the aircraft but it's Sunday night and they are having to get someone to come in and find the paperwork . . ."

"Get on with this, Jon," the president urged. "This is superfluous information and you're making excuses again. Why is this important?"

Looking at the screen on his PID, the Acting FBI Director resumed. "The aircraft took off from DFW at nineteen thirty-one CDT tonight after filing a flight plan as a 'humanitarian aid shipment' en route to Mexico City. But after dropping the humanitarian aid equipment or personnel at MEX, it took off again. Now its flight path indicates it is headed for the Yucatan Peninsula."

She nodded and said, "Go on."

Keker continued, "Shortly before I called Muneer to ask for this meeting, the aircraft went silent on its radios and shut off its transponders but we have determined the sat-comm equipment aboard and its frequencies are licensed to a company in Australia. Our analysts say the aircraft may have some kind of military significance because various weapons have been mentioned by A-Jay and Bruno."

Now Murad—the tech-savvy chief of staff—asked, "What sat-comm system are they using?"

Keker looked again at his PID and said, "Our SIU says the A-Jay person in Mexico and this Bruno character are using the Iridium satellite array. So is Caperton for his encrypted data exchanges. We don't know about the aircraft because we can't intercept satellite communications from or to Australia without violating the UN Space Treaty."

"To hell with the UN Space Treaty," said the president, who had lobbied for its Senate ratification. She turned to her lawyer. "Larry, don't we have a Presidential Emergency Action Directive that authorizes us to do whatever necessary to prevent a terror attack?"

Nodding in the affirmative, the White House counsel said, "Pretty much. We're already using your emergency authorities to intercept the Caliph's and Senator Caperton's PID and MESH communications. We used the same PEAD to detain the Navy aircrew that located Cohen's PERT signal in Mexico and to search the Newman properties in Virginia and South Carolina. You have national emergency authority to order the SIU to listen in to just about anybody. We used those same directives to expedite issuing the Capture/Kill order for James Newman on such short notice."

"Good," the president said, smiling for the first time as she arose. "Larry, get me whatever pieces of paper I need to sign authorizing us to intercept or jam whatever communications necessary. Tell the Secretary of Defense I want this pirate aircraft en route to Mexico found, intercepted, and forced to land in U.S. territory or shot down. And get me a Capture/Kill order for Senator Mackintosh Caperton."

At this Keker's survival instinct kicked in and like a

good presidential lap-lawyer he asked, "Why do we have to kill Caperton and shoot down the aircraft?"

"It's simple," she said. "This Swiss-owned aircraft communicating on Australian satellite channels is clearly a drug cartel plane. It probably has perpetrators of the 9-11 attack on Houston aboard. As for Caperton, he is obviously part of the Anark–drug cartel conspiracy with James Newman—a known, wanted terrorist. We have visual proof from the vid you sent me last night. It's also evident the Anark senator is interfering in our effort to rescue Admiral Martin Cohen—a valuable national asset. We certainly don't want anyone to disrupt our effort to rescue the world's expert on fuel cell technology."

As Keker opened the door and the three men headed for the exit she asked, "Muneer, how long will it take to get me the necessary paperwork for all this?"

Murad looked at his PID to check the time and replied, "Jon can take care of the satellite communications intercept order verbally with the SIU when he gets back to FBI headquarters. We can paper that over in the morning before you take off for the campaign fund-raiser in Chicago. But we can't just jam the Iridium system or the Australian uplink overnight. I'll have to check with NSA on what it's going to take."

"How about taking down this suspicious aircraft heading from Texas to Mexico and the Capture/Kill order on Caperton?"

"I'll call the Pentagon and see what military assets are available to deal with the suspect aircraft. The Capture/Kill order for Caperton will take longer because—"

"How long?" she interrupted.

The chief of staff suppressed a sigh and said, "We can't do this on a verbal. Caperton is an American citizen. The

Attorney General and Turner at DNI have to sign off on the authorization order based on the bill of particulars Jon sends us from the FBI. As Acting National Security Advisor, I can sign for the NSC. To avoid putting this in message traffic that others will see, the order will have to be hand carried. Unless Turner or the AG have a hang-up, I should be able to get their signatures and have the order to you by WHCA courier before you take off from Chicago tomorrow morning."

"Good," the president said; then she added, "See to it they don't have any 'hang-ups,' as you put it. We need to clean up this whole Newman-Caperton cabal tomorrow. These people are getting in the way of progress."

As the three men hastened down the stairway, none of them glanced at the Secret Service agent silently holding her breath in the corridor's muted light.

**SON RIVER RANCH**

P.O. BOX 633

FORT SHAW, MT

SUNDAY, 19 SEPTEMBER 2032

2120 HOURS, LOCAL

Mack, we're getting too old for this stuff," said Peter Newman with a smile. He and his old Naval Academy roommate were seated in Caperton's "Ranch Office"—the one the senator preferred over all the perks and privileges of his plush Washington workplace.

"You're right, my friend, it's been a long few days," Mack responded with a nod. "But as you are fond of saying, 'Age and experience trump youthful exuberance every time.' I'm praying we have thought of everything that needs to be done."

"Well, I'm hoping Rachel and I didn't leave anything behind at Cair Paravel to compromise James or you. When you sent Officer Carter to warn us they were coming with a search warrant, we only had a few minutes to pack up, get in the car with him, and head to Charleston."

"Peter, we've known each other for more than fifty-eight years. Don't be concerned about anything left behind. There is nothing we can do about it now anyway. And no matter how this turns out, we will eventually leave *all* this behind."

"Yeah, but—"

"No 'buts' about it, Peter," Caperton cut him off. "Today was a great success. All our alternative communications channels are working. Your ops people were able to get a CSG aircraft to pick you, Rachel, and Carter up at Charleston Air Force Base before the Homeland Security goons tossed Cair Paravel. Your daughter Elizabeth, her four kids, and your sister Nancy all got the word and cleared out of Narnia before the DHS search party showed up. They are all in good hands with fellow Believers who would die before giving them up. Best of all, you and Rachel are here with Sarah and her boys."

Newman nodded and said, "You're right, Mack. But I'm still worried about James . . ."

"Well then, pray for his safety—don't worry. Worry doesn't help anything. Prayers do. If anyone knows that, you and I should."

"Okay, roomie," Newman said, smiling again. "Don't bilge me. But don't you wonder where all this is heading; how this all ends?"

Caperton leaned back in his chair, thought for a moment, then said, "Sure I wonder. But I don't have the gift of prophecy, nor do I believe I'm the smartest person on the planet. I just have some very good friends like you. The people who think they are running the world from Washington are full of institutional arrogance. They have convinced themselves they can regulate and control everything—even the human spirit—by pushing buttons, listening to our conversations, intercepting our communications, taking polls, feeding us tailored information, controlling the MESH, telling us what to believe.

"For decades politicians have told us that topics such as the sanctity of human life, the definition of marriage, and freedom of religion are 'social issues.' They're not. For tens of millions of us, these are deeply held moral and spiritual concerns—matters of faith, not politics.

"What the president and her minions no longer grasp is the American people aren't sheep. We don't want government intruding in every aspect of our lives. The Bill of Rights—those first ten amendments to our Constitution—still mean something to most of us, no matter how much they have dumbed down public education. In their guts, most Americans understand that our rights to life, liberty, and the pursuit of happiness, as Jefferson put it, really are God-given—not a gift from government."

"What does our country look like after all this comes out? When the dust settles will we even have a sovereign country?"

"Sure. There will still be a United States of America—a place blessed with bounty and resources beyond measure. We will still have a Constitution and that Bill of Rights. What we have to hope for are people in government—elected, commissioned, and appointed—who will support and defend our Constitution; people who know the difference between rights and entitlements; people who will abide by the moral and spiritual standards of the brave

Americans who drafted those documents. That will only happen if people of faith participate in the political process. Will that happen in the time we have left? I certainly hope so, but I can't see into the future."

"Nor can I, Mack. But I sure don't like leaving a mess for our kids and grandchildren," said Peter as the senator reached for one of the unregistered PIDs pinging on his desk.

Caperton looked at the screen, pressed the corner of the device, held it up beside his ear, and said, "Hello." He listened silently for almost thirty seconds, then said, "Thank you." After pressing the corner again to disconnect, he deposited the PID in the chemical-bath shredder beneath his desk. As the machine quietly ground the device into biodegradable mulch, Caperton looked at Peter and said, "That was Captain Terry Sullivan—an old Navy SEAL and one of our 'trusted messengers' in Florida. Looks like we have to put Plan C into effect. Tomorrow the White House is adding my name to their Capture/Kill list."

**FINCA DEL GANADOR**

3 MILES EAST OF DZILAM DE BRAVO
YUCATAN STATE, MEXICO
SUNDAY, 19 SEPTEMBER 2032
2150 HOURS, LOCAL

When Bruno Macklin heard the faint whine of jet turbines being throttled back seven miles above him, he knew exactly what it was. The old SAS officer checked his watch, said to himself, *Twenty minutes late*, and gently nudged Felipe awake. He then flicked on his thermal glasses and peered up, looking for the glow of the engine exhaust in the star-speckled sky.

The sound of the jet had already faded by the time he heard the first *thwoop*—as a parachute opened several thousand feet above. Listening intently, Macklin picked up the sound of six more chutes "popping"—and then silence again. He immediately cracked the four infrared chem-lights he fashioned into the outlines of two ichthys ⟨fish symbol⟩ shapes, handed one of the recognition signals to the boy, and said, "Lie flat on the ground, hold this up over your head, and don't move."

Two minutes later he heard the swish of riser cords being pulled taut against the nylon skin of a parachute, followed by a thump twenty yards away—almost atop the T pattern. He watched silently through his thermal lenses as a helmeted, dark-clad figure gathered up the chute, shoved it into a kit bag, took a knee, and started scanning around the field with his weapon. But when the red beam stopped on the center of Felipe's chest, the old commando quietly said, "Winston."

"Churchill," came the reply as the red beam went out. The paratrooper arose, walked slowly to Macklin and the boy, and said, "I'm Dan Doan. Who are you?"

"I'm Major Bruno Macklin, formerly of His Majesty's Special Air Service, and this is Felipe."

"Good job lighting up the DZ, Major," said Doan, lowering his weapon and holding out a hand to help them to their feet. "We should have six more of us here in a few minutes. Sorry to drop in on you with so little notice."

"Think nothing of it, mate. On a beautiful night like this, good company from a former colony's DEA is always welcome."

\* \* \* \*

It took just ten minutes for the rest of the team to gather one at a time at the assembly point in the tree line just

south of the pasture. Doan introduced them to Macklin
as they arrived:

Communications Specialist: Steve "Coyote" McNaughton

Sniper: Kenneth "Killer" Connor

Demolition Specialist: Zane "Fingers" Felton

Team Medic: Daniel "Doc" Smith

Weapons Specialist: James "Newboy" Lehnert

Scout/Spotter: Ken "KK" Knapp

Instead of taking time to explain they weren't really DEA,
but in fact contractors from the Centurion Solutions
Group Hostage Recovery Unit, Doan focused on the
mission. Referring to the overhead imagery the jump-
ers loaded into their PIDs before launching from DFW,
he told Macklin to describe the interior of "Objective
Alpha"—Felipe's house—then proffer a summary of what
the boy knew about the four Iranians and Admiral Cohen's likely location.

As they lined up in patrol formation, Doan quietly
reminded them: "Remember, our primary mission is to
rescue Admiral Cohen. If we can, we are to bring back as
many Iranians alive as possible. Bruno and KK will take
point from here to Alpha. They should be the only ones
with ball and AP ammo locked and loaded. Everyone
else should have TASER XP 762 rounds chambered in
their rifles and the next four rounds in their magazines.
Sidearms should have XP 45 rounds in the chambers and
the next four rounds in their magazines. Everyone should
have suppressors screwed in tight. Check?"

Each man did as ordered, then gave him a thumbs-up

sign. Doan continued: "When we get to Objective Alpha, Bruno and KK will cover our right flank and take out any squirters. If we have to E-and-E, the rally point is Bruno's house—Objective Bravo. I have sat-comms with the aircraft. During movement and at the objective, I'll be last in column with Felipe in front of or beside me. Any questions?"

There were none.

Twenty-three minutes later the little patrol arrived at the damaged shed behind Felipe's house. When Doan pointed to the mound of freshly turned earth nearby, the boy said quietly, "That is where my brother is buried."

Bruno gave him a quick hug and whispered, "I know you miss Jorge. But he is in a far better place now, son." Then he and Knapp moved out to position themselves along the edge of the tree line to establish a base of fire. McNaughton and Connor headed left to get around to the front of the house while the entry team of Smith, Lehnert, and Felton crept toward the back door. Doan and Felipe stayed put, crouching near the shed to cover their six.

McNaughton was the first to call, whispering into the lip mike of his tac-set radio: "Coyote and Killer are in position but we're negative for thermals and it looks like the front door is open."

Doan replied: "Roger, hold your pos. Fingers, you copy Coyote?"

"Roger. No thermals here, either. We're ready. Shall we rush the back door?"

Doan thought for a split second and then said, "Go for it, but no stun grenades or firing unless you have a target."

"Roger."

Five seconds later he and Felipe watched as Felton's three-man team sprinted the twenty-five meters to the back door of the house and disappeared inside. For fifteen seconds there was silence, then the radio call:

"Rover, Fingers. We're clear. The place is empty."

Doan shook his head and said over his helmet mike: "Everybody hold in position until I call our eyes in the sky."

He grabbed the Australian-built sat-radio handset out of its pocket on his armor vest, keyed the button, and said, "Big Eye, this is Rover."

There was a slight delay as the signal bounced halfway around the world and back: "Rover, this is Big Eye, go ahead, over."

"Roger, we have a dry hole at Objective Alpha. Are you picking up any thermals on your FLIR?"

Again a pause, then: "Rover, we're orbiting over you at forty K, watching on high-res. Be advised, there are five thermals about one klick west of you moving toward Objective Bravo. There is also what looks like an old-fashioned auto rally about eighteen kilometers southwest of Bravo on the road from Dzilam Gonzalez. We count twelve SUV-sized vehicles and at least as many motor-cycles, most with their headlights on. They are stationary now, but they were headed toward you until a few minutes ago. You copy?"

Doan's mouth went dry and he swallowed hard before responding: "Roger, copy. Looks like we're about to have a lot of company. How much time do you have left on station?"

"At this burn rate, we bingo for Mike Echo X-Ray in ninety minutes; less if we have to do a lot of fancy flying. We can stay on station longer if they get a runway at Mike India Delta open. How can we help you between now and then?"

"Wait, out."

Doan switched to his helmet-mounted tac-com radio and said, "Objective Alpha is clear. Rally on me ASAP at the shed."

In less than a minute, all six shooters, Macklin, and the boy were circled around Doan in the shed. His "Frag-O" was brief: "Big Eye says we have five thermals a klick west of us, headed toward Objective Bravo. Bruno, that's your house. My guess—five thermals equals four Iranians plus an American admiral. The aircraft also has eyes on twenty-plus SUVs and motorcycles clustered about eighteen klicks southwest of Bravo. I figure that's the Federation Cartel gaggle en route to take out the admiral. We need to check out the five thermals between here and Bravo. If the admiral is with them, we need to get him to safety before the Federation thugs show up at midnight. We will head out with the same order of march and same comms. Any questions?"

Once again there were none. But as they lined up to move out, Felipe said to Doan, "Señor, I know the fastest way to Señor Macklin's hacienda."

Later, those who survived agreed: in the contest between good and evil, timing, technology, and wise words from a child make all the difference in the world.

* * * *

It really wasn't a fair fight. Felipe's shortcut, their thermal NVGs, and updates from the FLIR pod overhead helped Doan and his team arrive, breathing hard, at Bruno's back door in just under fifteen minutes. The SAS officer showed them where he placed the ten claymore mines and Doan quickly deployed his men:

"KK, you, Major Macklin, and Felipe stay with me. Coyote, Killer, and Newboy, you cover the approach from Alpha. If those five thermals are the Iranians and

the admiral, you know what to do. Fingers, you and Doc
cover their six. Remember, TASER rounds first. Bring the
admiral and any live Iranians here to the house. Bruno,
can we get up on the roof to a place where we won't be
seen from the ground?"

"Sure enough, mate. Upstairs is an internal stairway to
the roof. The roof is flat and there is an adobe wall about a
meter high all around it."

"Good. That's where I will be so I have good comms
with all of you and sat-comms with the aircraft. Any questions?"

When nobody said anything he said, "Move out."

As the two teams headed off, Bruno led Doan, Knapp,
and Felipe inside and they raced upstairs. On the second
floor he opened a hall doorway to a stairwell that exited
on the roof beside a chimney. In a low crouch, Doan immediately headed to the north side and peered over the
wall looking for thermals from his teammates. He was
watching them move silently into their assigned positions
a hundred meters in front of the house when his sat-radio
emitted a ping.

"Rover, this is Big Eye."

"This is Rover. Go ahead."

"Be advised, the five thermals on foot we've been tracking from Alpha are about two hundred meters south of
Bravo, on the road from Alpha. It looks like three of them
are held up and the other two are slowly approaching
Bravo. We have two friendlies and two others without IFF
on the roof of Bravo. There are five other friendlies in two
locations about one hundred meters east of Bravo. We are
transmitting our FLIR pod imagery to the bird so you can
see it on your sat-pac, channel three."

"Roger, Big Eye. The two friendlies on the roof of
Bravo are KK and me. We're with the two locals without

IFF. They will stay with me. Anyone else out there without IFF isn't ours. I'll come up on the sat-pac viewer
ASAP."

With Knapp kneeling beside him scanning the ap-
proaches to the house through a thermal scope on his
suppressor-equipped NEMO "Omen" Sniper Rifle, Doan
sat down behind the wall, pulled another satellite transceiver and a thin, five-by-eight-inch flat-panel wireless
viewer from a pocket on his armor vest, and pressed the
power button.

As the screen activated, its full-color glow revealed
everything being picked up by the FLIR pod overhead.
He watched for a few seconds and then came up on his
tactical radio: "Coyote, this is Rover. There are two armed
bad guys approaching Bravo from south of your pos. Let
them pass unless they spot you. We will deal with them
here. The other three are holding back on the road. I'm
guessing the admiral is one of the other three. If you copy,
key twice."

In his helmet-mounted headset Doan heard a double
*ping-pshht* when McNaughton keyed his tactical radio.
On the screen, Doan watched two figures pass Coyote's
position and furtively arrive at Bruno's front gate. As the
two scaled the fence, KK whispered, "I have two assholes
carrying what looks like AKs approaching our pos. They
are seventy-five meters out. I have subsonics loaded, not
TASERs. Do you want me to take them out?"

Doan peered at the screen again and said, "They're
both armed. Kill 'em."

KK's rifle spat twice—the action of the bolt opening
and closing made more noise than the projectiles leaving
the six-inch-long suppressor on the end of his barrel. On
the sat-pac there was a slight delay. Doan heard Knapp say

quietly, "Two down. Head shots. No movement," before seeing them drop on the screen.

Just seconds after Knapp fired, McNaughton was on the radio in a whisper: "Rover, Coyote. We have three individuals approaching fifty meters south on the road. Two have visible weapons. The one in the middle appears to have his hands bound behind him and a noose around his neck. Do you want us to engage?"

Doan glanced quickly at the screen and said, "Affirmative. TASERs only."

It was over in an instant. Ebi, walking in front, was hit by three TASER XP 762 rounds and immediately dropped to the ground, completely incapacitated. Ahmad, third in line and holding the end of the rope around the admiral's throat, had time to shout "Die, Jew!" just before he was felled by five TASER rounds.

The Iranians were still twitching when "Newboy Lehnert" raced to the hostage. With a flick of his knife he severed the rope around the man's neck and hands, helped him to his feet, and said, "Admiral Cohen, I'm James Newman. My father sent us to bring you home."

# CHAPTER SEVENTEEN

# LIGHTS OUT

**FINCA DEL GANADOR**

3 MILES EAST OF DZILAM DE BRAVO

YUCATAN STATE, MEXICO

SUNDAY, 19 SEPTEMBER 2032

2330 HOURS, LOCAL

McNaughton was immediately up on the tactical radio: "Rover, Coyote. We've got the admiral. Newboy is bringing him to you. They're moving slowly because the admiral is barefoot and his feet are a mess. The two bad boys are still out of it. We have 'em flex-cuffed but one of 'em took a high-voltage dump in his pants. I'm going to wait until he can walk 'cause he stinks and I don't want to have to carry him."

Doan, watching it all unfold on the sat-pac screen, smiled and spoke into his helmet mike on the tac-net: "Bravo Zulu everyone. Rally on me as soon as you can. We have more company coming to this party, so replace your TASER ammo with ball and AP rounds."

Then he spoke into the mike on his voice sat-comm:

"Big Eye, Rover. Pass to 'Tour Guide': the 'navy brass' is safe and sound with us. Now all we have to do is get out of here."

Turning to Bruno, Doan said, "Sure don't want to impose, but I'm hoping you have a spare pair of shoes or boots for our admiral and a couple of vehicles we can use for our exfil to link up with Tour Guide in Merida."

"Tour Guide?"

"Sorry, sir. That's our code for the person you know as A. J. Jones. We were instructed to never use his real name when it could be picked up by locals, the enemy, or in our communications."

The old SAS officer nodded and said, "Ah, yes, I know your Tour Guide very well. He's a very brave man. The boots are not a problem—soft British calfskin. Just the thing for sore feet—particularly for an admiral, if you know what I mean. As for transport, I have a 2030, methanol-powered Range Rover SUV and a 1975 diesel Land Rover lorry in the garage. Both are in excellent condition and fully fueled. But looking at your FLIR device, it appears to me the *cartelistos* are already this side of the intersection to Dzilam de Bravo. We would have to drive right through them to get out of here."

"Well, sir," Doan replied, "if flight is not an option, we're going to have to fight it out with these guys right here. Depending on how many there are and how well they are armed, it's likely to mess up your place a good bit."

"Don't let that bother you, mate. Nothing a little paint and stucco won't heal after the gunfight is over. Besides, I thought I was going to have to do this all on my own until you Yanks showed up."

Doan shrugged and keyed the sat-comm mike: "Big Eye, Rover. How long before the dirtbags get here?"

"Rover, looks like they are posting roadblocks behind them at every intersection. At the rate they are moving, the lead vic will be at your pos in about fifteen minutes. Some good news. We're monitoring a Mexican commercial aviation channel and just heard one runway at Merida is now open. That means we can stay on station for about another hour. Remember, we have six nice new Hellfire missiles aboard that we will have to jettison in the Gulf of Mexico if we don't use them."

"Well," replied Doan, "I hate to waste good missiles. Guess we'll just have to wrap this up before you guys have to break for happy hour."

As it turned out, they needed every one of them.

\* \* \* \*

At five minutes before midnight the first two Federation Cartel vehicles—motorcycles with two riders each—appeared at Bruno's gate. On the roof, peering into the FLIR monitor, Doan counted eight more motorcycles and nine SUVs at ten-meter intervals on the road behind the scouts. He keyed his tac mike and whispered, "Everybody stay down. Looks to me like these guys have AKs, RPGs, radios, and NVGs. Let's hope they're not thermals."

McNaughton, Connor, and Felton were crouched around the parapet—each of them armed with suppressor-equipped AR-10, 7.62mm automatic rifles and two AT-9 anti-armor rockets apiece. One story down, Doc Smith and Knapp were concealed in the large front bedroom, well back from the now-open windows. Newboy and Admiral Cohen were positioned in a back bedroom covering their six while Major Macklin sat on the floor of the hallway with a wireless, portable monitor display for the six cameras pointed at his ten radio-controlled claymore mines.

Felipe, seated on the floor of the dark hallway beside Bruno, had the task of keeping watch through his
thermals on the two Iranian captives. Ahmad and Ebi,
stripped to T-shirts and undershorts, were handcuffed to
the plumbing in the hall bathroom with pillowcases over
their heads. Major Macklin, ever the gracious British host,
was kind enough to provide the prisoners with clean underwear, pillowcases, and handcuffs.

On the roof, Doan watched on the FLIR viewscreen as
the four motorcycle scouts dismounted from their bikes
outside the gate. They peered at the dark and apparently
empty house and tried to force the heavy steel portals
open. Failing to even budge the gate, one of them pulled
what looked to be a handheld radio out of his pocket and
held it up to his face.

Suddenly the entire cartel convoy began moving up
the road toward Finca del Ganador. The first five SUVs
and four of the motorcycles pulled past the entrance and
stopped on the road leading to Felipe's house. The sixth
SUV stopped directly in front of the gate. A large man
emerged and began to gesture and point toward the house.

For Doan on the roof and the pilots in the Gulfstream,
all this was like watching a green-tinted silent movie without subtitles. The big man was apparently a cartel *jefe*, for
after he waved his arms about, the four scouts helped each
other scale the fence. They dropped inside and began to
warily approach the house.

Doan sighed, said to himself, *Here we go again. Dear
Lord, please protect us*, then simultaneously keyed both his
tac-set and aircraft sat-comm mikes: "Everybody listen
up. This is Rover. There are four dirtbags inside the wire
and fifty to sixty more in and around vehicles on the roadway outside the gate. Big Eye, on my command, put one
Hellfire on each of the last three vehicles in line so we can

block their escape route. Newboy, tell Bruno to be ready to take out any vehicles parked near his claymores to the right of the gate. Doc and KK, your targets are the four dirtbags inside the wire. Coyote, Killer, and Fingers, use AT-9s to take out the first three SUVs to the left of the gate—then everyone take down all visible enemy personnel with rifle fire. Stand by."

There was a quiet flurry of activity as everyone moved into position, searching through thermal scopes for their assigned targets. Doan, peering at the FLIR image on the sat-pac, waited until the lead cartel scout encountered the two dead Iranians on the driveway. The *cartelisto* stopped and motioned for his three comrades to join him. It was a fatal mistake.

When all four were standing over the bodies, Doan said quietly into his tac-set, "Doc, KK . . . Take 'em out."

Their subsonic rounds dropped all four cartel scouts in a fewer number of seconds. As they fell, Doan was on both radios again. "Everyone: engage your targets."

Five of Bruno's claymores immediately detonated in rapid sequence from right to left on the roadway in front of the gate. One of the SUVs must have been parked directly atop one of the radio-controlled mines, because the vehicle erupted in a pillar of fuel-fired flame. Then the three AT-9 rockets launched by McNaughton, Connor, and Felton found their marks.

Seconds later, the Hellfire missiles from the Gulfstream struck. Their fifteen-pound warheads tore into the last three SUVs in line, showering the *cartelistos'* escape route with burning debris. In less than a minute, nearly half the cartel killers were dead or dying.

There was a brief lull in the firing and considerable shouting and running around outside the gate as the attackers tried to regroup. Every time Macklin saw movement in one of his cameras he triggered another claymore, until he had fired all ten.

Over the course of the next fifteen minutes the Federation assassins tried to summon reluctant reinforcements from roadblocks they had positioned along their route. Doan told the pilots in the Gulfstream to use two more Hellfire missiles on cartel SUVs moving east toward Finca del Ganador, out of range of the AT-9s.

A few minutes later, a group of *cartelistos* fired a volley of six RPGs from a defile four hundred meters west of the house. Though the missiles caused no injuries to the defenders, Doan eliminated the threat by unleashing the last Hellfire missile on the RPG shooters' heads. That finished the attack—proving drug cartel killers are long on brutality but short on courage.

Doan immediately dispatched Felton, McNaughton, and Smith on a foot patrol around the perimeter of the house to confirm that none of the nearby hotspots visible on the FLIR were still a threat. On the tac-net he said: "Listen up, people: As soon as Fingers, Coyote, and Doc get back, we're heading to Objective Charlie in Major Macklin's vehicles. Rally on me at the garage in five minutes. Bring the Iranians. Big Eye is going to run out of gas soon and I want their help getting out of here."

By the time they were all assembled, Bruno had pulled the two vehicles out of his garage and opened the front gate with a remote control. Doan quickly issued his exfil plan:

"Vic number one, the green '75 Land Rover. Strip the canvas off the bed, cut it in two, and wrap an Iranian in each half. Tape the canvas around 'em so they can't move. Lower the windshield and fold the bench seats in the back.

"Driver is Lehnert. Shotgun: Knapp. Gunner in the front center of the bed, Felton.

"Doc Smith, you get in the back of the truck with me. Place the three remaining AT-9s at the front of the bed so we can get at 'em if we need 'em. Put the Iranians faceup in the back of the bed and make sure they can breathe. I don't want anyone accusing us of abusing detainees.

"Vic number two is the gray Range Rover. It's armored, so the windows don't go down, but it has a top hatch/sunroof that opens.

"Driver is Bruno. Shotgun, McNaughton; left rear seat: Admiral Cohen; gunner in the top hatch: Connor.

"Felipe, you're in the right rear. Put all the extra gear, ammo, and the Hummingbird UAVs in the space behind the backseat.

"Vic one will lead out until we reach the ring road east of Merida. When we get there, vic two will take the lead since Bruno knows the fastest way to get to the airport to link up with Tour Guide. We're moving lights-out at ten-meter interval using thermals until I say otherwise. E-and-E plan is to rally at Tour Guide's home address in Merida—the one I gave you on the airplane. We will all stay up on the tac-net until we get to the airport. I have sat-comms with Big Eye for as long as he can stay on station. Questions?"

Felipe spoke up for the first time since the shooting started: "*Sí*, Señor Doan. I have to pee. May I do so now?"

Instead of laughing, Doan looked down at the lad and said, "That's the second good idea you've had tonight, Felipe." Then to everyone he said, "You heard the boy. Do it now and load up."

They did as ordered.

\* \* \* \*

As the two vehicles pulled through the gate and past the shattered cartel convoy, there was no celebration. Eight of the Federation SUVs were still smoldering and the smoke was filled with the unmistakable stench of burning flesh.

Newman, driving the lead truck, carefully maneuvered through wreckage and bodies for almost a mile before Doan tapped him on the shoulder and said, "Hold up on the rise just ahead. Big Eye is painting some hotspots on his FLIR. He thinks it might be an ambush."

James stopped just short of the crest and killed the diesel so they could listen. Behind him in the truck bed he heard Doan, talking quietly on the satellite radio, say, "Roger, Big Eye. Let's try it."

Then on the tac-net Doan told them all: "This is Rover. Big Eye has an SUV, two motorcycles, and eight dirtbags at an intersection seven hundred fifty meters in front of us. They appear to be trying to figure out how to set up an ambush but Big Eye is out of ammo. Vic one will press on and when we're one hundred meters out, Big Eye will put on a low-altitude air show for 'em, and we'll bust on through. Vic two, stay fifty meters behind us and be prepared to QRF. Let's go."

James started the truck, threw it into gear, then headed over the crest and down the long slope toward the intersection, now clearly visible on their thermal NVGs. As they closed on the hotspots, lights suddenly appeared just above the treetops and the Gulfstream came screaming right to left across the intersection going three hundred miles per hour at an altitude of less than one hundred feet. Just before it reached the ambush, the jet pulled up with a horrendous roar—throwing a rooster tail of mud, dirt, and dead foliage into the air.

As Newman pulled through the intersection without incident, Doan suddenly shouted, "Stop!" Then, on the tac-net radio he said quietly, "Fingers and KK, check it out! Collect up any weapons and radios. Disable their vehicles. Vic two, close up on me."

Felton and Knapp vaulted out of the truck and instantly plunged into the undergrowth. Thirty seconds passed in silence, then there were two shots from what sounded like an AK, followed by more silence.

Less than two minutes later, Felton was up on the tac-net: "We have six terrified dirtbags who are now deaf. We have one dead dirtbag who shot at us without effect and we have his boss who just offered me five million gex to let him go. We put AP rounds into the two motorcycle engines. All their weapons are in the SUV and we have their PIDs and radios. We have a block of C-4 with a three-minute time fuse inside their vic ready to light. I have the keys to their car. What do you want us to do?"

"Roger, Fingers," Doan answered. "Good work. Flex-cuff the big shot and bring him with you. We may be able to trade him for something we need. Flex-cuff the others to a tree so they can see what happens without getting hurt and pull the igniter, lock the car doors, and hustle back here."

Felton and Knapp burst out of the foliage dragging a fat, bearded man babbling in Spanish. Using his combat knife, Doc Smith stripped the prisoner to his underwear, tossed away the man's shoes, stuffed his rolled-up socks into his mouth, and pulled the cartel *jefe*'s trousers down over his head and taped them in place. Smith, Felton, and Knapp then heaved the terrified drug lord—trussed hand and foot—into the bed of the Land Rover and stuffed him between the two Iranians.

They were three hundred meters down the road toward Dzilam Gonzalez when there was an enormous explosion and a fireball behind them. Doan reflexively ducked, then tapped Felton on the leg and asked, "How much C-4 did you put in that Federation SUV?"

Felton shrugged and said, "Just a couple of pounds. I told those guys it was dangerous to carry RPGs in a civilian vehicle."

Doan just shook his head and resumed peering at the FLIR image on the sat-pac. Five minutes later the G-VII called on the sat-comm to report two motorcycles about two miles in front of them, speeding away. He told the pilot to go ahead and "swoop them."

The Gulfstream made another high-speed, low-altitude pass, blowing the two bikes and their four armed riders off the dirt road. The two smashed motorcycles, four broken AK-47s, and three dead *cartelistos* were strewn in the ditch when Newman pulled up to the site.

Doan ordered Felton and Knapp out to pick up any PIDs or radios and they were on their way again when the pilots called on the sat-comm: "Rover, Big Eye. This is more fun than we can ever tell about, but we've got to get some fuel before we run dry. We're not seeing any more activity in front of you on the FLIR. We'll be at Objective Charlie waiting for you."

"Roger, Big Eye; well done," Doan replied. "Have a cold one for each of us. You've earned it."

They hit the "hardball"—Highway 178—thirty kilometers east of Motul, where Doan had Connor launch one of the Hummingbird UAVs to scout the route ahead. Doan watched for a few minutes on the monitor as Connor "flew" the tiny device with its fisheye thermal camera down their intended route. Seeing no visible threats, Doan told him, "Bring it back here and retrieve it." To the rest he said, "As soon as Killer has the bird in hand, vic one will take the lead and we'll go lights-on the rest of the way."

Moments later, Connor announced, "Bird in hand," as he landed the tiny UAV on the hood of the Range Rover. They started their engines and headed out, Bruno in the lead. For the first time since they parachuted from the G-VII tail ramp, the men of the CSG HRU removed their NVGs.

Bruno stepped on the gas and soon they were going 75 kph all the way to Highway 281, the Loop Road around Merida. There they finally encountered light civilian traffic. Doan had them pull off at the first exit.

When they stopped, Doan ordered Connor to drop down from the hatch on his vehicle. He then helped Newman put up the windshield on the ancient Land Rover to make their vehicle less conspicuous and appear to be somewhat normal. With everyone back aboard, and their weapons no longer in sight, they resumed their motor march to Merida.

At 0335, Bruno's Range Rover pulled up to the Sixty-Sixth Street Gate of Military Air Base #8, on the north side of Merida International Airport. Though the security building just inside the perimeter fence was dark, music was blaring from Tendejon Cindy, the little club just outside the gate on the right. As the two vehicles idled, a middle-aged male wearing a tan guayabera stepped out of the club, walked to the front of Bruno's Range Rover, and motioned for the vehicles to follow.

At the gate, the man in the guayabera reached into his trousers pocket, took out a garage-door opener, pressed the button, and the rollback gate performed as intended. He then walked before them to a second gate, entered the nearby security hut, and in less than a minute the gate opened. He then led them another fifty meters into the base, pointed to two parking places next to a one-story building beside the apron, and waited for them to pull in. The men in the vehicles noted the CSG Gulfstream was the only aircraft parked on the apron.

When Bruno, Doan, and the others disembarked

from their vehicles, their guide said, "Gentlemen, I am A. J. Jones. I work for the U.S. government—such as it is. Welcome to Mexican Air Force Base number eight. Please expedite bringing your cargo and equipment under the portico behind me so we minimize the time we're visible from overhead ISR and any local surveillance video cameras. This building is a Mexican Air Force Bachelor Officers' Quarters. Your pilots are already inside getting some rest. We're the only ones here."

It took Doan and the CSG team less than three minutes to offload their weapons, equipment, and prisoners into the reception area of the BOQ. After shackling the two Iranians and the overweight Mexican to a steel pipe in the kitchen, they gathered around A.J. in the dining area.

When they were all assembled, A.J. said, "First some administrative matters. I have given Major Macklin keys to nine rooms in this BOQ so you can get some rest. You should be relatively safe here, but I would suggest you keep someone on watch throughout the night.

"Since you gentlemen are here on a post-disaster humanitarian aid mission, the U.S. Consulate in Merida has already paid the per diem cost of your rooms plus two meals. I must remind you, this does not include any alcohol or other amenities. If you don't know what I mean by 'other amenities,' please refer to Secret Service Regulation 12-375B for your edification.

"It is my understanding you may also have with you persons of other nationalities. If this is correct, please complete Form 9375-P so the USG can seek reimbursement from their respective governments. A copy of the form is provided in Mr. Doan's and Mr. Lehnert's rooms. Are there any questions?"

"What time do we launch for CONUS?" Newman-Lehnert asked.

"I'm not sure yet. There are apparently some diplomatic issues regarding your aircraft—some kind of complaint about deviating from a flight plan. I hope to have this matter resolved by dawn. Just in case we need to find an alternative mode of transport, do any of you know the identity of the overweight, distraught Mexican gentleman now resting in the kitchen with a pair of socks in his mouth?"

McNaughton reached into a pocket, pulled out a PID, and said, "According to this, his name is Manuel Gustavo Lenin Felix."

A.J. smiled and said, "Ah, the notorious Machine Gun Felix. Number two in the Federation Cartel and one of the wealthiest men in the world. I am well familiar with Señor Felix, having overheard many of his instructions about eliminating various members of his own government and American citizens as well. You have caught a prize fish, gentlemen.

"I would be grateful if two or three of you would transport him down the hall to room eleven and place him faceup on the bed. Please do not remove his fetters. If one of you would be so kind to assist me, I need only a towel from the bathroom and a bottle of water for a brief conversation with Señor Felix."

Doan nodded and said, "KK, Coyote, Fingers, take the dirtbag down to room eleven. Stay with him until I get there with A.J. Doc, break out your little defibrillator thing in case I need you."

Knapp, McNaughton, and Felton left to do as ordered. That's when Marty Cohen asked, "Is there any way I can call my wife and children to let them know I'm alive?"

A.J. thought for a moment and said, "Yes, Admiral. I think I can make that happen. Please come outside beneath the portico with me, sir."

## OFFICE OF CHIEF OF STAFF, THE WHITE HOUSE

1600 PENNSYLVANIA AVENUE
WASHINGTON, DC
MONDAY, 20 SEPTEMBER 2032
0900 HOURS, LOCAL

Muneer Murad was at the very edge of complete exhaustion. In the nine days since the terror attack on Houston he had been at his desk or in the Situation Room nearly nonstop, day and night. Once, in a moment of extreme hubris, he told a media sycophant, "I use information technology to manage events." Now, overwhelmed with a deluge of "high-tech" information but almost no HUMINT, he had scant ability to alter outcomes.

Throughout the night of 19–20 September, Keker, encamped at the Special Intercept Unit pod in the FBI Command Center, kept Murad apprised of every intercepted sat-phone conversation to and from the "suspects" in Mexico. Though the SIU had yet to break the encrypted satellite data exchanges between A-Jay and Caperton, they dutifully recorded and logged each transmission to and from "Rover" and "Big-Eye"—which they concluded was the call sign for the Swiss-owned Gulfstream VII aircraft. By dawn Murad knew the plane landed at Merida International Airport and someone—they suspected it was A-Jay—had somehow short-circuited the effort to have Mexican authorities impound the aircraft.

At 0845, White House Counsel Larry Walsh delivered the Capture/Kill order for Caperton, complete with the signatures of Acting FBI Director Keker, the Attorney General, and Stanley Turner, the DNI. The chief of staff looked at Walsh, who simply nodded, and Murad signed the cover memorandum as "Acting National Security Advisor," sealed it in an envelope marked TOP SECRET—EYES

ONLY FOR THE PRESIDENT, and gave it to a WHCA courier for hand-carry to Air Force One in Chicago.

Once the courier departed, Murad closed his door and said to Walsh, "The Air Force is flying him in a T/F-35 to O'Hare. POTUS should have it before she takes off for her afternoon campaign event in Buffalo. Hopefully the veep won't see it and ask her what it is before she signs it. Stay here so we can recap where we are with Keker."

Walsh sat and Murad spoke to the digi-cube: "Secure . . . Jon Keker . . . FBI."

The cube glowed green. When the Acting FBI Director's face appeared on the screen, Muneer said, "Jon, I'm here with Larry. The Capture/Kill order on Caperton is on the way to POTUS. What's the latest?"

Keker, looking tense and tired, said, "The people we've been tracking in Mexico and Caperton have all gone silent. We haven't heard anything from any of them since early this morning, so we really don't know where they are right now."

"How can that be?" asked Walsh.

"It's simple," snapped Keker. "We don't have any HUMINT. We can track Caperton in real time only if he communicates—and apparently he's not doing that right now. It takes hours—sometimes a day or more—to ID him on voice pattern analysis when he uses an illegal, unregistered PID, and he apparently has an inexhaustible supply of them. We're trying to keep a DHS UAV constantly over his place in Montana but we're not seeing or hearing anything out there other than cows and horses."

"Well, how about sending some of your agents to his ranch to ask if he's there," Murad said sarcastically. "What about that Swiss-owned Gulfstream VII now parked at Merida? Your last report said FAA has verified the aircraft was contracted in the past to do classified work for the USG."

"That's correct," Keker replied with a visible grimace. "We don't know which agency or agencies have used it yet but we will. Overhead coverage from NGIA shows the suspect G-VII—call sign Big Eye—is still on the ground at Merida International, but there is no movement around it and we can't seem to get the Mexican authorities to pay attention."

"Why the devil hasn't the Mexican government impounded it yet?" asked Murad. "Didn't we tell 'em it was a suspect drug cartel aircraft?"

"Sure. We told them that last night but we don't know what the hell's going on down there right now. Fifteen minutes ago, President Rodriguez sacked his attorney general and then claimed credit for wiping out the leadership of the Federation Cartel in a secret operation last night on the Yucatan Peninsula."

"What the . . ." exclaimed Walsh. "Is Rodriguez talking about the mercenary unit calling itself 'Rover' that was communicating with that Gulfstream by satellite radio last night?"

"We don't know what Rodriguez is talking about, but he's going to hold a press conference this afternoon and he's promising to show proof of 'foreign interference' in Mexico. The Federation Cartel's MESH site in Monterrey admits their number-two kingpin is MIA and they claim to have evidence U.S.-made Hellfire missiles were used to attack Mexican nationals. I talked to Stan Turner a few minutes ago and he can't get through to anybody down there, either."

Walsh shook his head and said, "This is not good."

"Well, that's not all the bad news," Keker said. "Our SIU analysts think they now know whose voice that was on A-Jay's Iridium sat-phone at three fifty-five a.m. last night."

"Well, who was it?" asked Murad.

"SIU can't be certain because the number dialed was to an unregistered PID through a MESH node in northern Virginia. Our techs believe it was Admiral Martin Cohen calling his wife."

The chief of staff and the president's lawyer looked at each other in stunned silence for a moment before Walsh asked, "Where is she now?"

"We sent DHS agents to the Cohen residence in Arlington over an hour ago but there is nobody there. The neighbors haven't seen her since yesterday. We've put her PERT data up on the Global Watch System but no hits yet. She seems to have disappeared."

More silence. Then Walsh said, almost to himself, "Who the hell is running this operation against us? Is it the Caliph, the Iranians, who?"

Murad's response was chilling: "It's got to be Newman and Caperton. Here's what we need to do. If Cohen is alive and with this A-Jay character, that Swiss airplane in Mexico needs to be brought down if it launches and attempts to reenter U.S. airspace. I'll alert the Pentagon. Second, we need Caperton taken out—quickly. Jon, can you have DHS agents raid the Caperton place in Montana tonight?"

Keker was slow to respond but then said, "If the Mexicans let the G-VII launch, the Air Force or the Navy will have to deal with it—preferably over international waters. Since we believe Caperton is at his ranch in Montana, he's in FBI/DHS jurisdiction—but everyone around here is gun-shy after what happened Sunday night down in South Carolina. I have been reminded several times, 'If you want it bad, you get it bad.' I think it would be best to hit Caperton's place with some MQ-70 Marauder UAVs and then put some agents on the ground for a BDA."

"How many Marauders do you have available and what's their armament?" the president's lawyer asked.

At the White House Murad and Walsh watched on the digi-cube as Keker consulted another viewscreen and then replied, "Within range of Caperton's ranch outside Fort Shaw, DHS has eight birds total: two in northeast Washington state, two in Idaho; two more in North Dakota; plus the two birds in Montana we are using for constant stare over Caperton's place. It says here all of them can be equipped with four Hellfire missiles apiece. I'll have to check on how long that will take."

"Good," said Murad. "Let's plan on doing as you recommend. Get the ball rolling to arm up every available UAV for a strike tonight on Caperton's place in Montana. Tell DHS and the Air Force it's a confirmed Anarkterrorist hideout. I'll brief the president on this when she gets back from Buffalo this afternoon and get you a green light."

Keker nodded and said, "Okay, but before these birds can launch missiles on American citizens in U.S. territory, we need her authorization in writing. And remember, if Caperton and Newman are involved, expect the unexpected."

That turned out to be an understatement.

## BACHELOR OFFICERS' QUARTERS

MEXICAN AIR FORCE BASE #8
MERIDA, MEXICO
MONDAY, 20 SEPTEMBER 2032
0930 HOURS, LOCAL

The fresh tamales A. J. Jones brought for their breakfast were nearly as good as the news he delivered.

Doan summoned his teammates, Admiral Cohen, and

the three-man Gulfstream crew to the dining/reception area by bellowing down the hallway, "Listen up, people! Rally on me on the mess deck. Our Tour Guide is here with chow and an update!"

Bruno and Felipe were dispatched to guard the three hooded and shackled detainees and the others filed out of their rooms to gather around the tables. Doan said, "Bow your heads. Coyote, it's your turn to say the blessing."

McNaughton did as ordered: "Dear Lord, thank You for this food. We ask that You bless it to our use and us to Your service. And please give us a safe trip home. Amen."

"Good," Doan said. "While you all eat, listen up. Tour Guide has some news."

"Thank you, Sergeant Major. Gentlemen, we have new travel arrangements," Jones began. "Your guest, Señor Lenin Felix, has offered to fly us to the United States. When he and I were chatting last night he shared with me that he owns Vuelo Mexico—his latest venture in laundering cocaine money into legitimate businesses.

"It turns out he was telling the truth for a change. Vuelo Mexico has a brand-new Boeing 737 MAX departing here today at ten thirty on a certification flight to Las Vegas, Nevada. Señor Felix had the foresight to place some two hundred fifty million dollars in U.S. currency and gex aboard the aircraft—funds he planned to invest in a casino.

"After talking things over with Sergeant Major Doan and your pilots, I borrowed some of Señor Felix's cash, purchased appropriate travel attire for you gentlemen, and rented the bus parked outside against the portico. The bus will transport us to the main terminal. It is very important none of you be observed by surveillance cameras or overhead ISR, so stay under the portico while loading the bus. We will offload beneath the terminal overhang. We don't want anyone here or in Washington testing out their new facial recognition software on us.

"One final note: DEA Special Agent Marcia Quintero and I will be accompanying you on the flight. She is already at the terminal and will use her diplomatic passport to escort us through airport security. She is armed. Her husband is a U.S. Marine officer. She dislikes profane or vulgar language. Sergeant Major, the floor is yours."

Doan stood and said, "Thank you, sir. Listen up, people. Fingers, KK, and Doc, in the baggage compartment beneath the bus there are three rolled-up carpets, nine rolls of duct tape, twelve duffel bags containing civilian clothes, and ten Pelican cases. Bring 'em in here in that order. Bruno, Newboy, and I will roll and tape the detainees into the carpets. Everyone else change into civvies and stuff your battle gear into the duffels. Put your rifles in the Pelican cases with five loaded magazines apiece. Keep your sidearms on your persons, beneath your clothing.

"Leave the AT-9s, the Hummingbirds, all your grenades, blasting caps, and explosives here in the kitchen. Major Macklin and Felipe are staying here to sanitize this place, then head home to find the kid's parents. One of Tour Guide's friends is coming here to drive the other vic for Bruno.

"The rest of us will board the bus at ten hundred hours and proceed to a covered offload point beneath the international terminal. On Special Agent Quintero's signal we will download our gear plus the three 'carpets' onto baggage carts and follow her to an elevator that will take us directly to the jetway for the aircraft. Put all the baggage including the 'carpets' into the aircraft cabin with us. We will be the only ones besides the nonhostile, four-man flight crew aboard.

"The aircraft is scheduled to take off at ten thirty. It's

nineteen hundred miles—about a four-hour flight to Mc-
Carran International at Las Vegas depending on winds
and routing. Once we're out of Mexican airspace, our
pilots will take over in the cockpit. When we land at LAS,
we'll be met by DEA agents who will take the detainees
off our hands. Follow-on transportation from there is
being arranged and we will be briefed on arrival at LAS.
Any questions?"

There were none until they were boarding the bus.
Each man filing by Bruno and Felipe exchanged hand-
shakes, shared an *abrazo* and a *mil gracias*. But Admiral
Cohen said, "You and Felipe saved my life. How can I
thank you?"

"Well, sir," Bruno replied, "since you asked, when the
time comes in a few years, you can arrange to get Felipe
an appointment to that Naval Academy of yours. He's a
bright, brave fellow—and he knows where he's going and
why he's going there. As for me, just send my boots back
when you're finished with 'em. *Vaya con Dios.*"

\* \* \* \*

The Boeing 737 MAX pulled away from the gate precisely
at 1030. As the plane taxied, the pilot came up on the
Mexican FAA Air Traffic Control frequency and reported:
"Vuelo Mexico Flight X-ray One Niner One, standing by
on Mike India Delta Runway One Zero outbound for
Lima Alpha Sierra with eighteen souls aboard, fourteen
pax, and four crew. Filing flight plan Romeo. Altimeter
three-zero-point-one."

Ten seconds later the Merida tower responded, "Roger,
Vuelo Mexico One Niner One. You are cleared for takeoff
on runway one-zero, report five thousand for handoff."

When the Boeing 737 MAX began rolling down
the runway, Canadian, U.S., and Mexican air traffic

controllers at the North American Union Flight Monitoring Center in Pueblo, Colorado, glanced at their video screens. All three confirmed X-191 was a previously scheduled international flight and "tagged" it for "routine flight following."

At the National Geospatial-Intelligence Agency headquarters at Fort Belvoir, Virginia, a watch officer in the BOLO pod listened to the radio transmissions and peered at the video feed from the KZ-35 satellite parked over the Gulf of Mexico. He zoomed in on Merida International, watched the 737 MAX take off, noted the Gulfstream VII he was supposed to be observing in real time was still in place, and resumed his conversation with the pretty young intern he'd hooked up with for the weekend.

Two hours and seventeen minutes later, as Vuelo Mexico Flight X-191 was flight level at 37,500 feet on a heading of 285 degrees over Pecos, Texas, America became the third nation on earth to be attacked with a nuclear weapon.

**ABOARD MV *SEA GODDESS***
LAKE ONTARIO, 44.2°N, 76.5°W
MONDAY, 20 SEPTEMBER 2032
1347 HOURS, LOCAL

All nine members of the Quds Force team aboard the 240-foot-long, Greek-owned, Liberian-flagged vessel were very pleased with themselves. It took them just nineteen minutes to erect the hydraulic launch rail and single-stage, liquid-fuel Shahab-7 missile from its lead-lined shipping container on the vessel's foredeck—a full three minutes less than during their training in Iran.

After checking the readings on the four-foot-diameter, forty-three-foot-long missile's instrument panel, the team leader connected a heavy electronic firing harness and waved to the ship's captain on the bridge. To this point, everything had gone the way they rehearsed it for months before loading on the *Sea Goddess* at Bushehr in July. But now, without waiting for the men on the foredeck to clear away from the missile and move aft, the captain flicked up a safety cover, yelled, *"Allahu akbar!"* and pressed the red button.

The entire Quds Force team on the foredeck was killed instantly when the missile fired. On the bridge, the captain, helmsman, and first officer were first blinded by shards of glass as the bridge windows disintegrated, then deafened by the roar of the rocket engines and finally asphyxiated by toxic propellant smoke as the missile accelerated to mach 5 and tilted south on its preprogrammed trajectory toward Washington, D.C.

The ancient, ground-based NORAD early-warning sites in northern Canada didn't "see" the missile launch, either. Their Aegis radars all pointed toward the Arctic—at the most likely flight path for incoming Russian, Chinese, or North Korean ICBMs. A FLASHPOINT geosynchronous satellite in stationary orbit over Baffin Bay, between Devon Island and the west coast of Greenland, did pick up the launch plume on its infrared sensors. But the aging computers at Cheyenne Mountain initially decided the sudden thermal flare over Lake Ontario was a natural gas explosion on Amherst Island in Canada.

One minute and forty-three seconds later, they knew better. That's when the eight-hundred-pound, twenty-eight-inch-diameter, spherical HEU warhead on the missile's tip detonated prematurely at sixty thousand feet, just north of Oswego, New York.

One hundred and fifty miles west of the explosion, Air Force One was descending from twenty-five thousand feet over Lake Erie on a heading of 060 degrees with clearance to land on runway 05 at Buffalo-Niagara International Airport. The last thing the pilots saw was the retina-destroying flash just above the horizon. In the cockpit and throughout the cabin, every instrument suddenly went dark as the electromagnetic pulse from the 450-kiloton Iranian warhead instantly fried the Boeing 747s supposedly impregnable electronic circuitry.

The blackout shades in the Executive Suite on the starboard side of Air Force One were closed, so the nuclear weapon's blinding flare didn't awaken the president. The sudden silence did. She lay still in her bunk for a few seconds, shook her head to clear the cobwebs from her fast-acting sleep inhalant, and listened for engine noise, the air-conditioning—anything. Nothing.

Her first instinct was to summon the steward—an Air Force master sergeant. She pressed the remote several times without effect, then tried the light switch beside her bed. Again, nothing.

She sat bolt upright in the bunk and manually opened the nearest shade. Bright sunlight poured into the suite and she grabbed the phone off her desk, expecting a WHCA communicator on the deck above to immediately answer. The phone was dead.

Furious at the lack of response, she went to the door and tried to open it, but its electronic latch refused to disengage. She began banging on it with her fist and yelling, "Open this damned door, now!"

Then, from the other side of the panel, she heard a male voice. "Ma'am, it's Flagler, your PSD chief. The plane has lost power. We're going to have to use emergency equipment to get you out. Stand back from the doorway and put on your life vest."

Anger suddenly gave way to panic. She scrambled away

from the hatch and fumbled, hands shaking, for a life vest beneath her bunk. It took two Secret Service agents more than twenty blows with two fire axes to batter through the armored door.

When the portal finally opened, she screamed at her rescuers, "What the hell took you so long? Find somebody who knows what the devil is going on!" The thought of praying never occurred to her.

It took nearly three terrifying minutes for the presidential aircraft, now just an enormous, uncontrolled glider, to splash down a mile south of Buffalo's Peace Bridge to Canada. Motorists, stranded on the span when the EMP burst killed their auto engines, watched in horror as the big white and blue plane hit the water, broke up, and sank. Of the twenty-six crew members and ninety-seven passengers aboard Air Force One, only thirteen survived the crash. The president and vice president were not among them.

WASHINGTON, DC

MONDAY, 20 SEPTEMBER 2032

When the Iranian nuclear weapon exploded at sixty thousand feet over Lake Ontario, the electromagnetic pulse produced by the 450-kiloton weapon burned out every commercial electrical and electronic device within the visible horizon of the detonation. All two hundred and eleven commercial aircraft aloft within a six-hundred-mile radius of the airburst experienced the same phenomena—and the same consequences—as Air Force One. Though few of their pilots or passengers ever knew why, engines, radios, instruments, and flight controls immediately stopped working and the planes plummeted from the sky.

On the ground, all exposed electrical generators, transformers, relays, and transmission stations in a radius of 470 miles instantly stopped working. From the western suburbs of Lansing, Michigan, east to Bangor, Maine, and south to Williamsburg, Virginia, nearly 120 million Americans were instantly without lights, running water, sewage, air-conditioning, refrigeration, computers, PIDs, motor vehicles, or any means of communication.

In New York, Boston, Baltimore, Pittsburgh, Washington, Montreal, Ottawa, Toronto, and scores of smaller North American cities, emergency lighting, backup battery systems, and generators designed to get people safely out of high-rise buildings, off trains, and ashore from ferries in the event of a power failure all failed. Every multistory hospital, clinic, and nursing home and more than 351,000 elevators within the EMP radius—all totally dependent on electricity—became dark death traps. More than twelve million children were stranded in schools, miles from home and unable to communicate with their parents.

First responders on duty—police, fire, and rescue personnel—had no means of reacting to the crisis except on foot, and in most cases had no means of being notified of fires, criminal activity, or medical emergencies. U.S. government agencies—including the White House and our military—were little better off. Though some systems were "hardened" against EMP, most of the government's electrical, communications, and mobility infrastructure was never designed to withstand the EMP effect of a low-yield, low-altitude nuclear explosion.

White House Chief of Staff Muneer Murad became aware of the attack when the lights went out and all vidscreens in his office went dark. He tried his PID, digicube, and the ancient "red phone" on the credenza behind his desk. When none of these worked and the emergency backup generators failed, he walked down the darkened stairwell to the Situation Room, where a Secret Service agent had to muscle open the door labeled WHSR for the chief of staff.

\* \* \* \*

The WHSR Log is a chronological, minute-by-minute, record of every call, message, meeting, and event requiring the attention of the president, vice president, or National Security Advisor. Similar to a ship's log, it is a dispassionate, straightforward, apolitical chronicle of happenings that affect America's "ship of state." The senior watch officer on duty each shift decides what will and what won't appear as entries in the Log. And because its existence has never been officially acknowledged, it has never been subpoenaed by a court or a committee of Congress.

The WHSR Log for Monday, 20 September, is unique. For the first thirteen hours and fifty minutes, the entries were made, as usual, on the SWO's computer. Entries after the nuclear detonation over Lake Ontario were handwritten on a yellow, lined legal tablet:

*1351:* ALL POWER & COMMS @ WHITE HOUSE INOP. SECURE INTER-AGENCY VID-LINK DOWN.

*1353:* WH COS ARRIVES WHSR.

*1354:* NMCC FOC NOW UP. BGEN JOHN BRANSON, USMC, NMCC SWO, REPORTS ON FOC "ELECTRONIC ANOMALY" VIC NORTHEAST U.S.-CANADA BORDER.

*1355:* NMCC SWO ON FOC INFORMS: "DISA SITES IN CO, PA, GA & VA CONFIRM LOCALIZED COMMS DISRUPTIONS & CASCADE OF POWER OUTAGES FM CHICAGO, EAST TO COAST OF MAINE, SOUTH TO RICHMOND, VA. CAUSE OF OUTAGES UNK."

*1402:* 89TH SPECIAL AIR WING @ JOINT BASE ANDREWS CALLED ON FOC THRU NMCC TO REPORT "LOST COMMS W/ AIR FORCE ONE."

*1404:* SEC DEF ORDERS LAUNCH OF NEACP FM OFFUTT AFB, NE.

*1408:* SEC DEF & CJCS CALL ON FOC FM NMCC TO REPORT FOC COMMS REESTABLISHED W/ ANMCC @ SITE "R" AND FEMA @ MOUNT WEATHER.

*1409:* SEC DEF & CJCS CALL ON FOC: "RECOMMEND PLACING ALL U.S. MIL FORCES ON DEFCON ONE."

*1410:* NMCC SWO REPORTS ON FOC: "ALL U.S. GPS & ISR OVERHEAD ASSETS OVER NORTHERN HEMISPHERE EAST OF KANSAS, WEST OF GREENLAND & NORTH OF MISSOURI OUT OF SERVICE."

*1411:* WH COUNSEL LAWRENCE WALSH & MG WILLIAM DUNCAN, U.S. ARMY, DIR WHMO ARR WHSR. GEN DUNCAN REPORTS "LOST NCA COMMS W/ POTUS & VPOTUS MIL AIDES & NO ABILITY TO EXECUTE EAM OR EWO TO NUCLEAR FORCES."

*1412:* SEC DEF ORDERS WASHINGTON-MOSCOW HOTLINE ACTIVATED. MOSCOW REPORTS: "NUCLEAR DETONATION OVER LAKE ONTARIO. NOT OURS."

*1413:* ACTING USSS DIR GEORGE SANDERS ARR WHSR, INFORMS "LOST COMMS W/ POTUS & VPOTUS PSDs."

*1414:* SEC DEF ORDERS ALL U.S. MIL. UNITS WORLDWIDE PLACED ON DEFCON ONE STATUS.

*1415:* ACTING USSS DIR SANDERS REPORTS: "ALL SECRET SERVICE CONVENTIONAL & ELECTRIC VEHICLES OUT OF COMMISSION EXCEPT FOR DIESEL-POWERED TRUCKS RUNNING 'WHEN LIGHTS WENT OUT.'"

*1416:* ACTING USSS DIR SANDERS RECOMMENDS DISPATCHING TWO DIESEL-POWERED VEHICLES TO CAPITOL HILL TO BRING

SPEAKER OF THE HOUSE OF REPRESENTATIVES & A FEDERAL
JUDGE TO THE WHITE HOUSE "JUST IN CASE WE NEED A NEW
PRESIDENT."

**1417:** SEC DEF & ACTING DIR USSS CONFER ON NMCC FOC. SEC DEF
CONCURS ON BRINGING SPEAKER OF HOUSE & FED JUDGE TO WHSR.

**1418:** NMCC SWO REPORTS ON FOC: "TWO USAF F−35S
LAUNCHED FM JOINT BASE LANGLEY, VA, TO OVERFLY BUFFALO,
NY, & LAKE ERIE @ LAST KNOWN POSITION AIR FORCE ONE."

**1424:** ACTING FBI DIR JON KEKER ARRIVES WHSR ON FOOT
FM HOOVER BLDG. REPORTS NO POWER OR COMMS @ FBI HQ,
NO COMMS W/ FBI FIELD OFFICES; LOOTERS EVIDENT ON **14**TH
STREET, **2** BLOCKS FROM WHITE HOUSE.

**1433:** ANMCC REPORTS ON FOC: "FIBER OPTIC COMMS
REESTABLISHED WITH **10**TH MOUNTAIN DIVISION HQ EOC @ FORT
DRUM, NY. EOC SWO REPORTS: BASE IS SECURE; TOTAL POWER
OUTAGE IN SURROUNDING AREA; NO COMMERCIAL VEHICLES
OPERATIONAL; NEARLY ALL MIL VEHICLES IMMOBILIZED; APPEARS
TO BE RESULT OF EMP BURST; NO SIGNIFICANT INCREASE IN
RADIATION LEVELS OBSERVED SINCE INITIAL EVENT."

**1445:** NMCC SWO REPORTS ON FOC: "EYEWITNESS SAYS ONE
COMMERCIAL AIRCRAFT DOWN IN POTOMAC NORTH OF PENTAGON.
PLANE APPARENTLY CRASHED INTO ROOSEVELT BRIDGE ON
APPROACH TO REAGAN NATIONAL AIRPORT. NO EMERGENCY
RESPONSE OR SURVIVORS EVIDENT."

**1450:** SEC TREASURY ARRIVES IN WHSR VIA TUNNEL FM
TREASURY DEPT. REPORTS TWO COMMERCIAL AIRCRAFT DOWN IN
POTOMAC SOUTH OF REAGAN NATIONAL AIRPORT.

*1452:* SEC STATE ARRIVES IN WHSR ON FOOT FROM STATE
DEPT. ESCORTED BY STATE DEPT. SECURITY OFFICERS. SEC STATE
REPORTS BEING ACCOSTED BY HOSTILE CROWD AT *17*TH STREET
ENTRY PORTAL TO EEOB & WH COMPLEX.

*1453:* ATTORNEY GEN ARR WHSR ON FOOT FM MAIN JUSTICE
ESCORTED BY FBI AGENTS. REPORTS ANGRY CROWDS AND LOOTERS
ON *15*TH STREET AND VIC OF ELLIPSE. SEVERAL CARS ON ELLIPSE
ARE ON FIRE AND A DOWNED AIRCRAFT AFIRE ON NATIONAL MALL.

*1458:* SEC STATE CONVENES MTG IN WHSR EOC CONFERENCE
ROOM W/ SEC TREAS, ATTY. GEN., WH CHIEF OF STAFF & WH
COUNSEL, ACTING DIR USSS & DIR WHMO. SECURE FOC VID-LINK
W/NMCC ESTABLISHED FOR SEC DEF & CJCS PARTICIPATION.

*1525:* SPEAKER OF THE HOUSE REP. JOHN TRUMAN CASSIDY &
U.S. SUPREME COURT JUSTICE BRENDAN SULLIVAN ARRIVE WHSR
ACCOMPANIED BY SECRET SERVICE AGENTS. BOTH MEN ESCORTED
TO WHSR EOC CONFERENCE ROOM TO JOIN MEETING IN PROGRESS.

\*   \*   \*   \*

It took twenty-seven Secret Service agents—most of them
on foot—nearly an hour to find John Truman Cassidy,
the Speaker of the U.S. House of Representatives, and
Supreme Court Justice Sullivan. They were delivered to
the White House in two diesel-powered, armored SUVs
through streets crowded with disabled vehicles and thousands of angry American citizens.

At 1526 the two USAF F-35s launched from Joint
Base Langley, Virginia, arrived over Buffalo, New York.
They overflew the city and the area over Lake Erie where
Air Force One was last reported. Unable to establish
communications with anyone on the ground, the aircraft

proceeded northeast over Lake Ontario to Wheeler-Sack Army Airfield at Fort Drum, New York, where they landed "without comms."

The pilots taxied to a hangar, shut down, and found a soldier who guided them, on foot, to the 10th Mountain Division's command post. Once inside, the flight leader was allowed to use the hardened fiber-optic circuit to call the NMCC: "We observed wreckage and a fuel slick in the water, south of Peace Bridge on the Canadian side of Lake Erie. It appears to be the remnants of a USAF Bravo Seven Four Seven. We cannot confirm any survivors.

"En route to Fort Drum, we overflew Oswego, New York, at high speed and observed significant structural damage, fires, and mass casualties on our FLIRs. Based on elevated radiation readings, it appears to be the consequence of a low-yield, low-altitude nuclear detonation.

"There does not appear to be any hostile activity in the area. We detected no other aircraft aloft en route but evidence of thirteen crashes. We are attempting to decontaminate the aircraft and refuel and will stand by here for further orders."

At 1635, the Secretary of Defense read the F-35 flight leader's report verbatim over the FOC secure video-link to the participants meeting in the WHSR EOC Conference Room. By then the nation had been without a commander-in-chief for nearly three hours.

When he heard the report, Justice Sullivan said, "Gentlemen, at a time like this, our country needs a leader. I believe it's time. Without objection, I will administer the Oath of Office to Speaker Cassidy, in accord with Article Two and the Twentieth Amendment of the U.S. Constitution as prescribed by Congress in Title Three, Section Nineteen of the United States code."

Cassidy, looking stunned, asked for a Holy Bible. It

took fifteen minutes but one was eventually found on a bookshelf in the Lincoln Bedroom. When it was delivered, the Speaker of the House placed his left palm on the book and raised his right hand as a solemn Judge O'Leary said, "Repeat after me: 'I do solemnly swear that I will faithfully execute the office of President of the United States, and will to the best of my ability, preserve, protect, and defend the Constitution of the United States.'"

The new president repeated the words exactly as written in Article II, Section 1, then added, "So help me, God."

The handwritten WHSR log entry for 1700, 20 September, reads simply:

*1700:* SPEAKER OF THE HOUSE OF REPRESENTATIVES JOHN T. CASSIDY ADMINISTERED OATH OF OFFICE AS PRESIDENT OF THE UNITED STATES BY U.S. SUPREME COURT JUSTICE BRENDAN SULLIVAN IN WHSR EOC CONFERENCE ROOM. ON SITE WITNESSES: SEC STATE, SEC TREAS., A/G, W/H COS, ACTING DIR FBI, ACTING DIR USSS, WHSR SWO. SEC DEF OBS PROCEEDINGS OVER SECURE EOC VIDEO-LINK.

Fifteen minutes after John Truman Cassidy became the forty-eighth president of the United States, White House Chief of Staff Muneer Azzam Murad went to his office, closed his door, and shot himself in the head. Subsequent forensic analysis determined the projectile was fired from the same weapon as the bullet that killed General John Smith in Lafayette Park on September 18, 2032.

Vuelo Mexico Flight X-ray One Niner One was 135 miles east of El Paso, Texas, at 1253 CDT on Monday, 20 September, when the Air Traffic Control Center in San Antonio called the aircraft: "We have a Homeland Security alert. Proceed direct to Echo Lima Papa and land immediately. Contact El Paso tower on frequency one-one-niner-point-one."

In the left-hand seat, Bill Stearman, the pilot who flew the Gulfstream VII over the Yucatan the previous night, keyed the radio button on his yoke and replied, "X-Ray One Niner One, Roger, proceeding direct to Echo Lima Papa. Descending from thirty-seven. Switching to one-one-niner-point-one." He then keyed the cabin address system and said, "ATC has ordered us to land at El Paso International because of a Homeland Security alert."

As the aircraft began a slow descent from thirty-seven thousand feet, James Newman jumped up and stood in the cockpit doorway in hopes of learning more. All the pilots could tell him was what they knew from listening to the radio: There had been some kind of attack on the U.S. East Coast and every inbound international flight and aircraft over the continental United States was being diverted to the nearest operational airfield or airport. Stearman added, "This is just like 9-11-01 all over again."

In the cabin, Sergeant Major Dan Doan arose and checked the three detainees, now shackled to their seats. Ahmad and Ebi, the two Iranians, said nothing. But the drug lord, Manuel Gustavo Lenin Felix, asked, "Does this mean we're not going to Las Vegas?"

"Can't say," Doan responded, trying not to let his concern show.

When the 737 landed at El Paso International they were directed to a holding area, where they were joined by more than twenty other commercial and corporate aircraft that received the same orders. The pilots kicked on the jet's APU and shut down the engines awaiting instructions. In the cockpit doorway, James pulled out an unregistered PID and turned it on. The screen lit up with the message: "NO PID OR MESH SERVICE."

After fifteen futile minutes, A. J. Jones came forward and said to Newman, "If we can get a ground crew to bring stairs or a ladder alongside, Special Agent Quintero may be able to help us out. EPIC—the DEA El Paso Intelligence Center—is on the other side of the field at Fort Bliss. She has a lot of friends here who may be able to give us a hand."

*    *    *    *

Jones and Quintero were gone nearly three tedious hours while the passengers and crew aboard the 737 strained to listen on various radio channels for news of the catastrophe on the East Coast. Then, at 1710 CDT, six black SUVs with smoked glass windows and flashing blue lights came racing down the taxiway toward their aircraft. They were accompanied by two white SUVs with TSA on their sides.

From the cockpit doorway, Newman shouted into the cabin, "Looks like we have company! Everyone keep your weapons down and hope these guys are on our side . . ."

They were. Quintero and Jones were the first ones out of the black vehicles. Accompanied by a half-dozen men carrying automatic weapons and wearing SWAT helmets and ballistic vests with DEA emblazoned on chests and backs, they pounded up the stairs, punched the handle release on the cabin door, and swarmed into the aircraft.

Quintero introduced the only one of the team wearing

a suit and tie as Special Agent in Charge Roberto Nieves. Without preamble, Nieves walked down the airplane aisle where Marty Cohen was seated and announced, "Admiral, welcome home."

Cohen replied, "Thank you. It's good to be here, but I'm not quite home."

"Yes, sir, I know that. But before we can get you there, we have a few formalities," Nieves continued. "We are here to take the two Iranians and Señor Lenin Felix into custody. Based on information provided by Special Agent Quintero and Mr. Jones, we have obtained warrants to arrest all three of them for crimes against the United States. It is my understanding they were all apprehended in the commission of said crimes. Is that correct?"

Doan nodded and said, "You can say that again."

"Good," Nieves said. "I'll need sworn eyewitness statements to that effect before we can get you out of here. Unfortunately, all commercial, corporate, and private aircraft in the U.S. have been grounded for the time being because of the nuclear attack on the East Coast—and this aircraft must be impounded for evidence. But we have made alternative arrangements to get everyone here where you need to go aboard U.S. government aircraft. Agent Quintero and Mr. Jones will remain here to process the evidence against the Iranians and Felix. If the Vuelo Mexico aircrew is clean, they will be repatriated to Mexico. The USAF is standing by to transport the CSG aircrew to DFW to link up with another of the company's aircraft on DEA contract—a Gulfstream V, I believe. They will bring it here to pick up Admiral Cohen and his seven-man security detail. It's my understanding you want to get to Malmstrom AFB in Montana, is that right?"

"Yes," Newman and Cohen replied at the same time.

"Very well," said Nieves. "By the time we have all the

paperwork completed, the G-five should be here from DFW. I will arrange with our SAIC in Great Falls to meet you on arrival at Malmstrom and take you where you want to go. Any questions?"

There were none. But there should have been.

No one mentioned the two white TSA vehicles waiting below on the tarmac with armed Homeland Security agents in them.

Admiral Cohen, Jones, Quintero, the two aircrews, and the CSG HRU were offloaded first. It took longer than expected because the senior Homeland Security agent had a vid-recorder and insisted on capturing each of their images and stating their names at the bottom of the stairs before they could proceed to the vehicles. Newman's image showed him wearing sunglasses, a baseball hat pulled down over his forehead—and a beard.

As the DEA agents escorted the three detainees with their hands shackled in front of them down the steps, there was a further delay. The portly Homeland Security officer in charge demanded each detainee be "imaged" between his agents before they could be placed in the DEA vehicles. He told Nieves, "Until they are off this airport they are in our jurisdiction. I want DHS agents beside them on the aircraft steps for the record."

Nieves, Newman, and the others waited in utter frustration as the DEA agents handed over each shackled detainee so a pair of Homeland Security agents could pose beside each prisoner. Ebi was first, then Felix, the Mexican drug lord.

Ahmad, feigning fatigue, watched all this from the aircraft doorway. When it was his turn, he hobbled down the stairs, the chains around his ankles clanking on each step. On the bottom step he slumped and waited while the DEA agents handed him over to two DHS agents, now smiling at the camera. The Quds Force commander suddenly bent down, reached across his front with both hands, grabbed the pistol out of the holster on the right hip of the Homeland Security agent to his left, and opened fire.

His first head shot hit the DHS agent on his right; the second took down the one on his left. The third shot was to the head of the agent holding the camera. Then, in a crouch, he pointed the weapon at Admiral Cohen, standing beside James Newman, and screamed, "Die, Jew!"

Newman and Doan both leaped toward the Iranian as the pistol fired. Doan, closest to the shooter, took two 9mm bullets in the chest, but his momentum carried him forward, crushing Ahmad against the stairs.

James and the DEA agents were on the pair in an instant. While Nieves and his men hastily disarmed the semiconscious shooter, Newman pulled Doan's limp body off the unconscious Iranian. Seeing bright red blood pouring from the retired Marine sergeant major's nose and mouth, James knelt, then sat beside him. Cradling Doan's head in his arms, Newman yelled, "Corpsman up! Corpsman up!"

"Doc" Smith was there in an instant, carrying his Unit One. As the medic began cutting away Doan's shirt to get at the entry wounds, he heard James saying softly, "Dear God, not again, not again."

## SON RIVER RANCH

FORT SHAW, MT

SATURDAY, 25 SEPTEMBER 2032

There were eight of them: Peter and Rachel Newman, James and Sarah Newman, Mack and Angela Caperton, and Marty and Julia Cohen—all seated on the Capertons' West Porch, savoring the sunset over Twin

Peaks on the Continental Divide. As the golden ball slipped below the crests and the temperature dropped, Rachel pulled a light sweater over her shoulders and said quietly, "It really is America the Beautiful."

"Yes it is," Caperton replied. "It gives new meaning to the words 'Purple mountain majesties' . . . Hopefully, the last two weeks will serve as a reminder why that poem by Katherine Lee Bates and set to music by choirmaster Samuel Ward is in so many hearts and hymnals."

At this Sarah said, "What do you mean, Uncle Mack?"

"Well, the entire song is actually a prayer for our country. In the days ahead we're going to need a lot of prayers."

Now the admiral spoke: "Give us your sense for how you see things going, Mack."

Caperton sighed, nodded, and said, "At least we now have a chance of doing the right things.

"It's pretty clear the decision to bring the Speaker of the House to 1600 Pennsylvania Avenue on the evening of September 20 was one of the few wise decisions made at the White House in the days after the attack on 9-11-32.

"President Cassidy seems to be off to a pretty good start under the most adverse circumstances. He immediately canceled all his predecessor's secret Capture/Kill orders and Emergency Action Directives. Though it looks like nearly a million dead from the September 20 attack, power failures, riots, and pillaging on the East Coast, he's not imposed martial law. The flood of National Guardsmen, law officers, food, water, and medical supplies from unaffected states in the West and South seems to be returning a semblance of law and order. But if electricity can't be restored in the Northeast between now and winter, things are likely to get a lot worse for tens of millions of Americans before they get better."

"Mack, there are so many Americans hurting right

now. Is that what the Iranians wanted to accomplish with the attack on Houston and their nuclear missile over Lake Ontario? Is it all about killing Americans and making us suffer?" Julia asked.

"That's the primary motive for what the Iranians did. Their apocalyptic vision is pure evil. They may have been hoping for a nuclear counterstrike," the senator replied. "At the very least the Ayatollahs were carrying out their threat to punish us for supporting a Sunni Caliph and for what we did to them back in 2025. Retribution is a big deal in Tehran. Looking back, we should have paid attention when they said they could stop the president from getting reelected."

"But why kidnap Marty?"

"Iran is running out of oil, and they know it. Their 'fall-back,' if we didn't annihilate them for attacking us, was to learn the secret to building commercially viable fuel cells and sell them. That's why they had their Quds Force assets in Canada kill Dr. Long and try to kill Dr. Templeton."

"How big is the Iranian intelligence network, Mack?" asked Rachel.

"Well, based on the numbers involved in the attack on Houston and corroborating information we're getting from the two Iranians and the Mexican drug lord James delivered to Texas, the IRGC operational arm is very extensive here in the U.S., in every European country and throughout the western hemisphere. That's why this 'drone-killing' program has been counterproductive. A 'take no prisoners' policy kills some terrorists—but dead terrorists don't talk and we get no new human intelligence. . . ."

"Was the White House chief of staff who killed himself one of them?"

"Apparently not. It seems he was very close to the Caliph—in many ways. But he was also a committed 'jihadi,' loyal to a foreign leader."

"What's going to happen to the other White House conspirators who are still at large?" Sarah asked.

"Well, Turner is in custody and singing to prosecutors in hopes of a plea deal. Walsh and Keker are on the run—but they will probably get caught and eventually tried. Given what we now know about what was going on at the White House, it's providential we were spared a very messy impeachment trial."

"There's no doubt about that," Peter added. "But the question remains where we go from here."

"True," said Mack. "I think Cassidy's decision to temporarily move the seat of government to Dallas was wise. Even though we lost our best sources about what was happening at 1600 Pennsylvania Avenue, it's pretty clear our new president has cleaned out the rat's nest from the previous criminal cabal in the White House and the top levels of the administration."

"What do you mean, 'lost' our best sources?" James asked.

"Well, your mom's friend Frances James quit the Secret Service in Chicago that morning and surrendered her badge and gun to her supervisor before Air Force One took off. And I lost my best source when the plane went down. He was the one I turned to when I needed to confirm information I received from others. He didn't always know everything the president was doing to break the law, because she and her coterie of liars and traitors tried to keep him 'out of the loop.' But he was a great help and we met regularly in his office on the Senate side of the Capitol."

"So who was it?"

Caperton arched his eyebrows and said, "The vice president."

There was a moment of stunned silence before James asked, "So why do you have any confidence Cassidy will do any better? He's a 'Progressive' just like his predecessor."

Caperton nodded and said, "True. But so far—and I know it's only a few days—he's doing a lot of the right things the right way. He's nominated a new cabinet. I know some of his nominees to be men and women of integrity and real-world experience who love America and believe in free enterprise. I know two of those he wants to bring in are "Believers"—they wear the sign of the fish and they are supporters of restoring the First and Second Amendments. Perhaps best of all, he has asked our old roommate, Dr. Cohen, to become our next Secretary of Energy."

At this Julia smiled and said, "He may not want Marty once he finds out that the fuel cell Marty and his colleagues were working on doesn't work."

"Is that true about the fuel cell?" Peter asked.

Cohen nodded and said, "Yeah. That's why I was in Houston for the big energy conference on September eleventh. The cesium rare earth 'hydrogen-oxygen separation device' Steven Templeton, Davis Long, and I were working on is far too expensive to be economically viable. I was there to make the announcement—and urge our best course of action would be to press ahead with conversion of abundant, inexpensive, domestic natural gas into methanol as a motor fuel—and of course build nuclear reactors for electrical power."

"Who else knew that's what you were going to say?"

"Only Drs. Templeton and Long. Thankfully, Steven is recovering. I talked to him this morning and he's agreed we will have a joint press conference to announce our findings after things quiet down."

Peter shook his head and said, "Maybe you should make that announcement before the presidential election." Then, turning to Caperton, he asked, "Mack, are you going to run? We've heard from a lot of people out here the last few days who want you to."

The senator shrugged and said, "I may not have to decide right away. This morning, before we went to the funeral, President Cassidy called for Congress to convene in Dallas and vote on postponing the election. He also announced he will not be a candidate. I think it was a smart move. If the election is postponed, I will encourage Texas governor Charles to run."

"Have you decided how you are going to vote?" asked Rachel.

"Not yet, though it's pretty clear to me that Article One of the Constitution gives Congress the responsibility for setting the time and manner for holding federal elections. Article Two specifies Congress may determine the date for choosing presidential electors—meaning the Electoral College. From my reading of the Constitution it seems as though Congress has the authority to postpone elections to the House, Senate, and presidency because of a national emergency. We are surely in the midst of a national emergency that is likely to continue into next year. But I want to hear the debate."

They were all quiet for a while as the shadows lengthened and the glow in the western sky turned gold, then orange, and finally deep purple. With night descending around them, Sarah said, "We better go retrieve our boys before they drive Beth and Sam crazy over at their house. We're so grateful to you, Mack, for what you and Angela have done for us."

As they all stood, Angela replied, "I'm glad we could. You all mean so much to us. The funeral service today was a reminder of how blessed we are as family, as friends, and as Americans. Funerals are hard for us ever since we lost John. But somehow our nation still manages to produce heroes like our son and your husband. They are the reason why the third stanza of 'America the Beautiful' is so powerful:

> O beautiful for heroes proved
> In liberating strife.
> Who more than self their country loved
> And mercy more than life!

"Even though it made me cry, it was important to sing that hymn at Dan Doan's funeral service this morning. He was one of those heroes."

\* \* \* \*

As Rachel and Sarah left to find the young Newman boys and the others filed into the house, James turned to Mack and said, "What did you do with those two lists I gave you back at Pawleys Island? I need to make some revisions."

Caperton smiled and said, "I lost them somewhere in the turmoil of the last few days. But you're right, they weren't very accurate."

"So what do you recommend?"

"I suggest you get down on your knees next to your wife tonight and every night you are with her. Thank God for all your blessings. Ask her how you can pray for her—and tell her how you would like her to pray for you. You have both been through an awful lot these past few years—particularly since the Houston attacks. Dan

Doan's heroic last act saved Marty Cohen's life—and very likely yours. All that has to affect you and Sarah as well. Your wife is a remarkable woman. I know of only one other American mother who had to flee when bad people came to kill her and her children because of her husband. She and her husband and their children kept it all together because they started over. It's time for you and your family to do so as well."

"Start over?"

"Yes. Start over. That's what all of us must do now. But we're God-fearing Americans. That's what we do."

## Glossary

**ACV.** Armored Combat Vehicle

**AFRICOM.** U.S. Africa Command

**AG.** Attorney General

**AHW.** Advanced Hypersonic Weapons

**Anark.** From ANARK, acronym for "Anti-American Religious Kooks"—a pejorative phrase devised by political progressives to describe Christians who put duty to God ahead of fealty to government. The term first appeared in U.S. public discourse in the early 2020s. During the 2028 presidential election campaign, I'M AN ANARK—GOD-FAMILY-COUNTRY bumper stickers, buttons, and yard signs were displayed by Christian conservative and Free-Congress candidates and their supporters. After the election, the U.S. Department of Homeland Security declared Anarks to be a "potentially violent, militant, extremist movement with global connections." In 2030, the Anark movement, estimated to include 12–18 million Americans and up to 30 million worldwide, was declared a "global conspiracy" by the United Nations and largely driven underground.

**ANMCC.** Alternate National Military Command Center. Also known as "Site R," it is located beneath Raven Rock Mountain Complex in Pennsylvania, about six miles from the Presidential Retreat at Camp David.

The ANMCC serves as a redundant U.S. military command center in the event communications are lost with the NMCC at the Pentagon. See NMCC.

**APU.** Auxiliary Power Unit

**ATF.** Bureau of Alcohol, Tobacco, Firearms & Explosives

**BDA.** Bomb Damage Assessment

**BOLO.** "Be on the lookout," notification issued by INTERPOL

**Bravo Zulu.** Phonetic alphabet for letters "B" and "Z." In the U.S. Naval Service (Navy, Marines, and Coast Guard) the signal "BZ" means "well done."

**Cair Paravel.** Name of Newman family beach house in South Carolina. Cair Paravel is a mythical place in the *Chronicles of Narnia* by C. S. Lewis.

**Caliph.** Title given to a successor or representative of Muhammad with temporal and spiritual authority to govern all Muslims

**Caliphate.** The lands and people governed by the Caliph under Sharia law. By 2032 the "Modern Caliphate," created by United Nations resolution, included all the "Lands of the Prophet" south of the Mediterranean Sea, the entire Saudi Arabian peninsula, Turkey, Afghanistan, Pakistan, Turkmenistan, Uzbekistan, the east coast of Africa south to Kenya, and Indonesia. The United Nations also mandated that Muslims living in the British Isles, Western Europe, the Balkan states,

Ukraine, Russia, Africa, and the Philippines were to be considered "citizens of the Caliphate" and subject to Sharia law as determined by the Caliph.

**Cas-Evac.** Casualty Evacuation

**CENTCOM.** U.S. Central Command

**CIA.** Central Intelligence Agency

**CONUS.** Continental United States

**COS.** Chief of Staff

**CP.** Command Post

**CSG.** Centurion Solutions Group. A privately held U.S. corporation headed by Peter Newman.

**DEA.** Drug Enforcement Administration

**DEA FAST.** DEA Foreign-Deployed Advisory and Support Team; a task-organized direct-action unit of 4–15 Special Agents, trained and equipped for special operations, dispatched from Quantico, Virginia, to carry out sensitive, high-risk counternarcotics missions.

**DFW.** Dallas–Fort Worth International Airport

**DHS.** Department of Homeland Security

**DIA.** Defense Intelligence Agency; military intelligence-gathering and covert-action arm of the U.S. Armed Forces and the Department of Defense

**DISA.** Defense Information Systems Agency

**DNI.** Director of National Intelligence

**DOD.** Department of Defense

**DOJ.** Department of Justice

**DOS.** Department of State

**DPS.** Texas Department of Public Safety

**DRS.** Device Recognition Signal

**DZ (Delta Zulu).** Drop zone

**EAM.** Emergency Action Message to Nuclear Forces

**E&E.** Escape and Evasion

**E-Cell.** A sophisticated micro-circuit electronic timing device used in electronic watches and by terrorists to arm or detonate explosive devices

**EEOB.** Eisenhower Executive Office Building inside the White House complex

**ELINT.** Electronic Intelligence

**EMAC.** Electromagnetic Analysis Computer

**EMP.** Electromagnetic Pulse

**EMS.** Electromagnetic Spectrum

**EOC.** Emergency Operations Center

**EPIRB.** Emergency Position-Indicating Radio Beacon

**ESG.** Expeditionary Strike Group; a task-organized U.S. naval force with an embarked Marine air-ground combat unit

**EU.** European Union

**EWO.** Emergency War Order issued by the President of the United States to execute a nuclear strike

**FAA.** Federal Aviation Administration

**Fatwa.** A legal pronouncement of Islamic law issued by a Muslim cleric

**FBI.** Federal Bureau of Investigation

**FBO.** Fixed Base Operation for noncommercial aircraft

**FCC.** Federal Communications Commission

**FCT.** Fuel cell Technology

**FEMA.** Federal Emergency Management Agency

**FISA.** Foreign Intelligence Surveillance Act

**Fitna.** Islamic civil war, or literally "a test of faith in times of trial." Also translated to mean schism, secession, upheaval, and anarchy. It refers to times of trial for Islam, as in the Christian Tribulation. The First Islamic

Civil War from 646 to 661 AD was a time of struggle for control of the Caliphate. The Second Fitna, or Civil War, was 683–685 AD.

**FLIR.** Forward-Looking Infrared imaging system

**FOC.** Fiber-optic circuit

**Frag-O.** Fragmentary Operations Order issued by a field commander in the execution of a mission. The order contains a brief description of the friendly and enemy situation, the mission, a concept of how the operation will be conducted, the tasks to be accomplished, and essential logistics and communications information.

**Free-Cong.** Abbreviation of "Freedom Congress"—an independent political movement in the United States. The first "Free-Cong" candidates for the U.S. House of Representatives and U.S. Senate appeared on ballots during the 2024 elections. In 2032, ninety-six members of the House and nineteen senators are declared "Free-Congs" in Congress. Progressives and members of the media often refer to them as "Freak-ongs."

**GEX.** Global Exchange Currency Units, the new global currency mandated by the United Nations. Singular = gec; plural = gex; symbol = ¤

**GPS.** Global Positioning System

**HESCO Barrier.** Barrier used by the U.S. military formed by filling a wire mesh container lined with fabric with sand and gravel

**HEU.** Highly Enriched Uranium

**HHS.** Department of Health and Human Services

**HIPAA.** Health Insurance Portability and Accountability Act. One of several laws enacted to protect medical and health information of the American people.

**HPSCI.** House Permanent Select Committee on Intelligence

**HRT.** Hostage Rescue Team of the FBI, based at Quantico, Virginia

**HRU.** Hostage Recovery Unit of CSG, a private company providing "specialized services" to the U.S. government

**HSV.** High-Speed Vessel

**HUD.** Heads-Up Display

**HUMINT.** Human Intelligence

**IAD.** Dulles International Airport

**ICBM.** Intercontinental Ballistic Missile

**IDF.** Israel Defense Forces; the name of Israel's armed forces

**IFF.** Identification friend or foe; a device used to discriminate between friendly and enemy units, individuals, weapons, and aircraft. In aircraft, an IFF device will display altitude, speed, and direction on an air traffic controller's computer display.

**IMF.** International Monetary Fund

**Interpol.** International Criminal Police Organization, created in 1923 with the mission of facilitating the exchange of law enforcement information among member countries. In 2020, responsibility for funding, tasking, and management of Interpol was transferred to the United Nations, which uses Interpol as an international police force to enforce international law.

**IR.** Infrared

**IRGC.** Islamic Revolutionary Guard Corps, the Special Forces of the Iranian regime

**ISR.** Intelligence, Surveillance, and Reconnaissance

**Klick.** Military slang for kilometer

**LAS.** Las Vegas International Airport

**LCAC.** Landing Craft Air Cushion—a high-speed U.S. Navy amphibious assault landing craft used to transport Marines and heavy equipment ashore from ships at sea

**LHA.** Landing Ship, Helicopter Assault—a U.S. Navy vessel designed to carry Marine combat troops, helicopters, and landing craft to a designated area for an amphibious assault

**LHD.** Landing Ship, Helicopter Dock—a multipurpose U.S. Navy vessel designed to carry Marine combat troops, aircraft, LCACs, and other landing craft for an amphibious assault against a defended objective

**LZ (Lima Zulu).** Landing Zone

**M&M.** President's derisive nickname for Chief of Staff Muneer Azzam Murad

**MARSOC.** United States Marine Corps Special Operations Command

**MEOSAR/DASS.** Medium Earth Orbit Search and Rescue/Distress-Alerting Satellite System

**Mercator Projection.** A map projection on which meridians of longitude and parallels of latitude are displayed as lines crossing at right angles

**MESH.** Multi-Element Semi-Autonomous Hypernet. This global, fourth-generation, broad-spectrum technology provides multiple, fault-tolerant connectivity for all wireless devices worldwide. There are more than four million MESH nodes in the United States and nearly a billion around the globe. MESH protocols are "managed" by the United Nations.

**MEU.** Marine Expeditionary Unit, an air-ground combat task force built around a reinforced Marine infantry battalion

**MIA.** Missing in Action

**MTF.** More to follow

**MTV.** Medium Tactical Vehicle; a four-ton, fully armored, four-wheel-drive vehicle built to carry seven combat-loaded Marines

**Mullah.** A teacher or learned man (Islam)

**MV-22.** Military designation for the Boeing-built, tilt-rotor Special Operations variant of the Osprey aircraft capable of carrying up to 32 combat-loaded troops at 240 knots airspeed, refueling in flight and low-level all-terrain flying

**Narnia.** Newman family home in Virginia, named for the mythical place in C. S. Lewis's *Chronicles of Narnia*

**NCA.** National Command Authority (POTUS, SecDef, and USAF, USN nuclear force commanders)

**NCTC.** National Counterterrorism Center

**NGA.** National Geospatial-Intelligence Agency

**NMCC.** National Military Command Center. Also known as "The War Room." The NMCC, beneath the Pentagon, is staffed 24/7 by the Operations Directorate of the U.S. military's Joint Chiefs of Staff as the communications hub for the Defense Department and the U.S. terminus for the Washington-Moscow "hotline."

**NOAA.** National Oceanic and Atmospheric Administration

**NORAD.** North American Aerospace Defense Command; a U.S.-Canada military organization headquartered at Peterson Air Force Base near Colorado Springs, Colorado. The NORAD command center beneath Cheyenne Mountain is responsible for providing early warning and protection against attacks from air and space against the U.S. and Canada.

**NORTHCOM.** U.S. Northern Command. The U.S. military organization responsible for defending the homeland, Canada, and Mexico against attack from air, sea, and land. Headquartered at Peterson Air Force Base, Colorado, with NORAD, NorthCom is responsible for coordinating military support for civil authorities in the event of an attack by air, land, or sea.

**NOTAM.** Notice to Mariners and/or Notice to Airmen. Warnings issued to vessels and aircraft regarding hazards and safety.

**NSA.** National Security Agency

**NSC.** National Security Council

**NVG.** Night-vision goggles; worn by military personnel to enhance vision at night

**OIC/POC.** Officer in Charge and Point of Contact

**OJT.** On-the-job training

**One-Time Pad.** A cipher or encryption system in which random numbers, words, or letters are used to signify meanings known only to the sender and recipients of a message. Once the message has been transmitted, the "code" is destroyed and never used again.

**OP.** Observation Post

**OPEC.** Organization of Petroleum Exporting Countries

**OPSEC.** Operational Security

**PAX.** Military term for "passengers"

**PDB.** President's Daily Briefing

**PEAD.** Presidential Emergency Action Directive

**PERT.** Personal Electronic Radio Tag. A government-issued radio frequency identification device (RFID), about the size of a grain of rice, designed to be surgically embedded in a host's body to positively identify persons through individual biometric data, including DNA. Originally intended as a replacement for passports, licenses, and medical insurance and Social Security cards, commercial PERT scanners now enable cashless transactions globally by ensuring accurate identification and location data. PERTs are powered by a micro-battery that is recharged by magnetic-resonance proximity pads. In accord with the UN Convention of Telecommunications Security, all PERTs can be interrogated by military, intelligence, border security, and law enforcement entities through MESH nodes and certain other ground, airborne, and satellite sensors.

**PID.** Personal Interface Device. Slightly larger than an old-fashioned credit card, PIDs are fabricated from multiple plies of high-tech ceramic and plastic embedded with microcircuits providing wireless digital voice, visual, and data communications through the worldwide MESH. Like PERTs, PID micro-batteries are recharged by magnetic-resonance proximity pads.

**Piezo-actuator.** A solid-state ceramic switch that can convert pressure and temperature of biometric data (e.g., a fingerprint) into an electrical signal

**POTUS.** President of the United States

**PSD.** Personal Security Detail

**PVS.** Passive Vision Sight

**QRF.** Quick Reaction Force (U.S. and NATO military term)

**Quds Force.** Special Operations force of Iran's Islamic Revolutionary Guard Corps (IRGC)

**RCMP.** Royal Canadian Mounted Police

**Red Phone.** Secure/encrypted, hard-wired, fiber-optic telephone service connecting the White House, Pentagon, State Department, FBI, Treasury Department, Department of Homeland Security, NORAD, and the ANMCC.

**RFID.** Radio Frequency Identification

**ROE.** Rules of Engagement

**RPA.** Remotely Piloted Aircraft

**RPG.** Rocket-Propelled Grenade

**SAIC.** Special Agent in Charge

**SAR.** Search and Rescue

**SARSAT.** Search and Rescue Satellite-Aided Tracking

**SAS.** Special Air Service; elite unit of the British Royal Army and Air Force used for special operations

**SCAR.** Special Operations Forces Combat Assault Rifle

**SCBA.** Self-Contained Breathing Apparatus

**SecDef.** U.S. Secretary of Defense

**Semtex.** A highly lethal plastic explosive material developed by the Soviets in the 1970s and widely copied by their surrogates and others because it can be produced in very thin, nearly undetectable panels not much thicker than a sheet of paper

**SIG Events.** Significant Events

**SIGINT.** Signals Intelligence

**Sit-Rep.** Situation Report

**Site "R."** Raven Rock Mountain Complex; site of the alternate National Military Command Center

**SIU.** Signals Intercept Unit

**SOCOM.** U.S. Special Operations Command

**SOD.** DEA Special Operations Division

**SPR.** Strategic Petroleum Reserve

**SSCI.** Senate Select Committee on Intelligence

**SSO.** Sensor Systems OIC

**SVT.** Secure Video-Teleconference

**SWO.** Senior Watch Officer

**TSA.** Transportation Security Administration, an agency of the Department of Homeland Security

**UAE.** United Arab Emirates

**UAV.** Unmanned Aerial Vehicle

**Ummah.** Arabic for an Islamic community living in accord with Sharia law

**UN.** United Nations

**Unit One.** Field trauma medical kit carried by U.S. military medics and Corpsmen

**USAF.** United States Air Force

**USCG.** United States Coast Guard

**USG.** United States Government

**USMC.** United States Marine Corps

**USMCC.** United States Mission Control Center

**USN.** United States Navy

**USSS.** United States Secret Service

**V-22.** Military designation for the Boeing-built, tilt-rotor Osprey aircraft capable of carrying up to 32 combat-loaded troops at 240 knots airspeed

**VIC.** Vicinity; also military slang for vehicle

**WHCA.** White House Communications Agency

**WHMO.** White House Military Office

**WHSR.** White House Situation Room

**WIA.** Wounded in Action

**XO.** Executive Officer

# Acknowledgments

## MOGADISHU, SOMALIA, 2012

A quarter of a century ago this year, the U.S. Congress held hearings on "the Iran-Contra Affair." None of the Americans involved in the covert activities being divulged wanted their names or faces to appear in print or on air. I was one of them. Brendan Sullivan, seated beside me through the ordeal, said, "This is like a novel." He was right then—and will be tomorrow.

The Americans and our allies I'm accompanying in Africa operate in the deep shadows of a very shadowy war. Mike D., you and the Soldiers, Sailors, Airmen, Guardsmen, Marines, Federal Agents, Clandestine Services Officers, and "contractors" with whom I have kept company for most of my life are the patriots who inspired this book. You are "heroes proved."

Those I accompanied then and now and the experiences we shared in difficult and dangerous places have made my life—and this novel—very exciting. Someday I hope to use your real names, but for now, you know who you are and where and when you really did these things.

FOX News president Roger Ailes and senior vice presidents Bill Shine and Michael Clemente have my gratitude for dispatching me to cover these extraordinary heroes all over the globe for more than a decade. Thanks to you, our citizens have come to know what it takes to protect our freedoms, even though they don't know the real names of our protectors.

Gary Terashita, my personal samurai, and your wife,

Kim—thank you for insisting that I write this book. My gratitude to MDs Gwillam Parry, Daniel Laurent, and Kin Sing Au for ensuring "The Big C" didn't finish me off before I finished this novel. Marsha Fishbaugh, my executive assistant of twenty-five years, made me keep all those appointments!

Andy Stenner, my "Terp" in Iraq and Afghanistan, again served as translator—converting my "military lingo" into English, compiling the glossary, and tracking down the real eyewitness participants in this fictional account of genuine bravery under fire.

Robert Barnett and Michael O'Connor, the "Spec Ops Team" at Williams & Connolly, completed their mission and forged the alliance with Louise Burke and Anthony Ziccardi at Simon & Schuster to make working on this book a joy.

Duane Ward at Premiere promises another covert operation to ensure this book is an even bigger blockbuster than its predecessors. George Fenton and the Smith brothers at TASER®™, many thanks for showing me your remarkable, lifesaving products and how you make them!

Most of all, thank you, Betsy, mother of our four children, grandmother of fourteen, my muse, my greatest advocate, and the only real American mother who had to flee when "bad people were coming to kill her children because of her husband." You're still my best friend.

# "AMERICA THE BEAUTIFUL"

*Words by Katharine Lee Bates,*
*Melody by Samuel Ward*

O beautiful for spacious skies,
For amber waves of grain,
For purple mountain majesties
Above the fruited plain!
America! America!
God shed his grace on thee
And crown thy good with brotherhood
From sea to shining sea!

O beautiful for pilgrim feet
Whose stern impassioned stress
A thoroughfare of freedom beat
Across the wilderness!
America! America!
God mend thine every flaw,
Confirm thy soul in self-control,
Thy liberty in law!

O beautiful for heroes proved
In liberating strife.
Who more than self their country loved
And mercy more than life!
America! America!
May God thy gold refine
Till all success be nobleness
And every gain divine!

O beautiful for patriot dream
That sees beyond the years
Thine alabaster cities gleam
Undimmed by human tears!
America! America!
God shed his grace on thee
And crown thy good with brotherhood
From sea to shining sea!

# FREEDOM ALLIANCE

HEROES SCHOLARSHIPS—For the Children of America's Fallen Heroes

The Freedom Alliance Scholarship Fund honors American military personnel who have been killed or permanently disabled in service to our nation by providing educational scholarships for their dependent children.

Since 1990, Freedom Alliance has awarded millions of dollars in college scholarships to the sons and daughters of U.S. Soldiers, Sailors, Airmen, Guardsmen, and Marines. These grants further education and remind all that their parents' sacrifice will never be forgotten by a grateful nation.

SUPPORT OUR TROOPS—Serving those who serve in America's Armed Forces

The Freedom Alliance Support Our Troops program provides direct financial and other assistance to active duty military personnel and their families. Priority is given to those recuperating from wounds and injuries and to their dependents.

Through relationships with military and veterans' hospitals and rehabilitation facilities, Freedom Alliance provides emergency grants to families enduring financial hardship while members of our Armed Forces recover from wounds, injuries, or sickness suffered in the line of duty.

The Freedom Alliance "Gifts from Home" project ships thousands of care packages to service members deployed overseas throughout the year. Here on the home front, we provide gifts and sponsor activities for the spouses and children of deployed personnel.

Our Healing Heroes program offers "Hero Holiday" vacations for injured military members and their families and "Hero Hunts," fishing retreats, and outdoor activities to aid in rehabilitation.

Freedom Alliance, founded in 1990 by Lt. Col. Oliver North, USMC (Ret.), and Lt. Gen. Edward Bronars, USMC (Ret.), is a nonprofit 501(c)(3) charitable and educational organization dedicated to advancing America's heritage of freedom by honoring and encouraging military service, defending the sovereignty of the United States, and promoting a strong national defense.

For more information, or to donate, contact:

FREEDOM ALLIANCE
22570 Markey Court, Suite 240
Dulles, Virginia 20166-6919
Phone: 800-475-6620
www.freedomalliance.org
www.facebook.com/FreedomAlliance

"LEST WE FORGET"

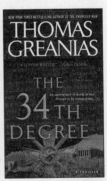

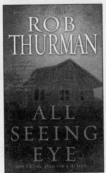
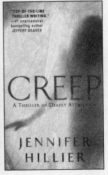